PRETTY JANE

OR, THE

VIPER OF KIDBROOK LANE

THE FIRST MEETING IN THE LANE.

CHAPTER I.

KIDBROOK LANE.—PRETTY JANE MEETS A GENTLE-
MAN LOVER THERE.—BELLA WARD AND BOB
HEAVISIDE.—THE HUNCHBACK BOY.

THE beautiful green lanes of Eltham were at
one time known only to the residents of the
place; but now Kidbrook Lane is known by
repute to the whole of England.

Known alas! not for its sweet-smelling hedges
—not for the melody of its birds that there build
and sing the spring and summer through—not
for the tangled home of myriads of gold-
burnished, buzzing, droning insects—but for the
ghastly murder of a too trusting maid!

Eltham is situated in Kent, and is a busy
little town about eight miles from the metropolis
and known in history for its being one of the
residences of Edward the Second, in which his
son, John of Eltham, was born.

The remains of the royal palace are converted
into a farm-house, and the once stately hall forms
the barn.

Kidbrook Lane has glorious peeps through
the hedges of many extensive country views,
stretching away over the range of the Kentish
hills. It has long been popular as the trysting-
place of country lads and lasses of all degrees.
And when early morn unfolds the curtains of
day, or the moon shimmers o'er leaf and tree, no

place could be so much in harmony with the tender passion, or fitted for the whispered question—"Will thou be mine?" and the trembling, hesitating reply—"I will."

Great charm for lovers, too, is the solitude and retirement of the place; here they might stroll for hours along the serpentine windings of this memorable lane and brook, and breathe their hopes of happiness with none to hear but the nodding birds that nestle in the sprays that fringe the lane.

But evil passion is so much allied with love, that many a trusting maiden has bewailed love-making in Kidbrook Lane.

Oh! love is cruel as well as kind. Though many a heart has been made happy in this lane, many a one has been broken, and the very loneliness of the spot has ministered to it.

These country lanes, too, are infested with vipers—vipers in human form, but who have all the stealthy cunning and deceit of the serpent race.

Pretty Jane found this late one evening as she was returning from seeking a situation alone through the lane—it was her nearest way to her temporary lodgings in Eltham.

It would have been well for her—she did not think so then—had she directed her footsteps by the highway, though it would have taken her ten minutes longer.

These human vipers, like the shining tenants of the brambly hedge, where they lie coiled up with shining fascinating eyes, to catch their unwary prey, prowl about those lonely spots to betray innocence.

When will girls learn to beware of flattery? It is the stock-in-trade of the seducer, who knows so well how to use it that it is hard to tell it from truth.

Let maids beware of praises of their charms by a stranger in secluded places. The fate of "Pretty Jane" should be a warning to them to close their ears to flattery, and hold no conversation with those who praise only to betray.

Pretty Jane—and if ever a girl's beauty deserved such a distinguishing prefix to her name it was hers, for her face was like a cluster of roses nestling sunbeams, with teeth shining like pearls of the ocean—was of lowly birth, nothing in the social scale but a servant girl, but one of the highest respectability, and trained by worthy parents and relatives to industrious habits and rectitude of conduct.

But she was cursed with vanity, and had too ready an ear for the viper's delicious poison. She was very susceptible, too, to the voice of love—what maid is not? She could not discern its counterfeit, and believed the viper's tale when he told her that her beauty was of the rarest—that her eyes outshone the stars—that her skin was fairer than "monumental alabaster"—that her figure was queenly, and the outline of her features a model for sculptors and painters.

The viper told her more: told her that her beauty had made an indelible impression on his tender heart—that he had never loved before, that he could never love again—that he was rich, and making choice of him as her husband, it would be equivalent to having golden carriages, and prancing steeds, mansions, and a retinue of servants!

Young ladies need indeed be strong-minded not to fall under such bewitching prospects—what surprise, then, that a poor unsuspecting servant, young in years, and ambitious that her well-known beauty should improve her social station, should yield her faith and virtue to such dark treachery with such a glittering surface?

"Oh! for a whip to lash such rascals naked through the streets."

And is he not a rascal who would make seduction the study of his wretched life? Who lives only to betray the young and innocent, whom he is bound by every human tie and instinct to love, cherish, and protect! Who for some low, selfish pleasure, would plunge himself and others into irretrievable ruin!

Jane had been seeking a service not far from Eltham, and as she had a good character, a genteel person, and engaging manners, she was accepted by the lady, who kindly invited her to take tea, and after tea she remained in pleasant conversation with the servants.

It was a spring evening, and the twilight was fast giving place to night, and the sky became overcast with a stormy face, when Jane left the mansion where she was that day week to take up her abode as under parlour-maid.

This kind of situation her face, figure, and manners well qualified her for. When she entered the parlour in her clean print dress, and natty cap and blue ribbons, with the tea tray in her hand, why she certainly was a dangerous attendant for any lady whose husband had an eye for beauty to keep about her.

Her new master and mistress had not yet reached middle age, lived in aristocratic style, and kept aristocratic company. They kept a carriage and pair, coachman and page, and several women servants. Jane thought herself lucky in obtaining so good a service.

She skipped homewards as light hearted as a fawn, until her onward way was intercepted by a gentleman of olive complexion, whose diamond ring and diamond shirt-studs sparkled in the moon's rays as it sailed from under the darkening clouds, as if to rival the brightness of Jane's eyes.

She carried in her hand a bunch of bright flowers, which the servants at Evesham House had gathered for her, and which she intended to present to Mrs. Oliphant, monthly nurse and landlady, to pacify her for the inconvenience she had inflicted on her in keeping her up.

Not that it was very late—Eltham bells had just struck nine.

But it was late for young women to be unprotected abroad in country lanes, for vipers are then about for prey; and it was late for Mrs. Oliphant, who was always more or less in a boozy condition. The old lady was very fond of a drop of gin, a pinch of snuff, and plenty of sleep, that is, if she had no one to gossip with to whom she might pour out her vials of scandal and superstition.

The gentleman who, to Pretty Jane's alarm, suddenly crossed her path and stopped her, was smoking a cigar, and he had a magnificent retriever dog at his heels. The dog, with his saucer-like eyes, surveyed the moon and the careering clouds travelling over it as intently as his master surveyed the alarmed face of Jane, who shrank back with instinctive terror as he laid his hand upon her waist.

"Why so alarmed?" he asked. "I should have thought you would have been glad of any society in a desolate place like this."

"Let me go, sir, or I will scream!" cried Jane.

"What good would that be, seeing that none would hear? Come, come, you need not be afraid of me; indeed, I have more cause to fear you—for what so dangerous to a man's peace as brilliant eyes like yours?"

"Do let me go, sir. If you are a gentleman, you would not detain a girl in a lone place like this."

Jane attempted to release her hand from his, but he bade her allay her fears, and believe in him as a friend who would see her on her way out of the lane and to her home, if she would permit him.

Jane felt herself in no enviable situation, and thought it best, seeing that she was in the stranger's power, with no one passing or likely to do so, not to oppose him, if he would only allow her to go on her way.

"The lane was really dark until your sparkling eyes illuminated it," said the gentleman, who never rose above the most commonplace compliments.

"Oh, I daresay," said Jane, who had somewhat recovered her composure, but who would have been better pleased had the stranger been ten thousand miles away. "Gentlemen like you should not condescend to speak to a poor girl."

"Poor, indeed. Ha! ha! ha! You are the richest woman in Nature's gifts that I ever beheld. With eyes as black as sloes, and their brightness as piercing as thorns; and such a sweet little mouth—don't let it pout so, for I would not offend you for the world."

"But you do offend when you talk such nonsense," said Jane, averting her head, and walking faster onwards through the lane.

These displays of anger or offence, the stranger, who was well acquainted with woman's weak nature, only attributed to coquetry. He could tell, he thought, when a woman was in earnest, and he decided that Jane was not, for he perceived that his flatteries were fast softening her towards his unmanly advances.

"Why, my beauty, you are sailing onwards faster than the threatening clouds above us."

"I should think I am, for I ought to be home before now. I shall get such a scolding!"

"You ought to be independent of any one. If you would listen to me, you might be mistress of yourself and a fortune to boot."

"What stuff!" exclaimed Jane, catching in her silk jacket that the wind was playing with.

"And pray where have you been to-night?" asked the stranger, devising plans to detain her.

"If you must know, I have been to Brockley after a place."

"I hope you have succeeded. But as I said before—and really I mean it—you ought to be independent of service. You may be poor in circumstances, but I swear you are of aristocratic birth, your small hand assures me of that."

As he spoke, he was about to take her hand in his, but the girl resisted the liberty, saying—

"Let me alone, if you please. You are a stranger to me."

"Not for long, I trust," he rejoined, interrupting Jane, who put on an offended look.

"Our meeting has been accidental," continued Jane; but the gentleman again interrupted her, saying—

"I love these accidental meetings. There is romance in them, and they are guided and willed by Heaven."

"No good comes of them, I'm sure of that," responded Jane.

"Tut! tut! Things that are thrown in our way without labour of design or deliberation, are always the sweetest, if we only give ourselves up to them, and not oppose our destinies. I came wandering with my dog to-night to watch the wild flowers sleeping in these hedges, and Heaven has blessed my path with the sight of a human flower more precious than any that dwell in brambly homes. I admire the one, but I love the other."

Jane gave a sweet little derisive laugh, and said—

"To talk of love to a girl you never saw before! That is rich! and you must think me very stupid to believe it."

"The more am I to be pitied. Tell me your name?"

"I am sure I shan't. I wouldn't have you know for the world."

"Nor where you live?"

"I should think not, indeed. My gracious!" she exclaimed, casting her eyes on the clock of Morden College, on which the moonlight streamed, "if it isn't nine o'clock! I shall be killed!"

"You seem to be in a vast hurry to get to those who would kill you, and to part with him to whom you have endeared yourself."

As he spoke, his large dog got in his way and nearly tripped him up. He gave the animal a savage blow across the muzzle with his fist, and the dog, in his resentment, gave a howl, leaped the hedge of the lane, and swam the placid brook close by.

His master in vain called him to his side. Onward he went, through the little water, and when he got on the other side he scampered off, no doubt towards his home, wherever that might be.

"All things appear to shun me to-night. I never knew him play me this game before."

"You should not have been so cruel to the poor creature," observed Jane, when he again hastened to her side, for she had hurried on while he, for an instant, watched the progress of his dog.

"Is it for cruelty that you shun me?" he pleadingly inquired.

"I have nothing to shun you for. I cannot help your walking by my side."

"Would you if you could?"

"Of course I would—at such a time of night, and in such a place."

"You have other lovers, probably?"

"Lovers, indeed! One young man is quite enough for a girl that is honest and true."

"And have you got this young man?" he smilingly inquired, gently taking her by the arm, while he smiled so broadly under his moustache, that he showed his white teeth.

"That's tellings," said Jane. "But I don't like you to touch me."

"You expect, perhaps, your young man to meet you?" he cross-examined Jane.

The girl was taken off her guard by this question, and without intending it, she grew communicative.

"Ah! he's too far away for that," she said.

"On the wide and open sea—eh?"

"You've just guessed it," replied the girl, who began to be lost in the sweet subject of her dear young sailor. "He's in Calcutta—been away for eighteen months."

"Which has seemed years to you, I swear," suggested the stranger, pleased that he had got his unwilling companion into easy conversation.

"Perhaps it has; I know I wish he was here now."

"I don't though," added the gentleman. "Sailors are formidable fellows to meet with when called upon to fight for their sweethearts."

"I certainly don't think William would like to see me in your company in Kidbrook Lane at this time of night. I don't like it myself; but I can't help it. And yet it is my fault for stopping so late. He's a strapping young fellow I can tell you, and I think——"

She paused.

"Well, what do you think?"

"I'm sure I don't know what I was going to say now. But you must please to leave me now, sir, for I'm close home."

She was quite pleased when a few cottages came in sight, that were built at the entrance of the lane.

"Don't be so unceremonious, there's a good girl."

"I don't know what you mean," she said, placing her hand behind her head to adjust her beautiful long hair, which was done up in the prevailing fashion.

"I mean that you might have thanked me for my company."

"Oh, I do, sir, I do—I very much thank you for seeing me safe out of the lane."

"You know had you met with any one with less gentle blood in his nature, and less true love for you——"

"Now, I don't like that. It is all stuff and nonsense to talk that way. I am very young, but too old to believe that tale, and you ought to know better than to talk so."

"It is your lustrous eyes that have wrung the confession from me. Pray don't go yet."

"I must! I will! Oh! do not detain me, nor come another step with me."

"When shall we meet again?"

"Never; except by accident. You know you like accidental meetings," added Jane.

"For *first* meetings only. First meetings are the work of Heaven; it is for loving hearts to carry forward what Heaven begins. Are you often this way?"

"Not at this hour; sometimes I walk here with a companion. But when I'm in a place I don't often get the chance of walking out."

"What a shame that a sweet girl should be the slave of some crabbed old mistress. Have you been long out of a place?"

"Oh, dear no; and no girl needn't be who cares for her character."

"Quite true. But I still maintain that a girl of your face and figure should aim above such low drudgery as is entailed upon servant girls.

Everything in its place. You are fit to adorn a gentleman's home, and to command his fortune."

"How you talk!"

"You are indeed. I scorn to flatter. What need have I to flatter you?"

"I'm sure I don't know, and I'm not going to stop longer to inquire," replied the girl, turning her head towards the hedge, and pretending to be dallying with some blue forget-me-nots, for footsteps approached, and she did not wish to be recognised by any one she knew. In a place like Eltham almost everybody was known to everybody, and her surprise was that she had never met the gentleman before who had accosted her in the lane. It was proof to her that he must be a stranger here.

Arm in arm and hand in hand came along a young confiding couple, who were as much surprised to find any one in the lane as Jane was to see them only now entering it.

But females have observant eyes for each other, and Jane could not conceal herself from the man and woman who passed her, although her back was turned upon them.

The woman knew full well Jane's best bonnet, trimmed with a red rose—for was she not with her when she bought it?

The strange gentleman was some paces in advance of Jane, slowly walking onwards, while he turned the front of his well-shaped hat low over his dark Spanish eyes, as if he, too, did not wish to be identified hereafter.

"Why, I declare, if it isn't Jane——"

"Hush!" cried Jane, looking round and preventing her friend from mentioning her name.

"Here's a pretty mystery!" cried the young woman, who was more stylishly dressed than Jane, and who had become acquainted with her through living with a widowed mother, who had a small annuity from the Funds, not far from where Jane lodged with Mrs. Oliphant.

"Look here, Isabella dear," said Jane, going up to the former, and resting her hand on her arm, and talking in low tones that the gentleman, who stood at a little distance, might not hear, although, without being noticed, he strained his hearing to the utmost, as he peered into the thick hedge with the affected enthusiasm of an entomologist seeking for rare insects.

"I caught the name of Jane," he muttered to himself, "I wish the little beauty had not cried 'Hush,' and stopped her friend from mentioning her other name."

"I don't believe one single word of it," said Miss Isabella Ward, who, compared to Jane, was rather a bold, off-hand, slap-dash young lady, and never stopped to study the proprieties of speech or sentiment. "You may tell that tale to the marines, it won't do for an old soldier like me."

"'Pon my word and honour, it is true," reiterated Jane, "I met him in the lane——"

"When the clock strikes nine," finished Isabella. "You have been found out, hasn't she, Bob?"

The person she addressed as "Bob," looked like a good-tempered potman, dressed all in his best to roam abroad with Isabella.

He had a well-trimmed beard, a clean shaven face, a tall white hat turned on one side of his thick head, and he carried in his hand an ivory-headed cane, and he was smoking a meerschaum.

His was a round Dutch-built figure, and he was very proud and happy in being the selected by Isabella from the lads of Eltham, and whom she intended to honour with her hand and small fortune—that is, if she did not change her mind, for she was as fickle as the wind, and without a dash of sentiment.

Now "Bob" was *not* a potman, but a ladies' shoemaker, and the sweet connection had sprung up through his measuring and fitting Miss Ward's pretty little feet with shoes.

He was good-tempered, and good-hearted, but really there was nothing in his face, figure, or manners, that could at all account for the dashing Isabella Ward's attachment to him.

But as this was a matter that so intimately concerned herself more than any one else, the subject was left undiscussed; but the general opinion was that Miss Ward wanted to marry a man whom she could lord it over, and be looked up to as a very superior woman, and above all the husbands in the world.

She did all the courting herself, and "Bob" was treated by her as a mere escort, and he had to take her where and whenever she deemed proper.

She would even dictate the style of his dress, and being shorter in stature than herself, she requested him to have the heels of his boots as high as possible without being noticeable; and further to add to his height, he had to wear for the sake of his imperious Isabella, a short cut-away coat, tight-fitting trousers, and a very tall hat.

"Bob" was not his name; engraved on his card was "Robert Heaviside, Ladies' Boot and Shoemaker."

He kept no shop, but his skilful manipulation with ladies' kid and leather "understandings," either plain or fanciful, brought him an excellent private connection throughout Kent, and had he been as enterprising as he was artistic in shoemaking, Robert Heaviside might have made a fortune.

But he sought no more work than what he could do himself, and although he charged a stiff price to everybody but Isabella, he earned little more than sufficient for his current expenses.

"You are more fortunate in getting sweethearts than I have been, Jane, although it is known that I shall have a fortune when my poor mother dies."

Miss Ward was very pompous, and called two or three hundred pounds a fortune.

"You have had a soldier and sailor, and now I find you with a gentleman in Kidbrook Lane."

"My soldier was a drunkard, my sailor is at sea, and as for the gentleman, Isabella, I assure you that he is a perfect stranger to me; that I *would* speak to me in the lane, and that I wished him to Jericho."

"Oh! you artful girl!" exclaimed Isabella, loudly laughing. "Look here, why did you pretend to be gathering hedge flowers when me and Bob came by? Why, because you did not want to be detected!"

"It was foolish of me, I confess," said Jane, deeply blushing. "But when I heard footsteps approaching, I hardly knew what to do. But it is always best to avoid concealment when you are conscious of doing no wrong. Had you been coming through the lane, he would have made love to you."

"Which I should have liked amazingly," said Isabella.

"For shame!" cried Jane. "But every one knows that you never say what you mean."

"I mean that, though. Gentlemen are scarce in this little poking place! and young ladies must put up with queer little fellows who make their boots and shoes."

Here, to make amends for her freedom of speech, and to heal Mr. Heaviside's wounded feelings, she pulled him by the arm closer to her.

"Do you see, Bob, how his ring glitters in the moonlight?"

"He looks a murdering Spaniard, and I shouldn't wonder if he is," replied Bob.

"Oh! pray don't talk of murder," shuddered Jane. "I have been thinking of it ever since I met him; and how strange that Bob should talk about it!"

"Don't listen to him, Jane, he's a fool!" said the refined Miss Ward. "He's jealous of everybody that's superior to himself. But never fear, Bob, you're all the world to me! Now you ought to say something pretty to me after that; but la! he's such a beauty to walk in green lanes with, for he can talk about nothing but kid and leather boots. How I came to love so much stupidity, I'm sure I can't tell."

"What a girl you are, Bella!" cried Jane. "It shows how much Mr. Heaviside must love you to stand it all," she added.

"We understand each other too well to quarrel. She says what she likes to me, and I say what I like to her. We are both very good-tempered, specially me," said Bob, chuckling at his own wit, which never rose above the most homely and the most hackneyed.

"Musn't throw away dirty water before you get clean, I've heard old Mrs. Oliphant say. You are only a makeshift for me—"

"A make-*shoe*, you mean," said Bob, with another chuckle, that resounded through the lane and awoke its echoes.

"What an abominable little fool you are!" exclaimed Bella Ward, who was tall and bony, and dressed in blue silk, and a white zephyr floating in the breeze, with a gipsy straw-bonnet perched upon the top of rolls and coils of well-oiled shining black hair.

"If I could get another beau I wouldn't put up with you. You only love me for my fortune," continued Miss Ward, whose strong peculiarity was plain-speaking, both in her merriment and anger.

"And you only love me that I make you such sweet pretty shoes, which show off your feet. People say that you have the prettiest foot in Kent."

"And people say right for once," said Miss Ward, tossing her head. "I don't choose to say it is the shoes."

"And if you did, you'd tell a lie. And if you think that, I won't wear your shoes any more."

"Dearest Bella, don't be hurt," said Bob, in mock adoration. "You have got pretty feet and pretty hands, but best of all, you've a pretty face."

"Indeed ! have I ? Well I never heard you say so much before," said Miss Ward, who was eminently pleased.

"Why, what d'ye think I love you for ? " asked Bob.

"For my fortune. I told you so before. Ha ! ha ! This is the way we court each other, Jane. Always wrangling, always loving. We never quarrel, yet ever saying something to hurt each other. How we shall get on when we're married, the Lord only knows."

"I can see one thing," remarked Jane.

"What's that dear ? " inquired Bella.

"That you love each other dearly. And nothing need be feared where there is true love. But men are mostly such deceivers—"

"And women," said Bob, "are so fickle."

"Men think so," replied Jane, "because a young woman has to be very careful before she gives a young man her affections. It is life or death to her. Many a young man has paid his addresses to me, but they are all too fast. Some are given to swearing, some to drink, others to flirting with other girls, so that I've been obliged to put them off. And then a young woman is to be called fickle, because she does not choose to throw herself away. Another thing, you cannot find men out till after you've kept company with them for a little while."

"What a cursed interruption ! " exclaimed the gentleman, who had strolled out of sight of the speakers, and waited in a turn of the lane, where he lit up another cigar, and beat the brambly hedge with his silver-mounted Malacca cane.

"This stranger that has now met me, he has said enough to flatter a girl out of her wits."

"Girls *without* fortunes have to be wide awake," said Bella Ward ; "but those who have got expectations ought to sleep with both eyes open, if possible. What has the stranger been talking about, Jane ? "

"Nothing worth repeating," was her reply. "Wants me to turn my back upon service, and says that my beauty ought to adorn the home of a gentleman."

"Aye, aye, to be a gentleman's mistress, I suppose," chimed in Bella, "and then to be tossed on one side like an old garment, to make room for some other beauty that has caught my gentleman's fancy."

"That's it, Bella," responded Jane, who lingered in this gossiping conversation as if she had forgotten all about the hour of the night and Mrs. Oliphant. "Oh, my gracious ! if my beauty could win me the son of a tradesman I should be very content. But these gentlemen, with horses and carriages and diamond rings, they are all very well if they mean fair."

"But they don't—they only mean ruin to poor girls," observed the wise Isabella Ward. "Not likely ! "

"Be—ware, Jane, be—ware," said Bob, in prophetic accents. "You are a very pretty girl—"

"Indeed ! Is she ? Then please to keep your eyes off her. You'd better go on, Jane, or this little fool will be falling in love with you, too."

"What nonsense, Bella ! " exclaimed Jane, who really drank in the constant admiration of her personal charms.

"Oh, let her go on. Bella likes to chatter and to teaze. She enjoys it, and it does me no harm. Had not Jane better walk with us up the lane, and then we can return together ? "

"Perhaps you and *pretty* Jane had better go by yourselves. I shall be glad to get rid of such a beau as you."

"How am I to take you, Bella ? " asked Bob.

"You won't take me at all," was the curt reply.

"I am ashamed of you, Bella Ward," said Jane. "I can hardly think you mean what you say. Bother this love rubbish ! It is the mischief of the world."

"I don't blame you, Jane, not in the least. But I think it very bad taste on the part of Bob to talk of your beauty before me. Now just hold your noise," she added, as her shoemaker lover was going to explain himself. "You only made the remark to annoy me, and I'll serve you out for it. I've had other offers, too."

"God bless my soul, Bella ! "

"Don't Bella me, if you please, sir," she interrupted, in indescribable tones.

"Why, I was only warning your friend against those snakes in the grass who lure girls, with diamond rings and flattering hopes, to their destruction."

"You seem to know all about it. But you needn't have coupled your warnings with praises of Jane's beauty. You'd better come on if you are coming. Jane is quite wise enough to take care of herself."

"Certainly, Bella," said Pretty Jane. "Besides, I must make haste home. You will be glad to hear that I have got such a nice place at Evesham House, and am going to it next week. But I've got such a lot to tell you, Bella, when I've more time. Shall I see you to-morrow ? "

"Perhaps," Bella stiffly answered.

"And you won't be cross with Mr. Heaviside ? He meant no harm."

"Oh, I've spoken my mind about it, and now it's all over with me. When I see anything wrong, I speak at once. I'm passionate, but not sulky. It was a very rude and thoughtless thing to speak as he did about your prettiness, and if he respects my feelings he won't do it again. You had better make haste, or you will lose your gentleman lover."

"Oh, bother him ! " cried Jane. "It's Mrs. Oliphant I'm thinking about. She'll wonder where I've been."

"Don't fear for her. She's happy enough at the bar of the White Horse. We saw her go in there, didn't we, Bob ? "

"That's right. She's a drunken old hag, and I wonder you went to lodge there."

"She was nurse at my last place, and I then thought her a nice motherly woman. But I soon found her out, and I shall be very glad when I am out of her house, where she will never have me for a lodger again. And as for that hump-backed half idiot son of hers—oh ! he makes me shudder to think of him."

"He'll come to grief," said Bob. "But it's well known that he is no son of Mother Oliphant's."

"So I've heard," said Bella. "He's a frightful ugly creature, who's ever son he is ; enough to frighten his mother, who is a great lady, some people say."

"A customer of mine was telling me the other

" Did her ladyship send any message to me ? "

" No, ma'am."

" Not very polite. How did she look ? "

" Of course, I don't know her at all to say, but she seemed to me to be sad, or ill, or something, I can't tell what."

Mrs. Oliphant's face darkened, then her ear was attracted by the buzzing of a disturbed blue-bottle in the window, no doubt drew forth from its slumber by the light of the candle.

" I hate that noise," she suddenly exclaimed, and then caught the fly with the merry horn, stuck a pin through the harmless creature, and burnt him in the candle.

Nor would the cruel woman be restrained by Jane's pleadings, that she might open the window and let it escape out of the room.

" You make a great fuss about a fly, Jane. The creature had no business to annoy me with his droning. You would not kill a fly, and yet you would marry a man whose trade it was to kill men! You were engaged to a soldier——"

" That is all broken off now," explained Jane.

" That I know. But you did not break from him because he would kill hundreds of men with the same heart as I killed this fly, but because he drank hard. Fiddle-de-dee ! it is nothing but mock humanity. Yet, I had rather not have killed that fly, for it is the first that I have seen for the season, and Nell Dod has told me that it is an unlucky thing to do. Now all this mishap is all through you, for had you been home, as you ought to have been, I should have been asleep in bed an hour ago," added the superstitious woman. " Well, well, what my fate is, that it will be," she muttered in tones so low that Jane did not distinctly hear the words, and then she clasped her hands across her stomach, and for a minute or two closed her eyes.

Then she suddenly said, retracing the conversation to Lady Duchesney—

" You had tea, I suppose, in the servants' hall ? "

" Yes. And after tea they kindly showed me over the house and grounds. But they told me there was an old barn in the four fields, next to the park, that was haunted. Such rubbish !"

" You are young yet, or you would not call things rubbish because you have not seen them."

" Have you seen anything ? "

" No, but I believe in the unseen things. You wouldn't like to sleep in the barn for all your unbelief !"

" Not likely ! But I am more afraid of living things than dead ones."

" Ignorant girl ! Nothing dies. That fly that I have just burnt before your eyes still lives in some shape or other, somewhere or other. But these occult things are beyond your mind. Did you see Mr. Duchesney ? "

" Not that I know of," replied Jane.

" He is a handsome man, with olive complexion, and brilliant eyes. Why do you start and change countenance ? "

Jane became confused. The description of Mr. Duchesney tallied with the gentleman she met just now in Kidbrook Lane. She hardly knew what to reply to Mrs. Oliphant's question, but she never allowed herself to palter with the truth, and she frankly answered that she had not seen such a person at Evesham House, but that she had met a gentleman in the lane exactly like him.

" Had he a retriever dog with him ? "

" Yes, black, and about that high," said the girl, placing her hand a distance from the floor.

" That's him," said Mrs. Oliphant. " And did he speak to you ? "

" He would. I tried to hurry away from him, but he would keep by my side, talking such nonsense."

" A dangerous man with a pretty girl like you. Yet how strange that you should have met the master of the house, and that he made love to you ! "

" Call it not love, Mrs. Oliphant," said the sentimental Jane.

" He called it so, did he not ? "

" All the men do ; they think it is pleasing to girls."

" And to nine out of ten it is," remarked the old woman,

" Then I'm the tenth ; it is not pleasing to me."

" I have but your word for that. But how strange, to be sure ! How foolish Mr. Duchesney will look when he finds you in the house as one of his lady's domestics. Was he drunk or sober ? "

" Oh, he was sober enough, but very wicked."

" I hope to gracious you will say nothing to her ladyship about such nonsense."

" Not I ; I am not a mischief-maker. But she would not care if she knew. She does not mind a pin about him. Let him flirt with the girls as he will, it hurts not her. The marriage ought never to have been contracted."

" For why ? " Jane naturally enough inquired.

" For why ? How should I know, only that it is plain they do not care for each other."

" Very strange that rich people should marry without loving each other."

" Strange it may be, but it is not our business to inquire into the affairs of others. And if you would keep your situation at Evesham House, be blind and deaf. Now that is a caution for you, which you don't deserve, for keeping me up, and now I haven't a bit of sleep in me."

The old woman then got from Jane all that took place in the lane, both with the stranger gentleman, and Bella Ward and Bob Heaviside.

" It is an evil thing for you that you have attracted his notice," said Mrs. Oliphant. " For a man in his position, and with his reckless, devil-me-care nature, will not be thwarted in his fancy by a poor girl."

Jane looked alarmed, and said :

" If I thought so, I ought not to go to service there. But I defy all the men in the world——"

" Don't be wilful, maid. You are not stronger in virtue than the rest of womankind in your position. Temptation——"

" But I won't be tempted, Mrs. Oliphant!" cried Jane, indignantly.

" Hasn't every maid said so ? " was the old woman's derisive reply.

" You ought not to talk in this way, Mrs. Oliphant. You quite frighten me. I wish I had never gone to Evesham House."

" You may wish, poor timid thing ! but you have your destiny as well as other people, and not all your wishing, nor all your fears, nor all your strength can set it on one side. But I have a letter for you from Calcutta——"

"Oh, from my dear William! Where is it? Why did you keep it from me so long?"

"Why did you stay out so late? I was half inclined to be wicked enough not to give it to you at all. But there it is," she added, withdrawing it from her bosom.

Jane kissed the letter—love will be demonstrative—before she broke the seal. Then drew her hand across her eyes to remove a film that tears and excitement had brought there. Then to herself, mid hopes and fears, she read the letter, which was much better in its composition than its orthography, which we have not followed, or our readers would not have been enabled to make any sense of it.

"*H.M.S. Firefly*, Calcutta.
"My Dearest Jane,
"This is the first port I have put into for a very long time, our ship having been knocked about at sea by all kinds of disastrous weather. You must have thought me dead or forgetful of you. I might have died, but I could never forget you. A sailor's life is a terrible cruel one, to have to leave so often and so long, all the treasure of his heart. Heart! oh! it would be well if sailors had none to love with, for it is torture indeed for it to be torn away when it has anchored near a sweet little craft that cannot be sailing with him. Your pretty face is always with me. I love too deeply not to be jealous of the land rats that crawl about after the treasures of others. My dearest Jane, oh! beware of them for my poor sake. My heart is in your keeping. For the love of heaven, hold it as a sacred trust! My first waking thoughts are for you and your welfare, my last prayers are for your constancy and our speedy meeting. You know our promise to each other, that when I return we are to be married. I was not well last night, and I got leave to go to my hammock, where I fell asleep with a burning brain, and dreamt a frightful dream about you."

Jane changed colour; the roses on her cheeks gave place to a lily's whiteness, and tear after tear dropped on the letter.

"I dreamt that you were stung by a viper while walking in a country lane, and that nothing in the world could cure you. But, ah! my dearest Jane, the worst, the most painful part of my dream has to be told. You were in the lane by appointment with a young gentleman far beyond your station in life, and that while he gave you a parting kiss, a viper stole from the hedge and stung your ankle. Here I came by, and, with a hammer in my hand, I killed the viper and then killed you. Upon this I awoke, my heart beating thump against my chest, and I was some time before I could believe that I had been dreaming. But I was thankful to find at last that 'twas but a dream, and dreams, you know, unlike most sailors, I don't believe in. But I could not have suffered more had it been true. Heaven preserve me from such dreams again as those, and blot them from my memory. It grieves me when I think that you are left in such an unprotected state. I shall be very glad when we have our home together, if it be but a room. Sailors must not be milksops, or home-sick, but 'pon my life, I wish I

had not gone this voyage. Something dreadful to happen hovers about me all day long. Our ship will be here till the next mail comes out; and if it does not bring me a long and loving letter from you, I shall be miserable indeed. Has my sister Betty got married yet? When you go into Essex give my truest love to mother and brother Ben. I have written to them all with this. I send this to Blackheath, to be forwarded to you if you have left the place; but I hope not, for you always told me it was a good situation, and that you were very happy there. Longing to kiss and embrace you, dearest Jane,
"I am thine and only thine,
"William Godwin.

"P.S.—Be sure and write at once, or you may lose the mail. Inquire at the post office for the latest day of sailing. But better write directly you receive this, for you cannot be too early. For to miss a letter from you would be distressing to me. God bless you."

CHAPTER IV.

JANE IS AGAIN RUTHLESSLY ASSAILED BY HER LANDLADY.—GHOSTS AND HAUNTED HOUSES. THE HUNCHBACK'S BREAKFAST.—NELL DOD. —THE DREAM INTERPRETED.—A VISITOR TO MRS. OLIPHANT.

The numerous unpleasant events of the evening, all coming together as they did, greatly bewildered Jane's brain, which was deepened by the melancholy tone and dream told in her William's fond letter.

She seemed, too, to loathe the presence of Mrs. Oliphant, and bidding her good night, she stole away to her bedroom, which the back parlour was converted into.

When she reached her room it was not for rest; her brain, through which the blood careered like wild horses, would not yield to the soft offices of gentle sleep. Placing her Sunday-out bonnet carefully away in the bandbox, she took a seat in a dilapidated rush-bottomed chair, and once more read her dear William's letter of love, warnings, dreams and omens.

Ugly dreams never fail to leave ugly impressions, whether we have any superstitious faith in them or not. Those who do not believe in ghosts or spirits from the dead would nevertheless shrink from sleeping in a reputed haunted house, and would go miles out of the way rather than go through a churchyard by night.

The truth is, that we all practically believe in the presence of spiritual creatures round and about us; for there are the ghosts and spectres of the mind, as well as the disembodied ones, which so many thousands avow they have seen, which so many eminent persons attest to have been the witnesses of.

Of course there are some closer disciples than others in the faith of ghosts and apparitions, but we believe that there are none but believe in them, while they affect to deny their existence.

So it was with Jane, who now pondered over her sailor's dream. She placed the letter on the japanned table, and began to take the pins from her long hair, and the cameo brooch from the top of her silk jacket, and otherwise to prepare herself for the little iron bedstead.

Indeed, Jane's was a poor and miserable lodging, and she thanked her stars that her stay in it would be short, nor would she have set foot in it, had she known what it was, or the character of the landlady, who, instead of making her home clean and habitable, and adorning it with some nice furniture, spent all her earnings in drink.

She had not gone far, however, in her preparations for rest, before she was thrilled by the voice of Mrs. Oliphant, calling from the garden, on which Jane's window looked.

"I will thank you to put your light out, and get to bed! Neighbours will think mine to be a bad house, to see lights in the window at this time of night. Nor can I afford the burning of candles through the night."

Mrs. Oliphant did not seem to remember that in her regard for the character of her house, she herself was burning a candle at the unseemly hour of ten, and the reflection of which might be seen from the Eltham main road, that led direct to London one way, and further into the county of Kent the other. But she was in spiteful, quarrelsome mood, and she cared not what she said or did to gratify it.

Besides, there were none there to see Jane's light, for the back of the house was surrounded with cherry gardens and apple orchards, the trees of which were now arrayed in lovely blossoms ripening for the delicious fruit.

Jane opened her window, to reply to the growling old woman, who stood beside a little bed of flowers that the hunchback boy had planted, while she looked up to the window with its six small panes of glass. The gentle wind blew into her room a most delicious perfume from the fruit-bearing trees, and played with the tresses she had unbound, and blew out the candle.

"I don't see why you should be so spiteful towards me, Mrs. Oliphant," she called out; "I shall leave in the morning."

"Don't you be so stuck up. That gentleman has turned your head, I think. Better be governed by older and wiser heads than your own. But for me, you'd have had no other place to go to."

"I won't go to the place at all, after what you've told me."

"Ah! you don't mean that."

"But I do, though," replied Jane, and closed her window; then, by the light from the moon only she went to bed, and after a while, strange to relate, with a very slight difference, she dreamt o'er again her William's dream, mingled with the distressing events of the day.

When she awoke in the morning, she was far from refreshed. Her young heart was deeply troubled, and her brain became filled with tragic presentiments in the future.

After she had dressed herself, she began to pack her boxes—but where to go she knew not. While she was thus deliberating this question, her landlady walked into her room and summoned her to the frugal breakfast. Spangled Dick had prepared as neatly as circumstances would admit.

The old woman had slept off the deadly fumes of the gin she had drunk the preceding day, and was far more congenial towards the girl.

"Let bygones be bygones, there's a good girl," she said; "I've a good bit of trouble on my mind, and sometimes really know not what I do.

Come along to breakfast, I've got some nice hot rolls for you and a beautiful cup of tea!"

Jane was wretched, but she bore no malice; she was neither a sulky nor a passionate girl, and soon yielded to the soft, kind tones of her changed landlady, and followed her from the back to the front parlour, and took her seat beside the round table, which the deformed boy had graced with a bunch of tall graceful weeds and fresh field flowers, which hung their smiling heads over the broken-lipped jug in which their stems were placed, and shed a charm over the dingy poverty of the room and its meagre appointments.

The dwarfed and hunchbacked boy sat at the table, but spoke little. He dared not. But he listened attentively to what passed between Jane and his mother. An admiring glance he every now and then directed towards Jane, when he politely buttered a roll for her, a luxury which was denied to him.

Jane began to feel some pity for the boy, and she told him to take one for himself, and that she would buy some more if there were not enough.

"Oh, dear no, bread and butter is quite good enough for him, a poor wretch of a boy, who is neither use nor ornament."

This dreadful speech from a mother to her son touched Jane's heart more than ever, and her repugnance to the boy's physical misfortunes was forgotten in her pity and sympathy for the unkind treatment he was subjected to.

"Dick shall have a roll if I go without myself," said Jane, pleasantly but determinedly; and she buttered one for him, and placed it by his teacup.

Poor Dick was quite overwhelmed. He had never had so much kindness shown him in his wretched life before. Hot rolls and butter! he felt himself quite unworthy of such luxuries, and would rather Jane had not invited him to partake Besides, saw he not his dreadful mother's grey forbidding eye upon him? How could he swallow food that was so much grudged him? It would choke him—that it would. And so Jane's roll and butter remained untouched, to be gazed at, but not to be tasted.

The sailor's letter now became the subject of conversation, and Jane retailed out the dream it contained, adding her own to it. Mrs. Oliphant, holding her cup and saucer in her hand, remarked that it was very strange, and only wished that she was as learned as Nell Dod in occult science, and then she would interpret it for her.

The old witch lives at Greenwich," she said, "and if you like to go there with me by-and-by, she will tell you all about it for a shilling."

"I'd give her twenty if she could," replied Jane. "But none but God can tell the future."

"Nell Dod can, I tell you. And you must come with me."

"I don't mind. We can but hear her notions. They'll serve for a laugh."

"You may yet have to weep, my beauty," suggested Mrs. Oliphant.

The afternoon arrived, the sun shone brightly and they took the rail to Greenwich, and were soon at Nell Dod's hovel beside the river.

The interior of the hovel was too filthy to be described, likewise Nell herself.

Mrs. Oliphant, with considerable reverence

and importance, introduced the subject of the dream, and the old crone with extended bony hand, while she looked preciously sharp at Jane, exclaimed,

"That dream means murder !"

Jane shuddered, even while she did not believe, and as she shrank by the table, she asked,

"The murder of whom ?"

"Have you ears to hear and heart to bear, while I reply the murder of yourself !"

"Come on, Mrs. Oliphant, I've heard quite enough."

"But there's my fee to pay, poor young leddy !" said the crone, in affected pitying tones, who well looked after number one, not that she was altogether selfish, for she looked religiously after her two grizzly grimalkins, whose witch-like oracular looks gave an additional awe to the crone's mystic rites and ceremonies.

Jane left the hovel, but Mrs. Oliphant lingered behind for a minute or two in whispered conversation with Nell Dod. She quickly overtook Jane, and the two strolled into Greenwich Park, sat under a grand old tree, and Jane, anxious to divert her thoughts from Nell Dod's interpretation of her dream, called two tame fawns to her side, and fed the agile things with biscuits.

Here they remained until the shades of evening approached, when they came down Royal Hill, and through London Street, to the Railway Station, and soon reached Eltham.

On their way to the station, Mrs. Oliphant refreshed the inner man with a little drop of gin, and was rather angry with her youthful companion because she would not join her.

"Don't be squeamish, child," remonstrated Mrs. Oliphant. "It isn't like as it you went into a public-house by yourself—that wouldn't look well for a pretty creature like you ; but with an old woman like me, no one would notice it."

"You can't persuade me, Mrs. Oliphant," persisted Jane. "I never did, nor I hope I never shall go to public-houses. I think it is so unwomanly."

"Hark at the chit ! Unwomanly indeed ! And pray what do you mean by that ? I have come a long way on your business, and in truth I feel some sinking at the pit of my stomach."

"Then by all means have what you like. I will pay for it, and wait for you. But it would do me harm to take any thing of the kind."

"Pish ! you must try and be like other females, or you'll never get on in this hard world. But it is the worst of you that you will be different to other people quite as virtuous as yourself. Come on !"

"Oh ! don't persuade me, there's a dear soul. I have had excitement enough to-day, and am just now getting myself again, and I wouldn't take spirits for the world."

"A glass of nice ale then ?"

Jane shook her head.

"Then you shall have a cool bottle of ginger pop, just to keep me company."

The old woman pushed back the heavy creaking door of the public with one hand, and dragged Jane in with the other. Jane, as she stood at the bar felt as if she were committing a crime, but her companion, old in sin, asked for her half quartern and the ginger beer, with the utmost familiarity and boldness.

"Say what you like ; but a drop of gin is a great mercy for the windy spasms, which I am subject to, and which, if you should ever be afflicted with, when you come to years, you will find nothing better nor nicer. My doctor recommended it to me, and it shows he well knew my constitution."

They reached home, talking a good deal about one thing and another by the way.

Outside the door of the house, the hunchback boy was sitting on the step, which he had well hearthstoned, revelling in a book of adventures, and so absorbed was he that he did not see his mother and Jane approaching, and was only made aware of their presence by the stern voice of the woman who assumed to be his mother, peremptorily ordering him in-doors.

"There's a gentleman in the parlour," said the boy, quickly getting on his dwarfed legs, and pushing open the door.

Jane started back. Could it be the gentleman she had met in the lane ?

"Why didn't you say so before, you imp ?" cried Mrs. Oliphant.

"I hadn't time to tell you, before," replied the poor little malformed boy. When addressing the woman he could never take the name of mother on his pallid lips.

"Whoever can it be ?" asked Jane.

"Somebody for you ; but you needn't be alarmed, I will take care of you," said Mrs. Oliphant, already leading the way through the short passage to the door that opened into the dim little parlour, followed by the trembling girl and the hunchback boy.

CHAPTER V.

THE STRANGER INTERROGATED.—A SCUFFLE.—
JANE ALARMED.—THE HUNCHBACK LISTENS.
—FEARFUL REVELATIONS.

"Who are you, pray ?" inquired Mrs. Oliphant, while Jane stood trembling behind her.

"Had there been more light in the room, you wouldn't have needed to ask that," was the reply of him who sat under the picture of the "Finding of Moses."

The speaker spoke in pleasant accents, but there was a Devonshire twang in his speech. His white wide-awake hat was on the table, and by the side of it was his stick, while the room gave evidence that he had been smoking—indeed, he held a brier-root pipe in his hand.

"Is it you, Josh Woodward ?"

"That's my name, old gal ; and Josh is devilish tired, too. And I don't think it's the cheese that you should fix your quarters so near Evesham House."

"Hush !" whispered Mrs. Oliphant, going close to his ear. "There's a stranger here. Will you come out and talk ?"

"That I can't for nobody," said Josh, "for I've been walking and riding all day. I've put my hoss up at the inn close by, and ordered a bed there, but I wanted to see you before I done myself up for the night. Get us a light—get us a light, woman, I've a horror of darkness ; besides, my matches are gone, and I want to light my pipe. Been out on the lush, I s'pose, haven't ee ?"

"Can't you be quiet I tell you !" said the woman, in hushed tones. She then left the room, closing the door behind her, and beckoning Jane into the back bedroom, telling her that the visitor was not a gentleman, but an old fellow-servant of hers when she lived at Earl Ashford's, in Grosvenor Square, and that as she had some private affairs to talk over, perhaps Jane had better go to bed. The latter, who was very very weary, readily assented to this.

"And as for *you*, you had better make yourself scarce, or it will be worse for you," she said to the hunchback, who looked her wistfully in the face of Jane. He then said—"Good night, Jane," and held out his hand to her, and slowly went up to his dark little room.

Mrs. Oliphant returned to the parlour, bearing in her hand a candle, which revealed to her eyes more particularly the young man who had been half an hour waiting for her. He was about thirty, with a round, clean-shaven face, and a smiling, open countenance. He wore a green cut-away Newmarket coat, and he had riding boots that came to his knees. A blue-silk bird's eye scarf round his throat, adorned with a horse-shoe diamond pin. If his coat had been unbuttoned, which it was not, might have been seen a white waistcoat, with a massive gold cable chain. His light-brown hair was cut short, and on the whole, he looked like a respectable young farmer, much disposed to be "horsey."

He was an excellent figure, and a homely, honest-looking man. But appearances are sometimes deceptive, and it was so, to some extent, in the case of Josh Woodward.

However, what he was, or what he was not, by some unaccountable means he had captivated the love and passion of his beautiful young mistress, who, when he first made her acquaintance, bore the title of Lady Mary Ashford, and was the third daughter of the Earl of Ashford.

He had been her groom, and as ladies are frequently in the habit of riding and driving about alone with their handsome, well-dressed grooms, so did Lady Mary Ashford knock about with Josh Woodward.

She conceived a low passion for Josh, who, not being gifted with much perception, was a long time before he saw the honour that was intended him.

Seeing that so many aristocratic young ladies have disgraced their families and tarnished their titles by amours with their grooms or male attendants, it really is surprising, that in the London season you meet with so many beautiful creatures riding or driving about alone with young, swellish grooms.

Servants and earls' daughters are but men and women in nature's parliament, and are subject to the same passions that attend all flesh and blood; therefore, experience teaches us that it is a dangerous practice to trust ladies and grooms too much alone together.

Lady Mary was very "fast," and Josh was a good-looking, simple youth of nineteen, the same age as herself, when he was appointed her groom.

It came to the Earl's knowledge that his daughter had been surprisingly familiar with her groom, and she was remonstrated with, and Josh discharged.

But the scandal began to be talked about in high circles, and Lady Mary pleaded that a great wrong had been done her by her father's haste in dismissing Josh, and thereby giving a serious complexion to nothing more than that one day she was seen by some of the other domestics of the Earl's establishment playfully slap Josh's face.

It certainly was a great freedom on the part of Lady Mary towards her lowly servant, and no doubt the Earl did right to resent such conduct in the manner he did. But as Lady Mary demanded that her character was at stake, and nothing but the recall of the groom, and his being reinstated as her body servant, would wipe away the stain, the Earl foolishly yielded, and Josh was recalled into my lady's service.

Not many months after this the voluptuous Lady Mary placed herself in the complete power of her favourite servant, and quite forgot herself as a woman, and her being a leading member of a high and noble family.

"Now we can talk, Josh, but you must talk low; for the girl sleeps in the next room," said Mrs. Oliphant, taking her seat in her accustomed arm-chair.

"Who is she?" asked Josh, lighting his pipe.

"Oh! nobody; a poor servant girl who has been out of place, and I took her in, and I have got Lady Duchesney to give her a birth."

"You're doing a d——d stupid thing, Mother Oliphant," replied the groom, crossing one high-booted leg over the other.

"How so, Josh?" inquired the woman, sitting bolt upright in her chair.

"The idea of your bringing anybody to live with you! By-and-by we shall all get talked about together; and then, blue blazes! won't there be an explosion!"

"What care I?" cried Mrs. Oliphant.

"You'd lose your money, wouldn't you?" asked Josh.

"Not if I know it!" said Mrs. Oliphant. "I'm too much a woman of the world to lose my money. The boy will yet have a position—"

"In a grave or the union," interrupted Josh, laughing.

"Since I saw you, what d'ye think I've discovered?"

"A gold mine, perhaps," answered Josh.

"Don't be flippant! Guess again," said the woman.

"Not I. This is not a Christmas party, and a game at riddles. I know a thing that you have not discovered—the way to become an honest woman."

"What, indeed! And that from the like of you! I'll throw the candlestick at your head if you insult or taunt me! What I am, your Earl's daughter has made me. Evil be to them who tempt needy women to commit crimes for money. But I haven't killed the boy for all that."

"The figure offered wasn't high enough for your greediness, or else you would have killed the boy."

"Liar! I wouldn't!" she exclaimed.

"You've been drinking, Mother Oliphant!" said Josh, and it is no good talking to you about anything when that's the case. "You told me to speak low, while you bellow like a cow that's lost its calf. But let's travel back to business. What have you discovered?"

"Don't know that I shall tell you now," said the old woman, who gave indications of deep offence.

"Then I'll come to-morrow morning. Although

I don't want to be seen here in the daylight,"—and Josh rose to go.

"Had you any business with me?"

"Yes, or you may depend upon it I should not be here, for you are not such an agreeable companion for a fellow to call upon in a friendly way."

"Your business, pray, and keep your insults to yourself."

"One thing at a time," said Josh Woodward.

"What have you discovered?"

"Don't mock me, and I will tell you. Those spangles on the boy's left breast I have traced out into the shape of a coronet."

"What of that!" said Josh, screwing his lip up to the tip of his nose. "He'll never bear one on his head."

"Don't you make light of those things, young man. That coronet on his breast—"

"Is a proof, you think, that he will yet wear one on his head? Ha! ha! ha! Go to, you silly old woman."

"What has Nature placed it there for then?" she asked.

"What the devil do I know about Nature? I never could make out why she made such an old frump as you," he added, laughing.

The insulted woman suddenly rose from her chair, and cast a flashing scowl at Josh, then sprang upon him, and seized him by the collar of his coat and shook him wrathfully.

"Hands off!" cried Josh, "or I'll throttle you, although you're a woman!"

He then threw his assailant from him with that force, that the table and all upon it was upset.

Jane had been much disturbed by the conversation, a good deal of which she had necessarily learnt, although she could make nothing out of it, only that there was some evil mystery between Mrs. Oliphant and her visitor. But when the scuffling began, and the table was upset, she began to be alarmed, and in her nightdress came and knocked at the parlour door, and asked what was the matter.

Mrs. Oliphant was saved from falling by the table, and when she had fairly recovered her equilibrium, with a face as tallow-white as a new-shorn sheep, she exclaimed—

"The devil take you, Josh!"

"The same to you!" replied Josh, arranging his bird's eye scarf, which had been much rumpled, "and may your devil be more of a devil than mine."

Jane had knocked again, and besought Mrs. Oliphant to go to bed.

The old woman opened the door and went with her to her room.

"This is all very frightful for me to hear," said Jane. "It quite frightens me. Do go to bed, and I will leave this house in the morning, or to-night if I knew where to go."

"Don't be alarmed, my dear," said Mrs. Oliphant, "the best of friends will quarrel sometimes."

"But such language is not fit for me to hear," said the timid Jane.

"Oh! we shall be friends directly, me and Josh. You don't know us."

"And I hope I never shall."

"Hush! my dear. Josh is more than you know. A word against Josh to Lady Duchesney would be destruction to you. But, between ourselves, he is a hasty, good-for-nothing fellow for all that. But my fit of passion is all over, and you will not be disturbed again. Get into bed and say your prayers!"

Jane had already made her peace with heaven before closing her eyes for the night, but she was amazed that Mrs. Oliphant could talk of prayers after the language she had been using, and her continued cruelty to the hunchback boy, and her drinking habits.

But the old woman was a strange mixture of good and evil, especially the latter ingredient. She did not, however, wish any further remarks from Jane, but made her exit from that room and her entrance into the front, when Jane locked her bedroom door and endeavoured to compose her racked brain to sleep, in which task she was aided by the lullaby wind which was soughing through the orchard trees at the back of the house.

Mrs. Oliphant was quite a master in the change of her moods; almost in the same minute she could be a storm raging like a wild beast, and a gentle summer zephyr. She was a woman hard to analyse or make out. Nature appeared to have given her power over all her changes.

But she was a woman, no doubt, ill at ease with herself for her continued wickedness, and living upon the infamy of others. She was a sinner of the first degree, a Newgate calendar of crimes embodied in her person. But by her cleverness she had escaped those chains that hung frowningly over the debtor's door of that gloomy prison pile.

Yet, in her more youthful days, she had had a heart to love, but her love had been taken advantage of, and it turned to hate of the object of her affections and all mankind.

Without being a wife she had been a mother. And if a certain garden in Walworth could disclose its contents, there would be found the remains of Rebecca Hart's baby. This desertion by the man she loved and trusted, infused into her blood the ferocity of a beast, and the first exhibition of it was made on her first born. From this tragic period of her life she became indifferent to crime, or anything but herself.

Her name was Rebecca Hart, and she was of Jewess extraction on the maternal side; but after the murder of her baby, when she was in service, she fled from Walworth, and took the name of Oliphant; and when she took up the position of a monthly nurse, it was then she became acquainted with Lady Mary Ashford, who sought the professional assistance of Mrs. Oliphant, while she lived in a dark slum of Whitechapel.

What a change from Belgravia to Whitechapel! Yet the earl's daughter was glad to go anywhere to hide the "misfortune" that had attended her love of her groom, Joshua Woodward.

CHAPTER VI.

A DARK CONVERSATION.—THE HUNCHBACK OVERHEARS DREADFUL THREATS.—THE LOVE BABY.—JOSH AWAKENED BY CONSCIENCE TO HIS CRIMES.

"WHAT a pity it is that we are both so excitable!" exclaimed Mrs. Oliphant, re-entering

PRETTY JANE

OR, THE

VIPER OF KIDBROOK LANE

"GIVE ME A PICK-AXE AND A SPADE, AND I WILL DIG THE GRAVE MYSELF!"
EXCLAIMED LADY MARY.

the parlour, as Josh, with his wide-awake on his head, and stick in hand, was about to take "good night" of it. "Say it's a pity, Josh?" she added, in somewhat endearing tones; at the same time, to give more effect to them, she seized Lady Duchesney's paramour by the hand.

"I shan't say it's a pity," said Josh, putting her on one side. "You should learn to behave yourself."

"That's right—that's quite right," said Mrs. Oliphant, clasping her narrow, yet tall brow, with both her hands. "But I have such distracted moments come over me, that no one is safe with me."

"It's all gin," said the uncouth man.

"Oh, dear no; the only spirit that moves my heart and brain is the spirit of grief. Sit down again, Josh—don't leave an old acquaintance in such hot haste and temper. What did you come for?"

"To take the boy away," was the blunt answer.

"You shan't! you shan't! The life of that boy is my witness and my living," said the woman, with some vehemence, although she spoke scarcely above her breath.

"Well, that is Lady Mary's wishes."

"Oh, indeed! And when did you see her?"

"I have just left her by the barn, almost as raving as yourself."

"Poor creature! I feel for her; but Spangled Dick, if he is to die, shall die before my eyes. He is asleep by this—go upstairs and kill him now."

"No, thank'ee; I can drown kittens, but not cats. Had he been an infant, I could have squeezed out his life with my finger and thumb," said Josh, bringing those two members of his body tightly together.

"I daresay you could."

"And why didn't *you?* Lady Mary meant it, and you understood that she did."

"The money was not enough to risk hanging for. And now, Josh, you have the truth, the whole truth, and nothing but the truth."

"Well, am I to have the boy or no?"

"Not by my consent," was the short answer.

"And if I took him without your consent, you'd blab! Eh? I know you."

"I must have a living for life out of the job. I've kept the ugly miscreant under my eye for twelve years upon a very poor pittance, and if the end must come, well then, I must have a lump sum down, or so much for life."

"You have had a good deal for doing nothing already. But you squander and don't know what you get, and you are always wanting."

"What have I had?"

"More than twelve hundred pouuds—more than a hundred a year. I know you have, Lady Mary told me so."

"And is that a great deal for keeping an ugly boy for that time, and an ugly secret?"

"I think so for persons in your position, who might have starved, or been a drudge without it. Lady Mary did not play her cards to rights, or you'd have known nothing."

"That's a question, and nothing to the point. I do know all, though she was confined with a mask on her face, to conceal herself from me. But the birth was a difficult one, and in her agony, screams, and delirium, she tore away the mask, and revealed her face."

"What of that? You were none the wiser as to who she was from seeing her face," said the man.

"But did I never tell you how I found her out?"

"Don't remember as you did," he replied, with some indifference.

"Then listen," she said, with that satisfaction in her tones that distinguishes the gossip when she has some tale to tell, and some one to hear. "You came with her to Whitechapel, did you not?"

"I don't care to hear anything about it now. That's not my business here to-night," he added, while signs of displeasure mantled his face. "It is a subject better forgotten than remembered," —here he rose from the chair, and with an uneasy mind he heavily strode the little room.

The woman observed the horseman's disturbance of mind, and wondered at the change that had so very suddenly come o'er the spirit of his dream.

"It's no use crying about spilt milk," she sagely observed.

"I want none of your comfort," he ill-temperedly returned.

"Can't understand you, Josh. You blow hot and cold with the same breath. But I don't see why you should be so quarrelsome with me. I have saved your hands from shedding the blood of your child."

"Speak not of the Hunchback as my child!" he exclaimed. "You know that I have never allowed my feelings ever to think of him as such—"

"But that wont do. Whether you love him, or loathe him, he is your son. If you love him not—"

"Love him!" mouthed the groom. "How can a fellow love a thing that he hardly ever saw? and only hears of with horror?"

"I grant you that the boy could not give the eyes of father or mother much pleasure, especially as it was born under the rose, and such a difference in station between sire and dam. But it must live on now—"

"Don't speak to me about him."

"You most unnatural father!" exclaimed this half fiend, half woman, jestingly.

"Don't you be quite so pat with your father. Had the child been anything but the monstrosity it is, I should have been proud to have acknowledged it."

"And so might Lady Mary."

"Not she. She is the most unnatural woman upon the face of the earth, and the most dangerous to be connected with. When it suits her purpose she will have my life."

"Dear me, no, Josh; you are her fancy man," said the woman, endeavouring to elicit as much information as possible from the horseman as to his relations with Lady Mary since her marriage with Mr. Duchesney. "Have your life! mine more likely."

"What have you to do with her, that she should harm you?"

"Don't I know too much for her safety?"

"She is too fearless to care for anything you or anybody else knows. She is a mad woman, and when she's drunk she defies Heaven and Hell."

"Does she drink as hard as ever?"

"Nothing but lapping all the day through, and she gives herself no time to eat."

"A fearful woman to be sure! Heaven has not made many such to curse the world with," she added, taking a drop of neat gin, for she had an antipathy to dilute her favourite beverage. "Drink, upon my life, seems to be the curse of so many men and women, rich and poor, that had I not some internal complaint, never a drop more should pass my lips, if only for example to others. And what says her husband to her goings on?"

"Never a word. They're a fine handsome pair, too—"

"So they are, so they are," chimed in the nurse.

"But, 'pon my soul, they don't care that for each other," bringing his finger and thumb together with a fillip.

"Strange!"

"Not a bit of it!" cried the groom. "She only married him to save some part of her fortune, and he only married her that he might put his paw on a few ready thousands as her dowry. What happiness is to be expected from such a union? He drinks as much as she does, and altogether they're well matched."

"Do they quarrel?"

"Quarrel! they fight like tom cats, and the

husband always gets the worst of it. From some cause or other they hate each other."

" Needn't hunt far for the cause. He knows she's had a child, and that she loves you."

" Make no blunder; she's too much of a fiend to love."

" See what she's suffered for you. Does her husband ever throw it up to her?"

" Daresay, but never heard him," he laconically replied. " They don't live together; got separate apartments; live under the same roof, I believe, only to annoy each other."

" Of course he don't know that you live at the house?"

" Of course he does; and when he comes into the servant's hall he's as jolly as a sand-boy. He don't suspect, of course, that I am the father of Lady Mary's child. He was given to understand by the earl, at the time of the marriage, that both were dead, and so Lady Mary told her father. But they don't look upon each other as man and wife—you understand what I mean— I can't explain myself nearer."

" Yoked together for money, that's what you mean, Josh?"

" That's just it. Money buys the best of us into any service."

" Natural enough, too, for we can't get along without it. I am bad only because I am poor. Nobody will starve for the love of goodness. Heaven, though, will deal with us, for all that, mark me."

" Don't you palaver of things beyond your reach. Heaven is many long chalks out of your depth."

The woman cast on her visitor those glances of anger that she had done when the scuffle ensued between them, and with constrained calmness she retorted to Josh's insinuations of her unfitness for Heaven—

" Perhaps not. But that again is a question. The gates are wide enough for the worst of sinners. I know I shall have to denounce a great deal before I can hope to enter, but I'm not without hope. But, look here, Josh. Woodward, we'd best be friends. We can't afford to quarrel with each other, nor can Lady Duchesney dare to quarrel with either of us."

" Don't trouble yourself about me. You can't hurt me," replied the horseman, looking her defiantly in the face.

" I can, Josh," rejoined the woman, giving him stare for stare. " But you don't know that I can."

The woman spoke so earnestly, that for the moment he believed that she knew his wickedness, and he started back and looked alarmed.

" I can hang you and your noble mistress any day I think proper. So best be civil—best be civil. True, I am a dependent on the bounty of Lady Mary—but she has yet to know that she is dependent on me for her life."

" You are raving, Mother Oliphant. Come, now, what d'ye know about me? "

" I shall bide my time, and reveal my secrets when they will do me the most good. I, and you, and Lady Mary are terrible wicked people. You may affect to laugh, but you know you fear me."

" The devil take you, I don't fear you. You are making a great mystery about nothing at all. The most you can tell is, that the hunchback boy is the illegitimate offspring of a groom and an earl's daughter, and that you hold them in your power."

" Is that my secret?" she derisively questioned the man, who, puffing out a volume of smoke, assumed an indifference that he did not feel.

" You could not be hung for being the father of illegitimate children, but you can for what you do with them. Their little lives are as much protected by law as those in wedlock born. Need more be said?"

As she asked the question she searched the man before her through and through with her dead grey eyes, and he could not meet her dissecting orbs, but cast his upon the floor, while he momentarily considered how and what to answer to her significant question.

She was not slow to see that confusion on his open country countenance which conscious guilt is sure to betray when it is challenged. She repeated the question, and Woodward at length found tongue to say—

" You're not worth wasting words upon," and then finished off with a meaningless boisterous horse-laugh, which moved Mrs. Oliphant to ask a still further disturbing question :

" There is an old barn in Evesham House, eh, Woodward?"

" Who said there wasn't?" he retorted, with rising temper.

" Do you want to know what is concealed in that barn?"

" Rats, cobwebs, and spiders," with assumed bravado, he unhesitatingly replied, and then repeated his horse-laugh, while he cleared out the ashes from his pipe in the grate, and then rose to go.

" And what else is in the barn?" she inquired, gently detaining the shame-faced man by the wrist.

" Burn the barn!" exclaimed Josh, withdrawing his arm from her hold.

" Don't you wish some one would burn it? You would sleep the better, wouldn't you, if that rotten old pile were blazed to the ground?"

The guilty man wriggled under the torture the equally guilty woman, by her inuendo and roundabout interrogatories, was inflicting on him. She evidently knew more than she ought, and he saw no use in longer fencing with her.

" Keep all your secrets for a good market, for I promise you that they wont suit me to buy," he said, beating his leg with his cane.

Mrs. Oliphant replied that she had but one secret that Josh did not know; but all the secrets that the barn would one day reveal he did know.

The man still pretended ignorance, and she then enlightened him further by asking him how many children Lady Mary had had by him?

This question unmistakeably proved to him that by some mysterious means she was acquainted with the crime which lay heavy on his soul.

He tried in vain to draw from the nurse and baby-murderess who it was that put snch stuff into her head about the barn?

Mrs. Oliphant had not the smallest inclination to gratify the curiosity of Lady Mary's well-dressed favourite, who sat crest-fallen before her, mentally struggling with his guilt.

The woman was satisfied. Her only object was to take the offensive bounce out of the high-booted man, and to treat her with more consideration. She paid out her coil of rope just far enough to make the man tremble, and to impress upon him that he and her and Lady Mary were all in the same black boat together, and that they must behave themselves towards her, or a single breath of hers would scuttle the boat and drown them.

All this she had now accomplished, and the poor young man, on whom had fallen the evil passion of a high-born wicked woman, now almost shrank with fear before the woman he had treated with contumely and insult during most part of the evening.

She was determined that both he and Lady Mary should be made to feel that she was far more necessary to their existence than they to hers.

What did they know of her? Did they, or any one else, know anything about what lay buried beneath that Walworth garden?

She flattered herself that without fear of contradiction she could stand before all the world, and lay her hand on her breast, and ask, who is there here to accuse me of crime?

Could Lady Duchesney or the now wan-faced man before her do this? Not if she were there to answer their challenge, and chose to speak.

She personally had more regard for Josh than his mistress, Earl Ashford's wretched daughter. A fellow feeling makes us wondrous kind, and it was her belief that the groom had been seduced by an evil woman into the pitfalls of crime, as she herself had been by the unhappy influences of a base and cruel man.

Her own misfortunes in the girlhood of her life elicited her sympathy with the young man, sitting before her, struggling with his grief for an atrocious crime which he was suddenly made to perceive had been discovered by a woman whom he as much feared as detested. He felt that his life now was not worth a pin's fee. That a threatening thunderbolt hung as it were by a thread over his devoted head, and that this woman had the power to release it to his destruction.

The torture dimly traced upon his face, was intensified in his heart. He was not naturally bad, but he was naturally yielding, and far too weak to withstand temptation.

Yet need he not have been strong to have turned coldly away from the warm advances of a fiend who wooed him in the guise of a beautiful woman?

And this outwardly resplendent creature, although a devil within, was his young mistress, too, which, of course, was another extenuating circumstance in the young man's favour. He was her servant, and it was her privilege to command, and his duty to obey; that was his simple interpretation of the Scripture dictum " servants obey your masters."

The simple-minded groom followed out the law as unconditionally as it was written, but his conscience, the unerring guide to all to steer us right if we would but follow its still small voice, now cruelly oppressed him for committing murder because, forsooth, his mistress commanded him to do so!

His sins no doubt will be upon her head, but his self-accusation was of the most torturing description. No one dreamt that Woodward—he who could caper and sing in the servants' hall, who could play cards, flirt with the girls, drink and carouse with the men, and keep the table in a roar—carried about with him the terrors of a guilty mind, and an upbraiding conscience!

That he who seemed to be the happiest, and the most favoured of men, could not sleep at nights because his eyes were appalled by the terrible apparition of a baby-girl, who was once as smiling as a June rosebud, and fair as a lily, but who nightly appeared to the unhappy Josh with its face discoloured as with ink, and a stable halter round its neck !

And that ghastly apparition was with him now as he sat in Mrs. Oliphant's old arm-chair, and not all her gin, nor all her balmy talk, could exorcise that spirit from his eyes.

But he was as anxious as possible to blind the peering grey eyes of the likewise guilty woman, who now sat in momentary silence before him, twisting round her finger that one corkscrew long grey curl, that hung adown her erysipelas-looking cheek—yes, from her he was solicitous to screen the perturbed state of mind her reference to the barn, and the bloody deed enacted there, had thrown him into.

It was quite enough for Josh to be made aware that she knew all, and that he and Lady Duchesney were in her power. He was desirous to show that he defied her to do her worst, and that he had an answer to all she could reveal, whenever her malice prompted her.

Mrs. Oliphant sat there toying with her long curl, with the self-satisfaction of an angler who had got a fish dangling at the end of his line. Although, as it has been observed before, personally she liked Josh well—he was so much like a brother of his who was at sea—but she was better pleased to have him in her power, if only to keep him civil, and it afforded her a selfish delight to see him struggling with the embarrassment that her evident knowledge of his infamy troubled him with.

She regaled her well-defined nose with a pinch of Prince's mixture, to give an additional perfume to which she always placed a tonquin bean amongst her favourite snuff, and then she said, examining the green glass bottle, which was well nigh empty—

" It don't want glasses to see that that's gone. Are you going to stand a little drop more, Josh Woodward?"

" I wish I'd never come," he ejaculated, then changing his position in the chair.

" Then you'd have nothing known," she rejoined. " But I've told you before you needn't fear me."

" Not that !" exclaimed Josh, snapping his finger and thumb together, while a diamond of the first water flashed in the candle-light as he upraised his hand before it.

" Then why wish you had never come ?"

Josh was puzzled what to reply, after making two attempts.

" It is only the guilty that stammer," said the woman. " You don't fear me?" she asked, half rising in her chair, while her two hands supported themselves on the arms of it.

Josh, with upraised arm, and upturned eye, was about to take God's name to bear him witness to a lie, when the woman suddenly seized his arm, and cried—

" Don't, Josh, don't! The roof will fall and crush us !"

" Why do you provoke me, then ?" he ejaculated, verily ashamed of himself after he had been saved the sin of false swearing by so bad a woman as Mrs. Oliphant.

" I won't say no more, Josh, that I won't," she said, while drops of sweat at her companion's attempted profanity festooned her tall but narrow brow.

Mrs. Oliphant was neither acting nor affecting ; she had been shocked by Josh's daring impiety, wicked as she felt herself to be. The man had perception enough to see that she was not feigning, when she placed her hand upon her beating heart, and wiped those drops from her brow.

Josh volunteered to drop over to the inn where he had baited his horse, and replenish the queer little bottle.

" I'm so glad that I saved you from taking God's holy name to a lie. That's the unforgiven sin ; now we're both bad enough, but let us do nothing that would place us without the pale of forgiveness. That would be awful !"

Josh shrugged his shoulders, made no reply, and went his way to the inn.

" You have forgotten the bottle, Josh," cried Mrs. Oliphant, as the heavily-booted man closed the parlour door behind him.

" All right," he returned, adding, to the woman's exceeding joy, " they've got larger ones over the way."

CHAPTER VII.

THE HUNCHBACK ALARMED.—PRETTY JANE REPENTS HAVING TAKEN SERVICE AT EVESHAM HOUSE.—JOSH AND MRS. OLIPHANT BETTER UNDERSTAND EACH OTHER.

IT was not the custom of the poor Hunchback Boy, when he was hunted to his room, to go to bed ; nor was there anything mean enough in his poetic nature to induce him to turn eavesdropper.

He would oftener, as it has been observed before, sit at the window, with the moon for his light, and the flowers for his contemplation ; for these beautiful blessings of earth and firmament were all his companions, and he ardently cherished them, and they seemed to speak impressively to him.

On the occasion of the scuffle in the parlour between Josh and Mrs. Oliphant, he was aroused from his window reverie by the alarming noise below.

He came to the door and listened, and continued to listen. But listeners we are told never hear any good of themselves, and we may be very sure after what we know that the Hunchback boy heard of nothing but harm and insult to himself.

Good, indeed ! had not his ears been thrilled by murderous threats ? The poor boy was so much terrified, so overwhelmed, by what he accidentally overheard, that he would have let himself out of the window into the garden and ran away from home, and the cruel people by whom it was haunted, had it not been for his wasting and debility, and the ugly load upon his back. For if his mother despised him, and if his father, whoever he might be, forsook him, why what could he expect from strangers ? Oh ! if his body was only as straight and sound as his mind, he would have gone for a soldier, or tried for service in her Majesty's navy.

" What could he do ? what could he do ?" This was Spangled Dick's silent pathetic cry from morn to night, but now his cry was intensified to the highest degree. Alas ! the only response to his prayerful cry was to submit with patience.

Yet amid his desolation he had dreams and hopes of happiness in the future, which were to him as grains of gold to a man of poverty and want.

Such visions as those helped him materially on his thorny way, and reconciled him to his present wretched fate.

He had heard enough concerning himself from the voices in the parlour to make him sick at heart. Could that be his father below ? No, no ! never let him live to know such a wretch as that for his father ! Heaven could not be so cruel as that to him ! Heaven who had tortured him with a fiend for mother, would surely temper his hard case by restoring him to a father who would love him, and whom he might acknowledge without a blush or a feeling of shame or regret.

And something, too, he indistinctly overheard about an earl's daughter, and a mysterious barn. He knew so little about social distinctions that he could not imagine the exalted rank of her they had been discoursing of, and quarrelling over. What would have been the deformed boy's feelings had he conjectured that on his mother's side he was of noble birth ?

Feelings ! why that he would rather have been lowly born, and herd with poverty, than call this abandoned high-born lady Mother !

Out of the jumble of disconnected sentences that he had been the listener to, he could make up his mind to nothing less dreadful than that by some mysterious agency, some ill-natured fate, he was associated with vile and dangerous persons, and that he had been deserted by both father and mother, for he never for a moment latterly entertained any other belief than that the woman passing herself off as his mother, was a sham and a counterfeit ! Nature, he instinctively felt, would not have permitted him to have loathed her as he did had Mrs. Oliphant been otherwise.

Thus unhappy, fearful, and perplexed, he turned from the one-flight staircase, kept so clean as it was by his own hands, and sought again his room, this time to bend his knee in prayer to God to deliver him from all evil and all evil people ; to discover to him his father and mother if they would love him, or hide them from his knowledge if they despised and fled from him for his deformity. Above all he prayed that he might find some companion in this wide wide world on whom his abundant affections might rest and find return. Then Heaven was blessed for making the moon now shining on his long black hair, and his companions the flowers, and then the little gipsey maid, Margery More, the Hunchback's prayers, like sweet incense ascended for her; nor was Pretty Jane forgotten by the grateful boy, for had she not shown him some kindness during the morning meal?

His childish devotions finished, he laid his mis-shapen trunk upon his pallet, and fell asleep with the determination that he would yet pluck up spirit, and run away.

Pretty Jane, too, as we have seen, had been wretchedly disturbed by the unseemly noise in the next room, and her curiosity was also stimulated to listen, She could hear more than the boy, and she knew more of the world, and was much older in years and understanding.

She shuddered at what she made out between the mysterious couple, and sickened at the disclosures about Lady Duchesney and the barn at Evesham House!

Then, could that really have been Mr. Duchesney that had intercepted her progress in Kidbrook Lane with flatteries and love nonsense?

She could not, dare not, believe it, and attributed it all to that love of scandal which these gin-loving women were prone to.

She was sure that if the master and mistress of Evesham House were the profligates that had been described to her, no honest servant would live with them. Jane was quite sure that she would not; her virtue and love of character forbade it.

But still she listened on to those smothered whispers in the adjoining room, and often they spoke so low, and disconnected, that she could understand nothing from it.

But the terrible references to the barn that Mrs. Oliphant made to Josh, these she distinctly heard, and the half-frightened girl wondered and wondered whatever could be the dreadful mystery that hung like a funeral pall over that grim dilapidated barn, secluded in an unfrequented part of Evesham Park, and round which grew innumerable weeds, and prickly outspreading bushes, while toads croaked, and snakes hissed, in the ditch at its base behind.

Sleep had deserted her eyelids, and fear had usurped its place. Could she do other than listen on to a conversation in which she was so much interested, and which might influence her future steps in accepting service with the Lady of Evesham House?

Yet she strongly regretted that she had ever been thrown in the way of Mrs. Oliphant, or been induced to accept lodgings in her abominable house.

Joshua Woodward was not long in returning, and delighting the eyes of Mrs. Oliphant with a quart bottle of rare Old Tom.

"Now just shut the door softly, and sit down by me, Josh. You needn't be afraid of an old woman," she added, for the sight of such a wholesale supply of her worshipped beverage inclined her to be facetious. "I declare if it don't have the appearance of water in the bottle, only blessed be Heaven it aint. Enough to tempt a tetotaller, very few of which there are, that's my belief. I judge of others by myself," she added.

Josh shrugged his shoulders, but ceased to use any further insulting observations. She knew too much, and he had to sing small.

"Oh, we are not worse than a good many of our betters, if all things could be brought to light. Draw the cork, Josh; it's no use to buy good things if we don't use them."

"Where's your corkscrew?"

"I buy my gin in quarterns and half-quarterns, and haven't lived up to a corkscrew. Use the carving-fork in the tray in the sideboard behind you."

"Your traps are all very bright, mother Oliphant!" cried Josh, surveying the cutlery articles spread out on a little japanned tray. And bright the few things certainly did appear.

"Don't be low and vulgar, Josh. I have admonished you before about calling me mother Oliphant. I don't like it. I am *Mrs*. Oliphant, and *will* be *Mrs*. Oliphant," she emphatically added. "I intend to stand upon my respectability before all comers. Besides, you are not a groom now, but a gentleman allied in love to a high-born lady, and therefore should drop the language of the stable. Take what I say in good part, Josh; the world will think better of us if we strive to be ladies and gentlemen."

"That's right enough, Mrs. Oliphant," said Josh, thinking more about the barn than what the garrulous old woman was saying. "But I say, haven't you got more than one glass?"

"I declare that's all," she replied, laughingly. "One glass is enough for one person, though, for I keep no company; and when any one does drop in, why I give them the glass, and I drink out of the bottle."

"Why a glass or two only costs a few pence," said Josh; "next time I come to Eltham I will buy you half a dozen; it's too late now, for the shops are shut."

"Leave the money, dear boy, and I will buy them in the morning."

"You won't?"

"I will."

"Gin more likely?"

"My sacred word is given, Josh," she said, placing her hand on the region of her heart, not in buffoonery, but as a sacred symbol of her earnestness. Even in trifles Mrs. Oliphant was always demonstrative.

Josh gave her a crown, and she expressed her gratitude.

"No call for all that," said the man: "before I go I shall give you money enough to set you up in a glass and chainey shop."

"So Lady Mary has thought proper to answer me at last. It is well for her that she has, or I and Spangled Dick would have been at the gates of Evesham House before sunset to-morrow. And how much has she sent?"

"Ten pounds. Let me tell you that she doesn't think the better of you for your threatening letter."

"I really cannot help it. She should have been more regular with her payments. I have now nothing else to depend upon."

"The more it became you to be civil," remonstrated Josh.

"I have been civil and patient too; but my lady provoked me past all bearing. And the mischief that follows provocation be on the head of those—"

"Never mind all that, mother—I mean *Mrs*. Oliphant."

"You must admit that it sounds better, eh, Josh?"

"This sounds better still," retorted the man,

drawing forth a canvas bag containing ten sovereigns, and jingling them before the wide-stretched eyes of the monthly nurse.

"To be sure she has done it handsome at last. Yet a good part of it is arrears, and I shall have little left against I've paid rent, and one thing and another. Nothing travels so fast as money. You find it as I say, don't you, my boy?" she pleasantly inquired, while one by one she counted out the coin, and then one by one re-counted them back to the bag, and then drew up her gown, which disclosed a capacious brown stuff pocket, into which she placed the bag of gold.

Josh handed her a glass of Old Tom, but she put it from her, and politely bade him take the glass himself, and reach her a teacup from the sideboard behind him.

"I call these happy moments, Josh," she reflected. "A purse of gold, a bottle of spirits, and a friend like you to share it. Your good health, Josh," she added, extending her hand to her visitor, who certainly took it, and shook it, but not very cordially.

"Who made my things so bright, you asked awhile ago. Give the devil his due—your Hunchback son."

"I have no Hunchback son!" cried Josh, with as much warmth as feeling. "I have told you before that I want no relationship made between us."

The woman gave an appreciative nod.

"It would be no joke, you see, if a boy like that was to grow round my heart. I must neither know him nor see him, and then it matters not to me what becomes of him. For that reason I hate to come here, and for that reason you should have remained in Whitechapel, where Lady Mary left the baby with you."

"The truth is, Josh, as I told you once before, there was too much haggling about the money, or the child need not have been above ground, and no trouble to nobody."

"The fact is," retorted Josh, "by some way or other you discovered that the mother was Earl Ashford's daughter, and wanted to take an advantage of her. Had it been a poor woman's misfortune—"

"And which, you artful dog, you tried to deceive me that Lady Mary was your sister, and that you was a very poor man, and that all the expenses would fall on your shoulders. You didn't play your part well, Josh, nor the mother either."

"Perhaps not; it was my first step in crime, and I daresay I bungled."

"That you did. To think that I could not tell a lady from a poor woman! Had the woman you brought me that rainy night in a cab been clothed in rags, it would not have blinded me to the fact that she was a person of high birth. What's bred in the bone comes out in the flesh. You looked common breed by the side of your stately sister! Ha! ha! ha!"

"The gin has made you merry and complimentary."

"No offence I hope, Josh," said Mrs. Oliphant, her face still lit up with those bright beams which laughter always leaves behind. "Better have been straightforward with me."

"A pretty thing to have been straightforward about, wasn't it? All the folks that came to you when you advertised lodgings, care and attention, medical and otherwise, they were all very straightforward?"

"Pretty near the mark, I'm thinking," she replied. "It isn't poor women, you know, who disowns their children, and don't care what becomes of them. Quite the contrary; they love and cherish them, and I believe that nine out of ten of the poor and middle-class women who fall into misfortunes through too much trust in men, would rather brave their shame than disown their offspring."

Mrs. Oliphant's memories on this subject for the moment saddened her. She remembered the time when she was Rebecca Hart; when she was deceived in her first love; and oh! the night when she dug the little grave in a Walworth garden.

Those recollections became more vivid, as now, when she had over-imbibed her "juniper," and during these fits of abstraction, she would cross her hands over her portly stomach, close her eyes, and drop her chin upon her breast.

She was now going through this operation before her equally guilty visitor, when Josh awoke her, by asking her how she found out who Lady Mary was?

"Eh? what? what did you say, Josh? Excuse me nodding before you. Don't think that I'm in the least weary of your company'"

"I'm quite weary of my own," yawned Josh. "Just another pipe, and I'm off," he added, bringing from his pocket a gold-mounted seal-skin tobacco pouch.

"What a lot of elegant things you've got, Josh," she said, examining the pouch. "Lady Mary seems determined to make a swell of you. She'll marry you yet."

"She hasn't the chance."

"She's a fearless woman. She'll make the chance when she's the inclination. She cares no more for her husband than she did for her children, and would soon dispose of him—"

Mrs. Oliphant was here interrupted by a shrill scream from Pretty Jane, who had been standing in her night-dress listening at her bedroom door. But on turning her head round she was alarmed to see the gentleman she had met in Kidbrook Lane peering in at her window.

CHAPTER VIII.

EVESHAM HOUSE.—LADY MARY MEETS JOSH BY THE OLD BARN.—THE MURDER OF HER HUSBAND PROPOSED.—PRETTY JANE MADE A DECOY TO LURE DUCHESNEY TO THE BARN.

JOSHUA Woodward had been made the despicable man he was by the extraordinary influences of a wicked mistress. He had been cast by circumstances quite beyond his control into a deep current, whose tide was so impetuous, yet fascinating, that it carried him far into the abyss of crime.

When those who employ others are wicked, those who serve are almost compelled to follow.

There is said to be a skeleton in every house, and Lady Mary was the skeleton, or trouble, of the house of Ashford.

She had been exceedingly wild, wilful, false

and cruel, indeed altogether unmanageable, from her youth to womanhood. Her life was continual rebellion against parental or any other control, and her scholastic tutors were nothing but sport to her.

Some said that she was mad, and it would be only common charity to cover her deeds with that interpretation, and view her as an irresponsible person.

Social restraint, and womanly propriety, she altogether ignored, and did what she could to bring it into contempt.

She had been twice summoned to the police court for furious riding in the Row; and once fined twenty pounds for assaulting her father's coachman with her whip, because, as she said, he had been telling tales to the earl and countess about her and Josh.

She was frequently so intoxicated that, though a wonderful horsewoman, she could hardly sit her horse.

It was truly appalling to find, besides her being fast and furious, how criminal she could become, and how easy she found it to drag her favourite servant after her.

Of course those of her own degree were compelled to shun her. What cared she for that? She had a fortune of her own, and defied every law human or divine.

She was an abandoned woman, though she was a good earl's daughter, and with hardly any characteristic to redeem or qualify the assertion.

She broke the heart of her aged mother, the Countess of Ashford, and the earl, her father, was often ashamed to meet his peers, or go into society, on account of the disgrace and scandal his daughter had brought upon his house, and dimmed its lustre.

She had no aspirations for Heaven, nor fear of Hell. She was wholly selfish, sensual, and permitted nothing to stand in her way for the gratification of her low corrupt tastes.

She was mean and illiberal, too, which are qualities that are not often found in association with the others that we have described. She never gave to the poor, and money had to be dragged from her for all things except those that ministered to her own gratification.

Her marriage with Mr. Duchesney, who was almost as abandoned as herself, had to do more with an eccentric clause in the family will than with any affection; the clause ran to the effect that she should marry some one approved by her father before she could inherit a very considerable portion of her fortune.

Now as there were none in her own rank who would have her, and as she knew it would be no good to offer Josh for her father's approval, it was proposed that she should marry the son of a banker, who was very needy, and to whom a wife's dowry would be very grateful, and she accepted him, with the same sentiment that animated Richard the Third after he had won Lady Ann, " I have her, but I will not keep her long."

After the birth of her Hunchback boy, and a long time before her marriage, she retired altogether from London life to Evesham House, the gloom and grim silence of which was often disturbed by song, and dance, and drunken revelry. Her fortune was large, but she lived up to her rank, and maintained an extravagan establishment.

Wicked women, as a rule, are either grea beauties or great wits. Lady Mary in her own person had a good share of both. She had a majestic face, with rosy cheeks, and a commanding figure. She dressed very richly, but it was quite after a fashion of her own.

She scorned to be the slave of another's taste She would lead, not follow; and lead in fashion she very often did, for she every now and then struck out some new idea in the fashion of la dies' apparel, especially that suited to horse women. She could ride, drive, hunt, shoot, swim and manage a boat or a yacht, as well as any sailor, or a jolly young waterman.

She was everything, could do everything, bu be a good woman; measured by that standard she was found far below it.

Josh, about a month after the events described in the preceding chapter, was commanded by his mistress to meet her one night, at nine o'clock, a the barn.

Josh wondered what could be up. He had al ready too tragic a recollection of that place to make the assignation agreeable. However, lan tern in hand, there he went, and sat sad as sad could be on the gnarled roots of an old black poplar, whose branches rose above all other trees as if peering into the mysteries of the sky.

Josh gazed upon the barn; he could not help it; he was fascinated by it as if by a snake's eye

There, in snow-white robe, before him stood an infant, with fair upraised hands, but purply black face, with a halter round its throat.

With both his hands he tried to shut out the sight, but the darkness he had thus created only made the apparition more palpable.

Thus his mistress found him, with the lantern on the ground, his head bowed on his knees, and his hands pressing on his eyes.

She had come close to him, before he heard the sound of her feet upon the dewy grass.

From the house to the barn was two miles; she would have rode the distance, had she not decided on taking a circuitous rout that involved stiles, and other obstructions to horse travelling. This she did to avoid observation.

" I'm so glad you've come, my lady, for I've had a creep of horrors come over me. Do you see nothing?"

" Yes."

" What, my lady?"

" Trees, bushes, a barn, and a fool!"

Josh made no reply, but with the lantern in his hand waited her ladyship's commands.

" I shall cease to care about you if you show the white feather."

She took from her pocket a somewhat ponderous key, and applied it to the rusty padlock of the barn, saying, as she did so—

" Those trembling hands could never dig a grave."

Josh shrank back from her, while she continued, in deep almost tragic tones—

" Give me a pickaxe and a spade, and I'll dig the grave myself!"

Josh was terribly bewildered, and his very knees trembled with alarm.

The lantern dropped from his hand, as he inquired—

" What grave, my lad ?"

PRETTY JANE

OR, THE

VIPER OF KIDBROOK LANE

PRETTY JANE ACCUSES HER MASTER.

The light of the lantern went out, and the two were left in darkness.

"I'm sure I heard footsteps!" cried Josh.

"Your hearing is disturbed by fear," retorted his companion. "You heard nothing more than the dry leaves chased by the wind. How could you be such a fool to drop the lantern?"

"I know not what I'm about," said the conscience-stricken man, while he fumbled in his pockets for matches to rekindle the light, but not succeeding in haste enough for his diabolical mistress, she drew forth a little silver vesta box, and handed it to Josh to strike a light.

But the man's hands trembled like an aspen, and he could hardly speak for his chattering teeth.

"You were never born for great deeds," she said, while she struck a light upon the silver box, and lighted the lantern, which, when reflected on the countenance of Josh, discovered it to be mantled with fear.

"It's none so pleasant, my lady," said Josh, while she unlocked the barn door, "to go inside that place again, or to be near it."

"Don't be a coward. We who have the power to give life, have the right to take it," replied this unnatural mother. "The child was mine, and I have laid it to rest. Nothing more. But had you been the man now as when you did the deed—"

"And which I'm not," stammered Josh.

"Fool!" she exclaimed, "what have you to fear? You are but a servant in the case. A woman in earnest beats all the men. Pah! how this place smells," she added, bringing her perfumed lace handkerchief to her nose.

"Let us leave it," said the groom, pleadingly.

"We will—"

Josh at once led the way with the lantern, but his progress was stopped by his mistress emphatically adding—

"When I have finished the business I came to do. Why what a milksop you have become, Josh!" she exclaimed, drawing herself up with a frowning countenance. "Couldst bear to lift those boards again?" she asked, pointing to a corner in which a barrel of slack lime was placed.

"Could your ladyship?" returned Josh, his eyes looking unutterable things as he intently fixed them on his abandoned mistress, who, stylishly dressed, stood as insensible as stone and impervious as iron before the conscience-smitten man.

"I could," she firmly replied to Josh's question. "But not while I keep a man-servant. As it happens I do not want that place to be disturbed, so I will not trouble you. What ails you, man?"

"I have serious thoughts of giving myself up," stammered Josh.

"Oh, you gallant fellow!" she derisively exclaimed, and could hardly keep herself from striking him. "Give yourself up indeed! Say but that again, and these boards shall cover you—and this little plaything of mine—"

When Josh saw an elegant diminutive pistol pointed at his head, he plumped down on both his knees, exclaiming—

"No, no—I am not fit to die!"

"Nor to live," she rejoined, drawing herself back from the man, who had completely thrown himself at her feet, while she still aimed the destructive toy, which was full cocked, threateningly towards her servant, who, still kneeling, besought her mercy.

"A brave fellow you for a lady to be spooney on! Ha! ha! But this will wean me. Henceforth be my servant, not my companion. Hallo! my head begins to swim," she suddenly cried, placing her pistol hand on her brow, and walking for air to the black poplar, followed by the half trembling man.

"Hold my pistol, if you are not afraid," she said, half leaning against the dark slim tall tree. "The abominable stench of the place has overcome me. The lime there should have sweetened it. Ha! that—that's reviving, and fits me for work again," she added, while she held her gold-stoppered vinaigarette to her nose.

"Now that your ladyship is better," said Josh, feeling more secure that he had the pistol in his possession, "let me ask a favour from you?"

"So brave a man should command favours. What is it?"

"I am too unnerved for ghastly work to-night. Let us return to the house. To-morrow I will serve you in any way you think proper to command."

"Don't you dictate to me. Bear yourself like a man, and I might listen to you. What have you to fear?"

"The life to come," he replied.

"Fear it then, if you are baby enough. Have I not told you before that mine is the responsibility. What you do, you do by command. Come hither, Josh," she said, in softer tones holding her handkerchief in one hand, and her scent bottle in another, and her servant, more inclined to flee the spot than remain, followed on her heels towards the barn.

"All my secrets are known to you, Josh, but the one I am now about to reveal."

This she said with the same indifference as if she were going to communicate some small flirtation.

But the trembling servant knew so well her dreadful insensibility to crime of all degrees that he felt he had no security from her serene and plausible manner, but that her sanguinary nature was still athirst for crime.

At length she said, while a really fascinating smile lit up her countenance with its beams while she placed her arms on the man's shoulder and locked her hands—

"Dear old Josh! I long to be a widow."

The man was not puzzled to know her drift he at once saw her meaning, although he pretended not.

"That will happen when your husband dies," remarked the groom.

"Exactly so. Now you know my wishes, will you help me to be a widow? Don't stare so man! I do not wish to be a widow that I might marry you! Pray be not alarmed. You are not my husband, so it is not you who are menaced. I have planned everything—"

"For what?" asked Josh, his old fears returning. "I don't understand your ladyship," he added, which was wide of the truth, for he perfectly understood.

"You should not ask me to speak plainer Yet I will if you like. The bonds of marriage are hateful to me, though I have defied them as much as possible. But I would and will be free of those chains which I forged about myself to please my father, but more to augment my fortune. Duchesney is not worth the smallest consideration at my hands. A drunken fellow, and there is not a wench safe for him. But were he the best man that ever lived I would not have him for husband. I'll have no husband! Husband means master, and I'll have no master! Must I speak further my meaning?"

"You intend to leave Mr. Duchesney?" inquired Josh.

"The same thing with a difference, Josh—I intend Mr. Duchesney to leave me," was her reply.

"I don't exactly see how that is to be managed; nor do I see what difference it would be to you whether he left you, or you left him."

"You are talking in the dark, and I must enlighten you further. Duchesney must die! and you must help me—"

"Not for the world, my lady!" exclaimed the man. "I have shed blood enough already."

"Cur! is my love for you to be set at nought like this?"

"Be advised, Lady Mary. If you are not happy—"

"No old woman's talk, man!" she exclaimed.

"There is the pick, and there is the ground. Dig me a grave."

"Is master dead?" inquired the terrified man, for how else could he understand her, and for what other purpose could she want him to dig a grave?

"Not yet," was her answer; "I want the grave prepared for that event. Come, set to work, and I will hold the lantern for you."

"I really dare not, my lady. I am every minute repenting the crime we have already done. To take the life of that sweet little cherub—"

"If you would be happy in this life you should not cherish tender feelings. Treat every event with indifference. 'Twas but a child of a day old, and its little life went out as easily as a butterfly's. That woman Oliphant swindled me, or that Hunchback brat should have perished too. His first cry should have been his death one. He lives, no doubt, to pull me down. He will arise, no doubt, to destroy me. for having sought to destroy him. Poetic justice they call these things. But the woman be cursed who deceived me!"

"We must be careful of her," said Josh, "for she knows, as I told you before, about the child in the barn."

"She thinks she does."

"I'm sure she does. She could not possibly think about such a thing without she had a good clue to it."

"She wont terrify me; yet it is very disagreeable to be living in fear of such a harpy. How difficult it is, Josh, to keep anything a secret! Light seems to shine everywhere, and that there is no such thing as darkness. If she knows, others know. A mere conjecture on her part, that is my belief."

"I thought so myself at first," said Josh. "But when she spotted the barn, why then I did not wish to hear any more."

"Very strange, I confess, and past all explanation. Let her take care, for there's room enough here for her."

"I should feel safer if she were under the ground. I could dig her grave with much pleasure."

"Trust me, Josh, and follow my guidance, and we will yet be secure, free, and happy."

"The Hunchback boy, I don't think he can live long."

"That is my hope,' rejoined the unnatural mother. "I would be free from children and husbands. Now look here, you quailing man. Your master, it is well known, is smitten with that girl Jane, who was recommended to me by the woman Oliphant."

"Pretty Jane, you mean?"

"Well, Pretty Jane, if you will. And the girl, too, has some attractions, that is, of the servant-girl type. Do you think she is pretty, Josh?" playfully asked Lady Mary, with the utmost indifference to the terrible things she had been communicating to her irresolute servant.

"I'm sure I don't know. She hasn't been here long, and I haven't thought anything about her," said Josh, thoroughly amazed that her ladyship could so instantly change her mood from grave to gay—from subjects in which murder was involved to the trifling matter of the beauty of a servant girl, whom she cared not one farthing about.

"How roundabout you are in your answers," said her ladyship. "Do you think she is pretty—that was my question."

"No doubt of it. Besides, everybody says so."

"Have you ever told her so, Josh?" asked the lady, quizzingly.

"Oh dear, no," replied the man, but in tones that betrayed that he was not quite speaking the truth.

"You are not good at telling lies," she said, surveying his face with the lantern.

"That I'm not, your ladyship."

"Then why do you attempt them?"

"Me! When, your ladyship?"

"Now. I am lynx-eyed, and know all your proceedings with that girl."

"Why what does your ladyship know? Bother the girl! I wish she was a thousand miles away for what I care! She's too vain for me to admire."

"Pray do not be unjust to her because your love for her has been discovered."

"Love! Your ladyship is joking," he said, with a little laugh.

"I am neither joking nor jealous. But beware of your trying to deceive me. Although you are my servant your fate is bound up with mine. Take heed to it, Josh," she imperiously added.

"I don't know what you mean, that I'm sure I don't."

"Then I will tell you. The wench had not been here a fortnight before these eyes of mine saw you kiss her—before these ears of mine heard you flatter her."

"How can you say so, Lady Mary!" exclaimed Josh.

"Enough for you to know that I have an unfailing method to discover what takes place with every member of my establishment. You sent her a letter—"

The lantern nearly again fell from his grasp. Here was a proof that by some mysterious means his loving mistress knew of his flirtations with Pretty Jane. Before she had given him time to recover from his surprise, to his further mortification she continued—

"In that letter you asked the girl to meet you in the willow copse—"

The man looked so frightened at this discovery that his fearless mistress laughed outright. Then the lady continued—

"You bade the wench to beware of your master—"

"Don't say any more please, Lady Mary!" exclaimed the terrified favourite of the earl's daughter.

"You have heard quite enough, have you, to make you sure that I have unseen means of watching you whenever I think proper?"

Josh could not help assenting to this, but he was greatly puzzled to understand how it should be.

In most confused manner he made an attempt to beg her ladyship's pardon, and ask her forgiveness.

He pleaded that he must have been drinking—that the deeds done in the barn every now and then obscured his intellect—and meanly and cowardly suggested that Jane was a dangerous and flighty girl, and that she should be sent about her business.

"That should be your punishment," she said sternly. "But never mind. I rather like the girl, and it is quite clear that you do also."

Josh denied this assertion, but his mistress persisting, he said that he had no more liking for her than for other girls, only that she was a bit better looking.

"You wouldn't marry her if you could?"

"Ah! Lady Mary, you know too well who has my heart to ask that question. Oh! I wish you would come with me beyond the seas out of the way of your husband, and that mother Oliphant, and that Hunchback boy, and that dreadful barn—"

"And that Pretty Jane of yours, eh?" asked the demon lady.

"Not mine, I do assure you. Say not so again!"

"It hurts your feelings, I suppose? Your meeting Jane in the willow copse—"

"Let all that nonsense pass, dear Lady Mary. She is really not worth thinking about. Since Mr. Duchesney condescended to flatter her in the servant's hall, why there is really no speaking to her."

"And so you thought you would declare yourself in a letter?"

"Just a bit of fun. I only wanted to tell her to beware of master," replied the terribly bewildered servant.

"Nothing more?"

"Well—well—nothing more than a bit of flummery, which every man is obliged to say to a new girl that comes into a place."

Josh stammered and stuttered as he tried to explain himself to her ladyship, for in truth he was afraid of her at all times, but more so now under the delicate circumstances.

"Only a little flummery, too, that you promised Pretty Jane a present from London when you went there, and begged her to sit for her photograph, and that you would pay for it?"

"She must have shown you my letter!" he exclaimed. "Oh! the vain mischievous thing. I declare your ladyship I wont stop longer in the place if she does."

"Enough about you. Just tell me if you think your master is fond of her?"

"All of us think so. And she is very stuck-up about it, and dresses herself in her best when she has no call to do so. You had better dismiss her."

"She shall yet be a friend of mine."

How Josh did stare! His mistress make a friend of the girl who had fascinated her husband and with whom she had just made such a discovery with regard to himself! Surely he must have misunderstood her! His wits must have been wool gathering.

He asked his mistress if she really said that she intended to make a friend of Pretty Jane, her new parlour maid?

Lady Mary, to the man's astonishment, replied in the affirmative.

"I cannot understand your ladyship. In what way can you make a friend of her?" he asked.

"I want this husband of mine brought at a certain hour to the barn."

The mention of the barn, with which he had such a tragic association, brought back the feelings that made the morn, noon, and night of his life a curse to him!

As we have elsewhere said, he wore a merry laughing mask upon his face, while his heart was the companion of an ever gnawing worm!

"How can Jane bring Mr. Duchesney to the barn? and for what purpose?" he not unnaturally asked.

"At length we have got back to the real business of this meeting," she said. "I have determined to be rid of the encumbrance of a husband. Besides, we thoroughly hate each other. As you and others know, we never meet but to abuse and even assault each other. And there is very good reason for this state of things. It was a marriage of convenience. The object attained, we now only live to despise each other. In short, he will have my life if I don't have his. I mean it to be the latter, for kingdom come, which parsons talk about, is not good enough for me. You must help me—"

"Pray don't bring me into any more trouble! I have enough already on my mind for a life time. What would you have me do?" he asked, while he was almost afraid to hear her answer, for he was conscious that she meant more blood to be shed.

In the most ordinary manner, as if she had been ordering her servant for a ride, and nothing more, she thus replied:—

"First of all you must prepare a grave, which is easily done by removing those boards—"

"I will do no such thing, though we part this instant!" he exclaimed. "I feel that we shall both be hung! You are an awful woman!"

This was the boldest thing Josh had ever ventured to address to her, though he had often said so to himself. She upraised her fist to strike him! he coiled beneath her, and begged her pardon for his audacity.

"No more of this contemptible nonsense! Do as I bid you, or the world shall quickly know what a scoundrel you are! You fear to die, you know. I do not."

"What would you have me to do?" he again asked, in more submissive tones.

"One thing I have already told you—pull up those boards."

"Y-e-s," stammered Josh, as well as his chattering teeth would let him.

"Then, when we return to the house, you must coax your Pretty Jane—you will like that job, won't you?"

"She is nothing to me, your ladyship," he replied.

"That is no concern of mine; evidences, though, belie your assertion, and I choose to believe the evidences. Stick up to her, Josh, and marry her if you can. Don't fear me; indeed, I will give you money to float you off."

"How can you talk so, Lady Mary, after all the love, and confidence, and crime that there has been between us! Had you been in the same station of life as myself you would have been my wife."

"That neither of us can tell. Sufficient for us we are not man and wife, and never shall be."

"That was my grief when you married Mr. Duchesney, for I had always hoped that you would have married me before our first child was born."

"Marry you and lose half my fortune? No thanks. Besides, I like favourites better than husbands. And to a husband I will not be tied, mark that!" she emphatically exclaimed. "And now for my plan to get rid of the dead weight imposed on me by a selfish stupid ancestor. The roué only married me to get hold of a little cash, and for money he would have married his grandmother. Tit-for-tat, I married him to remove a barrier between me and a fortune; and now I seek to remove him because he is a barrier between me and liberty."

Josh suggested that she should leave him if she was unhappy with him.

"What a fool you are! He would be my husband still though he and I were at the antipodes from each other. But I don't want your advice in the matter. My mind is made up. Just you coax that girl of yours—"

Josh interrupted her by protesting that Jane was no girl of his, and that he never cared a fig for her, and that his mistress would do well to get rid of such a mischief-maker.

"What mischief has Jane been the cause of?" she inquired.

"She must have shown you my nonsensical letter."

"She did not, and yet I saw it," replied his mistress.

"But how, your ladyship?" cried Josh, looking the picture of astonishment.

"That I shall not tell you. I have a method known only to myself of finding out all that passes within my house. Be warned. I want you, Josh, when you meet Jane in the willow copse—"

"I'm not going to do no such thing!" cried the hypocritical fellow.

"Pray don't disappoint the poor girl, nor yourself either, on my account. Indeed as you have made the appointment I beg that you will keep it, that is, if she accepts your invitation, which I daresay she will, for girls are such fools when they have the chance of a bit of sweethearting."

"I'm not a fool, Lady Mary!" exclaimed the man. "I would rather blow my brains out with this pistol of yours than have anything to do with Jane, or any other girl. My heart is yours, and yours is mine, and we oft to have been married, and kept our children, and lived happily together rather than this life of fear and misery!"

"Fear and misery!" sneered the abominable woman.

"Yes, indeed. I fear my very shadow at times!"

"Poor dear fellow! Pray blow out your brains—but upon my word I don't think you have any to blow."

"Ah, dear Lady Mary, you thought more of money than me, or I should have been your husband instead of that adventurer Duchesney, who you don't care the shank of a button for!" cried Josh, with warmth.

"Help me to get rid of him, then; you don't know my plans for your future. Your welfare will always be my consideration. By the bye, how is the mare?"

"She's all right. The mash did her a power of good."

"I must have her out to-morrow for a long ride. There's no creature like her in the world, don't you think so, Josh?"

"She's a rare bit of stuff. But I wouldn't ride her so soon."

"I shall. She's had good rest, and a gallop will do her no harm. I have business in London, and shall ride her there; be ready with her at ten."

It was wonderful that a woman, who was in this gloomy place, at such an hour, and for such a purpose, was so insensible to crime as to be able every now and then to talk playfully of matters irrelevant to it.

Josh could hardly believe her to be in earnest, and tried as far as he could to divert her from it by continuing to discourse about the mare.

But he was soon checked by his mistress, who again abruptly, much to his dismay, resumed her plans for the murder of her husband.

"Get Jane to write your master a letter that she would meet him at the barn— That won't do though, for that would be letting the girl into our secrets, and which, perhaps, she would shrink from being a party to. I want to bring him here at a certain hour, when I would plant myself in a favourable place and shoot him, while I should want you near to bury him out of sight, when he would soon be out of mind. How can we manage it? Speak!"

"I will have nothing to do with it—that's plain and plump!" cried Josh, in his native county phraseology.

"Then you can go about your business, and tell all you know for what I care."

"There'll be no call for that," he retorted, with much dejection in his looks.

"No—you are too great a coward to tell anything. You like your own neck too well for that!"

"Oh, let us be friends!" pleaded Josh, placing his hand on her wrist.

"Give me the pistol!" she exclaimed, throwing him from her.

Josh, not unreasonably apprehending that in her present desperate state she would shoot him with it, was about to fire it off in the air, and had his finger on the trigger for that purpose, when, like lightning, and with the ferocity of a tiger, she seized his pistol-hand, and arrested his purpose.

Fortunately for Josh, the dreadful threatening flash that animated the eye of his mistress when she had regained the elegant, but murderous little weapon, so alarmed him, that he took to his heels and ran as fast as the darkness would permit him towards Evesham House, leaving his lady love to remain or follow, whichever the devilry of her mind prompted her to do.

She looked after her gallant lover with contempt, and disgust and indignation rose in her mind against herself for ever having given him so much power over her.

"Would that he were dead!" she groaned, smarting with humiliation and rage at his want of courage to serve her, and gratitude for the serious sacrifices she had made for his sake.

She returned the pistol to her pocket, and for a minute or two went into the barn, and stood in deep reflection by the side of the old hogshead which Josh had half filled with slack lime.

"The dead," she said, casting her eyes down

on the rough and rutty planks that concealed her pretty infant's corpse, whose shroud was quick lime, "the dead are happier than the living. "Poor little thing! to have been born of a she wolf! Unconscious little creature! who even smiled and played with the ends of the rope round thy neck to strangle thee! Ah! yes, yes, it was a hellish deed. His child and mine, why did he not plead for thy life as determinedly as for this debauched husband of mine? Neither of us, father or mother, had one word, one compassionate look, for the little creature. It was doomed, and it was slain! Rest thee, babe, rest. But I fear that I am too near thy grave for that. If thou hadst a spirit why not now arise and accuse me! Here is thy evil mother in the dark alone—arise and speak to her, and let thy spirit's presence kill her! Come to me as fair as spring daisies, as when I saw thee first —not coal black as when I saw thee last!"

With her hands to her temples, she looked with affrighted face round the old cobwebbed barn, now as dark as her own soul, and every now and then her imagination, red hot with committed crimes, saw upon the wooden walls a luminous light coming and going like lightning.

Her imagination further shaped the light into the figure of a smiling infant.

At first she shrank from it, then she frantically tried to grasp it. But the smiling figure fled to another part of the wooden wall.

"How those smiles mock me!" she exclaimed. "If I stay longer here they will kill me. Spirit, thy guilty mother flees from thee. Oh! my swimming eyes, my heavy heart, what pranks you are playing with me!"

With faltering step she left the place, locked and padlocked the barn, and gloomily and leisurely wended her circuitous route towards Evesham House.

The dash and courage had been taken out of her by the events of the night. Josh had very much disappointed her, and her murderous designs had been thwarted by him.

It was always a pain to this wicked woman to be baulked in any of her plans or purposes, however daring or abominable they might be. She had designed that Jane should be the decoy to lure her husband to his death, and that her companion in crime should assist her in disposing of the body by burying it in the barn and covering it with lime.

But, reprobate as he was, Mr. Duchesney was saved from this ill fate by the conscientious scruples of Josh, who had now fallen low in the esteem of his mistress.

"That Hunchback boy of mine, too, lives," she mused, as she stole in and out between the trees. "And now I'm thwarted again. My plans must have been badly laid, or they ought not to have been so cut up. I have had too much trust in others. Future operations shall be done alone, or I'll have confederates with stouter hearts, and not those that are frightened by apparitions. What cowards conscience makes of us! Why had I not left that barn, I myself might have given way to foolish feelings, and weak imaginings. I could hardly have fancied that I could have been caught napping. When once those ghostly feelings arise, I find that it is not so easy to get rid of them; they hang

about one like feathers—if you brush them off one part of your dress they cling to another. Even now that baby form I see—but there's no such thing. It is but the upbraidings of a mind stimulated to a false action by the silly fears of another."

Musings of the character we have described, some tinged with remorse, and others with plans for other crimes, brought her to the iron gates of her home.

Evesham House was like what any one of imagination might conceive a haunted house to be. Pretty Jane, the first night of her service there, when she went through passage after passage, and up one little staircase and down another, with a gaping furnitureless room near by the one allotted for her slumbers, and when she drew her curtain aside and peeped forth upon the extensive grounds around, and heard the owl hooting from some dreary corner of this ancient rambling pile, why she heartily wished herself in more cheerful quarters, even if it were a humbler service.

That barn, too, and all she had overheard about it, by no means contributed to her comfort or her assurance on the first night of her engagement at Evesham House. But what alarmed her more than all was the evil character of her master, whose roof she now slept under, and who had so rudely intruded himself at her bedroom window while she lodged with Mrs. Oliphant. Hoping yet she should find that it was *not* her master who made love to her in Kidbrook Lane, and appeared again at her window at her Eltham lodgings, she fastened the window of her new home, locked her door, and barricaded it with a chair, and then went to bed, her ear listening to every sound, and her heart stimulated to a distressing action by strange fears, and nervous prostration.

If the master and mistress of Evesham House had been half so good as the building, Jane might have slept fearless. But she positively knew nothing about either, and had she been told that her master and mistress were the depraved and criminal persons that they were, why her innocent nature would not have been able to realise or comprehend such unfathomable guilt, and might have been well excused for not believing it.

Evesham House was a very deserted-looking edifice, frowning over a pair of iron gates, spotted with rust as red as blood.

The house was evidently built at a period when comfort and not security was the principal object.

The rusty entrance gates, the sombre group of Scotch firs just within them, and the long shadows of the brave old elms, would make the visitor wish to find himself in the bright sunshine again.

Yet the old gates, rust clad though they were, are fine specimens of forged iron work of Queen Anne's reign.

But the barn, or rather the dreadful rumours about it, was the terror to the servants connected with the place, and for the matter of that to all the village. The servants blessed their stars that it was so far away from the house, or one half of them would never have remained there. Balls of fire had been seen at night rolling from it, and children were kept in order by awe of it.

The dismal appearance of Evesham House is perfectly in keeping with the crimes that have been committed there.

Its gates are cumbered o'er with rust,
Its walks deserted, lone,
And through the rugged pine tree tops,
The night winds sigh and moan,
Like the wailing of a spirit
O'er the ruin and decay,
The pride, the pomp, the pageantry,
That long hath passed away.

The entrance hall of this house is paved with white and black marble; the hall opens to a spacious staircase, communicating with the upper apartments, and the balustrades are curiously carved to represent military trophies and weapons of ancient warfare.

Evesham House is reached from the highway through a grand avenue of trees, one mile in length. But a rich carpet of grass covers the carriage way.

A narrow footpath alone, winding through the dank grass, leads to the lofty iron gates which close the boundary of the perspective formed by two mile of trees.

The earl's abandoned daughter liked the place for the extent of the grounds by which it was surrounded, as well as the spacious rambling character of the interior of the old house, which had been shut up for a long period before she bought it.

She moreover liked it for its nearness to the Metropolis, where she occasionally resorted for a little dissipation with the bottle and cards and betting with men and women almost as abandoned as herself, yet moving in high and fashionable circles.

An ancestor of hers, more renowned for his infidelity then his good, here destroyed himself, and the floor of the room, it is said, has ineradicable stains of blood upon it.

Near this room, and entirely apart from her husband, Lady Mary had her suite of rooms, and placed conveniently near, were her steward's rooms and offices.

After she reached home, she had wine and supper served in the most profuse and elegant matter. She ate sparingly, but drank deep; and more like a sot than a lady, she rang for her maid to prepare her for bed.

CHAPTER VIII.

JANE'S ARRIVAL AT EVESHAM.—THE SERVANTS FLATTER HER.—SHE RECOGNISES DUCHESNEY AS THE GENTLEMAN WHO ACCOSTED HER IN KIDBROOK LANE.—JANE RUDELY ASSAULTED BY HER MASTER.—A WARRANT FOR THE ASSAULT GRANTED.

PRETTY Jane was so rejoiced when the sunshine morning came that was to take her to Evesham House! But the preparations for her departure brought anything but joy to the poor Hunchback boy.

He had for some time been growing fond of Jane, for she had lately taken more notice of him, and spoke to him more, especially when Mrs. Oliphant was conspicuous by her absence, for it was much against her rule and liking that any one should show the least friendliness to the unfortunate boy.

Spangled Dick, the night preceding Jane's departure to her new place, was ordered early to bed, with Mrs. Oliphant's imprecations that if he did not get up early she would give him a few more crooked bones than he had got already.

"I don't mind how early I get up, for I seldom go to sleep," said the patient cripple.

"That's another of your lies!" cried Mrs. Oliphant, throwing a slushy towel in his face.

The boy turned to go, when Jane, who caught his sorrowful eyes, now red and swollen with pent-up tears, said—

"Never mind Dick; you're a very good boy what I've seen of you. There's sixpence for you for the little errands you have fetched for me; and I shall want you to buy some rope for my boxes the first thing in the morning."

If ever boy showed pleasure and happiness in his countenance it was now. Ugly as he was to those who had not eyes to see the underlying goodness and tenderness of his nature, for the moment the grateful smiles for Jane's kindness that flashed across his countenance at once seemed to transform him into a being of beauty. It was not so much the sixpence, for he hardly knew the use of money for anything for himself, but it was for Jane's hearty outspokenness in his praise before Mrs. Oliphant.

The old woman looked mightily pleased too, as she sat bolt upright, toying with her long grey curl, her large tortoiseshell comb perched high behind her head, but *her* pleasure arose from the fact that sixpences were about.

"And that's how you spoil children is it, Miss Jane? You'll know better if you live to have children of your own—which I hope not, for they are a shocking plague, especially if they are such cripples as he."

The boy sloped off with bitter feelings. His cup of bitterness was filled again.

"Here you sir, come back with that money!" she cried. "You're too great a booby to spend it, or take care of it. Give it to me, and then be off with you."

Without much hesitation he laid it on the table, gave Jane another smile of thanks—he dared not speak—then up the stairs he went, glad to get out of the way of his so-called mother, of whom he stood in fear.

"I daresay you think I'm rather sharp with that boy?" she asked Jane, who sat by the table taking an egg for her supper.

"Well I really do, Mrs. Oliphant, as you ask me," was the honest girl's reply.

"Ah, you're just like the rest of the world. There's not one mother in a hundred as knows how to bring up children. Look at the obedience I get from that boy. No wrangling, no answering, no sulking, no frowning, but all my requests done with a willing cheerfulness."

Jane was unwilling to continue the conversation, for she did not care to come into collision with so detestable a woman that she believed her landlady to be, and she contented herself with saying—

"Poor little fellow! it would have been a mercy to himself if he had died at his birth."

"So it would my dear, and a mercy to his mother, too. But you see the mercy wasn't shown to him or her either. You know we can't have everything our way, or I would never have lived."

Jane, who was elated with her new prospects, and her heart full of youth, health, and a good deal of vanity, could not subscribe to the nurse's morbid wish, but she laughed outright, showing as she did so two rows of teeth of unparalleled whiteness, and said—

"Thank you for nothing! I'm glad I was born, and should like to live here forever and ever!"

Mrs. Oliphant took a pinch of Prince's mixture, then what she called a thimbleful of gin, and then, in the oracular manner of old Nell Dod, she upraised her finger, and said—

"That dream means murder! You know what she said."

"I do. But it is very unkind of you to remind me of such nonsense now. I don't know how it is, but you never like to see a person happy. If I'm out of a place in a week I shall never lodge with you again."

"And that after I've got you an aristocratic situation!" she cried, much inclined to lose her temper. "What did you come for?"

"Just because you asked me, otherwise I should have gone to my dear aunt's, where I am always welcome and happy."

"This is very ungrateful! For a chit of a thing like you to have sixteen pounds a-year, with tea, sugar, and all found, and yet to give me more sauce than gratitude for getting it for you."

"I am very very grateful to you for it," said Jane, "and I have bought you this new umbrella in return for it," she added, spreading out a gingham, with a nobby handle, as large as a balloon, for she had well considered Mrs. Oliphant's portly dimensions. "Take it, with my best wishes."

"I will, my dear; and a very pretty present too. Just the thing I wanted. This will keep me dry all over. I long for a shower of rain to sport it! It is a very thoughtful present, and shows you have sense above your years. Umbrellas are better than all your brooches or books or such useless things."

"I don't know about that," said Jane. "They are all good in their place."

"Right you are," said the woman, regaling her prominent nose once more with snuff. "But there are many young women who think too much of finery."

"You mean that for me," said Jane, smiling. "Well, I confess to a little smart dressing."

"And it well becomes you, too," said Mrs. Oliphant, whose flattering speech was under umbrella influences. "But, my dear, you must beware—"

"Bless my soul! every one is telling me to beware! Beware of what, I should like to know?"

"Of your new master," was the emphatic answer. "He is enough to corrupt all the girls of Kent—and he has a good many, I can tell you."

"Why should I beware of him more than any other girl?"

"Look in the glass," said the agreeable old woman, pointing with her new umbrella to a small glass, with a red-stained frame, lodged on the mantel-shelf, with a China ornament of a dreadfully-smiling shepherd minding two comic-looking lambs at play, on one side, and Taurus the bull, with tail in the air, and nose on the ground, as if he very much wanted to play at pitch and toss with anybody who was fool enough to join him, on the other.

"And what shall I see in the glass?" asked Jane, half understanding Mrs. Oliphant's meaning, but like other beauties of her sex, had ever an ear and appetite for flattery.

"Ah, Jane, you know well enough, that you would see a very pretty girl."

"Oh, what stuff, Mrs. Oliphant! Time to go to bed after that, I should say," said Jane, brushing some bread crumbs from her lap.

"Well, it is rather late," said Mrs. Oliphant, also rising. "What train do you go by?"

"I shan't be able to get away until the afternoon."

"And get to Brockley just in time for a nice tea with the servants in the hall, eh?"

"Oh, what a beautiful large hall it is! I never saw such a place before."

"I believe you. I've been there twice, that's all."

"Do you know I think I shall be very happy there. I like to be where there are other servants."

"No doubt of it, my dear; young folks like company," said Mrs. Oliphant, standing up before Jane, one hand leaning on her umbrella.

"One of the servants told me they got up a dance there among themselves."

"When a lot of servants get together, trust me, they'll be up to everything. I've been told that when Mr. Duchesney—"

"Oh, bother him! who cares for him? Good night, Mrs. Oliphant!" and without more words the pretty happy Jane skipped off to bed.

Spangled Dick was early astir as rigorously requested by his mother, and soon the little tin kettle was piping his song, and while he blew the fire the Hunchback began his doleful ditty about Margery More.

When he had got everything ready, Eltham bells had not chimed six. He had no instructions to awaken Jane, so he opened the garden door, and while the balmy morning breeze blew about his long black hair he turned to work in his garden.

Jane and Mrs. Oliphant, carrying a trunk between them, while the miserable little crookback attended on their heels between two tall bonnet boxes, trudged in happy spirits towards the station, whence the train quickly wafted the girl to Evesham House, or near to one part of the grounds.

Alas for her peace! the first person she saw in the grounds of the house was a gentleman in grey, relieved by a red neck tie, whom she at once recognised as the gentleman who accosted her in Kidbrook Lane!

This recognition for the moment stamped out her happy prospects. Her heart leaped to her mouth! The railway porter was on her heels with her luggage, or she would certainly have turned back, and fled the place.

Could she have read the future, it would have better for her had she done so, she would then have been saved the pain of accusing him before a magistrate for a rude assault!

PRETTY JANE

OR, THE

VIPER OF KIDBROOK LANE

MORE LIKE A MURDERESS THAN A DAUGHTER, LADY MARY DREW ASIDE THE CURTAIN.

"Why that's the little beauty I met in Kidbrook Lane! What the devil can she possibly want here! And come to stop, I swear!" exclaimed Mr. Duchesney, looking from Jane to Jane's luggage. "I wonder if she recognised me! No doubt she did, for she's tripping away as fast as her pretty little feet can carry her. If it is her, I'm a lucky fellow, for her face has haunted me ever since I saw it. I thank my termagant wife for feasting me with so much that is simple and attractive! She means it as a compensation, I presume, for her own infidelity.

While he thus mused he walked under some limes in an opposite direction to that in which Jane was making her way to the servants' hall.

No doubt Mr. Duchesney was a fine handsome gentlemanly man, and it was inexpressibly surprising that his wife should treat him with the scorn and hatred she did; and it was still more so that he should have been poor spirited enough to have married her when he knew that she had previously had a child.

But the power of money is great; for this he married her, and directly he saw that he had married a fiend more than a woman, he lived with her only to spite her.

While she, on the other hand, was conspiring with her groom to rid herself of him by taking his life.

Both, indeed, were sunk in the lowest depths of demoralisation and crime. They were both drunkards, gamblers, and adulterers, and on e

No. 5.

as we know, had murdered her own offspring, and was as insensible to the shedding of blood as a ferocious beast !

After Mr. Duchesney had followed Pretty Jane to her lodgings, on the memorable night that he met her in Kidbrook Lane, he took the train for London, and there he intended to have remained for the night at his club, or some other rendezvous of debauchery.

But as the wine stimulated his brain, Jane's loveliness haunted him, and the train not serving his purpose, he ordered a Hansom, and drove back to the little house in Eltham, in further pursuit of the fascinating servant girl.

With plenty of money at command, a flattering tongue, and a handsome person, he had, alas ! found girls of lowly position too yielding to his infamous plots and attacks.

He was a coward ! for he levelled his villainy at girls who could not defend themselves against his dazzling advantages of wealth, education, and social position, allied to a determined character, and a tongue capable of the falsest protestations, and that could talk by the yard of love and promises of marriage in such strains of sincerity that were enough to capsise the virtue of any ignorant unsuspecting girl.

Had he tried his seductive arts on young ladies of his own degree, he would have failed. Money or presents they are too well used to make them of any temptation to them. With them his wooing would have had to stand upon the standard of his personal merits and character, relied upon by the highest introductions; wanting in these, not all his wealth, nor all his position, would have prevented him from being kicked out of the circle.

This he knew, for he had already experienced it. Having wasted the fortune his father the banker left him, and having become a defaulter on the turf and at the gaming table, as well as being steeped to the very lips in debt with his numerous tradespeople, he was very glad to become the husband of Earl Ashford's wicked daughter, merely to lay hands on four thousand pounds paid to him as her dowry ; while she, to meet the conditions of a crotchetty will, did not hesitate to marry anybody that met with her distressed father's approval, and that by so doing increased her annual income by more than two thousand a year.

In a most excited and reckless condition, with furious driving all the way, he reached Eltham a little after eleven, and after having a " liquor up " with cabby, dismissed him at the ruins of the old palace.

Then, somewhat in a staggering condition, he picked his way through numerous blossoming orchards and gardens to the back of old Mrs. Oliphant's house.

But there appeared to be very little consideration in this step, for being there, he knew not the particular room in which the fascinating girl slept.

He reconnoitred for awhile, and then there appeared Jane's pretty figure, on the little white blind !

Those white blinds, with a candle behind them, are dangerous things for ladies to undress by, for prying eyes outside can see every action of their retiring operations.

" I swear it is her figure !" he exclaimed.

The window was quite low enough for him, with the aid of an old pail at hand, which he turned upside down to stand upon, to enable him to get hold on the sill and pull himself up to the window, his feet dangling in the air, and his knees fixed in against the brickwork.

In this most uncomfortable position he continued for some time to watch Jane by the sides of an ill-fitting blind, as she stood in her nightdress at her bedroom-door listening to the conversation between Josh and her landlady in the front parlour.

Jane, happening to turn round, saw the shadow of his head and shoulders on the blind, and half of his face peering into the room.

A loud scream from the frightened girl of course followed her discovery, which brought to her aid Mrs. Oliphant, and she and Jane, the latter throwing her dress over her shoulders, stood looking at the window.

But they saw no one, yet they heard the noise of the pail being turned over outside. Mrs. Oliphant rushed to the window, pulled up the blind, and looked out, when she saw the figure of a man receding as well as he was able through the orchard.

Mr. Duchesney, not knowing nor caring that he should be recognised, boldly turned round, hoping that he might have the felicity of making his bow to Pretty Jane, who stood trembling at the foot of the bedstead.

But when he saw instead the elderly face and figure of Mrs. Oliphant, he was prompted to exclaim, and the drunken boldness to do so, half paraphrasing Macbeth's passionate address to the witches on the " blasted heath "—

" Ye black and midnight hag, it is not you that I want !"

" What you want is a good horsewhipping, that's what it is, you impudent fellow !" exclaimed the exasperated woman, bending her fist, and shaking it at him, and rather a formidable fist it was, which Mr. Duchesney would have found could she have got at the defiant debauchee, who supported himself against an apple tree, the ripe blossoms of which fell, and decorated his hat and shoulders.

" Avaunt and quit my sight !" he cried, still profaning Shakspere.

" Do come away from the window, Mrs. Oliphant !" cried Jane, who felt like one in extreme peril.

" Indeed I shall do no such thing," snappishly replied the woman. " Hi ! Here ! Josh !" she bellowed.

" For shame, Mrs. Oliphant !" Jane exclaimed, flying to the door and locking it, for she heard Josh making his way to her room in answer to the summons from the landlady.

" No man shall come into my bedroom," she added, while Josh held the handle of the door, about to enter, but finding it locked against him he growled, while he retreated—

" I'm sure I don't want to come in if you don't want me."

" He has sneaked off now, Josh," said Mrs. Oliphant, letting herself out from Jane's room, greatly to Jane's relief.

When she rejoined her companion in the parlour, she said to him—

" A pound to a penny but that's your master, Josh !"

"Bothered if I know what you're talking about."

Mrs. Oliphant began to enlighten Josh, by telling him that she had a very pretty girl lodging in the next room, and that yesterday she got through her recommendation a place as under parlour maid at Evesham House.

"Why what a fool you've been, Mother Oliphant!"

"I won't be called Mother Oliphant, I tell you!" she vociferated, the gin she had taken beginning to work like yeast upon her brain, and exhibit itself in her speech and manners, to which she tried to impart dignity, which she ignorantly imagined to consist in throwing back her head, and thrusting her chin forward, almost far enough to break her neck.

"D—d if I care what you call yourself—".

"Hear me, Josh," she interrupted, "I *will* be treated with respect!"

"You should do something to deserve it," he retorted.

"I have, to *you*," she emphatically rejoined.

"What?" he defiantly asked, well guessing her meaning, though he scarcely expected that she would answer thus broadly—

"By saving your neck from a halter! Are you answered?"

Josh wriggled in his chair, bit his lip, then he jauntily filled his pipe, and said, his face the while radiated with a broad smile and a flickering laugh—

"You would have tried that on long ago, if you could have got anything by it."

"Don't know that I should," said the old woman, falling into a sentimental strain. "I'm not utterly a wretch. I've some mercy left in my breast. We've both been victims, Josh, so give us your hand."

"Are you going mad?"

"I've had enough to make me."

"What, gin?"

"No, not gin, Mister Sneerer, but grief that all the gin in the world could not wash out. I have, Josh—I have."

Here, whether she shed tears or not, she drew the corner of a speckled cotton apron to her eyes, while bending her head low, which pathetic attitude gave additional prominence to the tall comb which bound up her back hair.

"We've both been victims I tell you, Josh; you have been snared by an infamous lady, and I by—ah! me, what name can I give that disciple of the devil, who made me the wretch I am?"

"What has all this to do with the young woman in the next room, and who you say has got a place with Lady Mary? You ought to have had more caution."

Mrs. Oliphant had not sufficiently recovered from the grief of evil memories, so pathetically expressed in the attitude in which she sat before Josh, who looked upon her more frowningly than pitiful, for he attributed her display to the incoherence that is produced by the imbibification of gin.

Josh knew but little of Mrs. Oliphant, and certainly nothing of Rebecca Hart. She had told Jane that Josh was a fellow-servant of hers, but this was untrue, and was conceived in the moment of her anxiety to disarm Jane of all suspicion.

The groom made her acquaintance, same as a good many other people did, through the medium of her advertisement in a popular penny newspaper, the proprietors of whom should have exercised better taste, and more regard for the public morality, than to have inserted it in their columns. To have interpreted the advertisement in broad plain language, and stripped it of its covering, it would have read, "Ladies confined here, and their babies murdered at so much a head."

However, newspaper proprietors, anxious for grist to the mill, and oblivious to the dirty state of it, inserted week by week Mrs. Oliphant's murder announcements, and those of other baby farmers.

By the help of newspapers, baby farming not long ago became a large and lucrative trade; there was a little private establishment springing up in every suburb of London, where a small house with a roomy walled-in garden was to be had, the said garden to be converted into a God's Acre, or cemetery for the new-born children of shame.

Josh had no conception that the grieving woman before him was a bird of kindred black feather to himself—that she, too, in short, had been the red-handed Cain to her own illegitimate offspring.

"Don't fear the young woman, Josh," said Mrs. Oliphant, awaking out of her dreadful reverie. "Besides, I had the caution to tell you to speak low. And didn't I ask you out of the house?"

"But you never told me that she was going to live at Evesham House, and that she was lodging in the next room!" cried Josh, in an emphatic kind of whisper.

"I think I did—I think I did," she replied, as if recollecting herself, while she refreshed herself with a pinch of snuff, first politely offering her silver box to her visitor, who was not just then "up to snuff."

"I tell'ee what I think," said Josh, in his Devonshire brogue.

"What's that, Josh?"

"That it won't be long before the old kit of us are bowled out."

"Stuff o' nonsense! Don't give way to fears about this girl. If she heard anything, she can't possibly understand. She's too innocent for that. She couldn't have the least idea that there were such awful people in the world as me and you and Lady Mary."

"I didn't come here to be told that," said Josh, "and it will be a very long time before I come here again," he added, hastily rising, and taking his departure, while Mrs. Oliphant called out—

"Don't be so uffy, Josh!"

But the man was really constantly in a very troubled and unhappy state of mind, and the fact that Jane had been so near them all the evening, while they had been talking so incautiously of subjects that might at any hour hang him, by no means added to his equanimity of mind, and he breathed far more freely when he had got out of the house, and reached the little inn hard by where he had baited his horse, and where he had intended to take up his quarters for the night, but his long interview with Mrs. Oliphant, and the revelations that had grown out of it, altered his determination, therefore he had his horse saddled, and rode direct to Lady Mary at Evesham House, whom he found very jolly with a champagne card-party, made up of two of her west-end milliners, the racketty son of her wine merchant, a smart young lieutenant in the navy, and a "pious" clergyman of the Church of England, who knew Lady Mary when she lived with her father the earl, and who was very fond of the society of fascinating women, and unlimited loo.

And this middle-aged clergyman had plenty of opportunity of gratifying his tastes, for there were numerous fine women attached to his congregation who were always delighted to receive the reverend gentleman at their homes, and knock up little card parties for his delectation and amusement, in return for his arduous Sunday services in teaching them the way to Heaven.

The scenes and circumstances we have hitherto related between Josh and Mrs. Oliphant, our readers will please to remember occurred about a week before Pretty Jane made her entry into Evesham House.

Like a virtuous girl as she was, both in mind and practice, her hopes of happiness were much disturbed when she recognised in the grounds of Evesham House the gentleman who had met her in Kidbrook Lane, and who had dared to invade her bedroom-window.

She was received in the servants' hall by Mrs. Sterne, the housekeeper, whose name did not at all answer to her nature, which was sunny, kind, and genial.

Of course she was a favourite with everybody who knew her, and soon became one with Jane. Her boxes, under Mrs. Sterne's direction, were taken at once to the room designed for Jane, and which we have already referred to as being situated in a very lonely part of the building, and hither Mrs. Sterne herself inducted Jane, and bade her prepare herself for a good tea in the housekeeper's apartment, which Jane might not then have known was a very great privilege, but which afterwards another servant girl, between whom and Jane a very close acquaintance speedily cropped up, told her to esteem as an event to be proud of.

"All you have to do is to be a good girl," said the housekeeper, leading Jane into her snug apartment, which adjoined the servants' hall, "then I shall do all I can to make you comfortable. And now take a seat there, and we will have tea together."

Mrs. Sterne pulled a handsome bell-rope, and a stylish servant answered the summons, and the housekeeper ordered tea for two.

Jane was by no means at her ease at so much kindness and attention, especially when she caught a look from the servant, which unmistakably expressed—

"She might wait upon herself I think," while she walked out of the room after taking her orders from her superior, with her head tossed contemptuously high.

"Tea for two," she said, coming into the servants' hall.

The other servants could not comprehend her meaning, and asked her for an explanation.

"Tea for two. La! Ha! ha!"

The somewhat tallish girl, with a small olive-complexioned face, and not a very amiable expression, was repeatedly asked what she was grumbling at, but nothing could be got from her but—

"Tea for two. Ha! ha! ha!"

"Whatever are you laughing at, Tilley?" was the inquiry from more than one.

"At our new missus."

The servants could not make head nor tail to her meaning, and before many minutes had elapsed, the housekeeper's bell again rang for Tilley.

"Put some strawberries on the tray when you bring it in, Tilley; ask Wells to gather a few fresh ones; tell him they are for me."

"Enough for two, ma'am?" said the sarcastic servant.

"Yes, yes—just a nice plateful," said the housekeeper, who wore a handsome black silk dress, at the waist of which was suspended a silver watch and a bunch of keys.

"Any cream, 'm?"

"Certainly, cream," replied the housekeeper. "Don't I always have cream on the tea-table, Tilley?"

"Cream for two, 'm?"

"Why how strange you are acting, Tilley," said Mrs. Sterne. "When you are desired to prepare tea for two, I surely don't mean half the things for one, and half for two. The fact is that you are out of temper—"

"Not in the least 'm," protested Tilley, "I do assure you."

"Then you are out of your mind," rejoined Mrs. Sterne, jocularly. "But you are a good girl in the main, though there are a good many odd points about you?"

"Shall I help her, 'm?" asked Jane, very diffidently, feeling that the whole of Tilley's behaviour was levelled at herself.

"Not a bit of it," replied the housekeeper. "Now get along with you, Tilley, and make haste back with the tea and a smiling face. And if you cannot come back with a good temper you can send some one else with the tea."

This little bit of genial reproof cured Tilley's rising jealousy, and when she returned to the hall the half dozen other servants crowded round her to know what was the matter, and what the housekeeper rang her bell for?

"For strawberries and cream for two. I know that when I first came to service here, there was no strawberries and cream for me."

"They wasn't in season when you came, for we both came together, and that was in the winter time."

"What's that to do with it, stupid?" asked Tilley, at the same time spreading forth a very handsome tea-tray.

"All to do with it, booby!" replied the other, emulating Tilley's unseemly epithets. "You couldn't have strawberries if they wasn't in season!" and the matter-of-fact girl turned and appealed to the others for support of her undeniable logic, which was enunciated with as much gravity as if she had been giving forth some of the utterances of King Solomon.

"But the housekeeper's room was in season, I 'spose, and tea was in season, but I wasn't asked into her room, and another servant ordered to make tea for two—was you?"

"No, nor none of us," replied the other,

who had a good deal of common sense in her composition, though a coarse way of expressing herself. "But I hope I shall never be such a fool to care a button about anything that wasn't in my agreement, and I'm sure to take tea with the housekeeper in her room wasn't. Was it in yours?"

"Look here, E-liz-a-beth," said Tilley, dividing each syllable of her name, believing that it would savour too much of friendship to pronounce it in the usual short familiar manner in vogue amongst friends as "Lizzie," "you are the most unsentimental creature on the face of the earth. No wonder you haven't got a young man."

"Ma-til-da," rejoined the other, following suit in the spiteful pronunciation of her name, "I would have you to know that I'm rather pertikler about my young men. None of your red-coated rascals for me. who sponge upon you when courting, and when they are married desert you for another."

"Soldiers are a case of sour grapes with you —they're too tall for you to reach."

Fortunately, perhaps, for these tongue combatants, Lady Duchesney suddenly came into the hall, and her presence silenced them, and her group of discordant servants quickly scattered themselves to their several occupations.

Her ladyship was in the habit of making these abrupt entrances, and sometimes equally abrupt exits, and they were not taken much account of. With a letter in her hand, and dressed in light pink silk, with rich lace sleeves, and collar, she promenaded the hall, trying in a variety of little ways to make her presence agreeable to her servants, while yet she was thinking of something else.

"I hear that the new girl has arrived," she said, among other gossip. "Where is she, pray?"

"She is in the housekeeper's room your ladyship," replied Tilley. "I am just going to serve tea to them."

"With Mrs. Sterne, eh? Then I will just go and have another look at her, for when an old friend of mine sent her to me, I thought her a sweetly pretty girl. If my impression be the correct one, I would warn you, girls, not to bring your lovers to the hall, for men are very fickle to their plights and promises, when new blandishments cross their paths. Have any of you seen her?"

The answer was that they had all seen her, for the housekeeper brought her in the hall to tea after she was engaged to come.

"I have seen her two or three times within this hour, your ladyship," said Tilley.

"Well, and would you care to trust your lover with her?"

The servants tittered at her ladyship's affability and condescension, while Tilly racked her brains for an answer that should bear hard upon Jane.

She at length replied—

"If her character, your ladyship, isn't better than her looks, she'll soon corrupt young men and women too."

"Ah! I see. That observation tells me that she has either offended you in something, or that you are jealous of her already," said the lady. "Which is it?"

"I don't own to either, your ladyship," said the paltry-minded young woman. "She is nothing to me; and of course Mrs. Sterne can quite do as she likes about having her in her room to tea, and strawberries and cream."

"Ah, it is all out now," said Lady Mary, with a gentle smile. "Your eyes were too full of vexation at the sight of the poor girl being the guest of my housekeeper, to see any beauty of face or character in her."

"I never said anything against her character, your ladyship. I daresay she's quite as good as any other girl."

"I am told that she's a great deal better than most girls."

"I hope your ladyship may find it so," said Tilly, more enraged than ever with Pretty Jane because of the notice taken of her by Lady Duchesney.

But there was an under-current to the interest taken by her aristocratic mistress in Jane, as there was in the silly antipathy shown towards her by Tilly.

Lady Mary had heard of all the proceedings that occurred on the night of Josh's visit to Mrs. Oliphant, and as much as a fearless woman could know fear, from what Josh told her that Jane must have overheard about the barn and the Hunchback Boy, she feared Jane might innocently prove a serious enemy to her.

She had, therefore, a little game of tact to play with Jane.

Besides, too, had not her husband become enamoured of the girl?

The question for her was, how could she utilise that fact to his destruction?

"After all," she could not resist reflecting, "a wicked life is a life of fear and slavery. I am the slave of Josh—the slave of Oliphant— the slave of a hunchback boy lest he should discover me as his mother—and now I have become the slave of a little servant girl! Would that I could get the lot to sea—Josh and all— I'd scuttle the ship though I went down—down with them!"

While she mused thus, she rested her elbow on the mantel of an elaborate fireplace at the top of the hall, where she stood for a little time apart from her servants, who sat round a large oak table spread out with the luxuries of a good old English tea, in which a large ham and a fine round of beef were conspicuous, and there for any who chose to partake.

The hall now would have furnished a fine subject for a picture; Lady Mary's stately figure, arrayed as it was in flowing light pink silk and lace, with pale but tragic expression of face, would have contrasted well with the group of servants, men and women, in all kinds of costume, at their evening meal; and the beauty of the picture would have been much enhanced if we could have had Pretty Jane in the foreground, with her sweet face expressing goodwill to all, and marked by the diffidence she felt on being introduced into a new place.

The lady, as if struck by some thought that required urgent execution, with quickened step came down the hall, and bade one of the men look to her boat, as she wanted to use it within half an hour, and then she went to the room of her housekeeper.

Hastily opening the door of Mrs. Sterne's

room, she heard Jane talking to the housekeeper about the barn and the Hunchback Boy.

Jane rose on the entrance of Lady Mary, and made a lowly curtsey.

"Our new parlour-maid, your ladyship," said Mrs. Sterne, as radiant with smiles as if she had been introducing her own daughter to her mistress.

"I remember her well," said the lady. "You are the maid that Mrs. Oliphant sent?"

"Yes, your ladyship," said Jane, who had dressed herself as smartly as it was becoming for her to do, making use of blue riband in her cap, and a bow of the same colour, with long ends. She wore a natty black silk apron, with broad black strings that hung down behind, and both apron and strings set off, and contrasted well, with her stiffly-starched, and carefully got-up sprig-patterned cotton dress, which, for one in Jane's station, somewhat went beyond the usual amplitude of skirt.

Not content with this, she must further adorn herself with rather a large cameo representing the three Graces—and Jane might well have stood for the fourth, for certainly, as a common type of beauty, she was admitted to be unrivalled.

Had there been public prizes got up for the prettiest servant girls, as well as babies and barmaids, we are quite sure that Jane would have distanced all comers, and triumphantly borne off the prize.

Alas! that beauty should be surrounded with so many deadly perils! that so many parasites and vipers should hang about to feed upon it! that it should be betrayed and murdered by those who wooed it with the most sacred protestations of love!

"Sit down, girl, and make yourself quite at home. I am pleased to see, Sterne," she said to her housekeeper, "that you are having a little quiet drill with her in your own room before you turn her over to active service."

"Your ladyship has quite guessed it," said Mrs. Sterne.

"Father and mother both living, eh?" the lady familiarly asked.

"Not my mother, your ladyship," was Jane's reply, while sad memories were awakened in her heart.

"Mother dead, eh?" she said, with indifference—for what cared she about the death of Jane's mother?

"And your father—what is he?"

"I hardly know, your ladyship. He works somewhere in London, I believe. But I haven't seen him for years."

This was another sad memory awakened by Lady Mary's interrogatory.

"For years! you must have been a mere child then when you last saw your father."

"I was about fourteen. My aunt took care of me after my mother's death."

"Well, well, never mind since you found some one to take care of you. But, after all, your best guardian will be yourself. She's a very pretty girl, don't you think so, Sterne?"

"I have told her so, your ladyship, and cautioned her of the perils of beauty."

Jane blushed all over, but her vanity was mightily gratified.

"You were talking when I came in," said the lady about a hunchback boy—some brother of yours, I presume?"

"Oh, dear, no, your ladyship," interposed the housekeeper.

"Who then?"

"As far as I can make out—for she had not finished her story when your ladyship came into the room—this hunchback boy is more of a mystery than anything else."

"I am fond of mysteries, you know that, don't you, Sterne?"

"Yes, indeed," returned the housekeeper. "From a child you were fond of everything that other people shuddered at."

"Quite right, Sterne. Always did, and always shall, hate a tame monotonous life as well as people. The terrible for me! I can find no one like myself, and therefore I am companionless."

She here poured forth the air of a ballad from La Traviata.

"Now then, girl, what about this hunchback boy? Has he fallen in love with you?"

"Mrs. Sterne, your ladyship, was asking me what I knew about Mrs. Oliphant," began Jane, when she was interrupted by Lady Mary, who playfully exclaimed—

"Ha! Sterne; I find that you have the same curiosity that besets all our sex—only some of us think they are exempt from it."

"Just a little gossip over our tea, your ladyship—nothing more."

"We gratify most of our curiosity out of well-directed gossip," said the mistress. "Hand me a few of those strawberries, they look finer than those that come to my table."

"The gardener is to blame if they are," replied Mrs. Sterne, "for I always take as much care as possible that the best of everything is sent to your ladyship's table."

"Only my fun, Sterne, only my fun. You are about the truest old friend that I ever had; and the countess, my mother, could not possibly have left me a richer legacy than you for my housekeeper."

How emotional some women are! Now there was really nothing in what the lady said that should have made it necessary for Mrs. Sterne to weep. But Lady Mary's words brought to her memory the countess's almost dying words that she would watch over her wicked daughter, who had brought her grey hairs with sorrow to the grave.

She painfully remembered too that the countess on her death-bed repeatedly sent for her daughter, and that she would not come, excusing herself by telling Mrs. Sterne, who had for years been a valued domestic in Earl Ashford's family—

"I want no death-bed lectures about the wickedness of my life, and I am not going to be tortured to gratify the last moments of the countess, or any one else."

Still further, and more painful if possible, the good old housekeeper poignantly remembered that after all the amiable and aged countess breathed her last without seeing that vicious, hard-hearted creature, she was compelled to call her daughter.

After numerous entreaties of her father, the physicians, and Mrs. Sterne, she reluctantly consented to go to her mother, but on the condition only that no one else should be present at the interview.

She approached her dying mothers's bed, and with a proud stony countenance, grasped the curtain aside more like a murderess, as she was, than a daughter—but the life of the moth·r had fled; yes, there she lay in her stately bed more like one sleeping than dead.

Lady Mary kissed not the lips of the dead, she merely congratulated herself that she had been spared a scene, and quitted the chamber of death with more alacrity of step than she entered it.

She spread the news below that the countess was dead, then had her horse saddled, and rode abroad, attended by Josh as her groom.

It was the memory of these things that made Mrs. Sterne weep, not the praises that her mistress lavished on her.

She again brought back the conversation to the subject of the Hunchback Boy, but just as Jane was about to begin her recital once more, a servant announced that Lady Mary's boat was ready.

In one part of Evesham Park was a small ornamental lake, as pellucid as crystal, and the adjacent grounds were artistically arranged to give it an island appearance.

Here Lady Mary might often be seen, early and late, rowing herself about in her yellow boat picked out with the brightest of blues, and she would either be singing a song that resounded through the park, or smoking a cigarette.

" Look here, girl, you shall attend me in my boat, and there tell your story of this mysterious boy."

Jane shrugged her shoulders at her mistress' proposition.

She had a horror of the water, and dared not trust herself in a little boat upon it—no, not even if her own " sweet William " was the oarsman.

She hardly knew what to say, but the lady read her alarm in her face, and anticipated her, by exclaiming—

" You don't mean to say that you are afraid of the water ?"

" Horribly, your ladyship," she replied, after her confusion had subsided, and she had found words to confess her cowardice.

" I am surprised ! But you are thinking of an open boat on a stormy sea. If you were to see my pretty little boat on the pretty little lake, I am quite sure you would not be afraid," said her mistress, who had risen to go.

" I hope your ladyship will excuse me," said the trembling Jane, " I'm too much afraid of the water to go upon it."

" Then I wonder you are not afraid to wash yourself," rejoined her mistress, with a laughing sneer in her tones. " Don't be a coward, I pray you, if you care for my esteem."

" I don't know how to help it," said Pretty Jane, timorously. " I would if I could. I daresay it only wants a beginning, but I haven't the heart to begin."

" Better be brave than beautiful," remarked her mistress. " Women should be brave as well as men. But English girls nowadays have not the spirit of a fly. I am truly sick of such cowardice. Look to it, Sterne ; and amongst your gossip about Mrs. Oliphant, and things that do not concern you, see if some bravery is not to be imparted to this timid creature. I will not have cowards about me !"

Without giving either time to reply—not that Jane's beating heart would let her, whatever time had been given her—she made a quick exit from the room, hastily dressed herself for boating,—her costume being a gold-embroidered Grecian cap, a richly-worked white jacket trimmed with blue, and blue facings, with a pink tie round her white throat, tied with a sailor's knot.

She had a mad organisation, and all her cruel deeds, and base actions, and terribly uncertain temper, and wild manners, were but demonstrations of madness.

Mrs. Sterne knew her too well to take any notice of her. She knew her infamous career with her groom, but she did not know the secrets of the barn, nor the true history of the Hunchback Boy.

She detested her as a woman, and only lived with her in promise of a dying request made to her mother the countess, in order that not any opportunity should be lost of putting in a good word to check her in her downward career of sin and shame.

Mrs. Sterne was a very excellent woman, and a clever housekeeper, but not half strong-minded enough to stem the torrent of her mistress' guilty nature.

She knew her mistress to be an abominable woman, but she did not know her to be half so bad as she was. Had she known, she would have trembled to remain under the same roof with her.

Poor Jane, who did not understand this abandoned woman, dwelt sorrowfully upon her last words, and began to be apprehensive that she would not suit her ladyship.

" Don't you fret, my dear," said Mrs. Sterne, observing Jane's thoughtful expression of face, " at anything she might say. She meant it more to me than to you, for she knows that I too am afraid of the water. Take a few more strawberries, and think nothing more of her. You'll have to do with me, not her. You may not see her again for a month, except you meet her by accident."

" That is good news indeed !" cried Jane, " for she has quite frightened me."

" After all it is that man walking there that you have most to fear."

" What man ?" asked the terrified Jane, her heart in no condition to receive further shocks or surprises.

" He standing there by that lime. Sit where I am and you will see him plain," added Mrs. Sterne.

Jane for a moment changed her seat, and taking a glance from the window verified her worst fears.

She saw Mr. Duchesney, who stood, either by design or accident nearly opposite the window.

The dog he had with him when he met her in Kidbrook Lane was with him now, and the gentleman placed a newspaper under his arm while he appeared to be examining the dog's teeth, for he had drawn up the dog's lip.

Jane turned pale as death, and had she been anywhere else would have given way to her overwrought feelings, and swooned outright upon the floor.

The girl, by one circumstance after another, and now this strange remark from Mrs. Sterne, had been quite terrified in believing that this man was her evil genius!

She had had as yet no time to tell the motherly housekeeper of what had already passed in the Lane, nor of his rudeness at her window while stopping at Eltham with Mrs. Oliphant, nor did she intend to do so, but now she thought it best at once to make a confidant of the good housekeeper, and tell her all.

"Do you know who that is?" she asked the girl.

Much to the housekeeper's surprise, Jane answered that it was Mr. Duchesney.

"So it is, my dear! And he is the biggest wretch alive, and will yet get himself into some trouble. But how did you know him to be Mr. Duchesney?"

Jane here told Mrs. Sterne all she knew about him.

When she came to the part about the window the housekeeper lifted up her hands in amazement, and exclaimed—

"The impudent fellow! Why I wonder you had not been afraid to have taken service under such a master?"

"You see, ma'am, I had taken the place, and engaged to come, before these things occurred. I think now that I had better not stop," she added, while she looked up as if asking advice from the housekeeper.

"Pack of nonsense! You have been warned, and you now need only have your wits about you."

"But it is such an unpleasant thing to be living in fear of anybody," remarked Jane, who was now getting quite at home with the housekeeper, who was so different to that dreadful old creature, Mrs. Oliphant.

In Mrs. Sterne she seemed to have found a second mother, and she confided to her everything about herself, of course not forgetting her sweet William at sea.

And from her pocket came William's letter for Mrs. Sterne to read, and, woman like, the housekeeper never refused the chance of reading a love letter, although the sweet things therein might be for another.

Of course now the sailor's dream—and Jane's dream—and Nell Dod's interpretation thereof, became the solemn theme of conversation between the pair.

Unfortunately for Jane's peace, Mrs. Sterne was a thorough-going believer in signs, presentiments, dreams, omens, and apparitions; and she talked so eloquently upon these matters, that Jane was almost converted against her will to believe in them.

Mrs. Sterne did not go the length to profess to interpret those mysterious things that bore so much upon the future, a gift, in her opinion, that was given to very few, but she said enough to deepen the girl's interest in them.

"I should be sorry to be so presumptuous to say with Nell Dod that your sweetheart's dream means *murder*. So I wouldn't have you sad about it."

"I am not, ma'am. Indeed, I never think about such things."

"Ah! but dreams *are* things to think about," emphatically remarked the housekeeper. "We are in God's hands, I admit, and the Lord alone knows the future. But dreams are sent to set us thinking, and as warnings, and guides."

"You don't know, ma'am, how bewildered I feel. I shall go out of my mind!" cried Jane, and she showed much distraction of feeling in her manners while she spoke.

"After what you have told me, you shall find a friend in me. I had arranged that you should sleep in the detached room where you have placed your boxes—and there you must sleep to-night. But afterwards I shall arrange for your sleeping near my room."

"It was that troubled me. But I did not like to speak about it. I feel already that I am a trouble to you. I would rather not remain. I am too unhappy."

"Why should you be unhappy, more than any other servant in the house? Look here, my dear. You are a timid creature, and upon my word, while I laugh at you, I feel for you. You shall have my bed and room to-night, and I will sleep in the room that I had arrang d for you."

"I am timid—you see that I am," said Pretty Jane. "But rather than be more of a trouble to you, I would endure anything—sleep in a cellar —in the barn——"

"What! and have you heard something, too, about the barn?" said the astonished housekeeper, forgetting that Jane had already spoken to her before they were interrupted by Lady Duchesney, what she had overheard between Josh and Mrs. Oliphant about the barn.

Jane refreshed her memory by repeating what she had said.

"Truly—truly—I remember now. Well, it is no good concealing it—indeed, I never was a a good hand for secrets—you have come amongst wicked people."

Josh here opened the door, and put his head into the room, but directly he saw that Mrs. Sterne was engaged he withdrew.

"And that is not the least of them," observed the housekeeper, when the groom had politely withdrawn.

"I do believe that is the man that called on Mrs. Oliphant, on the night when Mr. Duchesney——"

Jane was sick to death on speaking of a subject so revolting to her feelings, and she could not finish her sentence. But Mrs. Sterne helped her by saying—

"Had the impudence to climb to your window. That man is Joshua Woodward, and whether he is steward, groom, or master, I cannot tell you. All is mystery here, and you must do the best you can to shut your eyes to it. You will have good wages, good board, and a good friend in me. But why I should take to you, I cannot tell, except it is that I fancy you cannot take care of yourself."

"Oh, but I can," said Jane, with more bravery of emphasis than she had used before. She had a horror of being thought weak or namby-pamby, where her virtue was concerned, and would fire up at such an imputation.

Josh here again put his head in at the door, and beckoned to the housekeeper outside.

PRETTY JANE

OB, THE

VIPER OF KIDBROOK LANE

SHE COULD NOT REACH THE BED AND FELL ON THE FLOOR.

The housekeeper could not imagine what Josh could want her so urgently for that he should call her from her room, not being able to speak before a third party.

Mrs. Sterne detested the man, and quite as much Lady Mary, for her extreme indelicacy in keeping the low creature in her service after the shame that had passed between them.

"Well—what is it?" she coldly asked, when she stood in the wide passage with Josh, whose face wore a harassed expression.

Before Josh told his business he led the way further from the door, beckoning her to follow him, which she reluctantly did, for she detested everything that savoured of mystery.

"Now then, what is it?" she again asked, when they had reached the furthest point of the passage.

"I met Lady Mary on her way to her boat,

No. 6.

and I can see she is displeased about your talking with the new girl about Mrs. Oliphant."

"And did she tell you to speak to me?" demanded Mrs. Sterne, with some warmth.

"No, she didn't—but I thought I would," said Josh, whose officiousness in the matter was more on his own behalf than that of his mistress, for he was full of fear lest what Jane might prattle about should awaken suspicion in the housekeeper.

"I really would thank you, Mr. Woodward, to mind your own business," she said.

"No call to lose your temper, Mrs. Sterne," retorted the groom, or steward as he was now promoted to be.

"Temper has nothing to do with it. I think it a great liberty, indeed I do, either for you or our mistress, to dictate to me what I shall talk about with my servants."

"I'm sure it doesn't matter to me what you talk about."

"I suspect on the subject of this Mrs. Oliphant it *does* matter to you," said the housekeeper, rather too significantly for the peace of Joshua Woodward, who retorted by saying in an off-hand manner—

"A woman who has lost her temper has lost her reason. I must leave her ladyship to deal with you."

"I am quite sure that it is not *your* place," she replied, and after this last word, which women claim as their privilege, Mrs. Sterne returned to her room and to Jane, and closed the door upon Josh, who had not at all succeeded in his mission to the housekeeper, but on the contrary, he feared that he had stimulated her curiosity.

In greater confusion than he came he sloped off dejectedly to his own room, which was situated on another floor, which was reached by two short broad carved staircases, and here he threw himself into an easy chair, tormenting himself with the thought that this girl—this Pretty Jane—was to be the means of bringing hidden things to light, and himself and his mistress to the gallows.

And Mrs. Sterne, by no means pleased with the conduct of Josh or Lady Duchesney, set to work with Jane to get from her everything possible about the hunchback boy and Mrs. Oliphant, carefully taking the address of the latter, deciding that one day she would go to Eltham and make the woman a call.

The chat and tea over, Jane was taken into the servants' hall, and there left by Mrs. Sterne to make her acquaintance in the best manner she could with the other domestics and her ordinary duties.

There were two sets of servants at Evesham House, one for the master, the other for the mistress, but both sets assembled together in the great hall, and there not unfrequently discoursed of the peculiarities of Mr. and Lady Duchesney, and when the home-brewed ale went about of an evening, there would sometimes be sharp words about the relative merits of their master and mistress.

Mr. Duchesney's servants, especially his valet, was vehement in the defence of his master, and spoke openly and insultingly of Lady Duchesney, generally concluding with—

"If she was my wife I'd give her a tidy horsewhipping."

"You wouldn't live to give her another," said Josh, who had peculiar reasons for sticking up for his mistress. "And as for your master, he is nothing better than a sponge upon the estate. I wouldn't serve such a man."

"Your mistress is no better than a—"

"Behave, if you please, sir," said Mrs. Sterne, interrupting the offensive epithet that rose to his lips. "You two are always quarrelling about your master and mistress, and the fact of it is neither of them are worth quarrelling about."

There was very frequently in the hall, an old woman, who, by Lady Duchesney's orders, was allowed to come in and out, and partake of anything going.

No questions were to be asked of her, indeed she was reported to be too deaf to hear anything spoken. She was present now, and was looked upon merely as a poor dependent of the mistress of Evesham House.

She was a most peculiar-looking woman, and although her bent body and grey hair showed age, there was a youthfulness in her face, which she kept averted, or bent down, as much as possible—concealed, indeed, from intrusive prying eyes.

She had a very cleanly appearance, and was always neatly attired in a pair of broad brass-buckle shoes, a brown cloak, a faded dark silk dress, just short enough to disclose a pair of clean white stockings, and a little Primitive Methodist black silk poke bonnet.

Mrs. Sterne's rebuke, although not at all complimentary to master or mistress, was yet free from partisanship, and the valet and steward seemed to agree with her when placed before them in that fair and conciliatory manner.

"Quite right, Mrs. Sterne," said the valet, a somewhat bumptious respectable-looking man about five and thirty years of age, who did not sport so much jewellery as Josh. "You have taken their measure exactly. They are both bad—but I know which is the worst."

Of course this last remark opened the ball again, and Josh replied—

"Your sponging master, that's who it is is the worst."

"A bad woman is worse than a bad man any day in the week. A million to one upon that! What say you, Jane?"

"I'm sure I don't know," replied the girl, who was honoured with a seat at the table between Joshua Ward and Mrs. Sterne. "Whatever do you ask me for?"

"Because you are the prettiest girl in the hall," was the ready answer, and which was more grateful to Jane's vanity than pleasing to the feelings of the four other damsels present, and who were not at all prepared to yield the supremacy to Jane in the matter of beauty, although they knew that Jane in that particular far distanced them.

Tilly, more than the others, resented the uncalled for observation of the valet, and fired up and asked him—

"Who made *you* a judge of beauty, I should like to know?"

"Well, Tilly," said the valet, who occupied the next chair to the speaker, "*I* think so—"

"You are nobody," said another damsel, who fondly nursed the idea that the valet was rather sweet upon her. "You are a shuttlecock. Not long ago you said that I was the prettiest girl in the universal world."

"Oh, you wretch!" exclaimed Tilly, leaning her arms on the long wide table, while she firmly looked into the face of the good-tempered traitor. "Haven't you often said that *I* was the prettiest girl in creation?"

"But then I didn't know that Jane was created."

This observation, of course, was stronger testimony in praise of Jane's beauty than the first; certainly the other girls thought so.

"Now a man like you, Mr. Brummell, ought to be well exposed before your beautiful Jane," said Tilly, producing a letter from her pocket. "Is that your writing?"

Mr. Brummell laughingly replied in the firmative.

", Now then Pretty Jane shall know what you wrote to me not long ago about my beauty, so that she mightn't think too much of herself, nor the deceitful Mr. Brummell."

She was just preparing to read, when the valet, whose face was suffused with blushes as well as laughter, exclaimed, while he made a vain snatch at the letter—

" Don't be a fool, Tilly !"

" You read the letter, Tilly," said the other victim to the valet's flattering deception, " and when you've done, I'll go to my box and get a letter that he sent *me*."

The laughter was now general.

" I should like to know what you're all so merry about," said the mysterious old woman, coming from her corner to the housekeeper's chair, while she made an ear-trumpet of her hand.

" All for love, granny." Mrs. Sterne pleasantly replied.

The old woman smiled when she asked, still bending her ear—

" Did you say that you were in love, Mrs. Sterne ?"

Of course general laughter followed the deaf woman's question, and the housekeeper laughed until she brought on a fit of coughing.

" How could you think such a thing, granny ?" returned Mrs. Sterne, when her coughing had subsided. " An old woman like me in love !"

" Hoity-toity ! why not, pray ! Why I love yet."

" You !" all present exclaimed, as well as their merriment and mirth would let them.

" I hope it is not with me," bellowed Josh into her ear, " for I'm engaged."

" To whom ?" inquired the old woman.

" That's tellings," replied the steward.

" Dear me !" said rather a pretty domestic, who sat by the side of a burly head-stableman, and who had been hitherto silent, " I don't see any need of your making a secret of it. He is engaged to me, granny."

" Well to be sure !" cried the old woman. " Secrets are coming out with a vengeance."

" But you mustn't believe all you hear," said Josh, looking rather darkly on the girl who had revealed so much.

" My deafness won't permit me to hear much, but I heard what the young woman said, and believe what she said. She is a nice girl, too, and you are lucky in having her love."

" How sly you've been, Ann," said Mrs. Sterne, which was echoed by Elizabeth and Tilly.

The latter said—

" I thought they were thick. Haven't I said so to you, Lizzie, dear ?"

" That you have. And don't you remember we met them one Sunday afternoon in the willow copse ?"

Pretty Jane, who sat by the side of Josh, was here observed to look strangely at the steward. She had not been many weeks there, but that was quite long enough for Josh to make love to her, and quite long enough for Jane to give willing ear to his flattering addresses.

While, trusting maid as she was, she believed in his sincerity, yet it had not positively ripened into an engagement. Yet she secretly hoped that it would, for was not Josh handsome, and

did he not hold the chief appointment in the establishment ?

Jane, at a bound, now saw through him, and after his engagement with the other girl had been so singularly brought to light, she thought her character would be tarnished if she concealed from her fellow servants the facts connected with Josh and herself.

Josh, who quite understood Jane's looks if no one else did, and who was afraid she was going to speak, nudged her elbow, and whispered—

" Take no notice. Never mind her."

But the scoundrel this time had mistaken the nature of the heart he was trapping to mislead. Jane was mercifully saved from the snarer, while she felt that she did not deserve it, for her vanity had too far led her to forget her sailor at sea.

She had done very wrong in listening to if not encouraging his advances, and the time had now presented itself of withdrawing from the pit that was dug for her, and on whose edge her vanity had led her.

How many maidens have laid down their purity and truth at the shrine of vanity ! The warnings are daily, but the bait that appeals to the palate of their vanity is too irresistible— they taste, and fall !

These engagements with sailors, and marriages with them, too often end in disaster. They are too often and too long away, and there are too many vipers about in their absence, for them to expect constancy in their sweethearts, or fidelity in their wives.

Jane was surrounded with temptation, and her lover was at sea ! Such a state of circumstances was by no means safe for a girl who was as vain as she was pretty, though she had a higher feeling of virtue than most girls of her age and class.

" The willow-copse was where Mr. Woodward promised to meet me, and there's his letter making the appointment, which I have not said that I would keep, nor do I think I should, for I am engaged."

" We are both in the same boat, Mr. Woodward," said the valet, when Jane had made her revelation.

" And a great pity but what the boat would capsize and drown the both of you," said Mrs. Sterne, the housekeeper.

" And so say all of us," said Tilly, in tones of indignation.

" Take your letter," said the much-aggrieved Ann, tossing Jane's letter to the floor, after she had read and satisfied herself of her lover's perfidy. The letter was read all round, and at last returned to Jane, who presented it to Josh, at the same time saying—

" Don't call yourself a man any more."

She at once left the side of the shame-faced steward, and went to the side of Ann, who, with a handkerchief to her eyes, was giving vent to her feelings in sobs and tears.

Josh pitched the letter to the floor, whence it was quietly picked up and read by the old woman.

" Ah," she sighed, " men are the same deceivers, as when I was young. Don't cry, silly girl," she said, gently patting Ann's back with her stick. " You have more cause to laugh that you have escaped entering into bondage with a villain !"

All looked amazed at such plain speaking to the steward of a poor old woman, who was dependent on the bounty of Lady Mary.

"I shall just take you by the neck and crop and put you out of the hall!" exclaimed the steward, rising from his seat.

"You would have to ask your mistress, young man, concerning that. Tilley-valley! I am here by her orders, and I only leave by her orders. Go fetch her, if you would have me away. Fill me a tumbler of ale, if you please, Mrs. Sterne. Don't think me bold for asking; you have been told by superior powers to let me have what I would for the asking."

"I say, granny, don't make yourself disagreeable; a little civility is becoming in all of us," said Mrs. Sterne, handing the imperious beggar the ale.

The valet here rose, and judging by his commencement of "Ladies and gentlemen," at the same time leaning forward, and placing his hands on the table, he was preparing himself for a long harangue. But the jilted girls, Tilly and Elizabeth, would not listen.

"Dear girls!—"

"Bother that! we've had quite enough of that!" cried Tilly.

"Fudge, I call it!" cried Elizabeth.

"Pray be *ladies*, whatever may have been your provocation," said Mr. Brummell, thrusting his thumbs in the arm-holes of his black satin vest.

"Hear! hear!" cried Josh, who knew the cleverness of the valet in getting out of a scrape, and also knowing that the door he was opening for his own escape, would also do for him to pass through—for was not his offence quite in character with his own?

"This is all a misunderstanding—" again the valet commenced, but he was interrupted by the young women, who added—

"Not on our parts. What about the two letters?"

"Bravo, girls!" cried Mrs. Sterne.

"Mr. Joshua Woodward," said the valet, and the steward answered to his name by nodding his head, "and you, Mr. Butters,"—a grave nod from the chief stableman, one of those men who heard much and said little, and who sat in silent state and apart over a long clay pipe, his hand thrust into the capacious pocket of a long dark blue waistcoat, which more than half concealed his corpulent form, "I say, gentlemen, if the ladies won't hear me, I must throw myself on your mercy. This is a case of character, gentlemen!"

"Heer-r-r! heer-r-r!" cried Butters, prolonging very much the guttural sound of the last letter, which came out from his half savage-looking mouth with clouds of tobacco smoke, who seemed as proud as Josh at being appealed to as "gentlemen."

"Yes, my character is lost—"

"Heaven help those who find it!" cried Elizabeth, and general laughter followed, while Mrs. Sterne clapped her hands at the girl's smartness of repartee.

Mr. Butter's gravity was, too, quite upset; his face became radiant with half-suppressed smiles, and he did his best to suppress them altogether. He lifted his eyebrows high to Josh, which action rightly interpreted, meant that the "game was up," that the girls had taken the "wind out of his sails."

"This is all jealousy," continued the valet, which assertion was rapturously received by the steward, on whom the old woman ever and anon cast a frowning glance.

"There has a jealousy sprung up, gentlemen, amongst the dear girls of this establishment, because we happen to appreciate the beauty of that young lady that now sits there drying the tears of Miss Ann. Have we not also appreciated *their* beauty?"

"Every one of them!" vociferated Josh.

"Gentlemen, is it not our habit to recognise beauty wherever we find it?"

"We shouldn't be gentlemen if we didn't," chimed in Josh.

"Wasn't beauty given to woman to delight men?"

Mr. Butters nodded his head approvingly.

"Jane is not only admired by us, but I don't mind telling her that she is admired by our master!"

"Let me tell you, Mr. Butters, this is very unpleasant for me to hear," said Jane; "and I don't think it right for me to stop in the place longer than I can help."

"Without doubt you have been the cause of a great deal of mischief," Tilly ventured to say, and the other girls supported her, which very much grieved Jane.

"And is it my fault, pray? Can I help these silly men from going on so at me?"

Mrs. Sterne took her part by saying—

"Certainly not, Jane. Nor does any of their admiration for you explain their mean conduct to the other girls."

"That's just what I was going to say," said Elizabeth. "Not that I care one fig for myself—"

"And I'm sure I don't," interrupted Tilly. "But I *do* feel for poor Ann, for her's was a regular engagement, and I think Mr. Woodward ought to keep it."

"Who said he oughtn't?" growled Josh.

"You shan't have the opportunity," said Ann, wiping her tears, and plucking up a womanly spirit. "I wouldn't have you *now* though every hair of your head was a diment!"

"Bravo, Ann!" exclaimed Tilly and Elizabeth, the former clapping her hands.

"Then there's a chance for somebody else," said Josh.

"You can now have your beautiful Jane for me," said the deeply offended Ann.

"Indeed but he can't!" replied Jane, tossing her head. "I am engaged to a great deal better fellow than he!"

"That's our master," said Mr. Brummell.

"No, better than the master either, or all the men in the world!"

"You don't include me?" asked the valet, smilingly.

"But I've seen so much of men this evening, that I shall think twice before I have anything to do with any of them," said Jane.

"But knowing that you were engaged, I blame you, Jane, for not sending his letter back with disdain," said Ann, who, unfortunately, had yielded her heart to the perfidious steward.

But had she known as much of Mr. Joshua Woodward as our readers, her heart would have leaped with joy at her escape from such a monster with so fair an exterior.

"I confess that I ought to have sent his letter back," said Jane, honestly. "But of course I never knew that he was wicked enough to make love to me while he was engaged to you."

"Yes, my dear," said Ann, "that is all very well, but you knew that you were engaged."

"Whew!" said the valet, looking from one to the other. "A little bit of inconstancy all round, that's the worst that can be said of it."

"I object to that way of putting it," said Jane, sternly. "Show me any inconstancy on my part?"

Jane here availed herself of woman's chief defence in battle, her tears, which always commands sympathy if not respect.

Besides, she could not help feeling that in the outpouring of the steward's love she had a little forgotten her sailor lad at sea.

"But you must own, Jane," said Elizabeth, "that you must have had a good deal of flirting with Mr. Woodward before he would have written to you to meet him in the willow copse?"

"Don't say a word, Jane," cried the steward. "They only want to know what they've no business to."

"I don't wish to be advised by you," said the still weeping Jane. "You've brought me into quite trouble enough."

"It's only those should cry, my dear, who are guilty of doing wrong, and I'm sure you've done no harm to anybody," said Mrs. Sterne. "You can't help the men flirting with you."

"But she can help encouraging them, 'm," said Ann.

"But how do you know that she did, you silly girl?" asked the housekeeper.

"I am quite sure that I did not," said Jane. "There he is, ask him if I did."

"Me ask him!" exclaimed the indignant girl. "I wouldn't speak to him again for the world! Hanging is too good for a man that would deceive a woman."

Hanging! the sound of the very word dashed the steward's gaiety. He shrugged his shoulders, and bit his lip. His thoughts were at once with the barn and the dead.

None present, but the old woman, noticed the sudden change in the man, who rose to leave the hall for the retirement of his own room.

"The girls have given us quite a good roasting for one sitting, Mr. Woodward," said the unconcerned valet, "and I propose that I and you and Butters go out on the lawn and refresh our drooping spirits with a game at bowls, or if that blessed mistress of yours—that half fiend, half woman, as I call her—"

"And you have no right to speak so of the lady whose bread we eat without stint," said Mrs. Sterne.

"You have spoken well, ma'am," said the old woman. "I would cudgel any lazy idle servant who presumed to speak disrespectfully of the mistress on whom he fattened!"

"Quite right, granny."

"I should like to know who gave you so much liberty to speak?" asked Mr. Brummell, coming close to her ear.

"She who fed you to-day," was the laconic answer.

There was a sudden stir among the domestics,

—Mr. Duchesney's quick firm step was heard advancing to the hall door. Presently he came bounding in, with two strong tawny-coloured bloodhounds leashed together.

He was always free and easy in the hall whenever he came in, which was not often.

He came in under the pretence of finding his valet, but in reality it was more to see Jane.

She was sitting right opposite the door, and when the master entered she was still weeping. Mr. Duchesney's eye immediately fell on her, and in an off-hand manner he exclaimed to his servant—

"What's this, Brummell? Beauty in distress? Don't gape at the old woman, stupid! I don't mean her. She may be in distress, but she's certainly no beauty. Not a bad sort, though, for an old 'un."

"Very likely not, sir," said the obsequious servant. "But she's a little bit impertinent at times."

"Let her go to —— ! Here, this is the beauty I mean," he added, going close to Jane, while the eyes of all were upon him, especially those of the old woman. "Tears denote sorrow—what is yours? Some one must be answerable for those tears—let me know who, and these dogs of mine shall tear him all to pieces!"

Jane was in a most cruel position; to speak one word she could not; she shrank away to the side of Mrs. Sterne for protection.

"What a perverse member of the body is the tongue! sometimes it rattles away like a steam-engine, at others so frozen up that that it will not thaw with the warmth of kindness. Will no one speak on her behalf, and tell me what's the matter?"

"It is something about Mr. Woodward," Brummell ventured to say.

"I knew there was a man in it," said Mr. Duchesney. "That fellow Woodward is a complete nuisance, and a sneaking sulky coward! Why he is kept here by my amiable lady, the Heavens above only know, except it be that they are both possessed of the devil."

"You ought not, sir, to speak of her ladyship in that manner before her servants," said Mrs. Sterne.

"I decline to be taught what I ought or ought not to do by you. If you are the housekeeper, you are not my keeper, and I beg that you will not assume the office."

"If I did," she courageously replied, "I am sure I should find it too troublesome to succeed in."

"Then have the kindness to mind your own business, and permit me to speak of my fiend-wife as I please."

"But I am not obliged to stop and listen," replied the housekeeper, and she rose to leave the hall.

Jane, of course, was about to follow, but he caught her by the arm, and the bloodhounds, which he held by the leathern leash, began to growl as Jane struggled to get her arm from his grasp.

"Tell me, then, what you were crying about?" he said.

"Let go my arm, sir!" exclaimed Jane, at length succeeding in getting her release.

"La! Jane, master won't hurt you," said Tilly, who, with the other girls, the valet and stableman, stood about the hall, and vastly enjoyed the fun.

"She makes too much fuss about nothing to please me," whispered Elizabeth to Ann. "I don't believe it's a bit real."

"I begin to think she's artful," whispered back Ann to Elizabeth. "Joshua would never have sent her that letter if she had not given him good encouragement."

"That's my belief, too," whispered Tilly. "Six to one and half a dozen to the other, there is no doubt of that."

"Do, sir, learn to set a better example to your servants!" cried Mrs. Oliphant, dragging Jane from him, while the growling dogs would have sprang at her had they not been held back firmly by their wild harum-scarum master.

During this short scene with Mr. Duchesney and Jane, the old woman silently and unnoticed made her exit from the hall.

While Mrs. Sterne was rescuing Jane, the hall door opened, and Lady Mary, with that toy-looking pistol in hand that she presented at the head of her groom in the barn, went also to the rescue of her pretty servant.

Jane screamed at the sight of the pistol, and the master gave back, while he still held Jane by the arm, for the pistol was levelled at him. To protect himself he slackened the leash of the hounds, one of which was about to spring on the lady, having his paws on her dress, and his capacious jaws wide open, but the pistol was speedily levelled at him, and in an instant he was shot dead!

"As the dog is, so you would have been, had you not released this defenceless girl—you most abject and contemptible coward! Touch her again, if you dare!"

"Well, I'm not exactly in the humour to be shot," said Mr. Duchesney, as much confused as man well could be.

"There," said Lady Mary, throwing the pistol from her, "now that I am unarmed, I dare you to touch her or me either."

"I certainly have no inclination to touch *you* —you are not pure enough for me. You are a mere dead weight that I was obliged to encumber myself with in order to get hold of four thousand pounds. Ha! ha!"

"Go into my room, Jane," said Mrs. Sterne, who kept herself peculiarly calm amidst all this passion and unseemliness.

"I forbid her!" said her mistress, "and let that be sufficient."

"I pray your ladyship," entreated the housekeeper, "break up this dreadful scene by leaving the hall with Jane!"

"Shame upon you, Sterne, for proposing such humiliation for me! Leave my own place because it is invaded by a rascal! When did you ever know me play such a coward's part?"

Master and mistress stood defiantly opposite each other, with Mrs. Sterne, on whose arm the pale-faced agitated Jane rested, on one side, and the dead and yet bleeding bloodhound on the other, his leashed companion looking on him with sorrowful and intelligent face, ever and anon making a low piteous whining.

"Reach me my pistol, Tilly!" cried the lady, for she had flung it along the large table to near the spot where stood Tilly, Elizabeth, and the jilted Ann, who were more interested than ter-rified at the dramatic scene being enacted before them.

Tilly, though, did not much like the job of handling the pistol, and while the girl hesitated, Mr. Duchesney, prompted by a sudden thought, sprang forward, and secured the weapon.

"It is not much good to me now that I have got it," he mused, "for the deadly contents are buried in the body of my poor dog. Would that they had been in the body of the wretch who killed the dog!"

"Take those keys, Sterne, and in the cabinet that belonged to the countess—you know it well —it stands in my boudoir—you will find a loaded pistol. Bring it to me. You hesitate?"

"I do, your ladyship," was the reply. "I will not assist in any way in which pistols are necessary."

"Will you? or you? or you?" she passionately asked each of the other servants, but all held back.

"Upon my word, I am blessed with a pretty lot of servants!" she exclaimed, while her eyes shot fire.

"A better lot than you deserve," rejoined her husband.

This speech fully kindled her rage. She must instantly give vent to it or die!

With a deep-drawn sigh, she first measured the man who stood before her coquetting with her pistol, then like a tiger-cat she sprang upon him, and dextrously seized upon the ends of his neck-tie, and would have strangled him but for the interposition of Mrs. Sterne and Mr. Brummell, his valet.

Directly they saw him becoming black in the face, while the pistol dropped from his hands to the floor, his hands powerless to hold it, they rushed forward, and pinioned Lady Duchesney's elbows behind her, while Butters the stableman and Tilly each seized a hand that was tightening the neck-tie round his throat!

The four servants had all their work to do, for she held on with all the strength and tenacity of one that was mad, and having in her deadly power the life of him she hated with the hate of hates!

Two minutes more, had no assistance come, it would have been a long farewell to the inglorious life of Mr. Duchesney. When he was released from the jaws of death, his head spun round, and he fell swooningly into a chair, and his head and arms dropped forward on to the table!

But his assailant still had no mercy for him. She instructed his two servants, Brummell and Butters, to remove him from her sight.

Each taking an arm, and supporting him round the back, they led him from the room, while the lady, with all the dignity conferred by triumph, her stature drawn up to its highest, stood in the centre of the hall, with extended finger directing the supporters of her husband to the door.

"I think I have now shown him, girls, who shall be master here," she said to the astonished servants, who, now the fray was over, began to applaud and titter to each other.

"And where is that fellow, Josh?" she inquired. "He is always out of the way when he is wanted. Really, Sterne, the servants are all becoming a pack of cowards, and I begin to think they wear your colours."

"Oh, no, your ladyship, I am no coward," said Mrs. Sterne. "You found me, indeed, contending with Mr. Duchesney for the release of Jane—"

"I did, Sterne, I did; and I gloried in your courage."

"But I cannot go the length of pistols," said the housekeeper, laughing. "If I cannot conquer with my hands, I must give up, run away, and live to fight another day."

"Get a man to move that unsightly dog out of the hall. The sight of the creature sickens me. Would it had been his master! and it would but for your officiousness."

"I saved your hands from murder," said the housekeeper. "What a pretty disgrace to the Ashford family, it would have been, for Lady Mary to have been tried for the murder of her husband!"

"No," she deliberately said, "it would only have been manslaughter; and a little false swearing, plenty of money, and clever counsel, no doubt would have got me out of the scrape altogether."

"But your ladyship's character?" suggested the housekeeper.

"When did you ever know me care about character? Now really, Sterne, that must be a downright piece of affectation of yours!"

"It is not indeed, your ladyship. Why the poor old Earl, your father, would clean break his heart if such a terrible thing had occurred."

"I shouldn't break mine if he did," she rejoined, with exquisite audacity and want of feeling. "Turn on the screw as much as ever you will, you will find no sentiment in me. As far as I am concerned the Earl may just as well be dead as living—for does he ever come to see me, or I go to see him?"

"But you must own that that unhappy state of things is your ladyship's own fault."

"Never mind whose fault it is. Practically it is the same thing—as we never see each other, and never can again—"

"That rests with your ladyship," interrupted the housekeeper.

"Be it so; it comes to the same thing, my good woman. There is a gulf between us that can never be crossed. I am a million times worse than what you or my father know about me. Send one of the maids for a bottle of champagne. Or stop, Sterne, I will have it in my own room, and you come there with me. That strangulation case has quite fatigued me," she added, laughingly. "I shall get use to it in time."

"Oh, for shame, Lady Mary! I hope I shall not live to hear of any more such cases that you are connected with!"

"That will all depend on circumstances. Now to the wine-room, and let us be jolly—eh? I and you and Jane and Josh—"

"Not Josh, your ladyship, if you would have me."

"Not good enough?"

"Nor for any woman who knows him, and regards her character."

"More villainy! Come with me, and let me know all about it. Let us bring all the girls with us, and give them a treat. They have had the tragedy, let us wind up with a bit of comedy. I feel dull, and expect no company. So come each and all of you, and cheer me up."

The housekeeper suggested that they should remain where they were; but Lady Mary overruled this by saying that the men would be coming in and out if they did so, and also that her beautiful husband and Jane's lover might return again.

"By the bye, has my old dependent been here this evening?"

"The whole of it, your ladyship, and gave Woodward some smart and sensible words."

"What has become of her?"

"That I don't know; indeed I never noticed when she went."

"I saw her leave the hall two minutes before your ladyship came in," said Tilly.

"I expect she was frightened," said Jane, who for some time had been sitting at the table alone, while her mistress had been standing. The poor girl was quite overpowered, and could not study decorum.

As she sat alone, while all else stood, she seriously pondered over the propriety of her remaining at Evesham House. But she decided on being guided by what the housekeeper might say on the matter.

Her own feelings were decidedly for going. It seemed impossible for her to remain, hunted as she now was, and not unlikely to be, by two unprincipled men.

Lady Mary and the housekeeper led the way to a spacious sumptuously-furnished room, the windows from each side commanding famous views of the park, and the adjacent hills and woods.

Lady Mary and her party of domestics seated themselves at a large table, inlaid with a diversity of rare and expensive woods; and the table was quickly spread out with an abundance and variety of expensive wines, of which the mistress drank deep, and would have had her servants do the same, could she have persuaded them to so much forgetfulness of female propriety.

"Wine is a good thing at all times, but to my mind it receives an additional flavour when there is a legitimate excuse for drinking it."

"I quite agree with your ladyship in that," said the housekeeper, "but I think we are wanting in that excuse to-night."

"Let us rack the imagination for one," she cried, drawing her richly be-jewelled fingers across her broad fair brow. "I have it. I shall take this opportunity of presenting you, Mrs. Sterne, my highly esteemed housekeeper, with this brilliant,"—taking one of the rings from her finger, and placing it on that of Mrs. Sterne, who was quite unprepared for such an event.

The lady was recklessly generous by fits and starts only, but she was more usually cautious in her gifts and liberality.

"Now then we have the fairest of excuses for the glass, and let every one of you follow my example by drinking off a bumper to the health of Mrs. Sterne!"

This was done, and done in champagne, and the housekeeper made a neat little speech in reply to her mistress' kindness.

The beautiful ring was proudly shown round to all the admiring girls by the housekeeper. Jane, who had an intense love for glitter and ornament, could hardly bear to part with it after it had come into her hands.

It was put on and taken off her finger twice,

and then she held it in a variety of ways and lights, that she might keep it as long in her possession as possible.

"Beauty unadorned, is adorned the most," said the mistress of the house, while Jane was admiring the glittering gem on her finger.

"I should like a beautiful ring, for all that, your ladyship," said Jane, with unusual animation.

"And wouldn't you like a plain gold one better than that brilliant?" asked the lady.

Jane smiled, but was shy to answer.

"That would depend upon who placed it on the finger, wouldn't it, Jane?" said Mrs. Sterne, who sat in the next chair to the pretty girl.

"I should think it would," she simpered, as she glanced at the other girls, who looked very jolly, excepting that they would rather a little more of the lady's notice was bestowed on them, and a little less on Jane.

"What if Mr. Duchesney placed a plain gold ring on your finger?" suggested the mistress, drinking champagne at very frequent intervals during the conversation.

Jane, with all her love of display and finery, could not conceive a worse fate for herself than marriage with a man who had caused her such misery. She could only answer the proposition by a tremulous shrug of the shoulders.

"He appears to be very deeply in love with you—"

"And every other girl, I should say," interposed the housekeeper. "Besides, your ladyship knows that he is married."

"I will sign away all my claims to him, and give any girl half my fortune to boot for taking him off my hands," cried Lady Mary, putting on a Turkish smoking cap, and lighting a fragrant cigarette.

"There's a good chance for some one," said Tilly, getting a little elevated with the champagne. "I wish I had a face that the master would fall in love with, he should have me, and I would have half the fortune. One man is quite as good as another for what I see. They are all of them unfaithful. Don't you say so, Ann?"

"I don't know about all, only I know that mine is," the girl replied, in somewhat melancholy tones.

"What does she say? The girl speaks so low that I cannot hear her," said the mistress, helping herself to more wine.

"She's grieving about Mr. Woodward," remarked the housekeeper. "Oh, she's a very stupid girl to fret about a man that all the while made love to another girl."

"Does any one know where Josh is? If I had him here, I would give him a good talking to. But what good? Make up your minds to one fact about men, that they are all libertines, only that some are found out and some are not. Those women who are too soft-headed or soft-hearted to make up their minds to the fact that men will not—perhaps they cannot—confine themselves to one woman, should make up their minds to the other thing, have nothing to do with them. Now I have put the whole course of man's love straight to you, I shall have much pleasure in drinking all your healths."

"If it be true what our mistress says—and upon my word judging from what we have seen of the double dealing of Messrs. Woodward, Brummell, and Duchesney—"

"And I know a million others!" exclaimed the excited lady, tossing her smoking cap on one side, and shaking out her hair, and letting it stream in the most abandon manner over the back of her chair.

"A million!" reiterated the simple-minded housekeeper. "Your ladyship is going on anyhow."

"Never mind the number. Every man I have known—and who has known so many?—has been a rake."

"Oh! I'm so thankful that I never got married!" exclaimed Mrs. Sterne.

"Why, pray?"

"Because I should like my husband all to myself," she replied, which caused much tittering among the domestics.

"And as far as you knew you would. It is the knowledge that makes the mischief."

"Your ladyship is a little too wholesale. The wine make you exaggerate."

"Watch it, woman. Cast your eyes abroad in the world, as I have done. And where you can show me one pure man, I will show you a thousand impure ones."

"I am glad to find that you have come down to thousands," the merry housekeeper said, as well as her laughter would let her.

"If the men are such rakes, why of course the women must be so also," said Elizabeth, the first time she had trespassed her voice in the conversation, which was becoming more animated as the wine flowed.

"Come, now we have a question before us that is well worth discussion. Elizabeth says, and very shrewdly too, that it would be no good for men to be rakes without women were so also. Now I must take a glass of wine, and then consider that question."

As she lifted her glass to her lips, the housekeeper gave her a scolding look, which the lady, who gave signs of intoxication, understood the meaning of, but it did not prevent her from another draught of the nectar.

She then addressed herself to Elizabeth's question.

"Women are not rakes, but they are weak and yielding, which in result is the same thing. Men always know that they can succeed with them, and while that is the case the rake will never be stamped out, but f-f-flourish."

The abandoned woman was now quite overcome with the champagne, with reeling brain and staggering limb, with the end of a cigarette in her mouth, she left the room.

The housekeeper was going to attend her, but she peremptorily forbade it, saying that she should return in a few minutes, and that she was quite able to take care of herself.

She was away some time, when the housekeeper went in search of her, and found her outstretched upon an adjacent bedroom floor.

It was evident that in trying to reach the bed she had fallen backward and stunned herself.

Where was Josh? When he left the hall, and had strolled into the grounds, who should he see there but the Hunchback Boy!

The poor fellow had run away from mother Oliphant, and had wandered hither in search of Jane. Josh went nearly mad at sight of him!

PRETTY JANE

OR, THE

VIPER OF KIDBROOK LANE

JANE'S PERILS NOW BECAME FORMIDABLE.

But before we follow further the fortunes and misfortunes of the Hunchback Boy, we will relate to the reader more of Mr. Duchesney's base plots and designs against the purity of Pretty Jane.

His attentive servants supported him, after the escape of his life at the hands of his infuriate wife, to a little ante-room near the servants' hall, where they laid him at length on a roomy couch, and supplied him with a glass of strong brandy and water.

The remedy proved a real antidote, as well as a palatable one, (for Mr. Duchesney was a true disciple of Bacchus) to the exhaustion attendant on the serious assault his wife had committed upon him.

After drinking three glasses he began speedily to recover. But the punishment he had received taught him no salutary lesson; it seemed rather only to inflame his wickedness against Jane.

With a dark, unmentionable oath, he rose up on the pillow of his couch, and exclaimed to his valet and stableman—

"I'll have that girl, come what may of it! You are a son of mischief, Brummell, and you must help me in the delicate matter. I will well pay you."

"You always pay me well, sir," said the fawning hypocrite, with a neat bow.

"Then I'll pay you better than well if you

No. 7.

will stretch your ingenuity to the point of getting this girl in my power!"

"You are my master, sir," said Brummell, with another obsequious bow—

"For Heaven's sake," interrupted the irritable and impatient Mr. Duchesney, "do not be so circuitous—so roundabout—but come to the point at once. Will you help me in the matter?"

"You are my master, sir—"

"I know that, you fool!" screamed the reclining man.

"Consider your health, sir. Such raving will do you harm, and me no good."

"This fellow will be the death of me!" exclaimed the master. "Deeds, not words—do you understand that?"

"How can I answer you, sir, without words?" he inquired, a question which he took to be a crusher to his master and the well-known motto he had quoted.

"Go to the devil with you!" exclaimed the master.

"He lives in a climate too hot for my nerves, and doesn't mix treacle enough with his brimstone for my palate," said Brummell, and which saying caused Butters the stableman to laugh more than he liked, or thought seemly, in the presence of his master.

Mr. Duchesney had no one to blame but himself for the freedom of his servants. For would he not often drink, joke and gamble with them, just in the same manner as his lady did with hers?

"What can I do to serve you, sir?" asked Brummell, after a short pause.

"I have already told you. Is it necessary for me to repeat it?" he added, while his eye flashed with displeasure.

"It was something about this Pretty Jane, was it not, sir?"

"You know it was," was the snappish reply. "And I wish now that I had not given you my confidence in the matter."

"You never found me betray it, sir. And you have trusted me, too, in some very ticklish affairs."

"That I have, and you have pulled me well through on all occasions."

The remembrance of these "ticklish affairs," appeared to delight this corrupt man. He became himself again, drank more brandy, and laughed outright.

"No, no, I am not complaining. Both you and Butters have been trusty servants—"

The savage-lipped stableman, who was so proud of notice from superior powers, here interrupted, by saying—

"I'd do anythink, I would, for your honour—that is to say anythink that a honest man might without rubbing his nose agin the law."

"All right. Now for business. Fill your glasses."

On tiptoe, Brummell stalked to the door, and peeped through the keyhole.

"What's all that pantomime about?" asked the master, after he had watched with surprise his servant's movements at the door.

"I thought I heard a sound like some one listening at the door, and it is still my opinion that I did."

"Let them listen," he bawled, rounding his

sentence with a vile oath. "We are not planning a murder, are we?"

"Lord! I hope not," exclaimed Butters, who looked as if no crime would come amiss to him, but he had a wholesome terror of the law, and always steered clear of it. But the higher law—the moral one—he was constantly offending against.

"Nothing like caution, sir," observed the oily-mouthed Brummell, pulling his satin vest well down, while he kept his eye on the door.

"I want action, not caution. I have made no secret of it that I am enamoured of this girl, and you may open the door if you will for all to hear while I say that I mean to have her!"

This he exclaimed with a flourish of his handkerchief, which he happened at the time to hold in his hand.

Brummell was very angry at such open proceedings, and could not restrain himself from saying—

"Such publicity is not the way to get your wishes, let me tell you, sir."

"How so?"

"The girl would bolt if she knew."

"And shouldn't I bolt after her, you ass?" he exclaimed.

"Master speaks to you, Butters," said the clever Brummell, neatly turning the "ass" epithet over to his fellow-servant.

The thick-headed stableman did not see the point of the joke that was so adroitly turned against him, and innocently said—

"I beg your honour's pardon, but I didn't know that you spoke to me."

"Nor did I, and he knows it. Let me tell you, Brummell, that I shall not much longer tolerate your cleverness. It is not in season with me, and the sooner you cease those liberties the better I shall like you as a servant. D'ye hear, sir?"

"Try as I may I cannot please you, sir. I never knew you so cantankerous before."

"You be—"

"Hush! hush! It is unbecoming for a gentleman to swear."

"It seems to me, your honour," said the pacific stableman, "that there is only a bit of a misunderstanding between you and my friend Brummell. I am sure he means well to your honour—"

"Who says he doesn't? Only let him keep down his infernal love of talk, and we should get along very well."

"I shall observe what you say, sir," said the valet, who was seated with Butters round a cosy table drawn close to the couch, and which was well supplied with pipes, cigars, wine, brandy, and other matters that betokened preparation for a snug convivial party.

"Let all this rubbish be blown away," said Mr. Duchesney, waving his hand to and fro. "The further we go in it, the greater entanglement we get into. Therefore, let us change the venue. Now then, Brummell, touching this servant girl—have you thought of any means by which I can get her in my power? Speak freely, but don't be funny."

"You see, I know nothing much about her, except that she is decidedly a very pretty girl," said Brummell. "Don't you think so, Butters?"

"Not quite stout enough for me," he replied. "I like substance better than shadow."

"That's right, good boys, travel away from the point. What to the devil do I care for your opinions about the girl's beauty? How to get her in my power is the question."

"Are you aware that Mr. Woodward is also sweet on her, sir?"

"No! How should I?" he sharply turned and inquired. "How do you know? Are you sure?"

They here informed the master of all the particulars that took place in the servants' hall before the affray with himself and wife.

"That fellow Woodward I hate! And this is another spur to get that girl! I shall rave until she's in my power! I am now stimulated by three different feelings for the pursuit of this object—each feeling sweet to me! Revenge of my wife—the humiliation of Woodward—and the passion I myself have for the girl! She shall be mine!"—here he raised his arm, cast his flashing eye to the ceiling, and swore to it with an oath. "If I cannot persuade her with presents, flatteries, and promises, she shall be mine by force!"

"It is a very orkard thing to force a girl. It comes within the law," remarked the sapient Butters, scratching his head, which was covered with a short-cut crop of coarse, tawny-coloured hair, having on the top of his crown a bald spot of the size of a crown piece, giving indications that ringworm had once taken up its abode there.

"I think I have a plan," said Brummell, with all the display incidental to a mind big with a great thought; he placed his hand on his brow, shading his eyes with his fingers, while he was in the throes of his idea. "Yes, I have a plan—"

"And you seem determined to keep it, too," interrupted his impatient master.

"I must say that you are a bit slow," said the drowsy stableman, pulling away at his long clay pipe.

"Let the man who thinks, think in his own way."

"For Heaven's sake no more argument," remonstrated Mr. Duchesney. "Your plans, Brummell?"

"You see Woodward has evidently jilted the girl Ann Orwell."

"Well?"

"Now what must be the feelings of that girl towards her rival?" asked Brummell, warming up to his subject, half in the vein of a Methodist preacher, and half after the fashion of an Old Bailey barrister cross-examining a witness for the defence.

"Her feelings, I should say, if it wasn't for the law, would run into murder," said the wise Butters.

"No doubt of it," said the valet. "Didn't her looks express so much when she dashed back the letter Woodward wrote to Jane?"

"That's jist the cir-cum-staunce that I myself noticed," drawled out the stableman. "That wicious hoss that you likes to ride, yer honour, and which is dangerous to come nigh, leastways except you're werry well up to his artfulness, never looked so wicked under curry-comb and dandy-brush, as did that ere girl Ann Orwell when she diskivered that Jane—I don't know her other name—"

"Servant girls have no names, except those given them by the family—"

"No discussion I say! What to the devil is her name to me?" exclaimed the master, with as much wrath as his strength would let him, which was sufficient to electrify the stableman, but failed to make the smallest impression on Brummell.

"I was going to say, yer honour—"

"Then why the devil don't you say it?" cried Mr. Duchesney, whose prolix servants were quite enough to have tried the patience of the renowned Job, much less that of an excitable, half-intoxicated man like the master of Evesham House.

"I had werry much better say nothink more," said the half-frightened stableman.

"You have said nothing yet, you fool, worth listening to!" exclaimed the master.

"Maybe not, yer honour. I can't tell now what possessed me to speak at all. It was only to say how werry fierce one girl looked at the other."

"Pardon me, sir, but if you did not interrupt so, both of us would be able to serve you. I have a good plan to submit, and a little preliminary conversation is necessary to the unfolding it."

"I would almost rather go without the girl than listen to your conversation—jaw would be the better term for it."

"Your humour, sir, is too hard to bear with. You are labouring under excitement from the violent assault of Lady Duchesney, therefore I do think we had better postpone further conference until after you have had a good night's rest."

"I want no rest! By the Lord Harry, whoever he may be, let me hear what you have to say! By the bye, do either of you know which is her bedroom?"

"That is just one of the things I could ascertain from Ann Orwell," answered Brummell, earnestly.

"If I knew her room, she might wake up one night and find a visitor there, and make a short cut of it at once!"

"Mark me, yer honour, that would be going clean agin the law," said Butters.

"What's that to you, you old fool?"

"Rape is hanging matter, don't you see, yer honour? and if you was hung, the hosses would be given up, and if the hosses was given up, why in coorse there would be no stableman required."

"There's a good deal of truth in what you say, but your interest in my not getting into a scrape big enough to hang myself, is uncommonly like looking after yourself rather than me."

"I axes yer honour's pardon, but our hinterests is united in the matter. You would find it quite as onpleasant to be hung as I should to be out of a place."

"There'll be no hanging, if you will kindly listen to me," said Brummell, pulling down his satin vest, and clearing his throat of a little phlegm, after the manner of a speaker about to make a long speech, or a popular singer on commencing a favourite song.

" Go on, Brummell, and don't be prosy."

" I will throw as much poetry into it as the subject will admit of."

" You quite distress me! Pray throw no poetry into it except it be the poetry of action —and as much of that as you please. Now then travel on."

" Ann Orwell must be dead against Jane," was the opening sentence of Brummell's oration on a proposed method of capturing a beautiful girl for the pleasure of his scamp of a master.

" And werry nat'ral, too," observed Mr. Butters, who could not keep his promise to be silent.

" Just you shut up, or I'll kick you out of the room !"

" I shall be werry glad to go, yer honour, if you don't want me," said Butters, rising to take his departure.

" Do your plans involve his services ?"

" Materially, sir. I shall want him to drive the trap," replied Brummell.

" A trap, eh! Ah! now I begin to think that you have a plan, Brummell, and it has quite put new life into me, and sent the laggard blood spinning."

" Yes, sir, I flatter myself that you may trust me for a plan to accomplish all you require."

In the delight and enthusiasm of the moment Mr. Duchesney grasped the hand of his servant, and assured him of his friendship for life, and a good money reward to boot, if he brought this Jane within his power without any law proceedings to follow.

" That's right, yer honour, bargain to steer clear of the law," exclaimed Butters, once more trespassing on his promise of silence.

" Shut up, I tell you! What to the devil do you care about the law?" cried the master. " How many bushels of corn has the law prevented you robbing me of in the course of a year?"

" Corn, yer honour! Me, yer honour! I wouldn't take a straw that was yourn?"

" Mind you don't then."

" Whatever put sich a thing in yer head, yer honour?"

" What is that to you? I'm a rum fellow, but I have got my eye about me."

" This dispersion on my character—"

" Aspersion, man alive!" corrected Brummell.

" Dispersion or aspersion, it's all the same if you knows what I mean. Does yer honour accuse me of dishonesty with the corn? Do you think that I would rob a poor hoss of his provender? Aint it my duty to look arter the poor dumb creeturs."

" Have the kindness to shut up, if you please. I was not born to-day, so watch it."

" This has knocked the life out of me," blubbered the stableman. " Can't you say nothink for me, Mr. Brummell?"

" Master is too irritable, and you are too sensitive, that is all I can see in the matter," said the valet. " But really all this is very irrelevant to the purpose of the meeting, for which I am sure, sir, you cannot blame me?"

" No more jaw, Brummell. The trap—what about it? Is Jane to be in it?"

" There is much to do before either the girl or the trap will be required."

" If this girl slips through our fingers it won't be through the want of jaw, which has been interminable. The girl will be dead and buried before our plans are arranged. And if they are so long arranging, the heavens alone know how long they will be in carrying out."

" I propose to get hold of Ann Orwell— To-morrow, if possible. And then work upon her jealousy of Jane—"

" I see! I see! Capital! Capital! Go on, good Brummell."

" Pitch such a yarn to her about Josh having his arm round her waist, and kissing her in the willow copse, and all that sort of thing, until her whole heart is turned against Jane, and she would do and dare anything and everything to crush and ruin her !"

" Glorious! Glorious! Iago's renowned attack on Desdemona was nothing half so good as that you now propose to set these two servant girls by the ears in order that one may fight the other into my embrace."

Butters had now other things to occupy his mind than the capture of Jane. His master's random shot about the corn had hit home. He knew he was guilty of purloining, which was more than his master did, although he had imputed so much dishonesty to him.

The stableman was a proficient in cant, and cant was an element that met with nothing but suspicion from his master, who was at all times a straightforward outspoken villain, and never cared to seem what he was not.

" Once having worked Ann into a fury, I should then show her the way how Jane might be forever got rid of."

Butters and his master well stared at the speaker.

Both of them interpreted his words to mean the murder of Jane !

Mr. Duchesney asked for an explanation of his meaning.

" To kill Jane will not suit my book. I don't care to sleep with a corpse. That would be too cold a bedfellow, however beautiful it might be."

Mr. Brummell laughed outright.

" How language misleads," he said. " And did you really think, sir, that I intended to murder Jane?"

" 'Pon my soul, I did," said the master.

" And so did I," said Butters.

" Not a bit of it !" exclaimed the valet, rocking himself in his chair, still laughing, and placing his hands in the pockets of his trousers.

" What did you mean by forever?"

" A mere figure of speech, sir. Still in fact it will be forever, for I don't think this pretty girl will care again to show herself at Evesham House after she has been at the cottage near Morley, near Gravesend."

" Have you taken a cottage for us, Brummell?"

" As good as taken it."

" Oh! how nice it will be to be in a cottage near a wood alone with this pretty girl !"

He clapped his hands, and could almost have hugged his servant for the anticipations of joy with which he was filled.

" There, with her, I shall revel in pleasure, revenge the attack of my wife, and torture her sneak of a steward !"

"Who is far too thick and familiar with Lady Duchesney," said the valet, while the stableman nodded assent.

"Do you mean so?" he gasped, leaning forward to his valet, with looks expressive of torture. "Why did you not tell me so before? Eh? Tell me everything without fear."

"Well, sir, it may not be much, but I don't think it looks well to see a married lady laughing with her steward, who was once her groom, as I've been told, in a lone part of the park."

"And you have seen them?"

"I have, sir, twice, and the lady had evidently been drinking."

"D—n her! she's never sober, that every one knows. I would that she would break her neck in one of her drunken frolics! But for a long long time I've had my suspicions about this fellow Woodward. He must be watched, and trounced, a pleasure I shall reserve for my own self."

"I went once to his room to complain of some of her ladyship's stablemen a taking my pails and gear, and to my werry great surprise her ladyship opened the door to me, while her steward was a sitting down as big as bull beef; and when I up and told my harrant, Lord! her looks were enough to knock me down."

"The beggars had been interrupted—d'ye see, Brummell?"

"I should say so, sir."

"The door, was it locked?"

"I wouldn't say as to that, yer honour."

"You would swear that it was if I wanted you, eh?"

"Any sich a little matter as that in coorse I would," replied the stableman, thinking of the corn.

"And that they were both in a considerable state of guilty confusion when you entered the room?"

"I can well swear to that, yer honour," he replied.

"And that there was a couch in the room, and that the man was lounging on it?"

"The steward, yer honour was sitting on a chair by the table."

"Who says he wasn't? But for the purposes of a law case—"

"I do abominate law," he said, interrupting his master, who was cross-examining him in the event of his getting up a divorce case against his wife.

"Will you swear that he was lounging on a couch?"

"If you wish it, yer honour."

"Good boy! Now you may stand down."

"Are you thinking, sir, of applying to the Divorce Court?" inquired the valet.

"Cui bono?"

"Ah, that licks me. It wasn't in my book when I went to school."

"In plain English, what good? So many adulteries have we both committed, that I fear no law would be elastic enough to divide us. Neither of us could come into court with clean hands. Besides, I knew all about her before I married her. She was a bad one, and no one in her own noble circle would have her. My father knew her father, we were a couple of children of the devil, they knocked up a match between us, paid me down on the nail four thou-

sand pounds, we went to St. George's, Hanover Square, got spliced, came out, and from that moment we heartily wished each other dead! Now you two fellows have had a nice little running history of the felicity that exists between myself and Lady Duchesney, who is a disgrace to my name, and her sex. I wish she was dead, and so make way for a better woman and a better wife. The fortune, too, that I had with her is spent and gone, and I am sick, sore and weary of the burden that my need of coin precipitated me into marriage with. Glasses round, boys, now that my exciting history is done with."

"Is it true, sir, that she had a child before she was married?" Mr. Brummell asked, emboldened by his master's recital of his domestic and private affairs.

"Why all the world knows that!" he exclaimed, in answer. "A dozen children for what I know or care! Love never entered into our compact, and nothing but a vigorous hate exists between us! Now then, for Pretty Jane. We are travelling by very slow stages towards the cottage at Morley."

"You will find it remunerative when you get there, sir. It stands on the brow of a wayside hill, and has commanding views of thousands of hop gardens. Oh! it is a charming spot! Just the place where I should like to spend the honeymoon with Mrs. Brummell, when I get her."

"D—n Mrs. Brummell! we'll talk about her when you get her."

"In a more affectionate manner, I hope," rejoined the valet, with a laugh.

"That will entirely depend on her beauty," retorted his rake of a master.

The trio were getting fast towards the first stage of inebriation, when everything passes before the toper's mind and eye in the loveliest of hues, and unalloyed happiness; when all doubts vanish, and all difficulties fade; when the blood runs fast, and youth again seems to return.

The valet's tongue ran more glibly, and in a less circuitous manner he delivered himself of his plans of abducting Jane, which, in few words, were as follows;—

He first of all, as we have already seen proposed to rouse up the jealousy of Ann Orwell against Jane, in order to convert her into an instrument to effect Jane's ruin, and Mr. Duchesney's purpose. That preliminary step accomplished, Ann was then to arrange a holiday with Jane, which they were to spend at the cottage near Morley, whither they should be driven by Butters. That Mr. Duchesney should conceal himself in the cottage until Ann had sloped away on her return home, and that he then should bolt and bar doors, and then make love to her over cake fruit and wine, and feast her eyes over a display of jewellery, which girls in her station of life were always attracted by.

"Your plans are perfect!" exclaimed the master when his servant had revealed them. "You must have helped in such a thing before," he added.

"I have," he unblushingly and unhesitatingly answered, "And at the same cottage, too."

"Not with the same girl, I should hope," said his master.

"Not exactly; but with one quite as pretty, and quite as troublesome to break into the ways of the world. And it all turned out well. I played my cards well, and the gentleman for whom I trapped the girl played his well, and I daresay she played hers well."

"The job—was it for your master?" inquired Mr. Duchesney.

"That I swore never to divulge," was the reply. "There was a child born of the seduction, and as the father has a title, there is very likely to be some legal row about the child, who is set up by the mother and her friends as the heir to the title and estates, for the father, I should tell you, has recently died."

"Ah, but how can an illegimate child claim the title and estates?" he very properly asked.

"There was a mock marriage—but I must say no more until I am paid for speaking. My evidence is most material, and it will be given in favour of the party who pays the most."

"Nor I don't blame you neither," said the stableman, getting much interested in the conversation, and more bold in his expression, the latter effect produced by the sundry glasses of brandy and water. "I wouldn't run my head agin the law for nothink, for nobody."

"It appears to me that we are about three of the greatest scamps out of hell!" exclaimed Mr. Duchesney, with more pride and pleasure in his tones than repentance.

"We are but types of the age we live in," said the metaphysical valet, who had been fairly educated by an affectionate father, besides leaving him a moderate fortune to squander amongst women and wine, which he found a very easy task. He soon knocked down his fortune, and not finding it easy to pick up another, was glad to get the appointment of valet to a gentleman who knew him well in the better off time, and such situations he had ever since continued to fill.

He was an eminent tactician; quiet, soft, and silky—but never sulky. Had he been found a place in any Government, he would have been found for lying, chicane, and ambiguity, an unrivalled diplomatist.

"You have a mighty fine opinion of the age if you set us up as types of it," remarked the governor.

"Show me better men if you can. I grant you we are wicked enough, but then so are all mankind and womankind, especially the latter."

"D—n it! I won't have that," exclaimed the governor, taking a turn or two across the room, by way of a change, while he tossed his black hair back from his burning brow. "Women are just what men make them."

"If they had any regard for their purity they would not associate with men in the free and easy manner that they do. They know that men lust after them, yet they are always ready to be found with them. The wise men of the East knew this, therefore to keep them pure unto themselves, they locked them up in their harems."

"A harum-scarum proceeding I should call it," wittily interrupted the master. "But if to keep women pure the locking-up system that you advocate should be enacted by law, I certainly should go in for the position of gaoler."

"There would not much purity spring from that arrangement, I guess," observed the valet, with a pleasant twinkle in his eye. "Every husband under my arrangement would become his own gaoler over his fair prisoners. Then there would be no need of Divorce Courts—then there would be no prostitutes thronging your streets—then men would have their own wives to themselves, which is not always the case now."

"Anybody is quite welcome to my wife, if they will only kindly take her off the premises," said the debauchee husband.

"I have kept from marrying through a limited faith in woman. 'She is a rake at heart,' as Pope the poet said, and he had had large experience with women high born and low born. Go into society, and you will invariably find indelicate subjects started by the women, and they never check them if men begin them, but think he the nicest man who can tell a story that shall bring a blush upon their cheek."

"You are a good hater of wives, Brummell."

"And I am sure, sir, you can say nothing good of them," retorted the valet, who was getting inflamed with strong speech and strong liquor, and who sadly wanted a dose or two of a strong-minded woman's tongue to set him to rights.

What could such reprobates as these men know about the wives or women of England? They had been living in muddy waters, and expected to find pure streams. Poor creatures! they judged women by such mad wretches as Lady Duchesney, who had not the vestige of a woman in her. A drunkard, a corrupter of men and women, an adulteress, and a murderess of her own children!

We sicken at such characters! and should never have brought them into our pages had not Pretty Jane been found among them.

"The last place I lived at, sir, oh! there was a duck of a wife there to be sure. An out and out Mrs. Potiphar! Ha! ha! ha! ha!"

"And were you her Joseph?"

"I was; but not quite so virtuous as he of Scripture history. Immediately master turned his back—and he was a jolly good fellow, too—she began her overtures to me, and I listened, and I forgot my master."

Roars of laughter!

"The husband of a woman once told me that his wife, a professedly religious woman, who never missed the Sacrament, late one night left his bed to go into another room that she might be nearer some impudent proceedings going on in the street between drunken men and loose women. So you see that religion even is powerless to restrain the sensuality of woman's nature when they can gratify it on the sly."

"I can't have it at no price, that women are all alike," said the stableman, scratching his head, and yawning.

"Some are coarse, and some are refined, but they are all sensual, and like other men better than their husbands, be they good or be they bad. Catch them at the theatre—see how they laugh at what they ought to leave the house for and never enter it again. It is for woman's delight that immoral plays and indecent novels are written. If women were as pure as they boast themselves to be we should have fewer indecent fashions, a drama that we could listen to without regrets and blushes, novels without bigamy and lust, and no corrupting comic songs!"

"Are you rehearsing for a May meeting at Exeter Hall? If you are, I object to any more of it," said Mr. Duchesney.

"I think I have exhausted my discourse, and I thank my brethren for their gracious hearing,"—this he uttered with a nasal snuffling twang, which the wife's libeller thought a good imitation of a Methodist parson. "Yet I must have the last word—"

"No more, no more,—on my soul, no more! I shall throttle you," and he here seized him by the throat, and gently shook him—"if you harp any more upon that string. Better for such rascals as we that women are as impure as you believe them to be—"

"But they won't have it—that's what riles me!"

"Not likely," said the governor. "D'ye think this girl that I am sweet upon would own to anything of the kind that you have been charging women generally with?"

"I don't know much about her; she's only been here a month. This I know, though, that I have kissed a million times all the other girls, and they have all seemed to like it."

"How can you tell?"

"They would have slapped my face if they didn't, and had me fined for an assault. Even this Jane, you see, had a love letter from Woodward, although she is engaged to some other young man."

"If all women are bad, what about your mother, and the governor's mother, and my mother?" pertinently asked the stableman.

"I would knock any one down who breathed a word against my mother!" exclaimed the gallant valet.

"And I would do the same!" cried the governor.

"And danged if I wouldn't butcher anybody who said a word agen mine, who was as good a woman as ever wore shoe leather!" earnestly exclaimed the stableman. "People may say what they loike about me or my wife, but not a word agen my mother!"

"The stableman's simple question about our mothers has floored your argument altogether, so now you had better shut up."

"Pardon me, sir, but I am not floored. My argument had to do with wives, not mothers."

This answer only provoked laughter, and very singular to relate the confused valet did not discover the cause of the mirth until the stableman in rough coarse country accents bawled out—

"Whoy dang my buttons! beant mothers woives, and woives mothers?"

"Well—ahem!—yes—no—that is to say, it does not always follow," replied the valet, whose vulgar tirade against the virtue of women was smashed up at a blow by one, compared to himself who was of clownish intellect, and an uneducated barbarian.

"You are licked, I tell you," said the master to his valet. "You say that all women are not a bit better than they ought to be, and when asked what about your mother—"

"And I submit, sir, that it was a very impertinent question for Mr. Butters to put. He ought not to have imported personalities into the discussion, and had he been a gentleman he wouldn't. What the devil do you or I, sir, care about his mother?"

"Nay, but I do," said the stableman, "and there's this for the man who would speak one evil word of her, though she's in the churchyard lying!"

While he spoke, the rough, but affectionate man, made up such a threatening formidable fist, and shook it so determinedly, that had not the valet been half-seas over, he would never have provoked the stableman to have given him a taste of it.

"Had her grave been here, I'd have spat upon it!"

This contemptuous speech brought the stableman to his half staggering legs, and off comes his long red jacket, then his shirt sleeves were rolled nearly up to the shoulders, and then he exclaimed, loudly slapping the rope-like muscles of his arm—

"It is all there, Brummell! and to be used agen anybody, master or man, who has a evil word to say agen my mother!" and then he placed himself in pugilistic attitude before the valet.

"If I haven't muscle, I have pluck and skill enough to set down such braggadocios as you!" he exclaimed, also taking off his black coat, and taking his watch and Albert chain from the pocket of his black satin vest.

"Go on for a round or two," cried the governor, eminently delighted at the scene before him. "Let us have a fair field, and no favour," he said, pushing the table into a corner of the room. "Ten to one on Butters!"

"Here goes for my mother!" was the stableman's war-cry, while he furiously but sprawlingly sparred up to the valet, and then hit right out.

"D—n your mother!" replied the valet, dextrously warding off the blow, which would have been a terrible disaster for his left eye had it been planted there.

"Another blow for my mother!" cried the stableman.

"Well meant, and well parried!" cried the governor. "Well done, on both sides. To it again, brave boys!"

"Right you are, sir," said the valet, who had not spoken long before a monster blow from the monster fist of the stableman felled him to the ground. The blow, and it was a savage one, caught him in the pit of the stomach, and it was sometime before he regained his breath.

"That was a good'un for my mother," said the stableman, a grin animating his savage-looking mouth as he exultingly stood over the downfallen man.

"Now we have had quite enough fight, and quite enough about our mothers, who I daresay were quite as good and quite as bad as other mothers," said the governor.

"There was no bad about my mother," insisted the cantankerous stableman, "and no one shall say it, guv'ner."

"Give me a little brandy, sir," pleaded the fallen valet.

"I wull, I wull," said the magnanimous Mr. Butters. "I knocked thee down for my mother, and I'll gie thee a hand up for old acquaintance loike. Here be the brandy."

The valet indignantly dashed it from him, and the glass was broken, and the spirit served to lay the dust on the carpet.

"I have quite demeaned myself enough already by fighting with you."

"D—n it, Brummell, you did the best you could, and I applaud you for it," said his governor, and I shall applaud you still more if you get up and give us a song."

"Aye, a song, Mr. Brummell, and I'll gie thee another," said the stableman, sitting down as when he stripped for the fight.

"Look here, my man, you have had quite enough, and you will please me better if you retire."

"I'm yer honour's servant," said the stableman, rising to go, and flinging his jacket over his naked arm. "One glass more to my mother's memory—"

"No you don't," said the governor. "You are getting impertinent and quarrelsome, and the sooner you get to your shed over the stables the better you will please me."

This reproof made the stableman pull himself together a little, and he touched the first lock of his hair that he could find, saying—

"I have forgot myself, yer honour, but I can be all there when I'm wanted. About to-morrow, guv'ner, shall I be wanted to drive the gal over to Morley?"

"You are getting sensible now, so you may remain, and discuss that subject with me and my valet."

The valet, who had risen from the ground to his chair, at first protested against working with the stableman, but the governor soon coaxed him into a better disposition with his fellow-servant, and eventually prevailed on him to grasp the stableman's proffered hand.

"Had we stuck to love, we should never have found time for war," observed the governor, opening anew his campaign against Jane, who at that moment, with Ann and Tilly, was assisting Mrs. Sterne in helping her inebriated mistress from the floor to the bed.

"When will you see Ann Orwell, and set the ball in motion?" he asked his valet.

"All shall be arranged to-night, sir."

"Nonsense—not to-night?"

"Oh, yes, sir, to-night: you like action, and so do I."

"Then hadn't I better put the hoss to in the single brougham?" suggested the stableman, pulling on his jacket.

"Do you suppose that we are off to Morley to-night? I intend to see Ann, only, to-night, and if I succeed in getting her help we will be off to Morley to-morrow."

"Quite as early as you can manage it, and I shall be as much pleased as surprised if you succeed then. It is now all in your hands. One bumper at parting."

"No more for me, sir. If I did, I might be tempted to run off to Morley with Ann, and forget all about Jane."

"Shall I see you any more to-night?"

"It is now past ten—I must get her alone—"

"Look here, I don't wish to bind you. It is impossible for you to promise anything. I shall be here for some time yet. Look in, and take your chance. If I am not here, I shall have gone to my chamber. Tap at my door, if I make no reply, conclude that I am gone to the land of Nod. So fare you well my own true love, and fare you well for awhile."

They were about to part, when the door was stealthily opened, and all three were surprised at the entrance of the Hunchback Boy! He came like an evil spirit, and vanished as quickly as he came.

They were all so terrified at his abrupt and ugly appearance, that they had not the courage to speak to or follow him. Had they done so, a great mystery, of importance to Mr. Duchesney, might have been explained.

But they thought it was an imp of the devil, and while they gazed at the door, their knees trembled under them!

Jane, when she first came, told Mrs. Sterne all she knew about the mysterious boy, and although that worthy lady had promised to sift out more about him from Mrs. Oliphant, she had not stirred further in the matter, for she saw Lady Mary did not like the subject ventilated, and she did not care to incur her displeasure by doing so.

Yet she was sure there was some terrible secret in the matter, and she was haunted with a terrible temptation to fathom it.

"Go and see what it was, Brummell," said the governor, after he had recovered the sensation that the apparition had given him.

"You go, Butters," said the equally frightened valet.

"If the devil wants me, he must come arter me, I don't go arter him. But I don't mind making one in three."

"Don't let us be children whatever it was. You two go; and I'll stop here, and valiantly guard the inside of the door that he don't come in here again. If it be the devil—"

"It wur he safe enough, guv'ner."

"We'd better all three keep close together, and not stir," said the valet.

"That won't do for me," said the governor. "Get me my gun, one of you, and I'll be after him, devil or no devil."

"Let us both go," said the valet to the stableman, and both did go, and they returned arm in arm, one leaning against the other for support, with the gun carried anyhow.

Then all three brave men sallied forth in quest of the apparition, which they honestly believed to be an evil spirit. If they had had the courage to have proceeded to the barn there they would have found the brutal Josh tying up the poor boy—devil as he was now supposed to be—by the leg!

"The barn—that's where he is," suggested Mr. Duchesney. "Who'll make one to go to that infernal—"

"Oh, pray don't swear, guv'ner!" pleaded the stableman.

"The devil is pleased with swearing, fool!"

"We don't want to please him. Let us go back and say our prayers."

"Let us go back and get drunk, and defy him, say I," returned the governor.

A shower of rain coming on quite decided their return to the apartment they had vacated. In the wide passage leading to the servants' hall, they met Pretty Jane and Ann, walking more like lovers than rivals! They had an arm round each other's waist, and smiling and pouring into each other's ear their love confidences.

"Hist! Lend me your help—get the carriage ready—and I will elope with her at once!

PRETTY JANE

OR, THE

VIPER OF KIDBROOK LANE

LADY MARY DEFYING THE TEMPEST.

You get the girl into conversation, while Butters gets ready the carriage! It is *not* too late! Night and darkness are the most favourable circumstances for the work to be done. So here goes!"

His servants seized him, and entreated him to be more cautious.

"Violence is dead agen the law," remarked the stableman.

"Who is to be master here, I should like to know?" he furiously asked, his lustrous coal-black eyes lit up with drink and passion.

"On this occasion, and to save you from danger, I will be master," said the valet, in soothing tones, while with difficulty they coaxed their refractory governor to return to the ante-room they had left in search of the hunchback boy.

"In the morning, sir, when the brain is cool,

and reason resumes her place, you will rather thank than abuse me for my seeming officiousness."

"I call it a most unprovoked and unwarrantable assault. To-morrow I shall instruct my solicitor to proceed against both of you."

"We've done nothing, sir, agen the law," said the stableman, who did not at all relish his master's threat, for many years ago—long enough, indeed, for the circumstance to have grown out of everybody's recollection but his own—he had suffered imprisonment for taking what "his'n his'n," and the correction then inflicted had given him a wholesome terror of the law.

"It will be better that you prosecute us, than that you give this girl occasion for prosecuting you," said the valet.

"I'm not a fool!" he exclaimed.

"Nor is this Jane. She has not been here long, but I and all of us have seen enough of her to perceive that she is rather more strong-minded than most girls of her class. Had she not been, her beauty would have led her into misfortune long ago. Remember, you are married—"

"To a fiend!—to a hound!—to a—"

"It matters not, sir. The law does not look at the quality nor quantity of the article you contracted with. You are married. Jane knows this. Therefore as a married man, and married to her mistress, you approach her under considerable disadvantage."

"Well, what of that? I tell you what it is, you fawning hypocrite! you want that girl yourself!"

"Oh, not I, sir," he replied, with a laugh. "You have already heard my opinion of marriage and women."

"Dust in my eyes, nothing more! You like the girl—you do! and you want to court her for yourself. Oh! what a trusting fool I have been! My eyes are open now—"

"You give no proof of it, sir. When did I ever deceive you?"

"Now! and you know it! I still hear the girls tittering somewhere—"

"Why there they be, sure enough, in the grounds!"

The valet winked frowningly at the stableman, while the governor suddenly sprang from his chair to where the stableman stood at the window, but in doing so his foot caught in the flowing velvet table-cover, and he went over on his head.

This accident lost him the sight of the girls, who were then passing, still in affectionate embrace, and breathing loving confidences, as they wandered on their moonlit way, in the direction of the willow-copse, and in and out between the lofty elms, that grew in stately pride and grandeur at the back of the house.

Leaving the half drunk men who were wasting their time in debauch, and concocting diabolical measures for the capture and ruin of a thoroughly honest innocent girl, we will play the eavesdropper, and slope along under the rustling trees the way they go, and listen to their free and unrestrained talk.

Ann, of course, was deeply anxious to know Jane's real feelings about the perfidious Josh, who had unhappily stolen her heart away, and to find out how far affairs had proceeded with he and Jane.

Under the sway of such a wicked erratic mistress as Lady Mary, why of course Evesham House was little better than Liberty Hall.

Had it not been for the gentle restraints imposed by Mrs. Sterne, the housekeeper,—she was incapable of strong ones, being a woman of too much amiability of mind, and too weak in moral purpose, for her high position—the place would have been pandemonium.

As it was the servants did pretty well as they liked, and their likings ran more in the way of their pleasures than their duties. They knew that there was in reality neither master nor mistress, and for their subordinates, Josh and Mrs. Sterne, they did not care one fig.

As soon as the little party which Lady Mary presided over was broken up by her over indulgence in champagne, the servants distributed themselves, while Mrs. Sterne had to be in attendance on her intoxicated mistress after she had found her outstretched on the bedroom floor.

Tilly and Elizabeth went to bed; they felt this step necessary, for they had such funny sensations in their heads. Could they possibly have been caused by the champagne they had drunk, and which delicious stuff they had not been used to? They remembered once before, at Christmas time, their gracious good-for-nothing mistress had allowed the champagne to flow freely in the servants' hall, and that then they had the same hilarious sensations, which allowed them to be very free with their kisses under the "mistletoe hung in the castle hall," and said things that, had their heads been freer of wine, they would have blushed to have heard or have uttered.

Then they said they would never drink such dangerous stuff again, and they kept their words until the second temptation came, and then they drank with the same gusto and merriment as at the Christmas time, and would have entrusted their blooming cheeks to any fellow who solicited them for a kiss.

But unhappily for their loving free and easy moments, when the wine made the blood flow faster and faster, there were no fellows present to increase their happiness.

Josh, in a suicidal condition of mind, was in the barn meditating about the destruction of the hunchback boy, while the valet and head stableman, as we know, were in consultation with their reckless master. While the three or four other males of the establishment were down at the Magpie playing at skittles.

"Men may be very false, and which we know they are, but, 'pon my life, we're poor lost creatures without them, don't you think so, Liz?" said Tilly, when they were left alone at the table, now covered with the debris of the mistress' entertainment.

"I just do think so, Tilly, dear. That Brummell is a nice chap, though, although he must be very dangerous for a young woman to know, when we found him writing to both of us at the same time."

"Oh! that was really and truly abominable! A great pity that he should be such a deceiver! Truth, I was just beginning to think that I should have liked him very well for a husband," mused Tilly, while she filled her small mouth with a handful of currant cake crumbs, and washed them down with a little champagne that Mrs. Sterne had left in her glass when she went to look after her mistress.

"If you drink any more I shall, too," said Elizabeth, whose pretty little cap lay at her pretty little feet, while the cap of her companion hung more in front of her head than behind, and gave sundry indications of also coming to the floor.

"Do, Liz! Let us be jolly for once! The champagne is all gone, but here's a half bottle of port, dear."

"No, my love, no. Champagne's my style! and if there's no more of that to be had, why I'll be a good girl, and go without, and go to bed."

"Bother bed! My feet itch for a good dance, don't yours, Liz?"

" Let's I and you have a turn, Tilly—shall we?"

" Lawks! what's the good of two gals a dancing together?"

" There aint much sweetness in it, I must allow. I wonder where all the men are?" inquired Elizabeth.

" Enjoying themselves somewhere or other, I'll be bound," said Tilly, who was in desperate mood for a little sweethearting, and quite angry with the men for being out of the way.

" They get on better by themselves than we can," said Elizabeth.

" A precious sight!" exclaimed Tilly. " They can do so many things that we mustn't. I wish to heaven that I was a man. They don't care a fig for us, only for a convenience, and then they treat us like a parcel of dressed up dolls."

" That's just it, Tilly, dear. What a great pity that we can't do without 'em !"

" It was never intended that we should, and therefore we can't, and that's all about it. A woman without a man is as bad as a teapot without tea, or a fryingpan without a bottom. We may bounce to them as we will, but Heaven has made us very dependent on 'em."

" And the worst of it is they know it, and treat us accordingly."

" So they do, Liz. Just like dolls before we're married, and then like slaves, while they go after other gals."

" I shudder all over at the thought of a husband of mine going after the gals!" said Liz, with considerable warmth of feeling. " But did you notice what her ladyship said, that all the men were faithless?"

" I'm not going to take notice of what she says. She's bad, and her husband's bad, and people are very quick at believing that other people are as wicked as themselves, they're so fond of company; but if they happen to do any good, why then they think there's nobody like 'em. I've known a many good men that I should like to marry."

" And so have I, Tilly, dear. Do you know I think Mr. Brummell means to propose to one of us."

" I wouldn't have him now at any price. I liked him very well once, and was hoping that he thought very well of me. But directly that I found he had eyes for other gals, why then I had no eyes for him."

" He's just the age and height I like."

" You're in love with him, that's what you are, Liz."

" Oh, not so bad as that, Tilly, dear. But his manners are very gentlemanly."

" He's a nice drake, he is—but I shouldn't now like to be his duck."

" Don't be hard upon him for one offence, Tilly, dear. It's that Jane that's done all the mischief."

" Rubbish! He was writing his false letters to us before Jane came here. He's a very deceiving man."

" Look at Mr. Woodward for deceiving!"

" Two blacks don't make a white, Liz. Mr. Woodward has not deceived us."

" He has other gals, though. He's nigh broken poor Ann's heart. And that was all through this Jane."

" I wouldn't say so before her face, but it was no fault of hers. And by what Ann said to me she don't think so either."

" Then she's deceitful, for she said different to me."

" They're both gone away together you see, Liz; so that looks as if they were friendly enough."

" Oh no, it dont," said Elizabeth.

" Then it don't—you shall have it your own way, Liz."

" Don't be a crab-stick, Tilly, dear. Ann is gone out with Jane just to know how far Mr. Woodward has gone with her."

" Bother you, Jane, Ann and everybody. Let's have a polka by ourselves. If the men ain't here, we can't have them."

" I do so wish Mr. Brummall was here," said Liz. " He is such a nice dancer."

" Oh, he's nice everything! You are downright in love with that man, Liz, that's what you are."

" Nonsense, Tilly, dear," she said, in a loving lackadaisical manner.

" Oh, but you are. And when I see Brummell I shall tell him so."

" Then you'll tell him a very great story, that you will."

" D'ye think I'm that silly that I can't tell when a gal loves a man?"

" Ah, but there is a great difference between liking and loving a man, Tilly, dear. I won't deny that if Mr. Brummell—who you must allow is a very respectable man—"

" The only respectability about him is his clothes," said Tilly.

" Now I must say you are too hard upon him, just because he said that we were both pretty girls. I begin to think you want to turn me against him that you might have him all to yourself."

" Do you indeed!" replied Tilly, sneeringly. " Then you are very much mistaken. It may be my misfortune to marry a faithless man, but it shan't be if I know it. Mind," she added, " I don't want to persuade you to be of my way of thinking about Mr. Brummell, but my opinion is that I can do better than have him, even if he would have me."

" I don't know Tilly, dear, but I say a bird in the hand is worth two in the bush."

" But the bird we are talking about, Liz, is not in the hand—leastways he's not in my hand—he's in the bush, and there he may stop, and pipe to you."

" Has he sent you more than one letter?"

" Yes—three."

" Oh, the wretch! he's only sent me two! That shows he likes you better than me."

" It shows me, Liz, that he don't like either of us well enough for marrying, but only to flirt with."

" I begin to suspect so. I want to get hold of a marrying man. Flirting leads to harm, but never to marriage."

" Men are growing shyer every day, to my mind, about marrying."

" 'Cause, my dear, they can get too many gals to flirt with. Gals make themselves too cheap, which makes men look down upon marriage, except it is with some woman who can maintain them."

" You're near the truth, Liz. Though I confess myself to having been the greatest of all flirts."

"A nice flirtation our wretch of a master is carrying on with this Jane," said Elizabeth. "Did you ever see so much impudence as his seizing her round the waist before us all, and wouldn't let her go even when his wife came into the hall!"

"Jane ought not to stop here in the way of such a villain, who seeks nothing but her ruin. Nor I don't think she would, only there seems to be something more than I can make out between her and her ladyship and Mrs. Oliphant. I didn't like Jane at first when I had to wait upon her in the housekeeper's room—'

"I remember. Oh, didn't you go to be sure, about the new missus, and tea for two? I nearly split my sides with laughing."

"I was vexed to be sure! But it was stupid my disliking Jane for it. My eye! what a thing jealousy is! I like Jane very well now though; and if the fellows don't spoil her by flattery, she'll turn out a very nice gal."

"I don't think she is so pretty as they make out, do you, Tilly?"

"Every bit, though I wouldn't say so to her face. You may go a day's walk and back again before you would see a prettier girl. I call her a great beauty, and it is a pity that she should throw herself away upon a common sailor man. There's many a gentleman would be glad of her."

"For his mistreee?"

"No—for his wife. But until she gets married she will be in danger."

"Oh, such fellows as master don't care about whether a woman is married or single; if they want her they'll lay traps for her."

"And whatever married woman is caught, I don't care, I say it is her own fault, and that she wanted to be caught."

Elizabeth began to yawn, and of course Tilly followed, and while with wide open mouths and outstretched arms, they were giving vent to their weary feelings, Josh came into the room.

He was very pale, and could not conceal his agitation. To his greater dismay the two girls noticed it, and spoke of it, but he denied that there was anything the matter with him.

He hurriedly inquired after her ladyship, and he was told that she had been inquiring after him.

"But where is she now, that's what I want to know?" he impatiently asked.

"Where you can't get at her," said Tilly, banteringly.

"Shall I do instead of her ladyship?" asked Elizabeth. "We were going off to sleep before you came in, and now if you like we will have a three-handed reel."

"I don't like," was the short reply. "I am on business now, and don't care for any tomfoolery. Where is her ladyship, can either of you tell me?"

"Dead—"

"Dead!" quickly exclaimed the steward, not giving the girl time to finish the compound word. "Don't jeer with me! Is she dead?"

"Oh, you disagreeable creature!" exclaimed Tilly. "Do let us get away from him, Liz!"

"I think so too. He was a different man when he was sitting in the hall beside his Pretty Jane." said Elizabeth, making her exit from the drawing-room.

"He has met Ann Orwell, I should say, and she has served him out," said Tilly, following her fellow-servant to the door, where they both laughingly turned round and said—

"Which served him right."

After the gossipping girls had retired to their respective rooms on the housekeeper's flat or storey, the wide passages resounding with their laughter and merriment, Josh flung himself into a chair, half mad with rage and perplexity.

He felt that that boy being abroad was the precursor of serious events to happen. Though he had bound him hand and foot until he could consult with his evil mistress, he was afraid lest his cries might attract some chance passer-by. Yet he knew that the dreaded barn was situated in a part of the park where no one ever had any business, and if they possibly had, they would have been terrified to have gone to that spot or near it at this time of night.

But his fears would not be stilled or stifled. Guilt had destroyed all the hope of his mind, and robed it in the black pall of fear. His very reason reeled upon its throne, and was near toppling over.

"What could those girls mean by telling me that my abhorred companion was dead? I wish she was! I wish she was! She will kill the boy if I let her know that he is in the barn, and I don't know what to do but to tell her. But where is she, I wonder? She has given me up, that's plain. I am not cut-throat enough for her. I wish to Heaven her fancy had dropped upon some other man, and then I might have slept without the vision of a strangled baby at my bedside!"

Those wretched thoughts drew forth from his heavily-laden heart sobs and a flood of tears. There was no one to see or hear them, and he did nothing to repress them.

In this extraordinary condition he was found by Mrs. Sterne, who had returned to the room after seeing that her drunk and raving mistress was properly tucked up—had it been by the neck instead of in bed it would have been a great public benefit—and soothed to sleep.

She was surprised to see Josh there alone, and he was equally vexed to be found by her in such a suspicious state of mind. Her entrance disturbed his grief, and he quickly rose, and feigned sleep and weariness, by yawning and stretching out his arms, and then trying to pull himself together in a more natural condition.

But he was not quick enough to elude the vigilance of Mrs. Steroe's eye and ear. She had seen the tears, had heard the sobs, and not all the fine acting of Josh could now deceive her.

"And pray what is the matter with you?" she coldly asked, when she saw the man with head bowed down with woe and care.

"A little bit sleepy, that's all, Mrs. Sterne," he replied, at the same time he began to yawn most unnaturally, and rub his tear-swollen eyes, and shrug his shoulders.

"Then why not go to bed?" was her pertinent question.

"We cannot always do what we should like," he replied. "Before I go to bed I must see her ladyship. Where is she?"

"Where you cannot see her," replied Mrs.

Sterne, who had not the smallest friendship for the steward, for she felt that there was some guilty connection between her ladyship and her steward.

"I have urgent business with her about the estate."

"If urgent, why were you sitting down here sobbing and crying?"

"Ha! ha! ha! Mrs. Sterne! you must have been drinking! And the numerous champagne bottles about is a confirmation of it."

"Not very polite. But I really have forgotten myself in having anything to say to you."

"And all these airs because you cannot have your way that I had been sobbing and crying! I 'spose I ought to know best."

"And you *do* know that you had."

"Then what call had I to conceal it?"

"That's what *you* know, and I do not know," she significantly replied.

"I know now what you mean. Just before you came into the room the girls—"

"What girls?"

"Tilly and Elizabeth. They told me that her ladyship was dead! Such news was likely to depress one."

"Easily said. But you want to see Lady Mary?"

"Urgently."

"She has retired, and must not be disturbed to-night."

"Tell her that I wish to see her."

"She is asleep, I tell you."

"You did not. You said that she had retired. But if you wake her, and tell her that I want particularly to see her—"

"I would not wake her for the Earl, her father, much less for one of her servants!" cried Mrs. Sterne.

"Oh, indeed! Then I have a good mind to relieve you of all responsibility in the matter by waking her myself."

"I dare you do that!"

Josh made no reply, but was quickly on his way through the room, when Mrs. Sterne held up a key, and with a triumphant laugh, exclaimed—

"There is the barrier to your impudence."

"Oh, you've locked her in, have you? For this, to-morrow, you may be locked out! Her ladyship shall hear of this."

"You are a miscreant! and the time is coming on when the world will know your blackheartedness!"

"Explain yourself, Mrs. Sterne!" cried Josh, every muscle of his body quivering with alarm and terror.

"You know your guilt. I only know it imperfectly, but I have the clue to the whole, and shall not rest until I know the whole."

She paused a moment to hear what he would reply to her insinuations.

Josh stared—trembled—bit his nether lip—but he had no power to reply.

"You cannot, dare not, say a word now! It is not me that accuses you—it is your own heart, Joshua Woodward!"

"You are good at raving, Mrs. Sterne. But I am ignorant what it is all about," said Josh, tamely, for all the bluster was taken out of him, and he felt like a lost man, who saw nothing before him but the gallows here, and the bottom-

less pit hereafter! He feared to live, and feared to die.

His mental sufferings were just now of the intensest character. He was indeed paying dear for being the favourite of a profligate woman.

"Your looks belie you, then. They quake and answer to every word I say."

"I wish her ladyship was here!" he earnestly exclaimed.

"Can't you defend yourself without her?"

"I don't choose to have anything to say to you, Mrs. Sterne. Had you been a man, I would have knocked you down for half of what you have said!"

"Knocking down will not wipe out your guilt. It was a bad Providence for you that directed the steps of Pretty Jane here."

"Oh, oh! I am up to your meaning now."

"Then I don't envy you your feelings."

"You mean about me and Ann Orwell and Jane what's-her-name? Oh, I shall soon be able to put that little affair to rights. Don't you trouble about that, Mrs. Sterne."

"But what about the barn, and the—"

"Enough!" cried Josh, "I've heard enough! You must remain with me, now, until her ladyship rises."

"With you! Not if I know it," said Mrs. Sterne, in the most cool and fearless manner sallying toward the door.

"Promise me, then, before you leave," said Josh, stepping before her, locking the door, and taking the key therefrom, "that you will not speak a word of this to anybody until after we have seen our mistress?"

"I am no coward, although a woman," said Mrs. Sterne, plucking up. "As your prisoner I promise nothing. Give me my liberty, I then, perhaps, may grant your request."

"Take it," said Josh, unlocking the door, and throwing it gape open. "Now go tell all you know, and to whom you please. You cannot harm me, but it may be serious for Lady Mary. It is for *her* sake that I am most concerned."

"Not one bit of it. You care nothing for her but to live on her, and sport diamond rings and gold chains at her expense. Oh! my infatuated mistress, I can do nothing but weep for you,"—here Mrs. Sterne brought her handkerchief to her eyes.

"Yes," said Josh, "you can do a better thing than cry for her—keep your tongue between your teeth."

"Keep your advice for those who want it," she replied. "To think that the noble house of Ashford should have been disgraced and ruined by one of its lowest servants!"

"What good has it been to me?" asked Josh, with passion. "My worst of curses on the Ashford family, and you too!"

"Your curses, like chicken, will yet come home to roost."

"It was passion only that made me curse you. I believe you to be a very good woman, Mrs. Sterne, and did you know all I am sure that you would pity me!"

"I know enough to make me hate you!" she scornfully replied.

"If I could but get you quiet enough to talk the matter over with me, why then—"

"I should be dragged into it. I'll hear no

more. I fear that I have heard too much already to keep secret without criminating myself. The innocent are sure to suffer for the deeds of the guilty."

"But you have not as yet told me of any guilt," said Woodward, hoping that she knew nothing positive, but that she had heard something, and had conjectured the rest.

"I am aware of that, nor do I know of any," she said.

At this confession the murderer could have jumped for joy at the relief he experienced, and with a jaunty air he said—

"Of course not, nor no one else. You have been dreaming, Mrs. Sterne."

"My friends must judge of that."

"Have a care for our mistress, I repeat. I have nothing to fear. As for that Jane—"

"I have better authority than her for what I have heard."

Woodward was amazed at this. He gave the girl credit for all that Mrs. Sterne had been darkly hinting at. If not her, who then? It was she he knew from his mistress who had been talking about the hunchback boy and Mrs. Oliphant—and it was Jane alone who could have overheard his conversation about the barn with her landlady at Eltham. It must be Jane—except, perhaps, Mrs. Sterne's curiosity had led her to visit Mrs. Oliphant.

"If not Jane, who was it then that has slandered me to you?"

To the man's astonishment, she replied—

"Your own companion in guilt!"

He stared at her first, and then exclaimed, with a dash of fierceness in his tones—

"She! Never! That won't do, Mrs. Sterne. You have been troubling your head with mother Oliphant, that's what you've been doing."

"I don't know such a woman, only by name. Hark! Lady Mary calls," she cried, flying from the room, with Woodward on her heels.

While this scene was going on between them, Pretty Jane and Ann Orwell had lovingly sauntered into the willow copse, which was situated at the back of the little lake, indeed the forest of those graceful trees drooped over the lake, and divided it from the copse.

No wonder Josh had made this the appointed rendezvous in which to steal Jane's heart, for it was a most pretty and romantic bit of woodland, where all the accents of love breathed there could not fail of receiving a new charm from the beauty of this unrivalled bit of landscape, that any artist would have revelled in.

Jane, although a town-bred girl, had a quick appreciative eye for the picturesque; and when she entered the copse, she was completely bewitched with the delicious scene before her. While the pale moonlight bathed her feet, and the soft wind refreshed her brow, she stopped, arm-in-arm with Ann, and gazed upon the peeps of moonlit lake that shimmered here and there through the willows and brushwood.

There were, too, the snow-white swans sailing and sleeping on its almost unruffled bosom; and now, in a wide opening between the trees, the pair came upon a broader view of the lake, on which the moon shone down with all its might and power.

In this opening three granite steps were laid, at the bottom one of which was moored Lady Mary's boat, which now lay there dancing up and down like a thing of life.

"Oh! isn't it a sweet pretty place, Ann?" exclaimed Jane, as she stood upon the second step, the skirt of her light cotton dress hanging over the boat.

"I thought so once," replied the mournful girl, "but I shall never think so again after what I have found out about the man I dearly loved."

"I do indeed feel for you with all my heart," responded the sympathising Jane. "But take heart, things may come right yet."

"Never, my dear, never! To think of his baseness to write and ask you to meet him here in the very place where he proposed to me, and where we both swore to be true to each other."

"It really is shameful how men can be so artless!"

"Yes, dear, almost on this very spot where we both now stand, just such a lovely night as this, not six weeks ago, we made our vows to be man and wife."

"How long had you been courting, Ann?"

"Well, Jane, not so long as I should have liked. Marry in haste, and repent at leisure, I couldn't help thinking about the old proverb when Joshua pressed me on for an engagement with him."

"Whatever could be the man's motive, I wonder?"

"He said he was anxious to be settled, and that he couldn't love me more than he did if he was courting me for a million years. I told him that I was not at all aversed to be settled—what girl is?—but said that I thought we had better keep company a little longer, to know each other's tastes, and ways, and tempers. But the deceitful fellow stopped my mouth with kisses—now I'm telling you every single thing that occurred between us, Jane—and said that was all fal-lal, and that he would chance all about my temper if I would chance his. So what could I do, Jane?"

"Just what you did, dear, and what I or any other girl would have done, had we liked our young men, accepted them."

"Of course you would. It would have shown great mistrust, don't you see, Jane, if I hadn't, and I'm sure I had no mistrust in Joshua then, I had no occasion."

"A very good job you've found him out," said Jane.

"It's a good job for you," replied Ann, "for had his soft sawder gone on with you, he might have got your affections."

"My dear Ann, that would have been impossible. My heart is out of my own reach, much less his."

"My Joshua—leastways my Joshua that was—has some very winning ways with him," remarked Ann, almost implying that her swain's winning ways would have been irresistible to Jane, or any other girl.

"Why, Ann, you must think me as faithless as Mr. Woodward."

"I should be very sorry, dear. Never be inconstant, Jane."

"Why whatever are you talking about, Ann, dear?"

"'Pon my life I hardly know. Going crazy, I think. Do come away from the horrid water, for I feel half inclined to throw myself in, and end my troubles, for they are getting greater than I can bear."

"Don't give way so, Ann. No other girl would," said Jane.

"If she has loved as I have loved she would, though," rejoined poor Ann. "Dear me! whatever shall I be able to say to my mother in Bristol? She'll break her heart, grieving for me, that she will. We were going down home for our honeymoon. Oh! Joshua, Joshua! however could you have been so false?"

She rounded off her interrogatory with a flood of tears.

Jane's sympathetic heart overwhelmed itself at her friend's distress, and she, too, gave way to tears.

"I'm sure I wish I had never come nigh the place," sobbed Jane. "I won't stop, that I won't! I seem getting mixed up in everything without any fault of mine," sobbed Jane.

"I don't blame you one bit, Jane, about my Joshua. I did at first, and so I told you."

"I know you did, and it hurt me very much indeed."

"I only wish that you had never come, Jane, then this misfortune to me would never have happened. However he could have had the imperence to write to you, after your telling him you were engaged, is a good deal more than I can understand."

"But I blame myself now that I was not more disagreeable with him. I should have been, too, had I known that he had been engaged to you."

"None of the girls knew that. That's the one thing about my Joshua—leastways that was —that I was not satisfied about."

"What was that, Ann?"

"He would have me keep our engagement secret. And I did from every person but my mother."

"Secrets are always suspicious in such matters. Engagements ought to be owned to. How beautiful the lake looks with those swans upon it! I don't think that I ever saw a swan before. They are a good deal like geese."

"Dear Jane you wouldn't be thinking about lakes and swans if your affections had been blighted as mine have been."

"I can't tell what I should do. But I know what I should like to do."

"What, then?"

"To let the deceiver see that I cared nothing at all about him."

"That's all very fine, Jane. But you couldn't do that with the man you loved, I'm bothered if you could. To tell you the truth, Jane, I don't think you are a girl as could love deep," added Ann.

"Don't know but what you are right, Ann," said Jane, rather flippantly.

"I can see the men like you better than other girls," observed Ann.

"I don't know for why then?" said Jane, coquettishly, for she well knew that it was her beauty that gave her such pre-eminence over other girls of her station.

"Because men say you are prettier."

Jane laughed; she had for answer what her insatiable vanity craved for.

"Besides my Joshua—leastways that was—

see how smitten master is with you. Nobody ever saw such a thing. Right before his own wife, too!"

"I don't know what it was for her, who I don't think is a bit better than she ought to be, but I know it was very disagreeable for me, and I was very much frightened."

"You must have been all that," said Ann. "I was surprised to see you keep so cool. I wonder you hadn't a fainted."

"I should but for Mrs. Sterne. What a nice woman she is."

"There would be no living here but for her," said Ann. "She's quite a mother to us girls, that's what she is. But as for her ladyship, the Lord help us! she's an awful woman!"

"Pray don't call her a woman. But there, she pays good wages, and a girl can dress a bit smart on good wages."

"Besides, we haven't much to do with her, have we, Jane?"

"Oh dear, no. If we had I for one would soon be taking my leave. Mrs. Sterne is our proper mistress, and her ladyship is our improper one," said Jane, with much vivacity, laughing at her wit, which the doleful Ann had failed to see. "Fancy her wanting me to go out in this boat with her! But I didn't seem to see it."

"She'd have drownded you, that's what she'd have done," suggested the melancholy Ann.

"What for, pray?"

"Because she sees that her husband is fonder of you than he ought to be."

"She didn't know that when she invited me out in the boat."

"Why we all knew about his meeting you in Kidbrook Lane, and his getting up at the window of your lodgings, a week before you came here."

Jane was surprised, and marvelled how such things could have been known at Evesham House before she came there. She had very often suspected that Mr. Woodward was the man who had the quarrel with Mrs. Oliphant a few nights before she left her lodgings, and what Ann now told her seemed to confirm it, for no one but Mrs. Oliphant knew about Mr. Duchesney's pursuit of her until after she came here, and amongst other things mentioned it to the housekeeper, Mrs. Sterne.

She had but caught half a glance of the man who sat that evening in the twilight in Mrs. Sterne's little parlour, but it had helped the impression that he and Mr. Woodward were one and the same person.

If she could be sure of this she would have had no hesitation in letting her grieving fellow-servant know that she had escaped the clutches of a villain, and one, as far as she could make out from their conversation while she listened at her bedroom-door, who was living in adultery with her ladyship.

"Did Mr. Woodward ever speak to you about a Mrs. Oliphant?" Jane inquired.

"Not that I remember. Who is she?"

"She was the woman I lodged with before I came here; and she was a very bad woman, although she got me this place."

"But what made you think that Joshua knew her?" inquired Ann, who was still fond of talking about any matter in which the name of her false lover was associated for good or evil. Her love was not a shallow, but a depth.

Jane took her arm, and they sauntered on to another view from the willow-copse, and as they walked onwards through this forest of willows, which were planted in rows or tiers high up one above another, and the branches from the highest downwards mingled with the rest, and to look up at them from a distance they fed the imagination and the eye to believe in them as a huge green waterfall.

As they walked on, Jane confided to Ann her reasons for making the inquiry she did about Mr. Woodward's knowledge of Mrs. Oliphant. But as she could gather nothing from Ann of any consequence on that head, Jane then inquired who it was that told her about Mr. Duchesney's treatment of Jane?

That she couldn't tell. It was no one in particular. As far as she remembered all the servants were talking about it. She only recollected that her Joshua was there sitting by her side, and that he said to her—

"You see, Ann, Mr. Duchesney is very fond of a pretty girl, therefore I hope you will look after yourself."

"And then, just in play like," said Ann to Jane, "I pulled his whiskers, and told him he had no call to be afraid. He knew who had my affections."

Jane was again baffled in finding out anything that should identify the man she partially saw at Mrs. Oliphant's as Mr. Woodward.

Jane then spoke about the barn, and asked Ann how far they were from it.

"Whatever made you think of that awful place at this time of night? You've made me shake all over, Jane. Let us get back to the house, for we may be near the barn for what I know, and I wouldn't be for the world! Oh! dear no, not even if Joshua was with me!"

"Has Mr. Woodward ever said anything to you about the barn?"

"Why of course not. What should he know about that horrid place? I wonder, Jane, that you can talk about it without a shudder, and only us two selves here alone. Do let us get back."

"By all means, Ann, if you wish it. But I could stop among the beautiful willows all night, I do believe. And that blue water, too, puts me in mind of my dear lad at sea. I wish I had him here now! He would enjoy this place as much as I do; and wouldn't he soon be in that boat, carrying me in his arms! and then he would row me about the lake, while I sang his favourite songs. I don't deserve to be a sailor's wife, seeing that I am so timid of the water."

"I don't see that at all, Jane, no more than if your lover was a butcher you should like to kill sheep."

Jane could not help smiling at the comparison, forcible as it was, and called herself a great donkey for talking such silly nonsense that because she loved a sailor she should therefore love the sea.

But Jane's was a sentiment, and not at all to be taken in the common sense literal style in which Ann Orwell understood her.

"How old is your young man, Jane?"

"Twenty-two on the twenty-eighth of next December," replied Jane, without any hesitation or thinking. How cold and frost-bitten must be that maiden's love who had not her lover's birthday at her finger's end?

"A very nice age, I should say. My Joshua that was is nigh ten years older than that, but then I'm older than you. His age would have been just the thing for me. His birthday, too, is in December; but it won't be remembered never no more by me. I always used to send him a token of my affection."

"What a deep thing love is, Ann!" cried Jane, in rather a light-hearted fashion.

"Yes, aint it, Jane?" responded Ann.

"Look at you; you've positively found your Joshua a false man, and yet you love him still."

"And shall do to the day of Resurrection! If I married any one else, it would only be out of respect. I could never love again."

"I shall try with all my might not to love anybody more than as they behave themselves."

"That wouldn't be worth the name of love," said the more serious Ann.

"Oh, there's plenty of happiness in the world without love. Love makes you too much of a slave to one person."

"I daresay, Jane, you've had so many offers—a pretty girl like you would—that you've had no time to love one man more than another."

"Don't I though! What would my William say if he heard you?" And then she laughed, which made her companion think that although Jane might love her sailor, it was not of that kind that she would have broken her heart about had he been washed overboard. And she said as much to Jane.

"Don't talk that way, Ann. I can't tell what I should do if my William was drowned."

"I know, though."

"Why get another beau."

"It would be the wisest thing for any girl to do. But we are talking great nonsense. My dear William is not drowned yet, and he is too good a sailor for that."

"There are as good sailors as he drowned, take my word for that. You should hear Lady Mary tell about the shipwreck she was in once coming from Jersey to Plymouth."

"And it would have been a blessing had she gone to the bottom," remarked Jane.

"I quite agree with you, dear. But she told us that while some of the passengers were about the deck praying, and the sailors being washed overboard, she clung on for hours to the ship's rigging and defied the storm! That after awhile the storm went down, and she was left alone in the ship, which she got into Plymouth by herself. Her pluck saved her she said."

"I don't believe one half what her ladyship says. But we are obliged to listen. She is mad, that's what she is, and her husband too."

"I think they are well matched," said Ann.

The girls soon reached the house, which Jane, on the morrow, was destined to be abducted from by the villainous plots of her master, and Messrs. Brummell and Butters, with the aid of Ann Orwell.

On the road to Morley, where poor Jane believed she was going to spend a pleasant day, she saw her master from the carriage window following them on horseback! Her suspicions were at once aroused, she felt frightened at first, but afterwards nerved herself for danger!

PRETTY JANE

OR, THE

VIPER OF KIDBROOK LANE

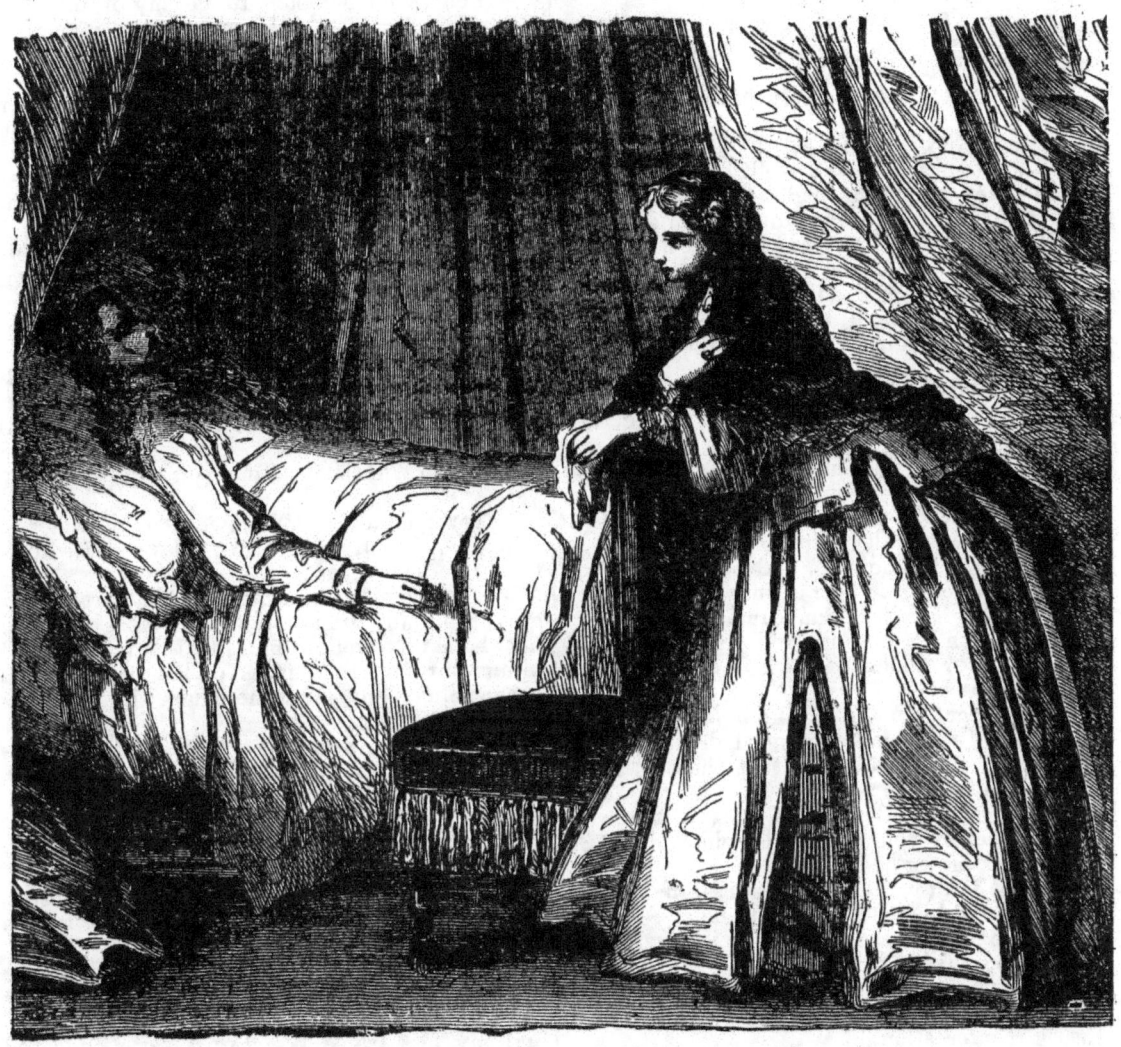

SHE WATCHED HIM DYING THROUGH THE NIGHT.

Jane, who was dressed somewhat beyond her station in life, her amplitude of skirt giving her more the appearance of her ladyship than her ladyship's servant, made known her well-founded fears to Ann Orwell, who sat, also in holiday attire, by her side in the brougham.

Ann innocently made herself a party to the proceedings, and she was not at all surprised to hear from Jane that Mr. Duchesney was in attendance, although she regretted that he had allowed himself to be discovered by her.

Brummell had taken horse, and galloped on before the party to Morley, there to prepare for their reception. He was the devil's trusty serving man, and had acquitted himself with so much energy and serpentine adroitness in this delicate transaction, that his master promised him no end of reward and preferment.

He had his work to do, however, to win Ann Orwell over to his views. She would not—could not believe that Jane had been encouraging her Joshua to tear his affections from her, and bestow them on her more beautiful rival!

"It is all true that I tell you," said Brummell. "What interest have I, pray, in telling you that she has been repeatedly seen by me and others in close conversation with Mr. Woodward, if it were not so?"

"I'm sure I don't know. But I shouldn't like to believe that Jane was so wicked a girl. Another thing, Mr. Brummell, Jane nor no one else, knew that me and Joshua was engaged; therefore however forward Jane had been it could not have been to harm me, but to please herself. She had a right to receive his attentions if she didn't know that he was engaged."

" That matters not," said the wily man; " the result is the same to you, is it not?"

She was obliged to allow that, while a tear moistened her eye.

The tear told Mr. Brummell that she was beginning to feel, and he further worked upon her feelings by saying, in a forcible argumentative manner—

" Had not this fascinating girl come amongst us, you would never have had to complain of Mr. Woodward, would you?"

" Oh, no; of course it's all through her being here."

" Don't I say so?" appealed the valet, as the two stood together at the trellis-work entrance to the dairy, where he had happened to meet her on the morning succeeding the night that she had had such a long conversation with Jane in the willow-copse.

" Now as long as she is here," he continued, " Mr. Woodward will be estranged from you. She is an artful girl, and knows the power of her beauty over men."

" More shame for them, then," spoke out the girl, " especially when they are engaged to others."

" We all know that, and despise ourselves for our weakness. It is but momentary, though, the coquette's power over a man's heart. There is nothing solid, real, or durable about it. It is a mere flash in the pan. Ah! how different from pure affection. One is undying, the other is transient as a winter sunbeam. The coquette is forgotten in her absence, while absence makes the heart grow fonder with those we love. Once get Jane out of the house—"

" I can't get her out of the house even if I cared to do so. I talked a good deal with her last night, and I could see that there was not the least fault in her."

" My dear girl, there must be fault in one of them, in her or your intended—which was it?" he asked, starting back.

" What fault could there be in Jane? She did not know that Joshua was engaged—"

" Nor cared—there, slap! that is my opinion —now you have it straight."

" I don't see why you should be so bitter against Jane, for you said that she was the prettiest girl in creation."

" Who wouldn't that saw her? And her beauty has brought no end of trouble upon the establishment. Every member of it—the married and single—the engaged and disengaged— has she brought into hot water! Look at myself, Ann—"

" Well?"

" Well, you say! But wasn't my attentions to Tilly and Elizabeth—"

" And I blame you very much for showing attentions to both."

" You don't know what I was going to say now."

" But I know what you said. And how do you think any girl can respect such behaviour? The idea of writing to two girls at the same time! And then to go and pay compliments to Jane! It seems to me that you men are all alike!"

" You are very severe, Ann. Please to remember that I was not under engagement to any girl; that I had not trifled with the affections of any girl, and that my own were free. I may never again have the opportunity of saying it— hem!—but had I not known that there existed a close and honourable engagement between you and my friend Woodward—but there, perhaps I had better not say what I was going to say— hem! hem!"

" You've no occasion to be shy of me, Mr. Brummell," said the girl, an amazing amount of curiosity floating in her eyes. " Anything you may tell me won't go no further."

" Some other time, Ann, when I see further what are to be the established relations between you and my friend Woodward."

" They're all off, as I told you all when I found out that he had been writing in the manner he had to Jane."

" Ah! that Jane again," he said, pursing his lips. " She seems at the bottom of everything. We were quite a happy family until she came amongst us. You and Woodward were very happy—"

" That we was!" exclaimed the girl, her feelings overriding all the laws of grammar, which, peradventure, she had never been instructed in.

" If you will listen to me you may be happy yet."

" Never no more. Now what is it that you was going to tell me? I can't have worse news than I've had already."

Mr. Brummell was a master of the art of fogging, especially the ignorant, and those who had not the skill to follow him in his intricate ramblings through the mazes of language, which overwhelmed and astonished such simple minds as Ann Orwell's.

He was never straightforward, but would becloud his meaning with a multitude of words, and shroud it in ambiguity. He had the convenient habit, too, of beginning subjects, but not the habit of finishing them where it was inconvenient so to do.

But now he had stimulated Ann's curiosity, and the girl pinned him to know what it was he had to communicate:

" If you would know, it is this. As I before said, had I not known—and I confess now what has long been a silent sorrow to me—that you and my fast friend Woodward were endeared to each other, I myself—hem! hem!—no, no, no, it would be unwise and ungenerous to all parties to disclose it."

" What a tantalising man you are," said Ann. " I am burning to know what it is."

" The spoken word can never be recalled," he observed, still beating about the bush.

" Who says it can? But you must first speak your word."

" That is right. You must first catch your hare before you can skin him, as old mother Glasse said. But you are impatient to know what I have to reveal, isn't that about the size of it?" he asked.

The girl nodded her head affirmatively.

" I wouldn't have my friend Woodward know for the world!"

" La! me," cried Ann, " whatever can it be?"

" And mind," continued Mr. Brummell, " if my friend ever does know, it will be entirely your fault."

"I promise you I shan't tell him, for I shall never speak to him again."

"Yes, yes, you will; and, mark my word, marry him too," said Brummell, with mysterious air, still jumping from his subject.

"I'm not so fickle as all that. He has chosen Jane—"

"That Jane again!" he maliciously cried. "She must be got rid of, I tell you."

The girl started, and lifted her eyelids, while she exclaimed—

"Whatever do you mean, Mr. Brummell? I don't wish to hear any more from you, if that's all you have to say."

"Had you a larger acquaintance with language, you would not put such a limited construction upon words. Got rid of, doesn't always mean to murder."

She started again, and begged him for gracious sake to change the subject, or she should leave him.

"You seem singularly careful of Jane's interests, which is more than she was of yours. I begin to think that you did not love Mr. Woodward, and that you are pleased that Jane stepped in, and broke it off."

"You are talking a great deal, Mr. Brummell, and upon my word I don't know what it is all about."

"Tell me—would you like to be reconciled with my friend Woodward?"

"How you are jumping about from one thing to another. Let me know, first, what you have to tell me, before I have any further talk."

"That is easily told, sweet Ann."

"Come I say, none of that. No wonder you wouldn't have Joshua know," said Ann, who was much surprised at the endearing epithet by which he addressed her.

"We shall never get on while you continue to interrupt me."

"There goes Mrs. Sterne, and I saw her look at us."

"That concerns not me."

"Perhaps not," said Ann, "but it does me, and she is sure to ask the meaning of our being here together."

"Very impertinent if she did," observed the stately Brummell.

After a great deal more circumlocution, and dextrous fence, on the part of the valet, the girl got him to reveal that there was a time before h r unhappy engagement with Joshua that he himself was about to propose to her; but alas! his friend spoke first, was accepted, and Mr. Brummell's hopes were forever crushed.

"Silence you see is not always commendable. My backwardness lost me that most estimable of fortunes—a good wife. There, now my heart is all out to you."

"Of course," said the girl, who was almost breathless after the unexpected declaration made by Mr. Brummell, and she spoke with maidenly hesitation, while she smoothed one hand with the other, "of course, hem!—"

"Oh, yes, of course, I see," said Mr. Brummell, coming to the rescue of the faltering girl.

"I'm glad you understand me."

"You need not say another word, Ann. Your meaning is as clear as crystal."

"I'm glad you understand," repeated the girl, her face radiant with lackadaisical smiles.

"Then what have you to say to it, Mr. Brummell?" and while she asked, she hung her head.

"Hem! about what, Ann?" asked the confused man.

"You understand, don't you?" said the simpering girl.

"Oh, yes, of course—that is—what is it?" he was at length compelled to ask.

"I'm sorry that you didn't understand me."

"Oh, but I do though,"

"Then what do you say about it?" again the girl asked.

This interrogatory placed the valet in the same fix as before. He did *not* understand the girl; indeed, we don't see how he could, for she had said nothing. Perhaps, though, he had read her discourse in her eyes, as Romeo did in his Juliet's.

Mr. Brummell was not often at a loss to find his way out of a maze or difficulty, but he really was on this occasion.

The girl could not make his silence out, and under the circumstances she showed no little patience in waiting for answer so long as she did. She knew what Mr. Brummell did *not* know, that her meaning was of the most serious import, therefore she gave him credit for well deliberating the subject before he bound himself, whereas he had no subject before him to deliberate on, and his delay of answer arose out of his protracted but unsuccessful endeavours to discover what she meant without asking her, seeing that he had twice already told her that he perfectly understood her.

Everything, however, must come to an end, and so did Ann's patience, and she once more asked him—

"Well, Mr. Brummell, what have you to say about it?"

"Let me see, what were we talking about, Ann?" he asked, placing his hand upon his brow as if he were hard taxing his memory, and very anxious that the girl should come to his assistance before he had to ask her in a more direct manner, and she did.

"You said there was a time before I was engaged to Joshua—"

"Oh, yes, the rogue," he said playfully, rubbing his hands, "he completely took the wind out of my sails. My friend Joshua had a braver heart than me, but not a more loving one."

"But his heart was false, Mr. Brummell."

"Say not so. A little indiscretion, that is all."

"All, indeed! Trifling with a woman's affections, do you call that nothing?"

"May I never be guilty of such a crime!" exclaimed the finished hypocrite. "But in my friend Woodward's case, believe me he was not the guilty party."

"Oh, but he was, though, and I shall never forgive him for it."

"We have all been spell-bound, as it were, and been enthralled by a wicked but beautiful spirit," said the valet, leaning his back against the trellis-work of the dairy, crossing one leg over the other, while he thrust his two thumbs in the arm-holes of his satin vest.

"That's downright nonsense, you know it is," said the girl, somewhat annoyed.

"It is not, and I do not hesitate to repeat it. Myself, the governor, Joshua, and even that old file Butters, have been one and all fascinated by Jane ! It is not one of us, but all of us !"

" I am ashamed to hear that men can make such fools of themselves. They shall know, though, that they won't make a fool of me. I don't believe that either of you meant what was honourable to the girl, which was cowardly."

" I don't think either of us knew what we meant. It was the error of a moment when reason was out of the way. It was an assault from the enemy when we were unable to defend ourselves. She came upon us like a thief in the night."

Mr. Brummell's metaphorical peroration was by no means complimentary to Pretty Jane, but it sounded well to the ears of Ann, and she began to think Mr. Brummell a wonderfully clever man, only she wished he would talk more to the point; a little more, indeed, about herself, and less about Jane, whom she gave Mr. Brummell to know was engaged.

" So the artful girl told us when it was too late. She concealed that fact until after she had estranged Mr. Woodward's affections from you, between whom and himself there existed an honourable engagement."

" That there did," said Ann, piping her eyes.

" Don't cry, good girl," said the valet, patronisingly. " I am here to make the wrong right. I am your friend, and Woodward's friend—will you be my friend ?"

The girl now certainly thought that a declaration and a proposal was at hand. She blushed, looked coy, hung her head, and her hands toyed with the corner of her apron, while she simpered, without raising her eyes from the dairy floor—

" In what way your friend, Mr. Brummell ? Did you wish, hem ! did you, Mr. Brummell—"

" Wish what, Ann ?"

" To take Joshua's place in my affections ?"

" By Heaven, no ! What a wretch you must take me for ! I am here to make peace, and how could you think me base enough to supplant my friend in your affections, even were such a thing possible ? Oh ! Ann."

The girl gave signs of disappointment. She was quite under the impression from what he said that she had two strings to her bow, and she was just in the humour to have marked the galling treatment of her old love by taking up with the new. The valet, however, had no such aspirations, nor never had ; the sole object of his long interview with the girl being to get her aid in the abduction of Jane to Morley.

" Then I see no reason for any further conversation," she said, coldly. " And I'm sure I don't know what we've been standing here so long about. What did you want to say to me, Mr. Brummell, for I have my business to attend to."

" In truth I have mine also to think about."

" Then I think we'd best separate at once."

" I had a thing to say," he slowly observed, when the girl sharply rejoined—

" Then why don't you say it ?"

" Would you like peace between yourself and Woodward ?"

" How can that concern you, Mr. Brummell ?" she asked, with impatience.

" Does not the misery of our friends concern every one ? I know that Joshua is in the depths of grief caused by that momentary infatuation of Jane ! I know that he cruelly feels that he has injured you !"

" Do you really think he does ?"

" I tell you I know it. If you care for the broken union to be cemented again, why then leave the affair to me."

" I do so most willingly, of course I do. I fear, though, that you have undertaken more than you can carry through."

" Give me all the encouragement you can, and not encumber me by want of hope."

" Joshua might have come to me I think without troubling you. It was quite his place to do so, for he is the offender."

" He says it was Jane, and I say so too. But never mind that, but do, pray, keep down an antagonistic spirit, if you would have peace."

" Mind, Joshua must speak first. That I do insist upon."

" All shall be transacted without wounding the pride or susceptibilities of either."

" He ought to have known better—"

" Hush ! here he comes," cried the valet.

Joshua did come along, his countenance dark and oppressed with the marks of care. He was too absorbed to observe them until he got very near, and then he would not have spoken had not Mr. Brummell addressed him with a cheery—

" Good morning, Mr. Woodward !"

" Morning," he glumly replied, and with hang down head he passed on his way. He could scarcely have seen Ann, and it was quite certain that he did not wish to, for she had receded into the dairy, and stood peeping out behind some large pans of milk, until her false lover had gone on his gloomy way.

" See what misery that man is made to suffer," said Brummell, turning the dejection of Joshua to account with Ann.

" Serve him right, for I'm sure that he has made me suffer enough," said the girl, who was now under the impression that Brummell was sent by her old lover to make peace with her, therefore she thought that what she said would be repeated to him, and she was careful that he should not think her over anxious for reconciliation, at all events that she was not breaking her heart about him.

The valet at length got the girl into a very tractable mood, but not being altogether a stupid girl, she saw that there was something more in the valet's proceedings than what met her eye, which she kept well open to observe.

He plainly told her that Jane would have to be found a new service, and that she must go this very day to Morley, where he could introduce her to a very respectable family ; and for a holiday, if Ann was so disposed, and if she could get Mrs. Sterne's permission, she might accompany her in the brougham which he would get Butters to drive.

The generous Ann expressed her sorrow that poor Jane should have to be hunted out of the house into a new service merely because a lot of men chose to misbehave themselves. Nor did she altogether believe that Jane was to be disposed of elsewhere because she had been unfortunate enough to captivate the admiration of Joshua.

No, no ; it would not altogether wash, Mr. Brummell. She was sure that there was some plot being hatched against Jane, and if possible she would stand her friend, for she was quite satisfied that she was a good girl, and that she had done her no harm.

Let us here relate that Joshua Woodward had not the smallest honourable interest either in Jane or Ann. He was merely flattering the latter on, by making an engagement with her, to her ruin. Upon Jane also he had the same cowardly design.

There was a time when Joshua was a very respectable lad, for he was but little more when his profligate mistress, whose groom he was, made him as corrupt as herself. But she had not the power to make him as callous, as insensible to crime. He had done deeds under her prompting that now fearfully troubled him, and inspired him with all kinds of fear, which was deepened by the knowledge that the Hunchback Boy had broken from his keeper, and found his way to Evesham House!

Yet it would appear that his mind was not so occupied with his guilty deeds as to prevent his augmenting them, by demoralising innocent girls. In the persons of this man, and Mr. and Lady Duchesney, there was lodged infamy sufficient to corrupt a city.

Ann at once went to Jane, and told her every word that had passed in the long interview between herself and Mr. Brummell. Jane was very much obliged to the valet for the numerous ill-natured things he had said of her, but she was really obliged to him for introducing her to a new situation at Morley. She expressed to Ann that she was so uncomfortable here, hated so many of the people about the place, that she declared she would rather be in the commonest service, at half the salary, than remain in this wicked house.

"I fear now," she said, "that there is something in this that is not real. What do you say, Ann, dear?"

"That there is some plot in it. But as we have both got our suspicions, we can be on our guard against foul play. A woman on her guard is worth a thousand men plotting against her."

"I think so too," said Jane. "Mind, you must go with me. I won't budge a step without you."

"That you sha'n't!" heartily cried Ann, skipping off to get the sanction of Mrs. Sterne to accompany Jane.

"I ought also to see the housekeeper, for she has no idea that I want to leave. She has been very good to me, and I would not offend her, or give her any cause to complain of my conduct, for the world."

"Then we had best both see her together—what d'ye say?"

"To be sure we had. So come along," replied Jane, taking Ann's arm.

Never walked together two truer friends, and they were soon closeted with the portly housekeeper, who heard them both with patience. She quite approved Jane's leaving if she could find a comfortable situation, for she was in very considerable danger here with her master, who was unquestionably a desperate man.

"Mind, however," she added, "I smell a rat in the affair, and it will behove you to be cautious. Don't separate from each other on any account. Look here, girls, let us see what her ladyship says. I know she takes an interest

in Jane. Stop here while I go find her. I won't be a minute."

Mrs. Sterne found her ladyship on a close-shorn lawn playing at croquet alone. When the housekeeper walked across the lawn, her ladyship called out—

"Well, Sterne, what is it? Have you come to challenge me?"

"I'm rather too stout for croquet. But if I did not interrupt you, I should like to speak to you about Jane."

"That girl has become quite the heroine of my establishment!" she exclaimed. "She is certainly a plump little rustic beauty, and will yet make a noise in the world either for good or evil. What is up with her now? Have the men been fighting or duelling for her?"

Mrs. Sterne told her, and after she had heard all, she cried—

"And are all of you so blind that you cannot see through it?"

"There's something in it, that I'm sure of."

"And I am sure there's a man in it—and I am sure that that man is he who lives upon me, because I was fool enough to marry him!"

"Upon my word I shouldn't wonder. Then doesn't your ladyship think it would be very dangerous for the girls to go?"

"Not at all. I wish he would do something with the girl that would hang him! And so he would if he had the chance."

"But the poor girl, your ladyship! She must be considered."

"La! I would take care of her, if she could only get that fellow hung!"

"Your ladyship ought—"

"Never you mind what her ladyship ought. She doesn't want any of your antiquated lectures. Let the girls go by all means."

"Not by my consent."

"And who are you pray? You think nothing of your mistress being clogged with a wretch of a husband whom she now and ever despised?"

"Your ladyship knows so much better than that. Your revered mother, the countess—"

"Let the dead rest, I beseech you."

"I was only going to say that the lamented countess would not have begged me to be with you had she not known the deep interest I had in you."

"Show me your interest by ridding me of this Duchesney—this sponge—this reptile!"

"I advised you against marrying him."

"I was compelled to marry somebody of my father's approval to get hold of a fortune that my stupid old grandfather left. But I would rather now be without the fortune and without the man. You know that I had plenty without it, whether my father leaves me any or not."

"And I'm afraid he won't," said the old lady shaking her head.

"I have not been good enough for him. I don't care! I have grown indifferent to everything in the world—but this husband of mine!"

She spoke the latter clause between her teeth, adding to herself—

"But he shall surely die by my hands!"

"If the girls are to go, your ladyship, they must go on your responsibility not on mine," said Mrs. Sterne.

"Oh, to be sure; let them go, if you can spare them. Surely the girls are old enough to take care of themselves. Besides, I may be wrong—there may be no false play intended. Caution them, that is all you can do in the matter. If Jane is uncomfortable with us through the men why of course we must not stand in the way of her getting another appointment. If anything wrong does occur, tell her she will always find a friend in me. Yet she is a poor timid thing. Fancy, afraid to go in a little boat on a lake !"

"She is young yet, your ladyship."

"Don't set up excuses for imbecility. Do what we may we should ever be fearless, and defy all consequences. Men and women that are not brave are not fit to live."

"Mr. Woodward—"

"No more of him, pray. It is *you* that have made him the miserable wretch that he is."

"His own conscience more likely, your ladyship."

"What do you know about his conscience? Only a few hours ago I told you before him that I should have slapped your face had you said half as much to me as you did to him. And I meant it too."

"I, in reply, took the liberty to tell your ladyship that in saying so you made a very unladylike remark."

"I know you did, Sterne ; indeed it was all that you could say. But it has not in the least altered my opinion. I tell you what it is, my good woman, Evesham House is full of cowards and fools."

"And wicked people," added Mrs. Sterne.

"Do you mean that to me ?" exclaimed the wrathful lady, raising her croquet mallet.

The housekeeper, of course, did mean it to her as well as to her husband and Joshua. But Lady Mary's looks and action made her shrink from answering her question, and she remained silent as she stood in front of the haughty woman.

"You have grown presuming, Sterne. Neither my father nor mother could alter my character, therefore I am sure it will never be your prerogative. If you must keep school don't let it be at Evesham House, at all events do not expect me for one of your pupils. Let me tell you another thing, if you are not happy here you can pack and go."

"And this to an old servant— !"

"Old servant or young servant, you shall keep your place if I don't mine. What if that fellow Woodward has some crime on his mind, what is that to you, pray ? Does he concern himself with your private affairs ?"

"I have done nothing in all my life that I need be ashamed of," said poor Mrs. Sterne.

"No doubt you are a very goodey-goodey woman. But you are not indebted to yourself for it. Don't you believe it, Sterne, people have no hand in making themselves good or bad."

Mrs. Sterne might well look amazed as she listened to doctrines that made her orthodox mind tremble.

"It is Heaven, of course, that sets our hearts in the right direction," she ventured to say.

"Don't be a fool !" exclaimed her mistress. "Do you think that Heaven concerns itself with our hearts or our affairs ?"

"I do indeed, your ladyship. Who else, then, if not Heaven ?"

"Outward circumstances acting upon the breed, or organisation. If Heaven interfered, how is it, pray, that there are so many Lady Marys, and so few Mrs. Sternes ?"

"Oh, I am not so over good."

"Don't descend to cant, but stick close to the argument. You ought to be a very good woman, or ought not to presume to lecture me and others on our wickedness. But waiving that ; if, as you say, Heaven guides our hearts, how is it that there are such myriads of wicked people in the world ?"

Now had Lady Mary asked the Archbishop of Canterbury, and all the clergy at his back, that same question, they could only have replied to it after the same fashion as did the less erudite Mrs. Sterne, that "that was an inscrutable matter, and belonged to God."

"It is no good continuing an argument if you shelter yourself under such nonsense as that. To think that God made me an earl's daughter, and you a lowly housekeeper ! Monstrous ! Such a belief is fraught with wickedness, if you like. You here make God the author of everything ; and if He be the author of everything He must be the author of evil."

"Oh, dear, no ; He permits it, but He did not create it. But such subjects are not to be talked about by me."

"Now that you are beaten in the argument, you become humble. How convenient ! You pack up your humility for state occasions, and this is one of them. Let me tell you that while here we are entirely the creatures of circumstances. As to good and bad there is no such thing in the eye of Heaven, it is a myth we have introduced among ourselves to frighten children with."

Mrs. Sterne deeply regretted, and well she might, speaking to such an ingrained graceless wicked woman upon the holy subject of religion, which is a thing to feel rather than discuss. She closed the discussion, if we might be allowed to dignify their conversation by such a term, by asking—

"What about the hereafter ?"

"That's a subject none of us know about."

Mrs. Sterne was shocked, and left her ladyship to her irreligious belief and her croquet.

She went direct to Jane and her companion, who, taking it for granted that they were to go, had already began to dress themselves " all in their best " for their trip to Morley.

Jane's last mistress presented her with one of her stylish half-worn dresses, with open bosom and flowing skirt. Had the girl seen herself in this dress with our eyes, she would not have been so proud of herself. We like to see the fitness of things ; we do not care to see beggars upon horseback, nor servant-girls attired in their mistress' dresses. Such pictures in human life incline us more to laugh than admire.

Everything in its place, was not Jane's motto in respect of dress. She was the reverse of a flighty girl, yet had she been judged by her usual style of dress, she would have been pronounced both fast and flighty, anything, indeed, but what she really was, a steady, cheerful, respectable servant-girl.

Jane, as she was driven along by the scoundrelly Butters, with Ann Orwell by her side, felt very happy, and laughed and chatted with her companion, wishing only that Ann was also going into service at Morley.

"We haven't known each other long, Ann, but if I get this place you don't know how much I shall miss you. I'd give a peck of diamonds, if I had it, if we were going to live together again."

"I should be gladder than you, Jane," said the melancholy girl. "What with one thing and another, and more of another than anything else, and now your going away, has made me very lonely."

"When I get settled I shall watch with all my eyes for a place for you!"

"Mind you do, Jane."

"Never fear," said Jane, all in earnest. "It can't at all be pleasant for your remaining where you are under the circumstances. My opinion is that the people at Evesham House, are a very abominable sort, and not good enough for either of us to live with if we have any regard for our characters."

"I certainly should wish to leave, and will, too. Mr. Brummell may talk as he likes, about Joshua and you—"

"Don't you believe one word of it, Ann, my dear."

"I don't, Jane, I don't."

"I'll now frankly tell you my opinion of that Joshua, if you will promise me that you won't be offended?"

"Why of course I will," she replied. "I want to know everything about him that I possibly can."

"I have the very worst misgivings about that man."

"Yes, my dear Jane, but have you good reason for your misgivings?"

"I am certain that he is the man I saw one night at Mrs Oliphant's?"

"But who is she?"

"I can hardly tell you that. But she is a very poor woman that I lodged with, and yet I can see she has some great power over Lady Duchesney."

"But what has that to do with Joshua, my dear Jane?"

"If the man that I saw there and Joshua are one and the same person it has a great deal to do with him, and if it is him, why then he is a very bad man."

"But don't you see, my dear, your suspicions have all to do with ifs. All I can say is, that I have never seen any harm in Joshua. He has always behaved very well to me until this last affair about you, which Mr. Brummell says that he can put all to rights directly you are settled in Morley."

"If you believe one word of that tale, Ann, then you are a great fool," said Jane, with unaccustomed fervour.

"I am watching it, Jane, believe me. I don't take for truth all I hear. But I thought it my duty to give Mr. Brummell's plan a fair trial, don't you see, Jane?"

"In truth, I do not, and that's plain. Friends, you know, should speak plain to each other."

"What! don't you think it's my duty to go a little out of my way for Joshua's sake?"

"Not in such a humiliating direction as this," answered Jane.

"I don't understand you, dear," said Ann, all aglow with surprise.

"Is it not humiliating, Ann, that I must be popped out of the way to keep the man you are engaged to from paying his addresses to me?"

"Indeed I do! but that is not exactly the way of it. Maybe Joshua knows nothing about it. I am sure that he doesn't. I am acting under his friend's advice."

"My dear it comes to the same thing. You are yielding to that which you ought not. I would see all the young men to the bottom of the sea first, than submit to the removal of another girl because my young man could not keep from falling in love with her. Such a lover as that wouldn't do for me."

"I think now, Jane, you're a little bit too fast," said Ann, not at all pleased with her companion's uncouth way of putting matters; it was too straight for Ann's present state of feeling, and she turned the tables upon Jane by intimating that if she could be happy with Joshua she did not wish to stand in her way.

"However can you think such a thing?"

"What else can I think? Your words blame me for recommending or consenting to your being sent away."

"You are quite right, dear—"

"Ah, I thought so," interrupted Ann Orwell.

"Stay, stay; you are right only so far as you have gone. My words meant, that it was all very right and proper my leaving Evesham House—"

"Well, Jane?"

"But that it was not right and proper to yourself to consent to my leaving merely to part me and Joshua, whom nothing upon the face of the earth would now induce me to keep company with, or to marry, even if I were ever so free to do so."

"I'm sure I hardly know what I consented to. Mr. Brummell nearly talked my head off, first about one thing, and then about another. You mean to say, Jane, that I ought to have shown indifference to whether you went or stopped?"

"Of course you ought."

"I think I've made myself a bit of a fool, but upon my word I did it more on your account than my own, so I tell you."

"I can well believe you, for I never can think that any woman would have a young man because he couldn't have somebody else that he professed to love better."

"It is very mortifying, I confess, Jane. But I thought quite as much of you as myself in the matter, I do assure you, and my coming along with you for safety like shows that I am anxious about your getting into a good place."

It was about this instant that Mr. Duchesney gallopped past, and that Jane caught a glimpse of him.

Her fears for herself at once became in the ascendant, and instead of lecturing her companion for her want of self-respect in her conversation with Mr. Brummell, she now quite leaned upon her for protection.

"How strange that he should be gallopping on the same road that we are going—don't you think so, Ann, dear?"

"It is, rather."

"Don't you wish that we hadn't come?"

"For why?"

"I need hardly say, I think, after what both

of us know. I feel my heart in my mouth, and that's the fact."

"Well, it's no good meeting danger half way," remarked Ann.

"Then you really think there is danger?" asked Jane, real alarm stamping itself on her countenance.

"Are you sure that it was him that was on the horse?"

"I'm quite confident! Didn't you see him yourself?"

"I saw some one, but I couldn't see who it was, he rode so fast."

"I popped my head out of the window to look at a large garden of hops at the very moment that Mr. Duchesney gallopped along, and we saw each other face to face—so I am quite sure that it was he. I begin to wish that we had never come," she added, shiveringly.

"We mustn't meet trouble half way," said the philosophic Ann. "One thing I know—"

"What's that, dear?" asked Jane, sidling up to her calmer companion.

"That he is not after me. I'm not good-looking enough."

"Don't talk such stuff, there's a dear girl," said Jane. "If beauty only serves to bring such a pack of rascals as he after us, I would rather be as ugly as a witch. I very much regret now that we ever came, especially after we were warned by Mrs. Sterne."

"I also told you that I was not over and above satisfied."

"So you did, Ann. But a situation in view made me a little incautious."

"I tell you candidly that I should not have advised you to have come alone. But when Mr. Brummell invited me to accompany you, why then I saw no further harm or danger in it."

"That's just what I thought," cried Jane. "I said to myself that he would never have asked two if there was any plotting going on against either of us."

"There's something funny about it, but I can't tell what. I should say we must be nearly there now, for Butters has driven us very fast—but I'm sure I don't know anything about the road we are travelling."

"There's one thing," said Jane, who had well observed the fine scenery they were riding rapidly through, "we have seen some lovely gardens and country places, and we are having a nice long ride."

"That we have; and perhaps after all we shall have nothing to complain of. And I shall leave you at Morley in a nice respectable family."

"I do indeed hope so!" cried Jane. "But you won't leave me, will you, until you have seen me safe and settled?"

"I'll take care about that," was the decisive reply.

They were now driving over a rustic bridge that spanned a mill stream that worked a mill belonging to a farmer who owned a good many acres there and thereabout, and that were now golden with the yellow corn.

Beside the well-tarred mill, here and there smeared with the flour sacks rubbing up against it, stood a village public, overspread by a patriarchal tree.

Butters the coachman had been for some time longing for a refresher, and here was the golden opportunity. To the surprise of the young women he pulled up, and thrust his head in at the window.

"Is this the place Mr. Butters?" inquired Jane, looking at the old mill and the picturesque public.

"This is the place for me," he replied, while a smile came across his savage-looking lips.

"Why that's a mill, Butters," said Ann.

"Yes, that's a mill that grinds the corn, and there stands the miller that owns it. But that's not where I'm going neither. That's the shop for me and my hoss," he added, pointing with his whip to the tree-covered public, "and werry much we wants it. Now, then, young ladies, you're having a nice ride, what are yer going to stand to the coachman?"

The girls looked and laughed at each other, and whispered each other, and then out came their purses, and then they had a little altercation which should give the coachman a shilling. They both wanted to be paymaster, but they only wanted the man to have one shilling.

"Me, me, me!" cried Ann, and "Me, me, me!" cried Jane, both holding out a shilling to the man, and each trying to keep the other's hand back.

"Lord! it's a sin and a shame to baulk a generous feeling," said Butters, taking a shilling from each hand. "I couldn't take from one without offending the other, and as we are out for a holiday, we don't want any offence to any one. Now what would you young ladies like to have to drink? I'm goin' to have a nice glass o' hold hale, I am, which is a werry nice thing to travel on."

"Surely we haven't got much further to go."

"The next willage is Morley, and the next willage is seven miles ahead on us," he said, adjusting the horse's nose-bag.

The girls conversed awhile to themselves, and then asked Butters how long he was going to stop here.

"One half hour to rest the hoss, and refresh myself; which aint a bit too much, for we've come a purty good distance, at a spanking trot. And my old gal wants a feed, don't she,"—patting the neck of the smoking mare—"and I want a quiet pipe under that ere tree. And I should advise you two young women to jump out, and go into the parlour—they've got a nice parlour here, I knows the house well—have some refreshment, and then stretch your legs about the grounds, which are hawful purty. Now I'll patter ne more. Just please yourselves, and you'll werry well please me. Hoi! here, you sir!" he cried to a plough-boy looking waiter who emerged from the house, "bring me out here under this old tree a pint o' hold hale, and a clean pipe."

After he had given his magnificent orders, he sat himself under the old tree, took off his brown felt billycock hat, and wiped his steaming brow, and dusty flabby-dabby cheeks, in pleasant anticipation of the good things coming for him.

The girls got out, but as there were some men in the parlour they did not venture there, but strolled into the grounds, and there had some refreshment, with beautiful flowers outspread at their feet.

"Lord! if poor Jane only knew what was in store for her at Morley," mused the scoundrel

PRETTY JANE

OR, THE

VIPER OF KIDBROOK LANE

MRS. STERNE WAS PLEASED TO HEAR LADY DUCHESNEY LECTURED BY HER VISITOR.

Butters, who sat behind his pipe on an old seat fastened round the huge trunk of the tree, " she would never forgive me for bringing her here. I can hardly forgive myself. And shan't I get a jacketting from my mother when I go aloft to where she is."

Here he foamed up a glass of his favourite beverage, and held it up to his critical eye.

" Not what it ort to be," he said, shaking his head; "maybe, though, it is better than it looks. The proof of the pudding, arter all, is in the eating."

He applied his mouth to the tumbler—good, bad, or indifferent, the ale vanished in a moment down his capacious throat.

" By gum! it is a shade better than it looks. A leetle bit hard, perhaps,"—loudly smacking his tongue against the roof of his mouth—" but it is werry much harder where there's none."

No. 10.

While he was taking his rest and refreshment, and the girls taking theirs in the rustic grounds at the back of the house, Mr. Brummell and his master had met at the pretty, well-furnished cottage at Morley.

The house belonged to an old friend of Brummell's, and it had been for some time in the market to be sold, and the furniture to be taken at a valuation. It was taken charge of by a decayed agricultural labourer and Joan his wife, and Mr. Brummell frequently had out one of his master's horses for a ride thither, to look about the place on behalf of his friend the owner, who resided in London.

" It cannot now be long, sir, before the fair freight arrives," said Brummell to his master, the former of whom was setting out the table with cloth, decanters, glasses, plates, and in the centre, in tall elegant vase, he planted a delicious bouquet of flowers, which he had gathered from the rich garden behind, and arranged according to his own taste, which, judging from the effect produced upon the eye, the colours would seem to have been very artistically blended and contrasted.

"Flowers are the only things you have set on the table, Brummell, and we can't eat or drink them," said Mr. Duchesney, who was arranging his gay scarf before the glass, in which the repast of glasses and flowers was reflected, and which prompted the master's pleasant remark thereupon.

"No, sir, we can only feast the eye on flowers until the arrival of Butters—"

"And then you don't mean us to feast on him, do you?"

"Not exactly, sir," replied the valet. "When Butters is in season may I be out of it. His flesh may be very agreeable to himself but not to me."

"Nor to me," rejoined the governor. "And that's where I don't exactly see what advantage his arrival will be to us."

"Why, sir, he brings a hamper of good things with him," returned the smiling Butters.

"Hurrah! hurrah! I breathe again," cried the master.

"Yes, sir, a regular Derby hamper!" said the valet, piling up the delights to come. "Pies, ham, chickens, cakes, champagne—"

"I love you for that!" exclaimed the master, warmly shaking his trusty servant by the hand. "How much cham have you brought?"

"A dozen."

"Not much—but can soon get more if the campaign is to last over to-night. But many thanks for your excellent management. Would that the cham and the beauty had arrived! Oh! the delicious harmony between wine and women. These poets knew a thing or two, the dogs, when they sang their praises together."

Then he trilled out a couple of lines from Tom Moore—

"Can sorrow from the goblet flow,
    Or pain from beauty's eye?"

"That man deserved a monument for those lines, even if he had written nothing else," remarked Mr. Duchesney. "Take a cigar with me, Brummell, and let's have a turn in the garden as we have nothing better to do until she comes that has brought us hither."

He offered his seal-skin cigar-case to his valet as he spoke, and round and round the gravel walks, and in and out the shrubberies, they walked, and talked, and smoked.

"They should be here by this time," said Brummell. "And won't the girls, sir, be surprised when they do come!"

"To find no one here but members of the masculine gender to receive them! Ha! ha! ha! We shall have to be very discreet, Brummell."

"The discreet part must be left to your performance, sir."

"What do you mean, Brummell?" he eagerly asked.

"That directly Jane is landed within the cottage my work is done, my responsibility at an end."

"Would you desert me in the heat of the battle?"

"How can I further help you, sir?" asked the obsequious servant.

"That's just what we have to see. For instance, who is to receive her when she comes?" he asked.

"It won't exactly do for you to open the door to her."

"Lord! no. She'd faint."

"Not she. Jane is not one of the fainting sort. Put her at bay, she would defy you, not faint."

"A girl of a strong temper, I suppose you mean to say?"

"Not temper, but courage, sir. She would fight as bravely for her virtue as a soldier for his flag."

"Come, I say, you will make me think twice before I tackle so formidable an antagonist. But there, my passion is stronger than my fear, and I am not going to relinquish the game that has been so exceedingly well opened. Still, it will not do for me to be seen too early in the play, for my appearance would frighten her off the stage."

"You see, sir, you have shocked her twice already."

"Thrice, I think," he said, with much callousness and effrontery. "There was my first meeting with her in Kidbrook Lane—"

"That was no shock—nothing more than a little tender love-making and gallantry."

"Nothing more, Brummell. I was sober then, and knew how to court a girl without offending her."

"Just so, sir. But the shocks I mean were those committed at her bedroom window before she came here—"

"I remember well. That *was* a spree. I had had plenty of champagne that night, and could have dared the devil, let alone a pretty girl. You know well enough what I am when I am a little sprung."

"Nothing in creation so wild. When you held her by the wrist yesterday in the servants' hall—"

"Ah, but for the dogs I held, and my fiend of a wife, who shall yet pay dearly for shooting him, she would not have escaped so easily from me then."

"There is danger in force, sir. As Butters says you would run agen the law."

"He be ——! If we consult that nonsense we shall do nothing. If we run into law we must get out of it again. Easy enough if you know the way."

"Oh, quite so—if."

"Don't be craven, my man."

"It is for you that I speak advisingly. But you never could brook advice that ran counter to your wishes, therefore I'll no further trespass mine," said the valet.

"Come to that, aren't the whole of these proceedings against the law?"

"Oh, dear, no. This is but a mere trap—a practical joke—and if Jane likes to fall into it she can," he replied.

"But if she won't?"

"Lay not a hand upon her, but let her go. There, sir, that is my advice."

Mr. Duchesney looked white with rage at his valet. He paused in his walk, and, as he held him by the arm, he looked at him with that threatening passion in his eye, that would have alarmed any one who didn't know him.

"Let her go, did you say? Do you take me for a fool, sir?"

"Had I done so I should not have tendered my advice," replied Brummell.

"What! to take all this trouble to snare the bird, and then, because it flutters in its cage, to let it go again! No more—you must take me for a fool! And I would just have you to know that I am not."

"Hark, sir!" cried the valet, with head awry, and uplifted finger. "I think I hear wheels advancing. Yes—there's no mistake about it," he added.

"I hope you're not wrong. But even if you do hear the sound of wheels it does not follow that it should be my brougham. There are more wheels in the world than those."

"True, sir, but there are not many that travel this out-of-the-way road. Besides, the brougham is due. So putting this and that together, I have no doubt, sir, but that our two best friends, wine and women, are close at hand."

"It just occurs to me, Brummell, there are two girls coming, and as one is enough for me, why don't you make up to the other?"

"An entanglement of that sort, just now, would be inconvenient if not serious to me."

"Ha! What's up?" asked the master, his former rage subdued as easily as it was kindled by the unpalatable advice his servant gave him but a minute ago. "What's up?"

"I am about to marry—"

"Don't!"

"Oh, sir, it will be a marriage after your own —for money!"

"It will be paying a devil of an interest for it, though."

"The fortune is large, and the party is old," said the valet, and they both laughed a devilish laugh.

"In every thing you have your wits about you! Do I know the old party, who is going to bring her grey hairs with sorrow to the grave?" he inquired.

"Oh, she shall not find me unkind—only that I may be away a good deal," said the valet, with a leering smile.

"I understand," said Mr. Duchesney; and what he understood was this—that he would marry the old party for her money, and sport it with a young one when he was "away a good deal."

"It is not the brougham after all," cried the master, as a light country cart hove in view. "Confound that Butters, where to the deuce has he got to?"

"Behind a long pipe and a glass of old ale, confound him!" rejoined the valet, who had hit the state of affairs exactly.

"A great piece of impertinence if it be so," said the master.

"Mind, sir, he has not been yet too long without distressing the horse."

"D—n the horse! The man was engaged on an errand that admitted of no such puerile considerations. Men before horses, and it always would be so were it not for the asses."

"It is a long pull, sir, and a bait or two was really necessary for man and horse."

"Oh, I can understand a nip of ale for the man, and a bucket of water for the horse, but that wouldn't occupy a minute."

"It is a long journey, sir; the horse ought to have a feed as well as water. The time lost would be more than fetched up."

"You think nothing of my need of refreshment," he said, angrily. "I must wait until after coachmen and horses have been served. I'm quite parched for a draught of wine!"

"They cannot possibly be long now. You saw them yourself about ten miles from hence."

"What of that? They are not here now, and that is what concerns me."

"Suppose if the girls took alarm at sight of you, and would not come on?"

"Then they won't be here. There, that stupid question is soon answered. Look here, my man, what is to be the modus operandi when they do come?"

"As I said before, sir, that must be your part in the drama. My plan would be to treat Jane very quietly—"

"Begin at the beginning, do! You decided that it would not do for me to receive her, because that I had already shocked her."

"Then, sir, it shall be my task to receive her," said the valet.

"Good. What then?"

"They will naturally look for the family I was to introduce her to for a place."

"Of course. By George! I had forgotten all about that!"

"But the author of the piece was bound to remember it," said the valet, with a bow.

"You will get a call before the curtain, I am sure you will. Ha! ha!"

"That will depend how the actors play the parts that I have assigned them in the play," he said, significantly. "Let a dramatic author write ever so well, his success greatly depends on the manner he is interpreted by those who assume his characters."

"Especially the villain of the piece—eh?"

"Exactly so, sir."

"Which on this occasion is myself—eh?"

There was as much delicacy as fun in the governor's question, and the valet hesitated how to answer it.

"I think you have undertaken that celebrated character."

"And I am sure I shall play it to the life."

"Having had a large experience in the part —no, no, no, that is not what I mean."

"I know better than that."

"'Pon my honour, sir!"

"Honour! you wouldn't know where to find it were I to accept the stake and win."

At this they both laughed.

"When Nature shared out honour I and you were out of the way. So if you please we will not encumber our conversation with that which neither of us know nothing about. Let us go on and perfect ourselves in the part that we took in with our mother's milk, and which we have diligently studied over since."

"In playing your part in the new piece you will be under this disadvantage."

"What's that?"

"You have not been able to rehearse it with the lady who is going to play beauty in distress," answered Brummell, looking askance at his master.

"That's true. But for all that I think I shall come out naturally."

"And we may be sure the heroine will," said the valet, and they both looked at each other rogueishly.

They paused, as if they had exhausted the witty side of their wickedness, but the valet, still keeping up his part as dramatic author, found a last word to say about the new piece that was to come out to-night before a select audience at the cottage-theatre, Morley.

"Such a piece of real life, with actors and actresses in entire sympathy with the plot, would fill Drury Lane."

"But it wouldn't pay then, for it could only run one night."

"But the events of that night might serve for another good drama. There might be a child born—"

"What in that one night? How to the deuce can that be?"

"Not likely, sir. My play would have a period of ten years between the acts."

"And about this child—"

"The interest of the piece ought to hang," added the valet, who certainly showed that he had some good leading ideas as a dramatic writer, whether he had ever written a play or not.

"The said child would be a beautiful girl of course?"

"Of course," reiterated the valet. "She would be the image of her mother, Pretty Jane. And she would be left enormously rich by the father—"

"Who would be the villain of the second piece, as I am of the first?"

"No, that would not be exactly my idea, for I would not have the father of the child known, he should be hung up somewhere in a cloud of mystery; he should be suspected—"

"Now, old chap, I think you are losing yourself—"

"Not likely that I can give a perfect plot off hand. Besides, we had better see how the first piece goes off first; indeed, there are sure to be plenty of real events flow out of it for a good drama without taxing the imagination."

"There might be a murder in it," suggested Mr. Duchesney, with a broad smile.

"That event would bring the piece up to a tragedy. And if the piece is to reach the altitude of tragedy, which I hope not, sir, for your sake—"

"Why for my sake?"

"Because the villain of the piece is always sacrificed to poetic justice."

"Then under those circumstances I must decline the character you have assigned me."

"Or rather which you assigned yourself, sir," said Brummell. "But sometimes villains are too subtle, and escape this same poetic justice," he added.

"A good many of them do in real life, that I know. Yourself for example," he said, with apparent good-humour.

The valet blushed and laughed, and then he said—

"Not at all personal, sir. Cannot you multiply your examples?"

"Oh, you want company, do you? Well, you shall have my wife, it you like?"

"I am glad that you give me choice in the matter, and not make it imperative that I have her ladyship for companion."

"Not good enough, eh? I should think not, indeed," he added, while the valet hesitated what to say. "But as an example of a villain who escapes punishment, commend me to her."

He spoke the last sentence with much bitterness, and for the moment lost his vivacity.

"She is not dead yet, sir," remarked Brummell, significantly.

"Worse luck!" he exclaimed. "You think, then, that she will get punished before she kicks the bucket?"

"My belief is that most wicked people do get punished in this world."

"Don't believe a d—d syllable of it! It is only the fools who commit wrongs that are punished. I and you and my wife, we are all too clever to get in the way of punishment."

"Up to this time we have been," replied the valet.

"Why, what a croak you are! You seem to court punishment, you go in for it so strongly. You are not half a villain."

"Never was a truer word spoken, except by him who said that there was not a particle of villainy in me."

"And who was that wiseacre pray?"

"Your humble servant," replied the valet, with a bow.

"Then you are training yourself to believe a lie. Why you are the greatest villain out!"

"Oh, sir! how can you think so?"

"But I do though," answered the master.

"All things are comparative. By whom do you measure me, sir?"

"Myself, if you will. You would succeed in villainy where I should fail. You may laugh, but you would."

"Will you define a villain, sir?"

"He who would do a base action to another, and make him believe that you had done him a service. Now I can do the base action as well as you—"

"Do not underrate yourself, sir."

"Hear me out, if you please. I say that I can do a bad action as well as you or any other villain—"

"Thanks," said the valet, not much flattered at having a place assigned him among distinguished villains,

"Interrupt me as you will," said Mr. Duchesney, "you shall have it hot yet. I say you can do the bad action, and have got the art of plausibility so perfectly at your finger ends to make it appear a good one. Now I couldn't do that, and should only bungle and break down if I tried."

"You don't show good judgment in character, sir, if you class me among plausible people."

"The most plausible man that ever lived!" exclaimed his master. "You would coax butter out of a dog's mouth, and make the brute believe that he had swallowed it."

"What a graphic illustration! Ha! ha! ha! Oh, sir, you will never say anything better than that, if you live forever. The most comprehensive definition that was ever given. I only regret that I was the object of so much severity, but I more regret that I was not the author of the definition. So excellent is it, that it has made the journey to Morley remunerative. Ha! ha! ha! I shall never forget it. What is a plausible man? He who who would coax butter out of a dog's mouth, and make the brute believe that he had swallowed it. Oh! it was a capital hit, sir. I am delighted with the smartness of it, but levelled at me it failed of its aim. The cap does not fit well enough for me to wear."

" I appear to have amused you, if I have mistaken your character; but of that you cannot be so well a judge as others."

" Better, perhaps, in this matter be governed by Othello, when he said to the Venetian senate, ' but little shall I grace my cause in speaking for myself.' But I am not plausible, nor a villain, save and except in the service of others."

" Then what about this widow that you are going to marry?"

" Not a widow, sir; oh, dear, no; a maiden lady, of sixty-two, in whose gentle bosom my irresistible charms has fired the passion of love —and it might have fired it and consumed it, for me, had there not been a good rent-roll to back the dear creature's aged affections, and which rent-roll is to be made over to me at her death—"

" Which would be soon, if her life stood between me and the rent-roll."

" Fortunately for the old lady I am not so sanguinary. May she live long and enjoy herself! I can have whatever I want while she lives—why should I wish her dead?"

" To marry stuff young and beautiful," the governor replied.

" Lord, sir, you know there is plenty of that to be had without marriage. What is our errand on this occasion?"

" And yet you kick at being considered a plausible villain!"

" Of course if you call marrying an old lady for her property, villainy, why then I am a very proper villain."

" Ah, but I don't; but when you marry the woman, and spend her money upon others, then I *do* call it villainy."

" Tried by a very high Puritanical standard it might, perhaps, be so designated; but we, sir, are men of the enlightened nineteenth century, and must be tried by the customs of the age we live in. To live in one age, and our conduct tried by the ethics of another, is like asking a man to live in water without getting wet."

" Your answer is nothing more than a pretty array of words. When Solomon said ' you may know a fool by his much talk,' I suspect that the king must have been bothered by some such a servant as you, who seeks to oppress every one by a multiplicity of words."

" You see, sir, there are grave charges tumbling about one, and I have no other weapons but words to defend myself. If I am a villain, it is for the good of others, not for mine own."

" Such a distinction will not serve you in heaven, old boy."

" Heaven, in its judgement, will take every circumstance of a man's life, and his organisation into account; therefore he who works criminally for the pleasure or aggrandisement of others, is not so culpable as if he had been working for himself."

" Why of the two sinners the provider is worse than the instigator. But it seems un-

grateful for me to say so, seeing that you have been my provider on this occasion. But we are waiting a devilish long while for the feast, don't you think so, Brummell?"

" I cannot explain the meaning of it. Shall I saddle my horse, and meet them, and hurry them on?"

" Oh, no, let it take its course. If the girls have ' frustrated our knavish tricks,' all the better for them."

" And perhaps they have," said Brummell. " It was unfortunate that Jane should have seen you on the road."

" I don't know that she did; I only know that I saw her, and devilish pretty she looked, while the blue streamers of her bonnet floated in the breeze."

" Then her head was right out of the window?" said Brummell.

" And half her body. What she was looking at on the road, I cannot tell."

" Yourself, perhaps," suggested the valet.

" It might have been, for what I know. She popped her head out of the window at the moment my horse brought me to it, quite close enough to kiss her had I not been gallopping hard."

" Depend upon it, sir, that event has something to do with the delay."

" I'm rather cooling about the girl. The time and trouble expended over it, is really more than the thing is worth. It is the wine, the wine, I thirst for!"

" I really could drink a glass myself. I have had nothing since I had a nip of brandy at a house by a mill stream that branches off the road. I don't know whether you noticed the house or not?"

" Rather—and had a nip there myself, and watered the horse. But what about Butters?"

" That's what I can't make out."

" Surely he hasn't been ass enough, after I saw them, to turn about, and drive the girls back to Evesham?"

" I should say not, sir. He must have been an ass, indeed, if he has. It is altogether past interpretation, this delay. Was it before you came to the public by the mill that you passed Jane?"

" Lord! yes; five miles the other side."

" Butters, I know, has a great horror of distressing his horses—"

" Himself, you mean."

" Oh, yes, he is not a man to neglect himself etther," said the valet.

" I hate humbug! that man is precious fond of a pipe, and on journeys he pulls up frequently to rest himself, and takes credit from others that he is anxious about his horse. My word for it, he has stopped at every public on the road; and perhaps he and the girls have all got drunk together."

" The better for your purpose if they have," remarked the valet.

" That would be all very well if they were here—nothing I should like better. But I don't see the fun of my getting up this elaborate play for the benefit of my coachman, I'm d—d if I do!"

" Never fear, sir, there will be another explanation to it than that."

" No doubt of it. Thieves always set themselves up for honest men. He will tell every lie upon the face of the earth to cover the truth of the delay. The horse fell lame—a lynch-pin loose—a shoe come off, and he had to drive to a smithey—anything but the truth. Oh, I'm up to it all, though it is not always my cue to say much. But, 'pon my soul! were I behind him now with a horsewhip, wouldn't I lash into him, though I had to pay forty shillings for it! I am not a man to screw up servants like galley slaves—I give them a vast deal of liberty, and treat them like men—"

"I can sincerely subscribe to that," interposed the valet.

"But I like a quid pro quo—"

"They are pretty little words, sir—what do they mean?"

"Something for something—one thing for another—tit for tat—a Roland for an Oliver—there's a heap of meanings for you, so you can take which you like."

"They're much of a muchness, but they're all of them pretty clear, and cannot fail to impress themselves on my memory. It is a very convenient thing to have a few latin phrases at hand, especially when you wish to appear learned and fog those you are talking to—duns for example."

"I thought you had been up in latin," observed Mr. Duchesney.

"Never took to it. Got on with everything but latin, which I now deeply regret."

"Well, as you say, it is handy with those who don't understand it. But satis verborum."

"There, sir, you have me again—what is the meaning of the phrasa?"

"Enough of words, or, you need say no more."

"How well that phrase would serve a fellow with a talkative importunate tailor. Satis verborum! Why he would go away fancying that he had a check for his account."

"While it would only be a check for him to shut up."

"Just nothing more. Ha! ha! ha! Oh! I must get up some latin. A little of it would have served me well when I was pitching the tale to Ann Orwell."

"Look here, Brummell, I can't stand this any longer. Wine, or I perish!"

"Mine is a similar case of distress, sir," retorted the valet.

"That don't quench my thirst, does it?" he snappishly asked.

"I should be gratified if it did."

"But it don't, so it's no good talking. How far is the nearest public?"

"About two miles, sir."

"Saddle my horse. I'll ride on there. I'll wait ho longer."

"Shall I go for you, sir?"

"That wouldn't do, for if these snails came in your absence, there would be no one but me to receive them. And the sight of me, we both agree, would frighten away the birds. No, no, I must go on—"

"And I must go without," said the valet, turning away towards the stables.

But he had but taken a step or two in that direction before the sound of wheels was again heard.

"This must be the brougham without doubt," said the valet, standing on tiptoe to look over a high box hedge.

"Seeing is believing with me," said the governor. "You have sold me once already with the sound of wheels, but you don't do it again," he added. "Watoh no longer, but proceed with the saddling."

"Just one minute, sir," said the valet, straining his eager eyes over the well-clipped box hedge that divided the grounds from the highway.

"No good can come by watching, and if it be not them, I shall be angry that you have kept me still longer without the wine.

Hurrah! the brougham comes. The sight of the vehicle, with a tall black horse, his brow mantled with a white star, filled the watchers with a little more seriousness of the parts they had undertaken to play in this real life drama.

"There's no time to be lost," cried Mr. Duchesney, running forwards then backwards, his valet in his confusion doing the same. "You needn't be lost, because I am, you fool! Your part is easy enough—you have merely to go in, say how-d'ye-do, sit down, pour out the wine, and drink it. Don't speak—that's all you've got to do. But me—where am I to go? what am I to do?"

"I should say—"

"Hold your noise! you've said too much already. We've been talking and not preparing, and here we are like a couple of fools while they are ringing at the gate!"

"And they are ringing too!"

"Let them ring, and be ——! They've kept me waiting long enough!"

"Really, sir, you're losing yourself—" remonstrated the valet.

"How do you know what I'm doing?" cried the irritable man, bending his fist. "You are not me, are you?"

"And I am sure you are not now yourself," ventured the valet.

"Who am I then? There, come on let's have a round or two! Butters hasn't half taken the humbug out of you—he has left that for me to do! Come on!" he cried, sparring up to his servant like a madman.

Indeed there were times when Mr. Duchesney was a madman. His brain had been so much weakened by debauchery of all kinds, that the smallest perplexity or opposition completely estranged it from its normal condition, and left him like one bereft of reason.

Butters the coachman was now impatient of delay. He adjusted his whip and his reins, got off the box, and began ringing and kicking at the door in a most infuriated manner.

"If any one lives here," he said, "they can't werry well help hearing that, I'm jiggered if they can."

Ann Orwell suggested that there might be another entrance.

"Not a bit on it. Don't yer see that the house stands in its own grounds? This ere is the hentrance, and if we are to get in at all this must be the way. Wisitors, though, don't seem werry welcome. I'll give 'em another chance howsumdever, for the happiness of our company."

"It is a strange lonely place," said Jane to Ann, as they sat together in the brougham.

"Not very lively, is it, dear?" said Ann to

Jane. "But I daresay they keep a good many servants."

"Then they must be very sleepy ones," replied Jane.

"Here goes agen!" cried the coachman, seizing with both hands the long handle of the gate bell, and continuously pulling until the place was alive with sound.

This continuous ringing stopped the sparring propensities of Mr. Duchesney. The valet told his master that he had a great many lies to invent before he could possibly open the gate, and that he had not one ready.

"Nothing so easy as lying, you fool!" exclaimed the master.

"I really, sir, must ask you to be more of a man and a gentleman. You will put all the lies out of my head, and in my embarrassment I may perchance speak the truth."

"Oh, there's no fear of that. The truth and you never made acquaintance."

"For your sake, it is to be hoped that truth and me may not unite on this occasion. But say what you will, sir, only keep your temper. Hark at the bell—"

"The coachman's drunk, or he would not dare to ring like that."

"Drunk or sober, I cannot keep him another moment at the door," said Brummell, bolting off.

"But where am I to go?" Mr. Duchesney bawled after him.

"There!" replied the valet, and as he ran, he pointed to some place with his finger, which the master was slow to recognise where he meant.

"Where?" he still bawled, to his servant, now almost lost amid the trees.

"There!" was still the servant's answer, as he turned round and pointed.

"Why that's the washhouse, you fool!" replied Mr. Duchesney, bending his fist, and well shaking it.

But the valet did not see his master's kind intentions, nor hear anything about the washhouse, to which he did not point, but to the window of a small room near by that very domestic but very necessary outhouse.

While Duchesney rambled about the grounds cursing and swearing, perplexed with where to hide himself, his valet had determined his first lying apology to the girls for the absence of the family to whom he was there to introduce Jane to for an engagement.

When he opened the gate to admit the brougham, which was driven by Butters to the pretty English house, that stood in the centre of the grounds, surrounded by beds of flowers, and approached by a broad flight of the whitest of stone steps, he told the coachman, as he walked along by the side of the horse, in tones that the girls could not hear—

"The governor's like a madman at your delay, so look out for a tempest."

"He be blowed! He should have bought me a hoss with wings if he wanted me to be quicker. Look at the sweat on the mare now—the creetur looks as if she had come out of a washerwoman's suds! We've come along that ere pace as if we had been flying before a hungry lion, or a Dick Turpin highwayman! And now he's a growling too, is he?"

"You will soon have an opportunity to judge for yourself. We had well nigh come to blows, indeed we had."

"I'm always to be found in the humour at that game, 'special when I've right on my side, Mr. Brummell. For my mother, or my character as coachman, or sticking up for my perks, why anybody and everybody will find me all there, and no mistake! Whoa!"

"Here at last then, young ladies," said the smiling valet. "And I hope to hear from you that you have had a pleasant ride?"

"That we certainly have," said Ann, completely taken off her guard by the frank agreeable manners of the valet. "But it has been a very long one."

"I hope the coachman has been attentive to you in the way of rest and refreshment on the road?" he asked in the blandest manner.

"I don't think they'll say they've any fault to find with me," said Butters. "I've pulled up twice at werry respectable houses, and then give 'em the run of the house, while I did a pipe. I couldn't do no more for 'em, an' if they had been my own daughters."

"You've been very kind and attentive, Mr. Butters, and we are both of us very much obliged to you," said Jane, also pretty well at her ease, and void of suspicion.

"I'll tell you one thing, young ladies, the breezes coming across the numerous hop-gardens that you must have passed through, has given a new lustre to your cheeks."

This bit of pleasantry set the girls tittering.

"Let us come out after that," said Ann.

"It speaks well for your self-control, Butters, that having had so much beauty in your possession, and a fast horse, you had not bolted with it," continued the flattering valet.

"I've got a party at home, Mr. Brummell, who would have spoken her mind upon that ere argument. Mrs. Butters aint werry amiable at the best of times, and if such a thing as that was to happen, she would just murder me and the girls too. She's a woman of a werry warm temper, and don't like no tricks."

"Really, Butters, under so much temptation, I do think your wife would have pardoned you."

"She'd have had my life first, though. I know Mrs. B., and you don't, that's the difference."

"That's quite enough about such nonsense," said Pretty Jane, taking the proffered hand of the valet to alight from the carriage, and in the same manner Ann followed her.

"Where's the guv'ner?" whispered Butters.

"Don't exactly know. Find him, and take a bottle of cham with you, which will protect you from his wrath better than a revolver."

"I shall put up the mare first, I can tell you. Where is the stables?"

"I must attend to our fair friends first, Butters. I know you'll excuse me," he said, leading the way to the room where he had so elegantly spread out the table with glass, flowers, &c., which were to be followed by a spread of the more substantial things in the hamper that the coachman had stowed underneath the box of the carriage.

"Lord, it'll take no time to say where the stables is."

"Round to the right—at least I think so. Go and see; if not, come back and try the left."

"Then that's outside the gate agen into the road," said the coachman.

"To the left, I mean. Do wait a minute, for I want something out of the carriage before you move it." He here tipped a significant wink to the coachman, who winked back again, each assuming that they understood the other.

Jane and Ann could do nothing but follow, yet the former began to think it strange that she had not seen or heard a female about the place, nor indeed seen any other face than that of the valet's.

When they reached the apartment, the busy Mr. Brummell bade them be seated, and after they had taken a chair side by side, Jane naturally enough began to inquire when she would see the mistress?

It was now that Brummell was called upon for essentially the first part of the performance. Had he got his first lie ready? Oh, dear, yes; and a lie at which there was a perfect network of other lies to follow to make good the first, and give the colour of truth to the whole.

"I hope that you did not understand me that the mistress was to be seen here?" he said, leaning both hands on the table, and speaking across it to the girls who sat opposite, and who heard his question with considerable dismay and surprise pictured on their countenances, more especially that of Pretty Jane, who was more interested in seeing the mistress than her friend and companion. The girls looked at each other before speaking, as if to read each other's feelings and thoughts on Mr. Brummell's extraordinary question. At length Jane said, her tones unmistakeably marked with rising suspicion—

"I certainly did understand that the lady was to be seen here."

"You might, I grant, because you did not receive any communication from me at all. But you, Ann, you—surely *you* did not understand me that the lady to whom it was to be my happiness to introduce Jane, was to be seen here at Morley Cottage?"

"Why of course I did, or how could I tell Jane so?"

"I have had many surprises, many disappointments, many woes, sorrows, and cares, but this licks everything I ever experienced—it caps the lot I tell you!" he cried, striking the table with as much vehemence as a railway official slams a carriage door.

The poor girls, who were already in a half nervous half fearful state, started from their seats at the affected wildness of his manner, and the sudden bang upon the table.

"But where is the lady to be seen then, Mr. Brummell?" inquired Jane, with dejected accents, and glum looks.

"And why did we come here, I should like to know?" asked Ann Orwell, sticking to the interests of her friend.

"Now look here—quid pro quo, and of course you know what that means, and if you don't it doesn't matter—but to leave latin, and speak in plain old English—I must ask you, ladies, to confine yourselves to sifting how the error, if it may be called an error, arose in your minds. Was it your fault in misunderstanding—"

"But I'm positive I didn't misunderstand," persisted Ann, bristling up.

"Don't interrupt me, Miss Orwell, don't, for the love of truth. I am a man of very few words, therefore shall not detain you long—"

"Indeed you mustn't, for we're not going to stop," observed Jane, with much firmness of manner.

"Pray don't add ingratitude to your interruptions," he pathetically cried. "I can bear the one, but not the other. Let me show you that I have been your friend, and mean to be. I invited you to Morley as a sort of half-way house, —to the house of an esteemed friend of mine, where you might rest till morning."

"And do you think we're going to stop here all night?—not if I know it," said Ann.

"How can you go fifteen miles further? Besides, the horse couldn't do it without considerable distress, and that, as feeling women, I am sure you wouldn't like! Things will all come right, if you will make yourselves at home."

"If it is so far, why of course we ought to have gone by railway," said Jane.

"But there is no railway near. It is one of those beautiful, secluded, out-of-the way places, with a few villa residences sprinkled about, and where there are no residents but those who keep their horses and carriages. There is no traffic, and therefore no railway. But had there been, surely you must prefer a nice carriage ride like you have had, right through the lovely hop gardens of Kent, than have been stuffed up in a smoky railway carriage, even if you saved a little time by it. And there are such a lot of roughs now travelling about on purpose to insult unprotected females—"

"There, we'd have chanced all that," said Jane, who seemed indignant and unhappy.

"I wouldn't stop all night in a strange place for the world!" cried Ann.

"I'm so glad to hear you say so!" responded Jane.

"Certainly, it is pleasant to see friends of one mind, but I must claim a little consideration for my position in the case. Please to recollect that I have made arrangements for Jane to see Mrs. Harfleur, and a sweet lady she is, to-morrow at eleven—"

"You never said all that before, Mr. Brummell," remarked Ann.

"Nor was there any occasion. I told you of the first stage, and I wished the others to be a series of sweet surprises. I never told you that I had prepared a hamper of good things—but there it is you see—although Butters needn't have brought it in in that rude manner."

"What was I to do?" cried the coachman, throwing the huge hamper from his shoulder to the floor. "The guv'ner took out the cham— but I say he did, Mr. Brummell, so it's no good your lifting that knife agen me—"

"Are you drunk, Butters?" inquired the valet, who had shook the knife at the coachman to enjoin his silence when he began talking about the "guv'ner."

But the coachman's incaution had alarmed the girls, who were just becoming reconciled to their position. They both at once rose.

"We don't choose to stop here another instant!" cried Jane, rushing to the door, but the valet intercepting their progress, each of the girls caught up a dinner knife from the table, and during this scene Mr. Duchesney, heated with champagne, came into the room.

PRETTY JANE

OR, THE

VIPER OF KIDBROOK LANE

MR. BRUMMELL LIFTED THE FRIENDLESS LITTLE GIRL FROM THE STEPS.

Of course the entrance of Mr. Duchesney was entirely in opposition to the policy of his valet, who was most anxious that the girls should be brought into "form" as he called it, by which he meant that they should be placed entirely at their ease, and all suspicion removed, and made warm with wine, before the villain of the piece should make his appearance.

Now the fat was in the fire, for the girls at once saw the meaning of it all—saw that they were betrayed into the hands of the enemy.

"Let us be firm," whispered Jane to Ann, as they stood shoulder to shoulder, each holding a dinner knife.

Mr. Brummell made one vain attempt to get his wild master from the room, but with a withering frown he put his servant on one side with his hand.

"This is a most unseemly display," he said, his eye fixed on the girls, with their brandished knives. "You must have been playing the villain, Brummell, that could have made it necessary for the girls to defend themselves with weapons!"

"They are seized with fear, sir," said the valet. "Why or wherefore they best can tell you."

"We wished to leave this house, and you prevented us," said Jane, keeping down all semblance of fear, though none but herself knew the terror and alarm that was pent up within her, and which she was determined should not be seen by her diabolical and cowardly enemies, who stood before her like impersonations from hell.

"And has so small a matter as that exasperated you to the use of knives?"

"And we will use them, too," cried Jane, with heroic determination, "if either of you, cowards as you are! attempt to touch us, or prevent our leaving this place! Stand back, for your life!" she further exclaimed, holding up the knife like a dagger ready to stab, when Mr. Duchesney made a step towards her.

"This will be a case of law, I see!" exclaimed the coachman. "But, mind'ye, I'm not in it."

"You will yet find that you are in it, for you brought us here," said Ann.

"That was by my master's orders," replied the terrified man.

"That excuse won't serve you when the orders are to do what's contrary to law," said Jane.

"But I didn't know, I'll give you my word for that," said the terrified coachman.

"You know now, though," said Ann, who followed Jane, in word and action, and upraised the knife, or let it fall, exactly as she did.

"If you help us now," said Jane, "you will prove that you were no party to this infamous plot. But if you refuse, as sure as you stand there you shall be had up before a magistrate with the others."

"Let us have a bit o' dinner first, young ladies, and then I'll help you might and main," said the coachman, beginning to take out the things from the hamper, while the valet spread them out in order upon the table.

"I must say, Miss Jane, you are not at all behaving after a fashion worthy of your ladylike appearance. Suppose it to be all as you imagine—that there is no situation in view, and that the whole thing is a piece of deception from beginning to end—think you that it merits such stagey resentment as this? But let me tell you there is no deception in the matter. That if you will but quell your unfounded fears, and exercise your patience until the morning—"

"Never!" cried Jane, and Ann Orwell simultaneously cried the same. "We will leave this instant, except we are detained by force, which you will do at your peril!"

"Look here, lassie," said Mr. Duchesney, again advancing close to her, "I am more afraid of your beauty than your knife. The weapon I defy, but your lustrous eyes cut me to the quick!"

"I should like to quickly cut it," said Butters.

"Cut what—the ham?" said the valet, who could never resist being facetious, however inappropriate to the occasion.

While Mr. Duchesney spoke Jane turned her back upon him, and conferred with her companion.

The valet nudged his master, and whisperingly suggested that he should speak a little latin to them, adding, that people are always awed by that they do not understand.

"Aut amat, aut odit mulier!" he cried, following the advice of his valet, but neither Jane nor Ann were awed by it, although they did not understand it. "A woman either loves or hates," he added, interpreting his latin quotation, and then asking—"which is it in your case?"

"Better ask that ere question after dinner, sir," suggested Butters, which was backed by the valet, who had now all the contents of the hamper fully set forth on the table. And then he placed chairs for the young women, and invited them to be seated.

They disdained to notice the invitation, but made towards the door, and would have left the room and the house, had not Mr. Duchesney, this time, intercepted their exit.

"Let us scream for the police, Jane," suggested Ann.

"I object to that," said Butters, who had serious misgivings of any law proceedings, which the name of police strongly smelt of.

"Who cares for your objection, you slave of a scoundrel master! When you three cowards stand before the magistrate—"

"I see nothing to convict upon, except it be a crime to give you a drive in the country, and inwite you to a good dinner."

"You take a very proper view of the case," said his master.

"There is no other offence that I know of," said the valet, "except it arise out of my anxiety to serve the both of you, by getting one into a good situation, and making peace between the other and her estranged lover."

"You detestable liar!" Jane passionately exclaimed, "you dare to stand there before us, and keep up the cheat?"

"It is not a bit of good talking to them, Jane, dear," said Ann. "The cowards are very brave before a couple of girls, but wouldn't they fly before a policeman?"

"How fond she is of talking about policemen," said the coachman.

"Perhaps she has a lover in the force," said Mr. Duchesney.

"A deal of force in what you say," said the facetious Brummell.

Could they have known how dear they would have to pay for their fun, they would not have enjoyed it quite so much.

"My advice is, young ladies—"

"We advise you to let us pass, or you will rue it," said Jane, interrupting her profligate master.

"Pray be seated, and make better use of these knives than to stab me. God bless my soul! I mean you no harm."

"Nor I," said Brummell.

"Nor I," said Butters, "for I'm a married man. Don't be so quarrelsome, but sit down and have a nice little bit of dinner. Don't keep the company waiting."

"Understand, we are determined to leave this house—"

"Let us have the honour of your company to dinner," said Mr. Duchesney, "then the horse will be rested, and Butters shall drive you back to Evesham House, if you are so determined."

"We will leave this instant," persisted Jane, "and we dare you to prevent us!" she added, boldly walking to the door, when the governor placed himself between her and the door, and endeavoured to get the knife from her, which he succeeded in doing, after a sharp struggle, and not before Jane witnessed blood flowing freely from two of his fingers, as well as from her own wrist.

The sight of the crimson fluid, fast dropping drop by drop, as he held up his lacerated fingers, upon the rich Turkey carpet, sickened Jane, and she at once gave up the struggle, and as the door was still defended against her egress, she was led back by Ann to a chair, away from the table, and as far from her cowardly tormentors as the room would admit.

Ann Orwell had not Jane's courage, which was more than she had strength to carry out. Directly she saw the struggle between Jane and her master, the frightened Ann threw down her knife, and began to scream. She now took her handkerchief and bound up the jagged cut inflicted by the knife, which Duchesney had at length wrested from her.

Butters did not at all like the sight of these proceedings. He saw in them a decided case for the next Sessions, and that he would be arraigned as one of the prisoners, and that it would go hard with him on account of a past conviction.

After looking at the dropping blood, he made his way to Jane, whose face was pale with pent-up passion, and said to her in crawling abject tones—

" Mind, if you please, Miss, it wasn't me that did it."

" Get away from me, you scoundrel !" Jane exclaimed, hastily rising from her chair, and confronting him in that determined manner that the portly vulgar fellow fairly crouched and quailed before her exasperated eye.

Had it been possible for the moment for the mind to disassociate itself with the perils and sufferings of Jane, which it was not, on account of her youth and beauty, no one could help laughing at the ludicrous position that Jane's eye had reduced the muscular stableman to.

Butters was now the impersonation of terror. With open mouth, and staring eyes, his fat shoulders drawn up to his dark blue weather-beaten looking ears, he hung back from her, almost afraid to breathe or move.

" Do sit down, Jane, dear," pleaded Ann. " We have not strength to contend against these devils—"

" Don't be a coward, and persuade me to be one also," interrupted Jane, snatching her garment from the clutch of Ann, who gently held her back by it, fearing that she was about to strike Butters.

" I'd rather live with you a week than a fort-night, I'm blowed if I wouldn't," muttered the coachman, sloping back to that part of the room he came from.

" Have you quite done staring at the girl ?" asked his master, angrily, who still stood by the door, holding up his bleeding fingers.

" Yes, sir, my eyes have had enough on her, and to spare."

" Then, perhaps, you will be good enough to fetch me a bowl of water to wash these bleeding trophies to my love, and a bottle of cham to drink my love's health in."

" I'm a stranger in these parts, guv'ner," replied the coachman. " Besides, sir, I'm not your walley, I'm your coachman."

" Bless my soul, Butters, at such a time as this, you need not stand on ceremony," said Brummell. " I cannot leave the room myself at this critical juncture."

" For God's sake one of you go, or you will have the satisfaction of seeing me bleed to death."

" I say agen, I'm a stranger here," said the coachman. " I don't know where the champagne is, and I don't know where the water is."

" Who then should know where the wine is ?" asked the valet. " You took it from the hamper—"

" That's right enough, so I did, and guv the dozen bottles to the guv'ner, one of which he threatened to shy at my head for stopping on the road as he said, which was anythink but the truth. Ask either of the young women if I loitered, if you don't believe me."

" Where did you leave them, sir ?" asked the valet.

" Just where the fellow brought them," Mr. Duchesney answered.

" Why that was in the grounds," said the coachman.

" Who said it wasn't ?" retorted his impetuous master. " Go and fetch them here, and when you find them, don't stop and drink it all."

" I shouldn't ha' been so long in your sarvice, guv'ner, if you couldn't ha' trusted me."

" Here, here, I will go," volunteered the valet.

" Why you ? Do you think I would trust you more than him ? You don't fight which shall get the water—not a bit of it."

" You really, sir, are very hard on us. Would you like to fetch the wine yourself ?"

" Don't keep dogs and do the barking myself," was the snappish reply.

" You get the water, and I'll get the wine," said the valet.

" That is cool," said the coachman, with a knowing grin. " You amooses me, you does, Mr. Brummell."

The master's patience was exhausted, and he began to feel faint with the loss of blood, which still dropped—dropped—until it formed a little pool at his feet.

He cursed his valet, and swore at his coachman.

" My heart alive, sir, I can't get no water if I don't know where to find it. I know where the wine is, and the walley does not, and he knows where the water is, and I does not, which, guv'ner, ought to go for the wine, and which on us for the water ?"

" Look here, you two fellows, as far as the wine is concerned, I will be my own servant," said Mr. Duchesney, binding round his fingers with his pocket handkerchief. " But as for the water, if it is not on the table by the time I return, I will kick the pair of you out of this house, and out of my service ! Gather up all the knives out of the way of these refractory girls—"

Jane sprang forward to the table and equipped herself with a knife before his orders could be executed.

Ann had no mind for such serious defences with the knife, and would not have had courage to use it, happen what might, therefore she did not follow Jane's example by providing herself with one, and almost shuddered to see Jane again with a weapon in her hand.

Ann entreated her in the most earnest manner to put it down.

" Let me alone, Ann. Keep quiet by my side. Whichever of those contemptible scoundrels attempts to approach us, shall find me use the knife better next time."

" You'd best be warned, young woman, and not play with edged tools," said Butters. " Mind f it comes to the Sessions don't say I didn't warn you."

"Your conduct, Miss Jane, is something most unseemly," said the sneaking valet. "It is next to impossible now, after this murderous display of passion, that I can give you a character with my dear friend, Mrs. Harfleur, a lady of the highest respectability, and extensive fortune."

"I wouldn't enter the best place in the world that was got by such a scamp as you!" Jane exclaimed.

"Very well, then my good intentions on your behalf must be considered at an end. Your silly passion has lost you the best situation ever a young woman could aspire to. Indeed, I wrong my description by calling it a situation—it is a home, where the chief care of the mistress is to see that her servants in every way happy and comfortable; I may say, indeed, that her dependents are treated like independents; they do just as they like; eat and drink what they please—"

"I wishes as I wur a young woman," said Butters, "I should just like such a place. She don't want a coachman, does she?"

"Her coachman is a perfect gentleman,—"

"Then I should suit her in that pertikler, shouldn't I, Mr. Brummell?"

"If you were up to your own ideas of yourself you would."

"And don't you think I ham?"

"Certainly not, in my estimation."

"Hum! that's werry plain, but not werry perlite."

"I always give truthful answers, and those shouldn't ask me questions who flinch from hearing the truth."

"I s'poses as you would be gentleman enough for her coachman?" asked Butters, with a face screwed up quizzingly.

"I s'poses I should," replied Mr. Brummell, mockingly.

"Then why don't you go in for the sityation, as she's a pertikler friend o' yourn?" asked Butters, thinking that he had nailed his superior fellow-servant.

"First of all, the sityation, as you call it—"

"And what do you call it, Mister Schoolmaster?"

"Sit-u-a-tion. But your pronunciation is near enough for a coachman."

"But not for a walley I s'pose?"

"Well, no—not quite," he replied. "It is necessary for a walley, as you call him—"

"Oh! that aint right neither?"

"Good enough for a coachman's vocabulary," he replied.

"I shall just say this for coachmen, which is more than I can for walleys, that everybody they talks to understands 'em. Who can tell what a wocab—and there I'm brought to a cab-stand. Wo—wo—what was it you said?"

"Vocabulary, I said."

"And how is any fellow to understand that? Do you understand it?" he asked Jane and Ann, who stood together at the window, but who declined to be drawn into any conversation with their tormentors. "They're too sulky to answer me, though I don't know why they should be sulky with me, for I brought 'em here safe as ninepence."

"Their behaviour is too bad for me to have any further regard for them, at least for Jane, who, if she don't mind, will certainly get herself into trouble. I can see that her companion is quite ashamed of her."

"You wretch! no," cried Ann Orwell. "I only wish that I had got Jane's courage, we'd have fought our way out of this place long ago, though we had killed the lot of you!" she passionately added.

"You will always find discretion to be the better part of valour," said the valet.

"Werry good adwice," said the coachman, taking a chair, which by three jumps, or jerks, and a little wriggling of the back legs, he brought himself close up to the table, before a beautiful little Westphalia ham, supported by two fowls, roast and boiled.

"You really seem putting yourself in form for dinner before you are invited," remarked Brummell. "Perhaps you would like me to wait behind your chair?"

"I don't care a dump where you wait, but I'm not inclined to wait any longer, and that's the naked truth, which the young women will please to forgive me for the expression," said the coachman, with knife and fork quite prepared to cut his way into the bread-crumbed ham.

"I should advise you to wait until you are asked," said Brummell, who was by no means pleased with the coachman's boldness, and utter want of respect to his own superior position in Mr. Duchesney's establishment.

"I don't want no asking, not I, and if I did I shouldn't get it."

"In the absence of the master the valet I believe takes precedence of the coachman."

"Then take your precedence, and live on it, while I takes my dinner and lives on it, and see which will be the fattest first. Master's out with the champagne, and you won't see him no more till it's all gone—so he will want no dinner; you are going to have yourn off precedence, and the girls is going to have theirs off sulks, and I'm going to have mine off ham and chicken."

"And for your dessert, you will have the governor come and kick you out of the room."

"He'll be too drunk for that," said the coachman, and without further parley he cut into the ham, and then into the right wing of the fowl, and a thick crust off a new loaf; but, before he began to eat, he opened a quart bottle of Guinness's Dublin stout, and drank off a large glass of the creamy liquid as an appetiser.

"In a few minutes I shall be prepared for any man's kicks, only I would beg him to be prepared to have kicks back again. Would you like to open the ball, Mr. Brummell?"

"I have demeaned myself too much already by fighting with you. But I was drunk then, and forgetful what was due to myself."

"But I reminded you what was due to you, and paid you, too, in a d—d good hiding! And I've got plenty of muscle enough left to do it again."

"Fighting is the blackguard's stock-in-trade, and not one for gentlemen to engage in."

"Don't put yourself out of the way, Mr. Brummell, I only passed the compliment. Mind, you haven't got your master's bowl of wa er, and if it aint got we're both on us to be kicked out of the house. I shall h ve my dinner and mizzle, which will save the master a deal of trouble, for he will then only have to kick you instead of the pair on us."

"You are a mean fellow, and just taking advantage of the row these two stupid girls are creating in the house of my friend, that's all about it."

"Mind'ye, I have nothing to do with the girls, so don't mention my name with 'em."

"You will all have to suffer for this assault," said Jane, who was a little relieved to hear the rogues falling out among themselves.

"Do you hear that, Mr. Butters?" asked the gratified valet, his gratification arising from a little wholesome terror that Jane held over the coachman's head. "Your kicks and muscular power will serve you nothing at the bar of the criminal court—"

"And that is where he will be, and you too," cried Jane, from the other end of the room.

The coachman's pluck was knocked right out of him. He crossed his knife over his plate, and rose from his chair, then turned his back upon the valet who stood near, and mildly asked Jane for an explanation, telling her to remember that an assault on a young female was a very serious charge to bring against a respectable middle-aged married man.

"And that is just the charge I mean to make, and mean to prove," said Jane.

"What agen me?" he exclaimed.

"You brought us here did you not?" asked Ann.

"How can I deny it? Look here, Ann, aforetime I and you was werry old friends—"

"There, you won't blarney over me, so don't try it on," she interrupted him by saying, much to his discomfort, for he was conscious of a little blarneying, and regretted being bowled out in his favourite method of getting out of a difficulty when fight and bluster would not serve him.

"Why you gied me a shilling a-piece for bringing you on so nicely," he said. "And you seemed werry comfortable like the whole of the way, till now when we was all about to sit down to a little family dinner like."

"We have been brought here under false pretences—"

"That you have not had patience to prove—you are halting by the way," said Brummell, loudly, for with one thing and another, he was beginning to lose his temper.

"You know it to be all false!" said Ann Orwell.

"Don't speak any more to them, Ann. They know they are detaining us against our wishes, and they shall answer it before a magistrate," said Jane, with decision, and her words appalled Butters, and he said—

"Understand, I'm not detaining you. You're not agreeable company enough for me, I do assure you. As far as I'm concerned you can go. There's the door, why don't yer go?"

"You know that your wretch of a master has locked the door outside."

"I didn't know, did you, Mr. Brummell?" he asked.

"I would rather hang than tell a lie! I did hear him lock the door, and saw him take the key from the inside and place it on the outside," said the valet.

"Then you all of you saw and heard more than I did."

"It is a falsehood!" exclaimed Jane. "You are as bad as the others, and their punishment will be yours as far as I can do it."

"In any court of law they will hear what a fellow has to say—"

"Then you will soon have an opportunity of speaking, for directly I get out of this place I shall get a warrant against all three; so I don't deceive you."

"But let me know what for?" said Butters, mildly, and who was really trembling in his high-lows.

"You brought us here—and you knew your master, who you know has already openly insulted me—"

"Lord! I know; you mean in the servants' hall? Why that was only a bit of fun like. You ought to be proud to see such a gentleman as our master, as keeps his servants an' hosses, so precious fond of you—don't yer think so, Mr. Brummell?"

"My opinions on the whole subject are so thoroughly well known to both Jane and Ann that I must decline discussing it further. The motives that I had in bringing them here were of the most unselfish purest description. Parallels—"

"You do speak to rights, I'm blest if you don't, Mr. Brummell! Are them parallels as fine eating as muscatells?"

"Don't be a fool and show it," was the valet's answer.

"If that's a parallel I don't want no more on 'em, so you may give 'em to the girls, which you was a doing on when I interrupted you," observed the coachman, pouring out another glass of stout, which he offered to the valet, at the same time saying—

"Here, have a wet, and go on again with your parallels."

The valet disdainfully put the glass aside with his hand.

"Oh, you won't have none, eh? You are looking out for the champagne, I see what you are arter fast enough. Take my advice, neighbour, a bird in the hand is worth two in the bush. The champagne aint here, and the stout is—"

"Pray do not take the trouble to explain your meaning, it is quite obvious enough."

"I'm generally pretty easy to be understood. I never talk about parallels, which no fellow can make out, except univarsity men, which I am not, and never was. The only edication I ever had was the way to pick out perriwinkles with a pin, and swallow the winkle without the pin, and to shell peas without eating 'em. I easily learnt the first lesson, but mother said I never did the other."

After this rambling recital, he lustily fell to work at his dinner; and we leave him with both hands and teeth at the fowl's wing, his grey eyes at the same time fixed on Mr. Brummell while he oratorically explained matters to the dejected-looking girls, telling them everything indeed but the—truth.

"I cannot think what has happened to have inspired you both with these unnecessary fears," he began, addressing the girls, as they sat at one end of the room, while he harangued them as he stood at the other.

But directly he began to speak, they sidle d

their chairs round closer to the window, and obscured their faces from the speaker.

"I am told by the coachman who drove you hither that on the way you were happy, merry and contented—"

"So they was, Mr. Brummell!" exclaimed the coachman. "So that shows I did my dooty by 'em, don't it?"

"Honestly, it does."

"We never thought then that there were such men as you and your master upon the face of the earth!" cried Jane, turning her head round, and showing a countenance strongly marked with indignation.

"We are all servants here," he continued, extending his hand, "and to a very considerable extent are under the control of our master and mistress."

"Not to do wrong, though," said Ann Orwell, turning her head quickly round, and then averting it again.

"Servants are not employed to criticise their employers' doings!" he exclaimed.

"Don't he speak like a book?" interrupted the coachman.

"D'ye see, Butters," he resumed, pleased with a kind of applause which the coachman bestowed on him, "we mustn't be our master's master, nor must those girls be their mistress's mistress!"

"That's right enough, and they knows it," responded the coachman, knocking applause with the handle of his knife.

"I maintain—"

"Interrupting you once more, Mr. Brummell, but have a glass of stout before you begin again—I'm sure you want some, and you'll have ever so much better ideas arterwards."

"No, thanks."

"Don't be afraid of the guv'ner. I'll punch his head if he says anything to either of us. Besides, he's drunk enough before this, I'll bet a wager, and forgot all about the bowl of water that he ordered."

"And which we couldn't get had we been inclined to have done so—"

"For why?"

"Because he has locked us in!"

"Dash my wig if ever I thought of that! Why so he has! No wonder then that you've been so easy about the water! To tell you the truth I've thought a good deal about it to myself, although it wasn't exactly my place to get it, as neither of you were too civil about it, and I was determined that I wouldn't. But I didn't at the same time forget that we were both to be kicked out of the house; and knowing that master was a devil to keep his word in every brutal promise, so I thought I'd just get a bit of dinner before the kicking commenced, that I might be the better able to bear it and return it."

"Do not alarm yourself—the kicking is still in store for us, for he will swear the water should have been provided, although it was quite impossible to get out of the room to fetch it," said Brummell, who was again getting friendly and communicative with his cantankerous fellow-servant, although he still declined to eat or drink with him, which was not out of any disrespect to him, nor out of fear to his master, but because he wished his abstinence to be made a point of with the girls.

"Master is werry unreasonable, and if he didn't pay well it would be next to onpossible to live with him, that's my opinion."

"He has some good points though. But he never does anything under the government of reason. His good and bad actions are all of them performed under the influence of excitement and passion."

"I never heard of any of his good actions. They must be performed when he's asleep and knows nothing about it. Ugh! ugh! Did you ever know him do a good action Brummell?"

"Not many perhaps—but one certainly."

"Maybe that he had done some great injury to the party before. Once you know he threw some turps over my stable clothes and then set me on fire behind, and I was nearly cooked brown, and should have been too had not little Charley Saltmarsh—you know him—thrown a pail of water over me. As it was I was well scorched about the neck and shoulders, and had to go in to Guy's Hospital for above three weeks."

"I remember it well. It was a most diabolical thing to do. But he paid you well for his lark as he called it," said the valet.

"That's what I say—so he did. But I had to put the screw on him a bit; I had to threaten him, and then he came down with a twenty-pun note. He always has his pen'orth for his penny. He likes to kill you first, and bury you with kindness arterwards."

"Oh yes, he is fond of a spree and paying for it; but he is so often drunk that really half his time he is not an accountable being. But I can tell you of one good action that he did to a little girl, that we found one rainy night on a doorstep of a west-end house where she had been in the pelting rain all the night through"

"His own little girl it was I daresay," said the coachman, who had a very bad opinion of his master, and could never believe in his doing a good action to anybody except as compensation for some bad one, as in the case he had previously related about himself.

"Indeed it was not his child," said the valet.

"How can you tell that, I should like to know?" inquired Butters, uncorking a second bottle of the creamy Dublin stout.

"Do not be so incredulous," said Brummell. "I tell you the girl was not his child, and he said so himself."

"Did he rayly! Who'd believe anything he said? Not I, if he swore till he was black in the face, Mr. Brummell."

"The devil is not so black as he's painted," observed the valet.

"Can't say, I'm sure. Never saw him myself except that was him, and I believe it was, that came into the room yesterday at Evesham House when me and you and master was there. If it was him, he was werry little, werry humpy, and werry ugly, but I didn't see that he was black."

"This has nothing to do with what I was going to tell you. Mr. Duchesney may be a bad man, but he is a very good master."

"That's right enough."

"As servants that is all that we have to do with," said Mr. Brummell.

"That's right enough too. Oh, give the devil his due. But look here, my friend, the guv'ner has children in every parish in London that he don't know, so p'raps a kind thought just looked in upon him when he saw this little creetur in distress that it might be his'n."

"Take my word for it—"

"Oh, aye I will do that, for you're a werry hupright man like myself."

"Well then take my word for it, he knew nothing, thought nothing, of anything parental connected with this child, but acted solely from the generous impulse of the moment. He saw the fragile thing—"

"I thought you said it was a little girl, Mr. Brummell!" exclaimed the coachman, in surprise, which was truly unaffected.

"So I did," returned the valet, not for the moment comprehending his friend's difficulty.

"Then why do you now say that it was a fragile thing?" asked the sapient coachman.

The valet, who was a well educated man himself, was amazed at the ignorance of his fellow-servant, and then he took some pains to explain that a fragile thing was a poetic rendering of a little child in distress.

"I'm blest if I see it now you have shown it to me. But if you say it must be one and the same thing why then it must I s'pose. But arter this why of course words go for nothing with me. You may call my hoss a hass, or a cow a cabbage, as well as call a little girl a fragile thing. Don't say nothink more about it, but go on with your story, and if it's all the same to you just call a girl a girl, and then I shall be able to understand you to rights. You're a bootiful speaker, and it you'll only try an' make yourself understud, you'll make a fortin at it."

"Well, to please you, (and it should be the business of a speaker to please his audience). it shall no longer be a fragile creature that I and master rescued from misfortune, but a little girl. It was long before you came to live here—"

"I should say so, for I've heerd of no good action of his'n since I've been here."

"Very well. One night, while we were doing a week in London, I was attending master and another gentleman to his club, when we saw a fair and pretty girl about ten years of age sitting on a door-step in the rain, moaning as if in pain. It was midnight and very dark. Master's friend borrowed a light from a coffee-stall round the corner, while I lifted her up, master the while looking very sorrowfully on. Then a cab was called, and the guv'ner drove with the child to the station. He there discovered that she had been for some time abandoned by her mother, and that her father she never knew—"

"All right! I told you so! He was her father fast enough, and he knew it."

"That I don't believe. However he succoured her in her misfortunes—"

"And so he oft, if she was his child, only she oughtn't to have had any misfortins at all if they who brought her into the world had gied her a proper hand through it."

"Let us try and see as much good in each other as we can," said Brummell.

"That's right enough," growled the coachman. "But all the spectacles as ever was could never see any good in him."

"That is uncharitable. However, he saved this child from perishing, and he has well protected her since. She was a pretty little girl, with light wavy hair, and an aristocratic face. She is now in a capital school at Brussels."

"Werry sorry that she aint got a better father," muttered the coachman. "I'm glad your little story aint a long one, for it's werry nigh time for me to be travelling back to Evesham House, you know that was our arrangement, and that Ann Orwell—"

The girl looked round at the mention of her name, and was just in time to see the valet with uplifted finger impose silence on the coachman.

"The new and unlooked-for circumstances which the young women have introduced into what otherwise would have been a happy holiday for them and us, coupled with the misadventure of the guv'ner riding this way—"

"You did not know that your base master was to meet us here, I suppose?" asked Jane, sneeringly.

"'Pon my honour!" he exclaimed. "His visit here is as much a surprise to you as to us, is it not, Butters?"

"It nigh spilt my dinner, that's all I can say," replied the coachman.

"Is it not a wonder, Ann," said Jane, "that the roof doesn't tumble in and bury such liars?"

"A werry good job for you that it don't," said the coachman, with a chuckle, "for you are under it, and when roofs tumble in they are not werry pertikler in calling out 'below!' but come down swift upon everybody under 'em."

"Do you mean to say that you didn't see your master ride past the brougham that you drove?" asked Jane.

"I don't mean to say no sich thing,' said the coachman. "I've no call to tell no lies. But that don't mean that I knowed he was riding here. I met other gen'lmen on the road besides master."

"There are other places in Kent besides Morley, you must remember. And because the coachman saw him on the road hither, he had no right to infer that he was coming to this house; although I tell you candidly I should, because I have known him ride here twice before. But, I had no idea of his being here to-day.

"Pray say nothing more to them Jane, dear. The more you talk, only the more lies you will make them tell. Show yourselves true men, and help us homeward," said Ann.

"We are prisoners like yourselves," said the valet, extending both hands, lifting his eyebrows, and shrugging his shoulders.

"If you were men and our friends, you would break open that door, and give us our release!" cried Jane.

Both the scamps affected to burst the door open, by tugging at the lock, and making a great noise and rattle with the handle.

Jane saw their mockery, and became enraged with it.

She suddenly left her chair, and half frenzied rushed down the room, and with all her strength and impetus given her by the fury with which she came along, she struck with both her hands against an upper panel of the door.

But the door was as unmerciful as the men. It mocked her strength, and returned her nothing but a low hollow sound. Ann came up to her, when off she rushed again at the solid door, but this time, alas! her head and not her hands came against the door.

Her foot tripped in her long dress, and down she goes! her fall on the floor being slightly broken by her brow coming in contact with the door.

It stunned her, while a protuberance, like an egg rose on her fair well-formed brow. Ann and Brummell lifted her from the floor to the couch. The former began to cry out for water to bathe the brow and hands of her swooning friend. But there was not a drop to be had. " Water, water everywhere, but not a drop to drink !" The lock that had made them the prisoners of an infamous man, had locked all the water out of their reach.

" Oh! you cruel wretches, to serve us like this," cried Ann, as she beheld her helpless outstretched friend going cold and pale.

" That's right, be down on us for everythink," said the coachman, while he fanned Jane's face with the long tail of his coat, the valet doing the same, though not quite in the same feverish and excited manner.

Butters held the long strip of his dark green coat with both hands, and he fanned so hard that had the cloth come in contact with Jane's face it would have given her a pretty considerable slap, which we think would have done good service towards awaking her.

The terrified Ann knelt by the side of her friend, abusing the men, bewailing that there was no water, and exclaiming—"

" She'll die ! dear Jane will die !"

" There's nothing at all to be alarmed about except your alarming excitement," said the valet. " Keep quiet, and all will be well."

" I can't keep quiet, and see dear Jane like this. I'm sure she'll die ! Feel how cold her hand is."

" Bless my heart there's some winegar staring us in the face, and none on us saw it ! That's the thing to bring her to ! Here, hand it over, young woman ! Now then, you rub one hand, and I the tother, and you just a gentle leetle on her forehead—there—there, that'll do her more good than your crying, or abusing us," said the coachman, puffing and blowing.

Butters proved himself a capital family doctor, and under his treatment, the patient, to Ann's great relief, gave signs of returning consciousness.

" What do you think of just a leetle stout down her throat, Mr. Brummell, seeing that we have got nothink more suitable ?"

" Has the guv'ner got the port and sherry as well as the champagne ?"

" Yes, worse luck ; the pig would have all the wine."

" Ann, dear, what are these men doing here ?" asked Jane, in a state of semi-unconsciousness, staring wildly about her, and then she moaned and moaned, and her eyelids dropped again.

The coachman poured a little stout into her mouth, while the others continued chafing her hands and brow with the vinegar.

" That's right," said Doctor Butters, " rub in the winegar !"

" If she does get better, Mr. Brummell, pray do find some way for us to get out of this house, before that horrid man comes back !"

" And don't you think I should be glad to get out myself ?"

" And look at me, locked up here without a pipe, which I've left in the stables, don't you think that I would like to get out ?"

" I'm sure if you pleased the both of you together might burst that door !"

" But I don't please to do anything of the sort. This house belongs to a very dear friend of mine—indeed, hem ! I expect to have the felicity of marrying his sister, a lady of immense possessions—"

" That's the time of day, Mr. Brummell !" exclaimed the coachman. " When is it to come off ?"

" Soon, soon, but the day is not appointed. You will know in good time."

" I think she's coming to herself again. Dear Jane, won't you speak to Ann ?"

" My head pains me so," she said.

" I should say that's werry likely, seeing that you've something on it as big as a hegg," said the coachman.

" Do take me home to my dear aunt's !" Jane pleaded.

" My dear, we're all locked in," returned Ann Orwell.

" I thought I had opened the door. I'm sure I did. You go and try it, Ann, there's a good girl !"

" It's fast locked, Jane. You tried to burst it open, but you couldn't."

" I begin to remember," said Jane, dreamily, while she held her hand to her aching brow.

" Yes, dear," said Ann. " And then you tried again, and tripped your foot in your dress, and had a bad fall."

" Oh, my head ! Ask one of those men to be good enough to break the door open, for I shall never be better here."

" Persuade her and yourself to have a good feed, that'll do yer more good than bustin' doors open," said the coachman.

" Besides, as I observed before, this house belongs to a friend of mine—we are here on sufferance as it were—and I shouldn't like him to infer from smashed in panels that a lot of burglars had been here."

" They will do nothing for us, Ann. They are as base as their master ! We must help ourselves, Ann. Let us both force the door."

" My dear girl, you have no strength for it," said Ann.

" And if she had I should object," said Mr. Brummell.

" Can we get out at the window, Ann ?" inquired Jane.

" If you want to commit sooicide you can," returned the coachman before Ann had time to reply.

" You know, my dear, we thought of the window before, but it was too high to be safe," said Ann.

" Then I suppose we must submit to be prisoners, Ann, w th these wretches for our gaolers. I have strength for nothing more. Sit down by me, Ann."

" Not werry purty language ; please to remember that the wretches snatched you from kingdom come, where none on us are fit to go without warning."

Ha ! the door was unlocked, and, to the terror of the girls, in reeled Mr. Duchesney, looking so impudent, his hat awry, a cigarette in his mouth, and his arms laden with champagne bottles.

He was about to go to the sofa, when Ann raised a scream of " Murder ! Police ! Police !

PRETTY JANE

OR, THE

VIPER OF KIDBROOK LANE

EARL ASHFORD BY WILL DISINHERITS LADY MARY.

Police! Police! Murder! You shall not touch her! I'll scream my life out first!"

She at once threw herself between her master and the couch on which Jane was outstretched, and was now struggling with her strength to arise from it.

But the governor, who was now in one of his dare-devil moods, took her by the arm, and sent her spinning across the carpet.

Butters now became very uneasy, and he was very much inclined to make a bolt of it, and looked once or twice at the door.

While he was thus bewildered how in the world he should save his name from the Sessions, where it was already on the books for reference in case of need, and that most embarrassing of questions, "Well, prisoner, what have you to say to the charge?" Ann Orwell still continued to cry and scream for the Police.

Directly Mr. Duchesney held the hand of Pretty Jane, and was about to embrace her for a kiss, the girl went to make her wants for assistance known at the window.

These proceedings the coachman would not allow.

He caught her by the arm, and placed his hand upon her mouth, angrily exclaiming as he did so—

"Aint there enough here to take care on yer without any perlice?"

"I don't want your care! Let me go!" she screamed.

"Hold yer row, or I'll shake the life out on yer!" exclaimed the coachman, well shaking her by the wrist, which he tightly and painfully held.

"Police! Murder! He's threatened my life! Oh! you cruel wretch! Murder!"

"Who's a-murdering on yer! You want to get up a case, that's what you want. You're a hartful dodger, that's what you are! And you looks it too, don't she, Mr. Brummell?"

"Let her alone, you d—d fool!" exclaimed the governor, before his valet could reply, "or take her and yourself out of the room."

"I'll take myself, guv'ner, but I don't have nothing more to do with her. Jeeroosalem! she *is* a jibber! Mrs. Butters can kick over the traces now and then, but a back-hander across her mouth shuts her up; but you lick her into fits."

Jane still lay in a critical state; some few minutes previous to the half-intoxicated governor's entrance, she gave indications of revival, but now, alas! with closed eyes, and her hand across her brow, her countenance betokening mental and physical suffering, her pallid lips moving as if she wanted to speak but could not, she lay seemingly unconscious of what was going on around her.

Ann continued to be moved by the serious appearance of her friend, whom she was now powerless to help. She looked at her, while Mr. Duchesney sat on the couch by her side, with a glass of champagne in his hand, which he had in vain attempted to pass between her closed teeth.

Through the master sitting on the couch by her side, she could not approach Jane, and could do nothing but wring her hands, rave, scream, threaten, and ever and anon shout—

"Police! Murder!"

"Who's a murdering on yer? It aint me, is it?" said Butters. "Why don't yer speak to her, Mr. Brummell? I can't make none on yer out, you leaves all the work for me to do. You see how she's a goin' on—why don't you speak to her?"

"Cui bono?"

"I've heerd o' that stuff afore. Do you take it innardly, or rub it into the bones?"

"I'm not prescribing for the bones."

"You said cure bones, did you not?" said the amazed coachman.

"I did not."

"Then my ears are no good to me," returned Butters.

"They are pretty long ones, too," retorted the valet.

"Werry clever, no doubt. But I wish you would use your cleverness to stop the mouth of that noisy hussey. But you clever people I always find can do nothing useful."

"Let me enlighten you," said the valet, as proud and pompous as a hen with one chick, at the scrap of latin he had picked up from his dissolute master.

"I don't want no ligtningment, except that means a pipe of baccy, which is werry likely, seeing that a fragile thing stands for a little girl. Ugh! Ugh!"

"I said just now when you asked me to stop that girl's tongue—Cui bono?"

"I know you did, which don't seem to have done her much good."

"It was not intended."

"Then what was the good of saying it, I wan to know?"

"You're all at sea, Butters. Cui bono is latin phrase, and means what good."

"Or a pot o' arf-an'-arf, or anythink else tha you wishes to say that it means. Lucky I'v had my dinner, or I should go as mad as tha ere girl. Here goes off for a pipe. But do ye know that the day is a wearing on?"

"Let it! It has been one of the saddest o my life!"

"That's 'cause you've had no dinner," sai the brutalised coachman.

"Why a man must have a stomach like a hors to be able to eat under such discordant circum stances as have occurred to day," said Brum mell, affecting much sorrow and regret. "I ca bear anything but ingratitude."

"Lord! I can bear lots o' that," said th coachman, earnestly; "but a fly in a glass o hold hale, jist as you're on the pint o' drinkin it hoff, is a circumstaunce I can't a-bear; it hir ritates me that much that I'm safe to drink i hoff and have another."

"I don't see the necessity," said the valet.

"You would though if you had a fly stickin in your throat," rejoined the coachman.

"But I shouldn't have been fool enough t have swallowed a fly. I should have taken it ou of the glass before drinking."

"Lord love yer! I can't a-bear to be baulke when I've got the glass to my mouth. If a he lephant was to drop in I should swallow him, couldn't be baulked of my drink to get hin out. When once the glass is to my lips the hal must go down if a black-beetle went down wit it."

"It would soon come up again with me," ob served the valet, shrugging his shoulders, an making a wry face, as if he had swallowed som nauseous thing that his stomach loathed.

While this conversation had been going on the governor had abruptly left the apartment taking care, as before, to lock the door behin him. As soon as he had left the couch on whic Jane lay, Ann Orwell at once returned to he charge, and continued to bathe with vinegar he hands and temples.

She moved, and opened her eyes, and An took heart, and continued her healing process which eventually restored Jane to consciousnes and to her painful situation.

"Master's a cutting about like a parched pe in a frying-pan," said the coachman, with a grin

"I have not the smallest idea what he is u to," said Mr. Brummell.

The two men spoke low and confidentially careful that the girls should not hear, which the were not at all desirous of doing.

"I know this," said the valet in the goggle eyed coachman's blue-looking ear, "that he ha completely spoilt the little game—"

"And got us into a serous amount of troubl I should say," added the coachman, puffing ou his cheeks, which he had distended with air till they had the appearance of two small bal loons, and which to him expressed fear, but t those who saw him would have thought he wa making up a comic face for the entertainmen of little folks at a Christmas party.

"It'll be a case for the Sessions, don't yo think, Mr. Brummell?"

" No doubt of it. And he won't have the girl after all."

" Sarve him right. And I should like to know what we've got by it ?"

" Nothing but abuse," replied the valet. " He has promised something handsome if it comes off right."

" Which it won't, I'm blest if it will. But the girls have no occasion to indict us. We're only servants in the case."

" That's true, Butters ; but the law won't hold us harmless if we aid and abet our masters in anything unlawful."

" Then we're living under werry fine laws, that we are !" he exclaimed, with political zeal. " And we've got a Liberal Government, too ! Why don't servants kick up a row about sich onjustice ? Don't you think so, Mr. Brummell ? Why don't you agitate the question ? You'd get into Parliament if you did.":

The valet smiled, and returned for answer to the coachman's flattering opinions of his transcendant oratorical abilities—

" Just now I fear that we shall have more difficulty of keeping out of the hands of the police—"

" Eh ? What's that, Mr. Brummell ?" he asked, while alarm spread over his countenance.

" This is sure to be a police case—"

" I seed it from the first, and was a hass for having anything to do with it ! '

" There need have been no trouble in the matter, but the guv'ner has been so selfish—"

The coachman bent his fist, and said—

" Shouldn't I like a couple of rounds with him —I'll bet a penny he wouldn't want a third."

" Not if you came out upon him in the sledge-hammer fashion that you did upon me," said the valet.

" Don't remember that, there's a good feller," said the coachman, growing very affectionate towards the valet, as he thought that his being the superior man intellectually, he would be able to find some way out of this case with the girls supposing that it unhappily came to a trial.

" Oh, there was nothing in that; you proved yourself the better man, that's all. You are welcome to your laurels, my boy, I shall make no endeavour to take them from you."

" 'Twas but a friendly set-to—I mean there was no malice in it, was there Mr. Brummell ?"

" Oh, dear no ; we were both of us tight—"

" So we was—that's quite right."

" Then I don't think we should have fought at all only we were fools enough to knock each other about just to please the guv'ner."

" I forget now how it happened. But let bygones be bygones. We are fellow-servants, and must pull together, then we shall be strong. If this case comes off, why what one says the other must swear to."

" There's two of them against us—"

" That's werry orkard," said the coachman, scratching his head. " But then there's three on us," he added, thinking that he had stumbled over a very bright idea, but the hope of it was soon dispelled by his more sagacious companion, who saw the bearings of most things, and could unravel most complications.

" But the difference is this—our accusers will be in the witness-box, while we shall be at the bar."

Bar ! the very mention of it made the coachman inwardly groan. It carried his retentive memory back to certain transactions for which he was placed at the bar, and how his knees trembled under him as the eye of the judge fell on him when he sentenced him, and when the gaoler led him off to the cells below until Her Majesty's van came up to take him to the due performance of his hard labour.

" Were you ever brought up to a bar, Mr. Brummell ?"

" Do you mean the bars where a fellow is served with grogs and cigars by pretty girls ?"

The coachman shook his thick head, and replied in a very lachrymose style—

" Something werry different I do assure you, Mr. Brummell. No grogs and pretty girls at the bars I mean—more t'other."

" I know where you are now. No, thankee, I have always kept my little hands from picking and stealing."

" And so have I," said the coachman. " But I was once accused by a werry malicious man who wanted to do me a hinjury, and through a deal of false swearing amongst the perlice, they conwicted me. But the judge and jury knew I was hinnocent—"

" Of course they did," said Brummell, laughing to himself. " I have heard of such cases before where the innocent have been made to suffer through the false swearing of the police."

" Oh, the cormorants !" cried the coachman, fully believing that he had his fellow-servant's sympathy in the gull that he was putting on him, and he would have been very much surprised to hear that the valet's real opinion was that when he was at the bar he was the right man in the right place. In the fond belief that he was impressing the valet that he was an injured man, he went on with his tale, which he would have kept dark about had he not thought that this case concerning Jane and Ann would be sure to bring the other to light, when the magistrate or judge went into the question of character.

" My counsel asked the jury to cast their eyes on me, and then say if I was guilty or not ?"

" Your personal appearance certainly ought to have helped you," said the valet, his inward laughter very much increased with the bit of fun he was poking at the coachman, while the latter made sure that he was taking in the valet.

" The jury did look at me," he said, " but it didn't do me a bit of good."

" I am surprised !" exclaimed Brummell, affecting sincerity.

" And so was everybody else, the judge and all. My counsel stared as much as I did when they found me guilty, but, as he said, it's all over with the hinnocent when the perlice are agen 'em."

" What was the case ?" asked the valet.

" You shall just hear. But do have something to eat and drink first, you will find yourself so much the better for it. Come, here's some champagne, and I mean to have some whether the guv'ner likes it or not. Jine me in a bumper to the ladies, and then take your seat behind a knife and fork and walk into the affections of that ere ham and chicken, you will find 'em werry nice."

" In the matter of eating and drinking on this unhappy occasion, Mr. Butters, you have proved yourself a very wise man, while I have played the fool. A man who quarrels with his bread *is* a fool! Out of compassion to these girls who are sorrowing over imaginary griefs—crying before they are hurt, I mean—"

"They all on 'em do that," interrupted the coachman. "And turn on the briny for nothink but their own hartfulness, and to make people believe that they are hinjured creeturs."

"Out with the champagne!" gaily cried the valet. "I'll be a fool no longer! I'll eat, drink, and be merry! I have done all I could do for those two girls, and they've turned their backs on me."

"And so they have on me!" cried Butters. "I brought 'em down the road, too, in the most careful and respectful manner; never even guv 'em a sly wink or said an onproper word, which servants are liable to do one with another, especially when they are out for a holiday."

"Let 'em go hang! Out with the champagne, Butters, while I cut into this veal and ham pie, which I am particularly fond of."

"I can't abear weal," said the coachman.

"You needn't eat it. But pour out the wine, for my appetite has grown a little stale through long fasting, and wants a sharpener."

"Glad to see you more an' yourself agen," said Butters, handing his friend a bumper of the creamy stuff, and then doing a like good turn for himself. "I'll jine you in a glass or two. My werry best respiks to you, Mr. Brummell, and may the next good turn you do your fellow creeturs meet with more favour and more gratitude!" With this sentiment he gulped down the wine, and then complained that it was a pity such nice stuff should be drank out of such tiny glasses.

"The haristocracy don't know how to drink wine. They plays with it. They ort to call for a pot of cham, and wolf it, then they'd better know the taste on it. But now it's nothing but powering on it out—making two bites of a cherry, as I used to say when I was a boy."

"I don't care a fig how I drink it, whether out of a glass or tankard, so long as I get plenty of it, and a jovial companion to join me in drinking it."

"A werry hexcellent sentiment," cried Butters. "A werry old friend of mine, one Ned Trollop, used to sing a werry purty song about ' My friend and a bottle to guv him.' "

"I know it well, and a fine old song it is. But come, let us have the facts of the case in which a prejudiced jury, false-swearing policemen, and an unjust judge found you guilty, when you were as innocent as an unborn babe. Not of course, if you have any delicacy about it."

"Bless your heart, I haven't any delicacy, nor never had. Don't accuse me wrongfully."

"Fire away, or maybe our mad guv'nor will return and prevent your telling it."

"It's told in a werry few words," said the coachman, who felt as proud as if he were about to relate something that any one might be proud of. "It was all about a pair of top-boots."

"Well, what about them?"

"I was under stableman at the time with Colonel Finchberry, and me and the head stableman could never hit it, and that again was all through jealousy. He saw, and so did all the servants, that the colonel—who was a good old soul, and carried his heart in the right place—

was werry partial to me, and went out on his way to speak to me once or twice. The hupper stableman didn't seem to like it—"

"Began to think that one day he might get the sack, and you be popped into his place."

"That's jist the ticket! That's where the shoe pinched! You're a man of hunderstanding, you are, Mr. Brummell, and seizes the truth before a feller can say Jack Robinson! Well, we went on like two Cheshire cats for a little while, he always finding fault with me, and me not above telling him he was a liar, until at last we came to blows, and gave each other a pair of black eyes. The whole thing was then bound to come before the colonel, and he said as we couldn't agree, we'd best part."

"Don't see how he could say anything else, except becoming a partisan."

"Of course not. The head stableman told sich hinfernal lies on me to set the colonel agen me, but it was no go, the master saw through it all, as quickly as you did. However, I gave a fortnight's notice, for I didn't want his place—do as you would be done by, as Shikspur says—"

"An excellent aphorism, but it is to be found in the New Testament, and not in Shakspere."

"I can't read either, so I don't know which is which."

"You're a fine subject for the New School Board."

"A better, though, for board and lodging," said the coachman, and whether he meant his rejoinder for a joke or not we cannot tell, only that he laughed immoderately after he had spoken, so it may be supposed that he was tickled by fun, which his companion, if he saw, failed to appreciate.

Mr. Brummell was just now too well engaged either for talking or laughing, and he trotted the coachman into the relation of his story, on purpose that he might eat his repast in as much quietness as possible.

But the valet begs it to be understood, that when he stipulated for the coachman's narrative he had not the remotest idea that he would attempt to be funny, or he would have thought of some other way of getting a dinner in quiet, or have gone without if necessary.

But it was not the coachman's habit to emulate Joe Miller, which so many dining bores do, who have no more capacity for wit or humour than the illiterate coachman.

Mr. Brummell cut short his companion's laughter by inviting him to go on.

"I have heard nothing as yet about the top-boots?" he said, by way of a hint to him not to digress from the narrative of his wrongs.

"The top-boots come in at the last."

"Boots—last! Does the fellow mean that for another joke?"

The valet dropped his knife and fork, which for the past quarter of an hour he had been making excellent use of, and looked Butters sternly in the face. He was greatly relieved—the coachman had not the capacity to see that he had innocently made more than an average joke—but it was evident that he did not see it for he neither laughed nor paused, and the valet was not fool enough to encourage him in the nuisance of punning now so prevalent at social gatherings amongst gentlemen whose chief ambition is to be accounted smart nice men with silly women, who are the great encouragers of fripperies fopperies and unmanliness amongst men.

"All the time my fortnight's notice was going on, we didn't speak more than we could help, you might be sure. I felt werry deep—"

"Do you mean cunning!"

"Not I. I mean sorrowful like at having to leave the colonel's, for there was good wages and good Tommy—two things I'm werry fond on, and which you don't get everywhere. Well, the fortnight slipped by, and I had my wages and hooked it, and the colonel there and then wrote me a character, to take to a hinfluential friend of his'n."

"But what about the top-boots?" asked the valet, who had exhausted his appetite, and had grown weary of the coachman's discursive narrative.

"Well, three days arter I left, the hupper stableman missed a pair of top-boots, and took out a search-warrant at my lodgings. A werry imperent thing to do, don't you think so, Mr. Brummell?"

"Not at all pleasant to be suspected, certainly not. But an honest man, one who hadn't got the boots—"

"But I had."

"Ah, in that case, it would be inconvenient, of course."

"Werry, and so I found it."

"But how came you by the boots?" asked the valet, in surprise.

"There's the mystery! That's what I want to know!"

"It is impossible for me to tell you," said the smiling valet, who certainly looked jollier after his champagne dinner.

"When the officer came to search the lodgings I positively opened the door to him with the boots on! and a natty fit they was too! and I was just goin' arter a situation in 'em, but instead of that the hofficer marches me off to Marlborough Street!"

"But how did he know but that the boots were your own?"

"Because I hup like a honest man and told him."

"What before you knew his business?" asked the valet.

"How could that be, Mr. Brummell? Why no. He said to me, said he, young man, I've called about a pair o' top-boots. Then I said you've made a mistake this time, for I'm not a boot-maker, nor nobody that lives in the house is."

"Well?" said the valet, pouring out a glass of champagne, for he found it necessary to support himself under the infliction of the coachman's long story about nothing.

"I'll wet my whistle with you afore I goes on," he said, taking the bottle in hand, and replenishing his glass.

This the valet regretted to see, for it alarmed him that the coachman was going to spin a three volume novel without a heroine, and a pair of top-boots for the heroes.

Ann Orwell, supporting Jane round her waist, and taking her hand, led her to the window, and threw it up for air.

The two men had their eyes on their proceedings, and when the window was raised the valet,

believing it to be a case of jumping out, rushed forward, exclaiming—

"For Heaven's sake, don't!"

"It'll be a case of smash if you do!" cried the coachman, who did not move from his seat near the champagne.

The girls disdained to take any notice of the valet, who stood close by them, and when Ann placed a chair for her injured friend, Mr. Brummell was satisfied that their intentions were not suicidal, and he returned to the coachman, to hear the remainder of the novel, from which he had no escape, the door of the room having been locked.

"Well, what did the judge say in summing up?" inquired the valet, hoping by this question to have jumped over a few chapters of this wearisome novel.

But the coachman was not to be done. He would not have his work of art spoilt, nor shorn of one embellishment, through the valet's impatience. Certainly not. He had invited him to the narrative, and he should hear every word of it.

"Well," he continued, "I hup and told him that there was no boot—"

"Come, I say, you had got a long way past that!" cried the valet, sorely puzzled to find a way to exorcise the dreary spirit he had himself created.

"It was not much beyond I know," persisted the coachman. "But perhaps, Mr. Brummell, you don't want to hear it at all?"

"Oh, but indeed I do, though. It is a deeply interesting story, only you don't get on fast enough with it. I want to get to the end of it, which is always more interesting even than the beginning of all stories."

"Where was I then?"

"Let me see," said the valet, musingly, but as he had not been paying much attention to it, he unfortunately could not say where the narrator had left off.

"Oh, let us begin again!" challenged the coachman.

This dreadful challenge awakened the valet's memory, and he remembered now where the coachman had left off in his narrative, and he straightway gave him the cue.

"Aye to be sure, that's jist where I was. Well, then, said the hofficer to me, said he, where did you get them boots from that you've got on?

"That's just what I want to know, said I.

"Then come along with me, said he, and I think I shall be able to 'lighten you. Now mind, Mr. Brummell, I'm giving you word for word,"

"I know you are;" and then to himself he added, "and I wish you weren't."

"I said what do you mean about going with you?

"I'll take you to the man who owns these boots, said he.

"I said, will yer? Then you'll be cleverer than me.

"Then he hup and said, now look here, young man, I'm a hofficer, and don't try it on with me, for it won't do.

"Didn't my fingers itch, didn't my muscles boil over like, to knock him down?"

"Yes. Well?" asked Brummel.

"Of course there was no resisting a hofficer,

so I pulled myself together, boots and all, and went straight away, like a deeply hinjured man as I was, my only hope being that I should yet have justice done me."

" And so you had."

"No I hadn't, for I was conwicted!"

" I mean that you were tried."

" And found wanting."

Ann Orwell whispered Jane, if she would like a little wine, she looked so weak and deathly pale.

" I would sooner die first, than touch their wine," replied the heroic girl, loud euough for their tormentors to here.

" Cut your story short, Butters, for we must try and square it with these women, or we shall soon be at the bar again, for I see Jane means to ride rusty."

" There's a storm there, and no mistake, for which we have to thank our blessed master," said the coachman.

" He has indeed played the fool ! He'll never get me in an affair of this kind with him again, if I can only pull through out of this."

" It's a werry serous affair," said the coachman, " and drink as I will I can't get jolly over it."

" Clear your story out of the way, and then we'll see what's to be done with the girls."

" Burn the story ! let that stand over till we can get a quiet pipe together in the servants' hall. Don't let us lose more time about an old pair of boots. Directly, you know, we shall have our wagabond master popping in on us, and then there'll be the devil to pay."

" I cannot imagine what's become of him."

" Gone out for more champagne," suggested the coachman.

" Not likely when there was a lot here," said the valet.

" Didn't think of that ; but there ain't a lot here now, is there, Mr. Brummell ?"

" Fill the glasses, and we'll make it less !" cried the valet. " It's no good thinking about the governor. Reeled into the village, perhaps, and picked up with another girl."

" Hardly likely."

" Oh, he's wild enough for anything." replied the valet. " He is sure to come to grief."

" He'll be hung, that's what he will, mark my words."

" And a jolly good job. I am tired of his service. He is a selfish man, without the smallest discretion."

" That's what I said awhile ago. And then you seemed to stick up for him."

" I just said that he was not wholly bad, and that he paid well. But while we are his servants we are liable to be brought into very dangerous scrapes."

" And we have werry much to consider that, as respectable men," said Butters, with much gravity. " How was yer a-thinking to square it with the girls ?"

" Can't at all see my way clear."

" Women, you know, is weak, and a little blarney goes a long way with 'em."

" I know all that, my friend," said the valet, thoughtfully. " But don't forget that it was blarney brought them here, and that our fool of a master opened their eyes to it. So all the blarney in the world won't do with them again

—they are thoroughly on their guard not to be caught with soft-sawder again."

" I see. Once bit twice shy. What d'ye say to a bold step ?"

" A what ?"

" A bold step."

" I don't care how bold it may be, so long as it is safe. What is it ?"

" Bust the door, and let 'em out !" replied the coachman, uplifting his muscular arm, and bending his fist.

" My thoughts have been turned in that direction. In that case we should have to get some security from the girls that if we gave them their freedom they would not prosecute," said Brummell.

" They might go agen master if that was any satisfaction to 'em."

" They couldn't do anything of the kind. You don't know the law, Brummell."

" Law ! there's plenty of that, but werry little justice. Laws are now made to punish the hinnocent, and reward the guilty."

" In too many instances, it is so. Laws to be valuable should be simple ; the people they are framed for should be able to understand them. There is no justice in expecting obedience to a thing that is not understood."

" That hobserwation o' yourn, brings me right round to the top-boots agen."

" Then I'm very sorry that I made it," said the valet to himself.

" It was this ere way. I found a pair of top-boots one day in my trunk, and I was werry much obliged to somebody for putting 'em there, for I werry much wanted 'em. Now had I known the law, why of course I should have obeyed it, and taken the boots to the police station, and have said—here, these ere boots don't belong to me."

" You've grown wiser now."

" By Jove, yes ! but picking oakum for three months, and never a pipe, ain't a werry genteel school to pick up wisdom at, and it's paying rayther dear for it."

" That I did, as you'll believe a hinnocent man," he added.

" To whom did the boots belong ?" inquired the valet, determined now to have it all out, for if he postponed it to another time, he would, he knew, have to hear it all over again, which was an infliction not to be endured.

" Why the boots belonged to the werry willan who got me out of my sityation with Colonel Finchberry ! At least he swore they was his'n. Well, yer honour, I said to the judge, if they is his'n, how came they in my box ?

" Then the judge he says, that will be the question for the jury to decide.

" Well, then I goes in a buster to the jury, and although I explains everythink to my *own* satisfaction, I couldn't beat it into the thick heads of the judge and jury."

" What was your explanation ?"

" That the dirty fellow must have put the boots in my box before I left the colonel's !"

" Well ?"

" Why then he hup and swore that I had got no box, and called a pal of his'n to prove it."

" But why didn't you call witnesses to prove that you had ?"

" You see I didn't know that the case would

take that ere turn, or I should have said a bundle instead of a box, which it was."

"Then you hadn't got a box?"

"No, but I had a bundle, which is the same
thing to me or you, but the pig-headed jury
wouldn't have it. But the jury was agen me
throughout—there were some of the vilyan's
friends on it—and whether I had called a box a
bundle, or a bundle a box, it would have been
all the same, they was determined to conwict,
and conwict they did."

"They found you guilty then of stealing the
boots?"

"That they did—right bang out in the open
court, without any thought for my feelings,
which was more tenderer then than now."

"The jury always do that."

"More shame for 'em then. I thought that
an action would lie for taking away a feller's
character. Well, don't yer think I was a werry
ill-used man?"

"There cannot be two opinions about it, my
friend," said the valet, at the same time choking with constrained laughter, more especially
at the dreadful bowl out about the box, and his
ludicrous try-on that the prosecutor would put
a pair of top-boots in a bundle, and that the
prisoner should describe that bundle as a box !
and expect a jury to be satisfied of his innocence !

"You see they had me two ways—one for
stealing the boots from the prosecutor, who ort
to have been the pris'ner; and if they couldn't
find me guilty of that, the judge told me they
would have nabbed me for having property in
my possession that didn't belong to me ! D—d
fine laws, ain't they?"

Before Mr. Brummell had time to answer the
rough, ignorant question of his fellow-servant,
Ann screamed out—

"Why there he is again !"

"Oh, my dear, whatever shall we do?" exclaimed the enfeebled Jane, clasping her hands,
and withdrawing from the window.

The two men looked from another window,
and were not long in discovering Mr. Duchesney groping about the lawn, and in and out the
trees, his hands resting on his knees, and his
head bent low towards the ground, indicating
that he was evidently in search of something.

"What's hup, I wonder?" said Butters, his
curious eye following the proceedings of his
master below.

"I can't at all make his little game out," said
the valet, who watched his movements as intently as did the coachman. "He seems to
have cooled upon the girls, or he wouldn't have
remained away from them all this time."

"He's lost something."

"I hope it is his temper," said the valet.

"His pocket-book or purse more like," said
the coachman.

"I should say that it was something of more
value to him than his temper, or he wouldn't
be at such pains to find it."

They missed him amongst the trees for a few
moments, when he again came into their view,
not this time bent to the ground, but with head
erect, and a laughing countenance, carrying in
his hand what seemed to be a case of jewelry.

He came along with a dancing step towards
the front entrance of the house, the door of which
he had been thoughtful enough to leave open
for his re-admission when he returned from his
search after a blue morocco case of jewels that
he bought to dazzle Jane's eyes with, and, like
a villain as he was, to tempt her to her ruin.

But whatever his experience of women might
hitherto have been, he found this poor servant-
girl possessed a lofty virtue, and lion-hearted
enough to protect it from such loathsome vipers
as the master of Evesham House.

Pretty Jane, in common with her sex, had a
weakness for jewelry, but not so weak as to bar-
ter her innocence for it with a fellow whom she
never regarded, but now loathed.

She ever regretted taking service at Evesham
House. With the exception of Mrs. Sterne,
and poor Ann Orwell, she had a very great contempt for all its inmates! She resolved with
Ann to return to that place no more, save and
except for their boxes, and so say farewell to
good Mrs. Sterne.

These matters they had resolved upon while
seated in whispering conversation at the window
that overlooked the grounds surrounding Morley Cottage, and during the time that the scoundrels Butters and Brummell had been dining and
seasoning it with much small talk.

Rushing steps were heard along the passages,
and rushing steps came up the stairs two at a
time, and the door of the room in which were
the servants was swiftly unlocked, and Mr. Duchesney, a shade steadier than when he left, was
again one of the party, but, for different reasons,
the entrance of a monster would have been quite
as agreeable.

His coming was anticipated, but anticipated
with dread. The women were pallid with fear,
though the heroic Jane, after her first outburst
when she discovered him in the grounds, for
the sake of her companion, tried all she could
to conceal it.

"We have only to be firm, Ann, and the cowards will fly before us."

"But I haven't got a bit of firmness in me,
Jane, and that's the truth," she said.

"Then I must find enough for both of us,"
said the valorous Jane. "Only my poor head
aches so !"

"I'm sure it must, my dear. It was such a
fall you had right against the door," said Ann,
sympathetically.

"This was my favourite dress," said Jane,
"but I shall never like it again, for serving me
such a trick. Had it not tripped me up we
should have been free by this !" she added, with
considerable spirit.

"You never could have broke that door, dear
Jane."

"I seemed to myself as if I could have moved
mountains ! I fear I couldn't get up such courage again."

"I'm sure you couldn't, Jane, so we'd best be
still, and see what they mean to do."

"I suppose, my dear, we can do no other.
But if either of them touch me, they shall find
that I have some courage left. I had a knife—
where is it?"

"When you fell, the knife dropped from your
hand, and Brummell picked it up."

"My dear Ann, you should have prevented
that."

"You mustn't depend upon me for anything,

Jane. In trouble, I'm the weakest woman as ever was."

"Oh, I'm so vexed about the knife!" whispered Jane. "I had but little else to depend upon in case of need. Now what to do I know not. Is that window too high to escape from, do you think?"

"I shouldn't like to try," said the timid Ann Orwell.

"My dear, we must try something."

"I don't know what then, I'm sure. Don't I wish we hadn't come!"

"Wishes won't help us out of our perils," retorted Jane. "We should have been safe at home long ago, and these fellows in the hands of the police, could wishing have done it. We are hunted by wild beasts, Ann, and we must be women not children."

"Once for all, my dear Jane, you must expect no help from me. I feel myself quite a burden to you, that I do!"

"Oh, dear no. You have been quite a dear good friend to me. I should have had no courage at all but for you. I should have died no doubt."

"No, no, I think you would have done many things to have gained your escape had you been alone, and your bravery not been baulked every now and then by a poor timid woman like I am."

"Do not underrate yourself, Ann. The very presence of a friend to one in trouble is a great help. I should have died outright, under the circumstances, I do believe, had you not been with me."

"It wasn't then for what help I have been to you," said Ann, who was in that distracted condition of mind, which the inspiration of fear always more or less occasions, that she cared but little what became of herself.

"When the worst comes to the worst—"

"Which will be pretty soon now," interrupted Ann.

"Let it," cried Jane, whose brave sentiments, as we have said before, were partly uttered to reassure her friend, who was terribly sinking in despair.

"I hate suspense," she continued. "If anything dreadful is to happen, the sooner the better say I. Oh, what would I give if I could see my dear William coming in at that door! He would throttle the lot of them, while we poor things sit trembling here! But oh! vain wish. He is not here—"

"But we are, worse luck," added Ann.

"And haven't we wit enough to get out?" asked Jane, rather cheerily, considering the dark circumstances of their position, and the grave results that might flow out of it.

"I don't see no way out of it," said the despairing Ann. "Nor I don't think you do, Jane, or you'd have been off before now."

"That I certainly would. But I have made an effort to get away, although it failed. And I'll make others yet, believe me, dear Ann. They won't have it all their own way with me, I can tell them, the scamps! Though but a girl, I'll strike a blow in our defence, though my death followed it!"

"If I had only got your bravery, Jane, we needn't a bit fear. But it's no good talking, I haven't a mite of pluck."

"When the worst comes to the worst, you won't be found wanting more than me."

Jane's companion still persisted that she felt powerless to do anything now, or in any other emergency that might arise.

What a contrast was Ann to Jane! The spirit of the latter quite rose to the occasion. For so young a thing, under such exceptional circumstances, the height of courage to which she rose, both in sentiment and action, was truly wonderful!

Jane seemed completely a metamorphosed being. Her very language gathered strength and fullness out of the trying position these three fiends placed her in!

She more awed than encouraged her companion, who sat shivering by her side. She was weak and in pain too from the blow on her brow, which was still much swollen, and discoloured.

But it is ever so, the best souls are the heroic ones!

Ann Orwell was of far commoner nature than Jane. She would have yielded long ago to the circumstances had she not have been sustained by the virtue and heroism of her companion.

How different the character of Jane! In defence of her virtue, which was dearer to her than her life, which was but the casket to hold the jewel, she would have grappled with the deadliest circumstances, and either died or conquered them!

It was *she* that was feared by her captors! There was determination in her speech, and oh! such defiance in her eye, that the thief of a coachman might well quail under it!

"Were we alone with that window," she said to Ann, "do you know I think we might find a way to escape from it."

"Perhaps we might, if we could find a stout rope."

"If we couldn't find a rope, we'd cut and contrive something that should answer the purpose of one."

The girls carried on this conversation in the lowest possible key as they sat close beside each other, their backs facing the valet and coachman, and their faces the garden grounds.

"Now look out for squalls," said Lutters to Brummell, as they began to ship-shape the table in anticipation of the master's coming, directly they saw him making his quick way towards the house.

"The first growl will be that we have thought proper to dine without him," said the valet, smoothing out the cloth, and wiping the champagne glasses.

"He be blowed!" cried Butters. "Does he think servants have got no stomachs? I know I have, and he want wait for no masters neither, but will have grub if grub's about. And I don't blame him neither."

"Hush!" cried the valet, when he heard the lock of the door turned, simultaneously with which Duchesney entered. He was all smiles. He drew forth from the jewel case a pair of gold bracelets, and holding them up in each hand, he approached the frowning Jane with them, saying—"Here's a thing, and a thing, and a very pretty thing, and who shall the owner of this be?"

As he neared Jane, a terrible thought seized her!

PRETTY JANE

OR, THE

VIPER OF KIDBROOK LANE

SHE WAVED HER HANDKERCHIEF, BADE HIM FAREWELL, BUT THERE WAS LITTLE REGRET
IN THE TONES.

Before Duchesney, dangling the bracelets between his fingers, had reached Jane's chair, she had risen from it, and stood with a frenzy rolling in her eye that could not but awe every one that looked upon it.

The coachman and the valet stood together at the lower end of the room, which was a very noble one for a country house, and contained three windows, and a fireplace at each end.

"I'm werry glad that she ain't got no knife in her hand," whispered the coachman to the valet. "She'd stab him if she had."

"Her deadly eye shows that," Brummell whispered back.

"He is playing a fool's game I think," said Butters, shaking his head. "And he'll get us into a rare peck o' trouble, mark my word."

"No doubt of it," returned the valet. "He hasn't the sense to see that Jane is a good girl, and that all his gold and silver can never make a bad one of her."

"I've seen that all along, my friend," said the coachman. "She ain't a girl to be trifled with loike the t'other."

"Ann is but common stuff compared to Jane, who is a girl of good breed, and capable with education of being made a splendid woman of. Any man might be proud to call that girl his wife."

"She's swopped her affections with a sailor,

No. 13.

I heerd her say, when the rumpus in the hall took plaec."

" Happy sailor, that's all I can say. If Jane had some tin I should try and cut that sailor chap out, and be on to her myself for a wife."

Butters made up a face as if he had a nauseous physic in his mouth.

" What's the matter with you ?" interrogated the valet.

" No more wives for me."

" I didn't say you, but me," said the valet.

" Right you are. Only when you talked about a wife—"

" But not for you."

" I know that, don't I keep on telling yer," said the coachman. " No more wives for me arter I've decently interred Mrs. Butters. This earth would be werry much like a paradise without that woman."

During this little cobble-whobble between the men-servants, Duchesney had not moved a step nearer towards Jane. The girls took fresh heart. He had shown hesitation, and Jane recognised that a little fear had bespread his countenance. She took the arm of her friend, and made her way toward the open door, avoiding her master as much as possible. She had no eyes for him nor the bracelets, which the fool endeavoured to tempt her with.

The bracelets were very handsome and expensive, the goldsmith having fashioned them into the representation of serpents, with precious sapphires for their glistening eyes.

Jane had perceived that the room-door was slightly opened, and her hope and intention was that directly she had got a little way from the man who promised to intercept her progress, she would have taken to her heels, and make a bolt of it.

But her hope and intentions were to be frustrated. Her master accosted her, and stopped her further progress.

He took her by the arm, while he said, holding to her eyes the bracelets—

" For you, my love, these are to adorn your wrists. Receive them not with a frown."

That touch of his had the most maddening influence on the girl.

He was the most indecorous of lovers, and the wildest of men.

He either had no conception of character, or totally disregarded it.

He had no dread of consequences, nor fear of punishment.

As with his wife, so with him, the hereafter was a myth, and the love or fear of God was never with him.

He went through life as if the " world was made alone for him to revel in."

He was equally without heart as without conscience.

He was comparativey young, and decidedly handsome, and had been well educated, but he was a most unmanly man, and capable of all the social vices that crowd and disfigure the nineteenth century.

For money he had married a woman that other men would have loathed, and he still was contemptible enough to live under the same roof with a wife whom it was impossible to believe but that he knew she was still carrying on an adulterous intercourse with her own ser-

vant ! The familiarity between Joshua Woodward and his mistress he must have both seen and heard of.

His spirit was of the lowest type, while honour he had none.

It is not often to be found that two such dark and wicked people come together in marriage—if we do not profane that holy state by calling such an union as theirs by that name which none but lovers should engage in.

Was it to serve the ends of some justice for their wickedness that circumstances had conspired to bring them together, that they might embitter their days, and, in the end, like the Kilkenny cats, tear themselves to pieces !

Their careers were very much alike in kind and degree, with the exception of murder. Yet in the eye of Heaven Duchesney would also be adjudged a murderer—for had he not begotten children, and then forsaken them and their mothers to an outcast condition, and the chill penury of the world ?

Butters had shown himself, in our opinion, a man with more sagacity than the more learned Brummell, at all events as far as his master was concerned, for when he protected the child found on the door-step, he was actuated by a fit of remorse, and that for aught he knew the friendless girl might have been his own daughter.

If he could bring her down to his level—and in too many instances he had succeeded—no woman was safe from his corrupting influences.

It was a pitiful sight to see three men using their best arts and wits to destroy an unoffending innocent girl. But her heroic nature rode the storm, and their cunning devices to encompass her were bravely defied.

Life without virtue to Pretty Jane would be unendurable, and she was thoroughly prepared to lay it down rather than succumb to the temptations of the villain who now held her hand.

Jane remembered the manner in which Lady Mary seized the scoundrel by the throat when he in like manner held her in the servants' hall, and to free her hand from his, and do as her ladyship had taught her to do, was but the work of a moment.

No one expected what was to come, and certainly no one could imagine that such dexterity and strength was possible in so young a girl as Jane.

As quick as the lightning that shot from her eyes, she twisted her wrist from his grasp, and with both hands she tightly held him by his long cravat.

He flung the bracelets to the ground, in order to release his hands to protect himself from strangulation.

Poor Ann turned pale as death, and stood in remarkable contrast to the burning red that suffused the whole of Jane's face and brow.

Not being near so tall as Lady Mary, she had not that command over the throat of her adversary.

Ann began to scream, but not to help her companion.

While Jane was fearless, she was wholly paralysed with fear.

She was deficient in tact and energy, and had no courage wherewith to oppose existing circumstances. She was a good enough girl in her way, but if evil was to befall her—well—it must—she had no soul or energy to oppose against it.

She flew screaming down the room towards the open door, which seemed just then to have more attractions for her than assisting her friend, to whom help just then would have been so grateful!

Not that she cared less for Jane's safety, but that she cared more for her own.

Ann, in her silly fears, apprehended murder, and would neither stop to see it nor prevent it. Self-preservation was her law and guide just now, and she followed it.

She flattered herself that if she could get out of the house she could then raise an alarm, and send in a lot of people to Jane's rescue.

But she never considered that while that was being done her friend's life might be sacrificed, or that in the height of her frenzy, she might take the life of another.

She would do everything she could for Jane but run risks of personal maltreatment.

Ann's intentions were as sincere and honest as the day, but like a good many other young men and women, she was pigeon-hearted.

True friendship requires actions. Ann had none to offer except to scream for others to endanger themselves for her friend.

False friends, like insects in a summer's day,
  Bask in the sunshine, but avoid the shower,
Uncertain visitants, they flee away,
  E'en when misfortune's cloud begins to
    lower.

Into life's bitter cup true friendship drops
  Balsamic sweets to overpower the gall—
True friends, like ivy and the wall it props,
  Both stand together, or together fall!

Ann was not capable of such a friendship as the poet describes. She didn't care about falling with Jane. True, they had not long known each other, and friendship is a thing of slow growth.

But there was no depth in poor Ann's nature, and if she had known Jane, or any other person, for a thousand years, she would have been incapable of sacrificing or running into danger for the protection of her friend.

With her bonnet hanging behind her, as we have before seen, while the valorous Jane held her master by the throat, she bounded down the room, making the windows and floor shake with her not very light step, and filling the air with screams of an alarming character.

While the valet ran to the assistance of his master, whose life he saw was in peril from the tight grasp of the infuriated girl, the coachman sprang forward, and stopped Ann's progress by seizing her in his gorilla-like grasp, and placing his hand upon her mouth to stop her terrible screaming.

"No good comes o' noise, don't I tell yer," he said, and he spoke loudly, while there was a great deal of anger conveyed in his tones.

"Oh, do let me go and get a policeman!" she cried, endeavouring to emancipate herself from the man's hold.

"What do yer want to give yerself up for? Have yer committed a murder?"

"Let me go, you wretch! Police! Police!" she continued to cry.

Butters hated the very name of the police, and their presence was a terror to him.

"You may as well call for a shower of frogs as for the perlice! There are no perlice here! What are they wagabonds wanted here for d'ye think? to look arter the birds? For them is all the people that I see here."

But the terrified girl would call upon the guardians of the public peace, and the coachman as far as he could prevented her by applying his hand to her mouth.

"Shout out cold rabbit pie if yer want the perlice," he replied to her vociferous calling, "and if they don't come then you may be sure there are none there."

"Will you let me go?"

"No I won't, and that's flat, 'cause you're a loonatic, and ain't able to take care o' yerself."

"You are suffocating me!"

"That's a lie!" cried the brutal fellow, "for you couldn't speak if I was."

"Will no one help me?"

"Ain't I a helping yer?"

"Take him by the throat, Ann!" cried Jane, who still held on to her master's scarf, twisting it tighter and tighter round the jugular vein.

"No she don't," said Butters. "If any one has the honour o' hanging me it'll be Jack Ketch, whose got the reg'lar machinery, and is a werry hupright tradesman."

"Do pray let me go!" she entreated, holding back his hand from her mouth as well as she had strength to do.

"It is inconwenient for you to go alone. We all on us came together, and the same wehicle will take us back when we have become more of a happy family."

"I don't want to go back! I won't go back! I want a policeman!"

"And a very onproper thing too, and yer don't have a perliceman while I'm here. Come to that I'm as good as two of they common fellers any day."

Then he took her by both her arms, and shook her pretty severely, while she screamed out with pain and terror.

"I'll be with you directly, Ann," cried Jane, which gave the girl some encouragement, and for a brief minute or two the coachman felt a little more resistance, and more strength, on the part of Ann.

"I must take a high hand with you, I see!" he cried. "Just you sit down there," he said, lifting her in his arms, as a child would a doll, and bumping her into a chair which was brought up close before the savoury things on the well-spread table.

This treatment very much provoked the girl. She quickly rose from the chair he had dared to seat her in, and caught it up by the back, and held it threateningly towards him.

"I'll kill you," she cried, "if you don't let me pass out of the room!"

"Kill away," said the coachman, with a saucy grin, although he shrank a little out of the way of the uplifted chair.

During these proceedings between Ann and the coachman, Jane held long and fast at Mr. Duchesney's scarf, and would have so weakened him that he would not have been enabled to have prevented her escape had not his valet come up opportunely and assisted him in releasing her hands from his cravat.

When freed from her grasp he became furious, and without pause or hesitation he seized her in his arms, and as quickly as Jane's resistance would permit him, he carried her to an anteroom.

"Come with me, Ann," Jane cried with outstretched arms over the left shoulder of her infamous assailant.

"Keep that other girl back from following us, Brummell!" exclaimed Duchesney, "and then come to me with the bracelets and some champagne, for I can feel by her dead weight that she has swooned or fainted."

This was terrible news for Ann, who was now surrounded with both men while their master with his precious burden made his exit from the apartment.

Of course she made an attempt to follow her dear friend, and with more energy and strength than we supposed that she was capable of did she handle the uplifted chair when the men approached her. But what could she do against two wretches, when she had failed to win her way against one?

Of course it was the heroic influence of Pretty Jane, and her calls on her to be firm, that for the moment actuated Ann's display of courage, but as she was not to the "manner born," and had no native courage, why of course the fire of her valour soon consumed itself, and left her at the mercy of these cowardly men.

"I'm werry glad that the guv'ner has given her over into your charge, for she's a bit of a wixen," said the coachman to the valet, "and I've had enough on her, especially as she's now taken to the chair."

"And you shall have it on your head too if you do not let me pass," she gave back for answer.

"I'm not a hindering you, am I? I'm not your keeper now, you loonatic, to make such a row as this, rather than tuck in some of them good things afore ye."

More especially was the beset girl's eye and attention fixed on the man who was speaking to her. This the valet saw was his opportunity, and he at once ran in upon her, and quickly overpowered her, and took the chair from her.

Brummell was getting weary and irritable. He was disgusted with the whole proceedings of his capricious master, but as he dared not show him his feelings either by word or action, he let some of his steam off upon Ann.

"Come, I say, we have had quite enough of this unseemly display," he said, easily twisting the chair out of the girl's hands. "We came here to serve you—"

"You're a great cheat, Mr. Brummell!" said the girl, with new-found courage. "Serve me indeed!"

"Yes—to serve you, madam! and never had man a more ungrateful return. Think no more of Joshua Woodward!—he shall never—never—never be yours!"

"If Joshua was here now my opinion is that he would give you a good horsewhipping if he had his whip handy."

"Say what you will, Samuel Brummell was never provoked out of the way of being a gentleman."

"You've fine notions of a gentleman! To decoy two girls, whose character is their bread, away from their situations for purposes best known to yourself! A blackguard more than a gentleman, that's what you are, and your master is too much like you!"

"I'm werry glad you didn't knock me down with the lot, as the auctioneers say."

"Oh, you're all three alike, only that you are the stupidest of them."

"My eyes, Brummell, ain't she a-going it with the rancour of her tongue!" exclaimed Butters, puffing out his blue-red cheeks to a very considerable distension. "I'm a stoopid blackguard, am I? Werry well; but I tell'ee, if you only had on breeches instead of peddicoats, I should have knocked you right over, I should, and anybody as had taken your part. I've spent the shilling you gied me, but if I hadn't I would have guv it yer back agen. Mind'ye, I can owe it to yer, so there need be no hobligations."

"Why do you detain me here against my will?" asked Ann.

"Ax yer keeper, don't ax a stoopid blackguard like me," said the coachman, who was much stung at being called "stoopid;" the other epithet he did not care about, but he had some opinion of himself as being naturally an intellectual man.

Ann Orwell did refer her very proper question to the valet.

The plausible scoundrel, though, was equal to any emergency. Subtle as Satan, whose son he was, and gifted with a ready tongue, he replied, in the tones of an offended man—

"You have forfeited all right to my consideration."

"Then what about me, Muster Brummell?" asked the coachman. "I ort to be more offended than you. You're a blackguard—"

"It really is not worth repeating," said the pompous valet, throwing up his head, while he thrust his thumbs in the arm-holes of his tight-fitting satin vest.

"You flinch, you see, at only being called a blackguard," said Butters. "You'd have gone into fits, wouldn't yer, at being called a stoopid blackguard?"

"I have a repugnance to the word, and yet you will keep on using it," said the fastidious valet.

"I can't help my feelings, can I?"

"But you should keep them to yourself, as I do mine."

"I don't want to keep 'em—they're none so pleasant, I can assure you—I want to get rid on 'em."

Here Mr. Duchesney rushed in, exclaiming in furious tones, while he flew up to the valet as if he were about to strike him—

"Why to the devil didn't you bring on the wine?"

"Sir!"

"And sir to you! Why didn't you bring the bracelets and the wine, as I directed you?" he demanded.

"You did not!"

"I did!"

"You told me to prevent this girl from following you."

"D—n the girl, and you too! We're all at cross purposes here!"

"We're all very cross here," retorted the valet, his repartee not being at all in facetious tones. "I can only say again that you directed me to look after the girl."

"That's what I heerd," said Butters.

"You're an ass!" he exclaimed, rushing up in threatening attitude to the startled coachman.

"Well, I never!" was the man's meaningless response.

"No one spoke to you," said the passionate master.

"I only wanted to set matters straight, guv'ner."

"Try your skill on your legs—God knows they are crooked enough. And as for you,"—here he placed himself in front of the shivering Ann, "there's the door, you can go about your business. But mind, don't let me see you back at Evesham House again."

"I don't intend, you may be quite sure of that," answered the girl, rather fearlessly. "I and Jane, when we leave here—"

"When indeed!" he mouthed. "Jane is under that key," he said, holding one up, "and it will be some time before she will have her release."

"Let me go to her this instant!" demanded the girl.

"Not if I know it."

"Then the police shall soon be here!" cried the girl, about to hurry from the apartment, but her savage master caught her by the two shoulders, and exclaimed, while he shook her in a most discreditable manner—

"Ha! threaten your master, would you?"

Ann cried out in a manner that might be heard far and near—

"Murder! Police!" and these cries she repeatedly made.

And her cries were heard too!

As much to her surprise as the three men, at this instant there entered the room that mysterious old woman, who came and went whenever she liked in and out Evesham House!

She was dressed precisely as we have described elsewhere. She was the pink of neatness and cleanliness, but there was something about her that was unnatural, for every now and then a far more youthful expression was discoverable in her countenance that harmonised but little with her doubled up body.

Again, there was an unearthly whiteness about the face, while there were no wrinkles, and a good part of the cheeks were concealed by a broad strip of white linen tied round her head and under her chin; whether this was worn for ornament, or for the alleviation of some pain, or for disguise, no one inquired.

The broad steel buckles on her Florentine shoes looked very smart and aristocratic, quite in keeping with her features, which were of a noble order.

Had she not been so bent, she would have been decidedly tall and commanding—a figure quite imperial.

There were a variety of intonations, too, in her voice; there was a rich full sound at times, which she would suddenly change to the aged treble, with "pipes and whistles in its sound."

She entered so softly, her shoes being of list, that she came upon the scene like a ghost, and

Butters in truth was a little frightened when he turned round and saw the old woman by his side, although he knew her.

Nor was Brummell much less frightened than his fellow-servant when she looked up in his face, which just then wore the expression of dissatisfaction and misery.

"Just in time to do good!" exclaimed the little old woman in a little poke bonnet, while she raised aloft her crutch-like stick, and brought it smartly down upon Mr. Duchesney's knuckles, quite effective enough to make him release his hold of Ann.

"Mr. Duchesney, I declare!" she exclaimed, when he turned round upon her, with fiery anger in his eye, which was much increased when he saw the quarter from which the blow came, and the pain it possessed him with.

"Why, you—you—you," he stammered, but his passion was of that choking character that he could not get out the oaths and curses his evil mind was well stored with to bestow on the old woman who had so remorselessly tortured him.

"Lord, sir, pray forgive me!" exclaimed the old woman. "Had I known it was so great a man as yourself, of course I should not have taken the liberty."

"Oh! granny, I'm so glad to see you! Me and Jane have been almost killed by these horrid men!" exclaimed Ann, delighted that Providence had at length sent her a friend able to help her.

"What Pretty Jane down here too! Have all the people of Evesham House come over to Morley? On my life it seems so! Is my dear patron Lady Mary here?"

Mr. Duchesney was about to give her a backhanded blow, and had he done so, in all likelihood it would have killed the old woman.

He had bent his fist, and curved his arm, and taken his aim, and knitted his strength, when the woman's age, not her words, for she used none, pleaded for her with the valet; at all events he interposed between the threatened blow and the woman, while he ventured to say—

"Do not hurt her, sir!"

"No, I won't hurt her, I'll hang her! and only wish that her 'dear patron' was here to see, when she should hang on the next tree! and thus get rid at the same time of a knave and a beggar!"

"Let us hasten away, granny!" pleaded Ann, "and find poor Jane. She will be so glad to see you!"

As the girl spoke, having her arm linked in that of the old woman's, she pulled her on a foot or so, when she resisted going further with the importunate girl, saying—

"Ah, my dear, my age protects me from the master's wrath. He knows that I would not have rapped his knuckles with my staff, had I known that it was the master of Evesham House. I couldn't have believed that he would have acted improperly with his servants—"

"She is daring to preach to us!" interrupted Duchesney.

"I thought it was some knave of a servant who was insulting the girl," she continued.

"Seize her, and hang her on a tree!" exclaimed Duchesney, with unmeasured wrath.

"She is a spy, sent hither by that infernal patron of hers, as she calls her!—that adulterous wife of mine!"

"Ah, me!" sighed the crone, "no doubt she is a wicked wife, and a wicked woman—although she has been a generous friend to my grey hairs, God bless her! But what man that was a man would live with a wife carrytng on adultery under his nose?"

"Insolent hag! what do you mean?" he exclaimed.

"Come, I say, you had better hook it," said the valet, gently turning her face towards the room door.

"Your hands off, good sir, if you please," she said, with consummate dignity. "I am but a very poor wayfarer, that a breath would almost blow into her grave, yet I claim a little respect for my declining years."

"Do come away, granny," said Ann, who had no other name for the old woman.

"What brought you here, you hag?" inquired the master.

"A mere accident of my wanderings, sir. I am here, there, and everywhere, as fast as my aged legs and staff will carry me. A family that was very kind to me lived here last time I was this way—"

"She'll jaw your head off if you give her the chance, and you stand there, Brummell, dealing as mealy-mouthed with her as if she were your mother. Away with her! or I will take the office upon myself!"

No sooner said than done. Duchesney rudely and suddenly seized her, and was dragging her from the room, when she screamingly cried—

"Police! Police!"

"These women must think themselves in Scotland Yard, there's such a cry for the perlice—the wagabonds!" growled Butters.

"Out you go, so you may as well go quietly, old woman," said Duchesney.

A third time she called "Police!"

"There are no policemen here, granny," said Ann.

"Nor anywhere else when they're wanted," observed the coachman.

But there was magic in the old woman's cry for help.

The coachman was terribly started when he heard the sound of rushing footsteps coming up the stairs two at a time, but he was more so if possible when the very detective who had arrested him for stealing the top-boots, with another, entered the room, closing the door.

"Hallo! what's up here?" asked one of the detectives, a tall, keen-eyed, much be-whiskered man of about forty.

"What's the charge, and who called on us?" asked the other, who was the one that had made a former acquaintance with Butters upon the subject of a pair of top-boots.

The perplexed coachman had hoped never to have heard that officer's awful voice again. But our hopes are not always realised, and the coachman's sins had once more found him out, and now he stood again before those representatives of the law, whom he designated "cormorants," "wagabonds," and "purloiners of cold rabbit-pie."

"What are you doing with that old woman?" asked the detective with that voice which went through the very bones and marrow of the coachman.

"Thrusting her from the house, and whoever you are you won't prevent me!" said Duchesney.

"You had best keep a civil tongue in your head," remarked the detective.

"Yes, for all our sakes be werry civil," said the terrified coachman. "They're policemen out of huniform."

"Hallo! why yes, surely it is the same fellow!" said one of the detectives, coming round to Butters, who had somewhat averted his head from the officer's scrutiny. "It's the same man, only that he has grown a nobby pair of whiskers since."

"Are you speaking to me, sir?" said the coachman, in tones so meek and mild.

"Don't I know you?"

"It is not werry likely, sir. But if you do, sir, why then you've the adwantage of me," said Butters, in a feigned voice.

"People are generally shy of owning an acquaintance with detectives; it is not often to their interest to do so. But you don't give me a chance to look at you. Turn round and hold up your head. Yes—and you are the man."

"O Lord! O Lord! what's up now?" he cried, in his own coarse voice, which was tremulous with agitation.

"Isn't your name, Butters?"

"Not if I know it," said the coachman, with a little pleasant chuckle. "It won't do, guv'ner, I'm not to be caught that way."

"I don't want to catch you, my man. I only wanted to make good our acquaintance."

"There's no 'casion to take any pains about that," said the coachman.

"All right. But isn't your name Butters?" he again asked.

"Don't know, I'm sure. Never had any eddication myself. I'll ask my mother the next time she's out."

"Very funny, I daresay. Do you know anything—"

"No, I know nothink. I've had no eddication, don't I keep on telling yer?"

"The top-boots—"

"What on 'em?" asked Butters, throwing out his leg. "There's my master, ask him whether they are mine or not."

"Don't be so fast at interrupting me," said the officer. "I'm not speaking about the boots you've got on—"

"I've got none off—this is the only pair I've got," he quickly interposed, trying all he could to baffle the detective.

"I lagged you for stealing a pair of top-boots, did I not?"

"That's putting it straight to him, Ned," said the other officer.

"That's a purty question to put to a servent before his master! I think that's hactionable, for an inflammation of character," said the coachman.

"Aye, aye; but your actions are always to be feared—shall I tell you why?"

"I'm werry much offended, and want no further conwersation."

"Because your actions are always bad ones," said the officer, who was determined that the coachman should have the benefit of his smart observation.

"But what are we wanted here for, Ned?" said the be-whiskered detective to his brother officer.

"I s'pose you've reckoned me up enough," said Butters, "and that I can go?"

"There's no one will leave this room until we've had some explanation of our being called here," replied the detective.

"I didn't call yer, did I?" asked the coachman, who was getting more of himself again, for he began to think whether their visit and interrogatories had anything to do with the abstraction of sundry measures of corn that his master had referred to yesterday.

"You don't leave for all that," said the detective. "I told you we should meet again upon some other 'innocent' job of yours."

"So I was hinnocent!" cried the coachman, fairly taken off his guard.

"I thought he was the man who stole the boots—the man who was so innocent that he didn't know a trunk from a bundle! Your name is Butters? You need have no delicacy in answering—you see I know all about you."

"Come, I say, what do yer know about me?" he asked, bristling up, his face changing colours like a cameleon.

"Enough to know that where you are there is sure to be a case for a policeman, if you were only found out."

"That's hot, I'm blowed if it aint!"

"His name is But'ers," said Ann.

"I know that," said the detective, laughing. "And the man is like his name, very slippery."

A loud scream from some other part of the house penetrated the room. It alarmed Ann, and took the others by surprise, especially the two detectives.

Mr. Duchesney, who had released the old woman at the whispered advice of the valet, was about to rush from the room, for he too well knew from whence the scream proceeded.

The detectives, however, prevented this, but it was with considerable difficulty.

"You had better not be obstructive, sir," said one of the detectives. "We have told you before that we are police officers, and that we have been summoned here."

"By whom?" inquired the ill-governed master, while he was held back by the two officers.

"By me," said Ann, now coming well forward, while the old woman stood by her side in support of her while she detailed out to the detectives the whole of the circumstances from the beginning to the end, and made them thoroughly understand it.

"This is a clear case of abduction for felonious purposes against all three," said the detective.

"Not agen me!" exclaimed the coachman.

"Why you brought the girl here!" replied the other detective, with a little sneering laugh curling about his laugh.

"Master ordered me to bring the girls here," said Butters, in his defence.

"That's right enough," said his master.

"It won't be right enough for judge or jury he will find," answered the detective. "You charge all three of them, do you not?" he asked Ann, who, without any hesitation, replied that she did.

"Then all three of you may consider yourselves our prisoners."

"I say, Brummell, this is a pretty go!" exclaimed the coachman to the valet, with his eyes half starting out of his head.

"It will not serve any purpose making explanation to them," said Brummell, who looked as tranquilly as he spoke.

"You give him good advice, sir," said one of the detectives. "Pray what is your name?"

"Samuel Brummell," he answered, as proudly as if he were going to say Samuel Johnson; distinctly pronouncing every letter of his name.

"And there's my name and address," said Mr. Duchesney, presenting an elegant card to the officers. "And I think you will find you have made a great mistake in arresting us."

"Our duties, sir, are as onerous as they are disagreeable. We have no malice against you, and your arrest to us is nothing more than a troublesome duty."

"At all events I conceive that you have no right to detain these servants of mine."

"No more he aint, master, and you're a trump to say so!" exclaimed the coachman.

"I know nothing, sir, of Samuel Brummell, nor of yourself; but I know a good deal of this fellow Butters."

That scream again! that banging at a distant door! reminded them of poor Jane, who for the moment in the exciting conversation, they had seemed to have forgotten.

"Do get the key from him," said Ann, pointing to her master, "and let out Jane, and then you will find all true that I have told you, and see that lump on her head!"

"The key," demanded the detective.

"There it is," my fine fellow," said Mr. Duchesney, flinging it on the table. "And when you open the door with it, you will see a beautiful girl,—so beautiful indeed, that any man might well be forgiven for making an attempt to run away with her. But there, she proved herself too good for the lot of us. Not this champagne spread—which, by the bye, you are both of you welcome to partake—not these bracelets (and I was told that she had an eye and taste for jewelry)—"

"That is not at all singular," interrupted one of the detectives, while the other went straight away to release Jane. "All women, especially those of the lower class, are fond of gew-gaws."

"Fine feathers, they think, make fine birds," said Duchesney, talking as unconcerned with the detective, as if he had been a chum who had just dropped in to smoke a cigar rather than one who had him under arrest. "But I was just going to say for Jane—and I say it with some chagrin and mortification—that she has completely baffled my designs, and that jewelry and her master's admiration, have not been the weight of a feather against her self-respect and her virtue. She has triumphed—and she has been put on her mettle, too—and you are here to make us pay the piper! But I think we shall get over it, so cheer up, Sam! But in the event of our not doing so, let us partake of the good the gods provide us, before we come down to prison fare!"

"And werry queer fare you will find it too!" cried Butters, who was not by any means so gay as his volatile master, who was now cutting into the Westphalia ham with great gusto, and pouring out champagne—glasses all round.

But the detective, when he offered him a bumper, under the circumstances begged to be excused. It would be more than his office were worth, to drink with one under arrest.

"Had I been prosecutor instead of prisoner," he suggested—

"Then, sir, the boot would have been on the other leg," he replied, smilingly. "The law likes to see its representatives in respectable company," he added.

"Ah, yes, I see. By the bye, there is such a mob of us here, and there has been such a confusion of tongues, that I should like to know who is the prosecutor here?"

"This young woman at present," said the detective.

"Not old Mother Meddlesome?" he cried, pointing to the old woman, who stood apart, keenly looking on.

"Your sun is setting, sir," she said, prophetically raising her staff.

"You are good at that jargon, we know—but we don't want any of it. You'd better get under some tree in Greenwich Park if you want to tell fortunes. We know our own here, and just now they are d—d bad—eh, Brummell?"

"But you are bravely bearing them, sir. Only an innocent man could be so light-hearted."

"The shoe hasn't begun to pinch yet, nor the screw to turn," said the old woman.

"I'll turn the screw on you yet, if ever I catch you at Evesham House," he said, threateningly.

"I shall be at my lady's house when you wont be there to see. Those luxuriant locks of thine will soon fall into the hands of the prison barber —and your broadcloth changed to prison grey, made without measure by a prison barber—and your lazy riotous servants will share your happy fate. While Lady Mary—"

With a terrible oath he flung a champagne bottle at her head, and had it hit her its effects would have been serious, but at that instant, fortunately for her, she turned her head to whisper to the detective.

This action on her part excited suspicion, especially in the mind of Mr. Brummell, who whispered in Mr. Duchesney's ear that he had grave doubts that she was not what she represented herself to be.

Mr. Duchesney was much inclined to the same opinion, and began to think she was in disguise.

"Off with that poke bonnet of hers, and that strip of white linen bound under her jaw as if she were a laid-out corpse—and which I wish she were, and her patron too," he added.

"Better be as decorous as possible, for these detectives are expected to report all they see and hear in cases they have in hand."

"I suppose I know that," he said, snappishly. "But who's afraid? I'm not, are you?"

"Press the hofficer to have some champagne," whispered the coachman. "Get him drunk if you can, and then we might get hoff."

His master whispered back, and pretty loudly too, for all in the room heard it, although no remark was made—

"You're a d—d fool! and you think these detectives are like you!"

Butters, seeing his master in such merry mood, expected at the least a civil answer; but a reply like the one he received, was rather cutting.

He puffed out his cheeks, stared at everybody as if courting their opinions and sympathy upon the insult he had received—but the mortification was increased when he saw a smile, which he magnified to a grin, upon the face of the very detective who had "lagged" him for stealing the top-boots, and who had the further impudence to comment on his master's rude remark by saying—

"More R than F, I'm thinking."

"You've no right to hinsult your prisoners— I know enough of law for that."

"You don't like my company, I see. You won't be troubled with it longer than my mate coming with the other girl to see what she has got to charge you with."

"What can she have to charge me with? I'm a married man—"

"I hope a happy one," said the bantering detective.

"That's no business o' yourn," said the coachman. "I wish she was here now to give you a bit of her mind for detaining her husband, and taking away his character."

"Did I run away with you?" with much fierceness of manner he asked Ann, who at that moment came into the room with the pale Jane between her and the detective.

"She will answer you in another place than this," said the old woman, replying for the girl who had now reached her side.

"Look here, old creetur, you've been the cause of all the mischief—"

"That's right, my man, give the witch a dressing, for she well deserves it! It will save me the trouble of doing it myself!" said Duchesney, who was doing the good things on the table the most ample justice.

"Hadn't it been for you, you dreadful old party—"

The woman so addressed looked terrible things, and uplifted her staff to strike him.

"Oh, I'm not afraid on yer," said Butters, who received great encouragement from his callous master. "I say again, but for you we should have had no perlice here—"

"You shall be taught how to treat a woman as a woman. We have found a nest of scoundrels, and I and these poor girls will do all we can to stamp you out!"

"D'ye hear her, guv'ner? She's going to stamp us out," said Butters, suiting the action to the word, by raising his right leg as high as he could consistently with the laws of equilibrium, and bringing his thick top-boot heavily to the floor. "Is that your style to stamp us out, you beggar? Lady Mary don't know yer, or she must be a hass to feed yer!" he added, looking round on his master for approval.

The detectives here conferred, and Jane was then asked by them if she gave these men in charge. She answered "Yes," after giving them a "round unvarnished tale" of the infamous treatment she and her friend had received.

At this Butters became furious. He suddenly seized the old woman, and shook the bonnet from her head, and a grey wig followed it, and to the consternation of all present but the detectives, Lady Mary Duchesney stood before them! She drew up her majestic figure, and took from her pocket her elegant pistol, and then said—

"I also give these men in charge for abducting these servants of mine from my house!"

PRETTY JANE

OR, THE

VIPER OF KIDBROOK LANE

DUCHESNEY CONFERS WITH A MISERLY SOLICITOR ABOUT BAIL.

A great sensation was caused when the old woman was discovered to be no other than Lady Mary. She had for a long time past, unknown to every one, assumed this disguise whenever she wished to see and hear what was going on amongst the servants of her establishment, without being seen.

And she often heard truths of herself which were very unpalatable and insulting, aye, even from those who fawned and flattered her as Lady Mary. In this disguise, too, she had discovered the flirtations of her paramour, Joshua Woodward, with the other servants, and the contents of that letter which he had written to Pretty Jane, proposing to meet her in the willow copse.

But she thought a great deal too much of herself to be jealous of any one. Yet she liked to be well posted up, to use a commercial phrase, in the actions, feelings, sentiments and characters of all those, whether friends, acquaintances or servants, by whom she was surrounded.

She was unmistakably a majestic woman, nor did the poor habiliments in which she was now arrayed detract from it. Her face and figure, her imperial deportment, towered over all the considerations of dress. Those who beheld her were so entranced with the grandeur of her person, that her dress, except sometimes for its eccentricity, was seldom noticed.

When her bonnet and wig were taken from her by the rude hands of the coachman, she saw at once that her little game was up as far as the further maintenance of her disguise as a little old woman was concerned.

She was very sorry for this, for her little stratagem had been of vast service to her, and satisfied many a longing curiosity to know her friends from her foes.

When her disguise was broken in upon, she drew up her stooping figure to its stateliest height, flung aside the staff with which she mocked age, drew forth her pistol, and held it levelled at the head of the crouching coachman.

"Spare me, your ladyship! spare me! It was all a haccident!" he cried, in dreadful fear as much at the venom shot from her eye as at the glittering weapon.

This was no theatrical display on the part of Lady Mary, albeit her husband gave her credit for nothing else. She was too proud to affect; whatever she was she was always natural; but her nature was of no common kind—fortunately for the world she lived in, for a few more such fallen spirits as hers would have shocked if not corrupted a kingdom.

"I call on the perlice to protect me!" he vociferated, while the infuriate woman kept her fiery eye upon him.

"Shoot him, and get hung!" cried Duchesney to his wife. "You may as well have your desserts first as last!"

"Pauper! if you have no objection, I will have them last if they consist in hanging. In truth I have too many lovers to be weary of life. Joshua Ward shall call upon you with a horsewhip, after the prison authorities have done with you and your currish servants."

"You are a father's outcast, and you were sold to me at an outcast's price! Five thousand pounds they gave me to call you wife—"

"And you found me a bad bargain?"

"So bad—"

"Come, come, that's some satisfaction to one's revenge that you should live so long."

"Thanks to your good living, and to the sweet pretty girls you have surrounded me with, and the reminet of the tin that the earl your father gave me to get rid of you, why I am pretty well, thank you, and all the die you'll find in me will be found in my hair."

"You are the most profitable pensioner that I have. I was always accounted a woman of business, but I surpassed myself when I endured a little church mockery for the sake of three thousand a-year. Love, honour, and obey, indeed!—"

"Wasn't it a farce? Ha! ha! I was thinking all the time of a pair of bays that I had spotted to purchase at Tattersall's, to drive out that little party that I met the night before at the Argyle Rooms."

"My thoughts at the altar—"

"Were how you should halter me, I suppose, eh?"

"Many a true word spoke in jest. Truly my thoughts *were* in that direction—but sad to say I have not been able to work the oracle."

"Hear you, gentlemen of the law?—this wife of mine threatens my life. Will you take the charge?"

"And you saw me under fire of her pistol?" said the coachman, who had taken advantage of the amiable conversation that had sprung up between husband and wife to slope out of her sight, and quietly hide himself behind his fellow-servant Brummell, from behind whose back he now spoke, just showing his head from under cover of the valet's shoulder.

"And I think she would have been entitled to a medal had she shot *you*," said one of the detectives, which, under the circumstance of a pistol having been levelled at his head before

the officer's eyes, was rather a thoughtless bit of facetiousness on his part, and no doubt he would have been severely reprimanded for it had it been reported at head-quarters.

"Need we stop longer here, officer?" asked Lady Mary.

"I hope not, for your presence spoils the enjoyment of my dinner," said Mr. Duchesney, as gay as a lark.

"The last dinner that you will eat at my expense; for some time yet to come you will board and lodge at Her Majesty's cost," retorted Lady Mary.

"Which will be altogether compensated for by your absence," he rejoined. "But don't crow—I am not yet her Majesty's guest."

"Have no fear about that. My purse will be at the disposal of these poor girls, so that they will be able to employ eminent counsel to set your villainy clear before the jury, and if each of you don't get twelvemonths with hard labour, why then you will not get what I heartily wish you!"

"And werry hard labour it is, sir, so I don't deceive yer," said Butters.

"Who spoke to you, you cur?" cried his master, with much exasperation at his servant's display of the white feather before the proud and insolent Lady Mary.

"Cur! why that is your character," said his wife. "Three big fellows against one bit of a girl! Such brave men!"

"I am quite sure, officers," said the valet, who had been too much disgusted with his master's wilful proceedings throughout to speak much, "that having heard the charge against us, you have no business to detain us here to be abused by that woman for your amusement. You have duties towards prisoners as well as prosecutors."

"Are you in such a hurry to be locked up?" asked the be-whiskered detective, with a self-satisfied smile radiating his face, which was anything but agreeable to Mr. Brummell, who returned his smile with a frown of contempt.

"I daresay we know our duty," said the other. "The chief part of which is never to let a prisoner go when we catch him."

"I don't see the force of your remark, sir," said Mr. Duchesney. "I don't think either of us have shown any anxiety to escape, or give you any unnecessary trouble in our capture."

"We are not complaining, sir," said the detective. "But we object to be lectured by your servant."

"He is anxious, I suppose, to get to his new quarters, eh, Brummell?"

The valet heeded not the question, and the pause gave the coachman an opportunity to say—

"He don't know them ere quarters as well as I do, or he wouldn't be werry anxious to get to 'em."

"I object to any more of this trifling," said the valet, with considerable ill temper. "These girls have given me in charge for abducting them with felonious intent, and I am only anxious as quickly as possible to disprove it."

"What am I to do with the hoss and carriage?" asked Butters.

"Have you got such things down here?" asked the detectives, at the same time.

"That I has, and shall be werry happy to drive you and your mate anywhere as you pleases."

"We will be your coachman on this occasion, Mr. Butters. Gentlemen who keep their carriages, should likewise keep their coachmen. That office shall be mine, while my mate will keep you and your friends company with a little agreeable conversation on the inside."

Butters didn't seem to see it; he had not been used to such civility, and he didn't care for it now. It would be a very unpleasant ride for him when his coachman and companion were policemen.

"No thankee, sir," he said, "I would rayther do my own coaching. The mare—"

"Didn't you say it was a hoss?" asked the detective.

"What fellers you detectives are for picking up a chap for a word. What does it matter about the sex of a hanimal?"

"A great deal I should think, especially in the law."

"But what has the mare, pretty creetur! to do with law? D'ye think I stole her?"

"We presume the animal is your master's?" said the detective.

"Who said she wasn't? But what I was going to say was this ere, that the mare—for she is a mare—"

"She can't very well be a horse," cried both detectives at once, full of laughter.

"I don't know so much about that," said the coachman, not at all caring to be the subject of their laughter, and which only made them laugh the more. "It'll be a blessed good job for Englishmen when there is but one name for a thing, and no policemen."

"Yes, when we are not wanted—when some people have learned to keep their hands over other people's top-boots—"

"That's being windictive—which is a werry long word for me to spit out. What's top-boots to do with mares or hosses? But my mare, or my master's, is a hartful hussey, when anybody has got the ribbons over her but me. She's sure to bolt, so I don't deceive yer."

"Let her bolt as she will, when I drive her, with you inside, my life upon it she will pull up at a station-house, or within a prison yard."

"Can't yer talk of something else than perlice stations and prisons? Your trade aint a werry hedifying one, so I think the least said about it the better."

"Now that I have done my dinner, I can do all the talking myself," said the master to his servant, "so you can make yourself scarce as soon as you please."

Could it be possible that his master meant him to leave the room? and could it be possible that the detectives would let him if he tried?

Butters did try, but he did not find it possible to persuade the officers to accede to Mr. Duchesney's orders that he, the coachman, was to make himself "scarce," his interpretation of that word being in this instance that he was to leave the room.

"No you don't," said one of the detectives, stepping forward, when the man had got near enough to the door to show that his intentions were to leave the room.

"Well I'm sure!" cried the stopped man.

"P'raps you didn't hear my master tell me to make myself scarce?"

"Go back, and hold your noise," replied the detective, giving him an unceremonious punch in the stomach.

"I didn't mean you to leave the room, you jackass!" cried the master, lighting up a fragrant cigar.

"He knew that well enough, sir," said one of the detectives.

"No I didn't," contradicted the stableman. "I thought master meant me to go and saddle his hoss, now then!"

Mr. Duchesney took this low officious servant of his by the collar of his coat, and spun him out of the way between himself and the detectives, who again divided, not formally, the prisoners from the prosecutors.

Lady Mary, and her two servants, Jane and Ann Orwell, had seated themselves on a couch in the room, and had been engaged in earnest conversation, and had taken little heed what had been going on amongst the prisoners and the detectives, who had been brought hither in a post-chaise, and which post-chaise was now waiting in the pretty lane a little way from the house.

Poor Jane looked very ill, and Lady Mary, judged by the manner in which she sat, her face quite close to Jane's, while she held her hand, and talked to her, was consoling and encouraging her.

"Might I be allowed to speak to Jane?" inquired Mr. Duchesney of the detectives.

"Oh, yes," was the answer, to which was added, "only we caution you, that all we hear will be given in evidence on the trial."

"I cannot object to that."

Saying this, he walked straight to the couch where she sat between Ann Orwell and Lady Mary.

As he approached, the latter rose, placing herself in front of the girls, and almost hiding them from view.

"I do not fear your terrible looks, nor your pistol. They have no terror for me," said Mr. Duchesney, holding his lighted cigar between his fingers.

"I disdain to speak further to you than this," she said; "if you approach one step nearer those girls, I will shoot you!"

"Oh, your ladyship," cried Jane, rising, exhausted as she was, and holding the lady's pistol arm, "I beg of you not to fire! The constables will protect us now, won't you?"

"Aye, aye, you are safe enough now," they replied, one of them going up to Mr. Duchesney.

"I have permission of the detectives whom you have set upon me and my servants, to speak with Jane—"

"Speak then, but you shall not approach nearer to her!" cried Lady Mary.

"And what have you to say to me?" asked Jane, while she stood close to her mistress, and took courage from the nearness of the constable to her.

"How fortunate for my life that I am not susceptible to a woman's frown, or yours would kill me."

"Now, sir," said the detective, "what you have to say to the young woman, please say, for we must be on the move to scenes less congenial than these."

"A very good reason for not being in a hurry," replied the master, with a little laugh at the smartness of his repartee.

"I must go—"

"Pray don't let me detain you," he replied, with a gay laugh.

"Nor me," said the coachman, who had taken a seat at the table, with his back turned upon the company, and his brazen face towards the luxuries on the table, which he still kept picking at, although he had very recently fared so sumptuously.

"Who did you ever kill with that pistol?" Duchesney sneeringly asked of his wife. "You must carry it about with you to frighten children with."

"This man, officer, has nothing to say to the girl," said Lady Mary; "it was a mere pretext for delay. His prison quarters have no attraction for him."

"Prison indeed! I shall be at Evesham House before you now, if you don't make haste and take your unwelcome presence off."

"About that I am quite satisfied," said Lady Mary, throwing as much contempt into her tones as she was capable of, which was a great deal. "The wing of the house that you loafed upon, will be occupied by a better man than you, while you increase your stores of knowledge—which are lamentably poor—from prison springs,"

"Which he will find werry muddy," said Butters to himself, drinking the dregs of his master's champagne glass.

"Then that better man of yours, you strumpet! will have to try his strength with me, even with your do-nothing pistol support, to see which is the *best* man! A fig for the better man—I shall go in for the *best* man! The superlative degree for me."

"In his absence I will shake you well myself, you parasite!" she cried, while she suddenly sprang upon him, and shook him well, then threw him from her, something after the same manner as he had previously himself served Butters.

The attack was so sudden, and so vehement, that it quite overpowered him before he could resist it.

It was, however, not for lack of courage or strength that he was thus spun about for the moment; a stronger man than he would have had to yield to such sudden frenzy.

"Sarve him right," mumbled the coachman to himself, but quite loud enough for Brummell to hear.

The valet stood close by the coachman, looking as if the whole of the proceedings was totally unworthy of his notice.

He was very much disgusted with his master's conduct, and felt quite indifferent to any hard treatment that her ladyship might inflict upon him.

Mr. Duchesney was about to turn upon his Amazon partner, but one of the detectives held him back, saying—

"We really, sir, have had quite enough of this."

"You did not think so when you saw her fly at me!" he vehemently cried, but the detective did not lose his equanimity of temper.

"It was too sudden for me to interfere," he replied.

"Don't prevent him, officer," she said; "I am rather pugilistic myself, and that he would find were he to come within my arm's length. Do let him come!"

The detective took Duchesney by the arm and led him to the end of the room that he came from.

"Before my unpleasant duty—"

"Gammon," said Butters to himself, yet loud enough for the detective to hear.

"The duty will not be unpleasant as far as *you* are concerned," he said. "You may hang your thick head, and cover your long ears as you will, prison is your proper place, and no one—at least their property—is safe from you except the policeman's eye be on you."

"Cold rabbit pie," retorted the coachman, who now that he saw the game was up, and that the detective could do him no more harm, and was not inclined to do him any good, he became bold and insulting.

"D'ye see those pretty things?" asked the detective, holding up a pair of steel handcuffs, and jingling them.

The coachman did not condescend to turn his head.

"Won't you look at them?" repeated the detective.

"The sound's enough for me," growled Butters, still avoiding the sight of the handcuffs. "There—there, you needn't keep a ringing on 'em. They're no moosic to me if they are to you."

"Oh, they're very soothing to those who apply them to their wrists."

"Mind'ye, I'm not hobstroperous," said Butters, "so it'll be agen the law to use 'em on me."

"Are you an Old Bailey lawyer?"

"I know that you can't use them on a hinoffensive hinnocent man."

"Innocent! Wouldn't you like me to let you go?"

"No I wouldn't—there then! These ere gals have made a charge agen me, and I'll make 'em prove it."

"Your previous good character will be very much in your favour—hem!"

"Where's the good o' talking to you?"

"None, if it's about your innocence," said the detective.

"So I am hinnocent!" he shouted. "And them ere gals will find themselves in the wrong box for trying to take away my character, which ain't so easily got agen."

Jane was about to speak, but Lady Mary forbade her.

"Let them answer to the law, not to us," she said.

"You'll have to answer to the law yet, and your man, Josh Woodward too; and if he was here now I'd punch his head!" said the coachman.

Butters, who was now goaded beyond his control, spoke with a wrathful earnestness. He cared nothing for her ladyship—she was no mistress of his—and to give her a rap or two over the knuckles now that she had given him the opportunity, he thought would do him service with his master, by inclining him to shield him as much as possible from the consequences o the mess he had brought himself and his fellow-servant into.

"Do remove these fellows, officers," she said. "There presence offends our eyes."

"While yours offends my nose," said Mr. Duchesney, affecting her contemptuous tones, while he held his hand to his nasal organ, and the coachman did the same.

"There is no need for your ladyship to wait any longer, except you please," said the detective, submissively.

"I have been waiting for the satisfaction of seeing these fellows conveyed to prison," she ejaculated.

"A satisfaction that you will never have," rejoined Duchesney.

"How so?" inquired the detective, whose intention it was to convey the three of them then and there to prison, the only delay being that he and his mate could not decide what prison to take them to, the offence having been committed in a cross country.

But they at length decided between themselves that they should be taken to Gravesend, as being nearer then taking them back from whence they came.

The coachman and Brummell were both as much surprised and puzzled as the detectives to hear that they were not going to prison.

When asked for an explanation by the latter, Mr. Duchesney said—

"Because I shall be able to get substantial bail for the lot of us."

"I thought you knew better than that," said the other detective.

"How know better? What d'ye mean, governor?"

"Why you must go to prison before you can get bail, even if this case is bailable at all, which I doubt."

"You're not a magistrate, you're only a perliceman," said Butters, who became antagonist with every one who expressed any doubts against them.

"Don't be quite so bold, if you please," said his master, which saved him from a stinging reply from the detective. "We are not quite on an equality, though we are prisoners under a charge made by two silly maidens, and an old fool, to whom my counsel will put a few questions about certain matters connected with the dirty old barn."

"We shall be there, either in person or by counsel to answer all your questions, and to make our charges; and if we don't rid ourselves of you for a long time, then I shall never indulge in hope again."

"All right. Now touching this bail. Then you think it will be necessary for me to be locked up to-night?"

"I am sure of it."

"I had hoped that it would have been in her arms. Not yours," he added, addressing Lady Mary, "but that beauty by your side."

"Who instead of that will be your prosecutrix in a criminal court," said Lady Mary. "The men I have known—"

"And that has been half the general camp, pioneers and all," retorted Mr. Duchesney.

"But amongst them all I never knew so great a fool as you. Ha! to make such a great trap to catch a simple servant-girl, and the three boobies to tumble into the arms of two detectives instead of the arms of the girls! And they call themselves men! Won't Mr. Woodward laugh when I tell him," added Lady Mary.

And she laughed immoderately herself, and it proved infectious to the detectives, who concealed it as well as they were able.

"Those who engage in amours—"

"Those delicate affairs should be left to ladies and gentlemen, not to boors," she said, interrupting Duchesney, tossing up her head, and looking over her shoulder with ineffable contempt.

"Have you anything to say to either of the young women who make the charges against you?" asked one of the detectives of Mr. Duchesney, who was busy pouring out two glasses of champagne, one for himself and one for his servant Brummell, who looked anything but a man in a good temper.

"Wake up, Brummell, and drink with me to our better fortune!"

"I should like to jine in the toast," said the coachman, not particularly well pleased that his master should have forgotten his services in unmasking the old woman, and giving Lady Mary a jacketting.

"You be ——! your tongue has been oiled enough, and if you'll take my advice you'll set a lock upon it," said Mr. Duchesney.

"I don't want no lock-jaw, thank'ee. I had a brother as died on it," said the coachman.

"I will thank you, sir, to attend to my question," said the detective. "Have you anything to say to the prosecutrixes?"

"Yes, I have. But will they listen?"

"I won't," said Jane, with decision.

"Nor I," said Ann Orwell, following suit.

"You can't help listening," said the detective.

"But I can help staying," retorted Jane.

The detective was taken aback at Jane's quickness of reply, and looked at Mr. Duchesney, as much as to say—

"You have caught a Tartar—you have indeed. I pity you, but I can't help you."

"Oh, she is all there," said Duchesney, quite understanding the significance of the detective's looks about Jane. "And she is as good in her nature as in her spirit." This he added aside, and confidentially. "You need not fear me now, sweet lassie,"—Jane turned her back, and walked further up the room,—"for I am not going to speak of love but of law."

"I don't think, sir, that you should permit any more of this nonsense," said Lady Mary. "The very sound of the rascal's voice affects the poor thing, and really she has not strength to bear any more agitation. I have been waiting here for a purpose, but if it does not suit your convenience to remove the prisoners at once, I shall retire with my servants."

"We appear to have got ourselves in the position of that well-known man who, in his endeavours to please everybody pleased nobody. We haven't been even able to please ourselves, me and my brother officer having been for some time in dispute where was the proper place or prison to lodge the accused. No doubt we have tolerated too much conversation between prosecutors and prisoners, but there have been many peculiarities in the case which excuses the laxity we have exhibited."

Thus spoke one of the detectives, and when

he had finished, with note-book in his hand, he went and conferred with the other for a few minutes.

While he was thus engaged, Lady Mary conversed aside with Jane, who had received the first rude shock of her life, and it had left upon her great mental disquiet, and much physical exhaustion.

When Duchesney carried her from the dining-room, she swooned on his shoulder, and she, continuing in an unconscious state after he had reached with her to an ante-room, in an irritable state he locked her in the room while he rushed back for the bracelets and the wine.

He had not long left the room before she recovered her consciousness, and her alarm was great when she found herself alone in a strange apartment.

"Wherever am I? Where is Ann? How my head swims!" she cried, looking round the elegant room, while she bound both her hands round her brow and temples, her fingers avoiding that large discoloured swelling on her brow, which was too painful to touch.

Worse and worse—she found that she was locked in!

Her thoughts instinctively went to Heaven for deliverance from the perils which a fiend in human form was dodging her steps to pull her down to everlasting ruin!

She knew not what to do; and besides the depth of her mental agony her strength appeared to desert her.

She sat on the couch—she wept—she wrung her hands—she feebly called on Ann. But she had no response—no deliverer came;—and her calls upon her friend were only mocked back by the echoes of the room.

Her poor strength she repeatedly tried upon the lock of the door—but it was vain, and she left her task in despair. Then the window became her frantic study.

Oh! it was too high to leap. Wonder, though, that she had not toppled over, for as she looked out upon the gravelled walk below, her brain again grew dizzy, but she tightly held the sash, and thus saved herself from serious disaster.

"The window shall remain up, and in the event of that villain intruding himself, out I'll go through it, though I perish!"

Her ear was now quickened to every sound; and she thought she heard footsteps on the stairs. She took alarm, and now thought that the dreadful leap must be taken or the villain would defeat her!

For a minute or two she clung to the window, but no one entering the room she concluded that the sound proceeded from her imagination only.

Jane was not a girl to despair in difficulties—although she now really saw no way our of her captivity.

At length she fixed her anxious eyes on the long beautiful bell-ropes that hung down by the side of the marble mantle. An idea seized her. She would possess herself of these ropes, knot them together, and then fasten them to a bar of the grate.

Her idea, however, was abortive, for the grate was so far from the window that the distance would absorb the length of the ropes after so much of them had been absorbed in knotting.

But poor Jane was in a delirium of wild excitement, and had no brain to consider the fitness of things. She was mad to make her escape, and there were the window and the ropes inviting her with their help, and she gladly accepted it.

Upon a chair she stood, and then tugged at the thickly-twisted scarlet velvet rope, for she had no knife or scissars to cut it. She found it a tough job, though it was more a trial of patience than of strength. Had there been more resistance at the rope's fastening than that yielding dance-about wire, it could not so long have held its own against the incessant jerking, and tugging, and pulling, that Jane gave it. The bell, of course, rang furiously, and was heard all over the house, but there were none to attend, for the old labourer who was placed there to look after the house and grounds, and to show all comers over it who presented the card of the owner.

But Jane's determined perseverance was at length rewarded. Down came the rope and its fastenings, and Jane, having the rope and the wire to which it was attached now in her hands, she quickly severed them.

The liberation of the second rope became easier, for much of the labour expended on the first rope reacted on the second, and soon had Jane both ropes in her hand freed from their fastenings.

Her cheeks became flushed with the certain hope of escape, and the smile upon her sweet lips radiated and lit up with delight the whole of her matchless countenance.

She wished that her sailor lad had been there to "tie the knot" for her—not matrimonially, but to fasten the ropes together and to the grate, and then succour her to the ground.

"Ah, me, had he been here," she reflected to herself, while with all her might, and all her strength, she spliced the two ropes into one, and then fell on her knees before the grate to fasten it to the bar, "bless his heart for loving me! he would have had the house down before now if his Jane had been in peril. I wish he were a landsman, and be always with me. But then, perhaps, I should not love him so much. Why should maids love sailors so? Is it because their long absences make their hearts grow fonder? or is it that every time the wind doth blow, and the thunder crash, and hearing and reading of wrecks, so much romance is mingled with our fears for their safety? or is it that we think them braver and truer than other men? I don't know, I'm sure, why it is; I only know that I do love my own dear William! Oh! that he were captain of the ship, I would conquer all my fears, and sail with him over the seas, if he would have me for his wife."

Such, or similar, were the heart reflections of this true-hearted girl as she fastened the bell-rope to the bar of the grate, and they were deeper in feeling for their not rising to her lips.

After she had fastened the rope as well as her genius in knot tying would allow—which, as a rule, except there's a lover and a parson in the case, women are not very clever at—she took the middle of the rope, and tested how far it would bear by pulling it with both hands with all her strength.

It was well for Jane that she did so before trusting her dear self to it out of the window, for she would have been seriously hurt if not killed.

She planted her feet well in the floor, and then with both hands pulled at the rope. It proved treacherous—at least her knot did—for it gave way, and stretched poor Jane outright upon the floor!

She had received injury enough about the head without this further blow, which was rather a smart one at the back.

But after she had managed to get from the carpet, she more felt the disappointment at her knot giving way than the shock and blow she had received while trusting her strength to it.

She had taken great pains in tying the knot, but she knew nothing of the principle, and what seemed right to her proved in practice a delusion and a snare.

Jane was essentially a brave girl as well as a virtuous one, and, as we have elsewhere observed, those two characteristics in nine individuals out of ten go together.

Jane felt shocks and rude assaults as much as any of her sex, and she was keenly alive to all the feminine proprieties, and never permitted a liberty to go unrebuked.

She felt acutely that she had not played a more open part with Joshua Woodward. She thought sometimes that she should never forgive herself for not sending back his letter of invitation to meet him in the willow-copse, and at the same time informing him that she was engaged.

But there was ample excuse for her forgetting what was due to herself and to him, had his intentions been honourable, which they were not. Jane was new to the place and to the people; and no doubt, further, that she felt a little flattered at receiving a love-letter from so important a personage as the steward of Evesham House, who wore on his finger a glittering diamond ring, and his rather good-looking person further embellished with a rich gold watch and chain.

But in this matter of Joshua Ward she was much relieved that Ann Orwell had accepted her explanation, and had forgiven her, and was now at perfect peace with her, notwithstanding the attack made on her behind her back by that talkative scoundrel, Mr. Brummell.

Well, Jane was no coward, and when she saw that a thing was right and proper to be done she did not shilly-shally with it, nor hesitate over it, nor sit down and weep and despair at the difficulties in the way to be overcome.

But she was all these good and desirable things by nature, they came from the parent stock to her, and not from education; and therefore they were more easy of performance to her than to those who had been made good by training only.

The rope gave way, and directly after that she had recovered the fall involved in it—what did she do? did she sit down, and cry, and lament her hard fate, as too many girls would have done under the circumstances?

Not Jane. She might have lamented her hard fate, and indeed she did, and deeply felt the disappointment incurred by the knot giving way against her strength, but she was not foolish enough to let any of her feelings interfere with sensible action.

She would try, try again. She was grateful to find, however, on examining the cause of the disaster, that it was not the rope that had broken, but her own bad work that had thus given way.

She felt that she could improve upon that, but had it been the rope, Heaven help her! she would not have known what to have done in the emergency.

Without any further delay, she at once applied herself to the re-fastening of the bell-rope to the bar of the grate, and studied the science of it a little more.

Well, after a few minutes ingenious labour, she had made another fastening, and to all appearance far more secure than the last.

But appearances are sometimes deceptive, and Jane, considering that she was about to trust her life to this bit of frail rope, would not run the risk until she had used what means were in her power of testing it.

This time she did not put her whole strength at once upon it, for she had some consideration for her falling; by degrees she pulled, until at last, as before, she had her feet well planted in the carpet, and with both hands pulled with as much strength as she was capable at that time of exerting.

It proved in every way satisfactory—that is as far as the knot and the strength of the rope were concerned.

But " would you be surprised to hear " that the rope upon which she had cast all her hopes of escape was not long enough?

Jane, to use a naval term, " paid out " the rope to the window, when she found that there was nothing more left, or really nothing that was any worth to her.

If her disappointment need be told, we confess that we cannot adequately describe it.

Her first feeling was—and what could be more terrible?"—that she had been deserted of Heaven, and left without a friend in the wide world.

If ever she despaired in her life it was now as she still looked upon that rope which had proved so delusive to her hopes.

She sat upon the couch, and for a moment buried her face in her hands. Whether she was weeping over her disappointment, or studying some new means of escape, we could not say. Suddenly she sprang from this melancholy position and flew to the open window, and to have seen her thus any one might have been alarmed with the apprehension that she was going to commit suicide by leaping from the window!

But Jane had never been haunted by such cowardly unholy thoughts as deliberately taking her life. She would risk it in the defence of her virtue, but would never lay it down at the altar of despair.

While she clung to the window sill, her body in an attitude to take the leap therefrom if it be necessary, she strained her eyes upon the room door.

Her sudden alarm had been caused by the apprehension that she had again heard footsteps on the stairs.

But no one came, and she heard no further sound, and most likely had heard none before, except that heard through the agency of the imagination.

But she was now sorely puzzled what to do. She left the window, and once more essayed her strength upon the door. It made a little noise and rattle, but was as unyielding as before.

She then tried what screaming would do for her. And these were the screams that met the ears of Ann and the detectives.

Jane had not the happiness to know that the latter were on the premises, and her screams were made more with the view of reaching the ears of Ann than anything else.

But poor Ann was powerless to help although she was greatly troubled when she heard those cries.

But they helped the captive girl although she was not aware of it. No help immediately arrived, and Jane very reasonably concluded that there were none to hear, and she desisted from further efforts in that direction.

What could she now do to lengthen the rope? That was her next consideration. But it was a problem that she saw no means of solving. Nothing occurred to her, and she saw nothing with which she could lengthen the rope.

Hope was fast deserting her, while she still continued to rack her tortured brain. She cruelly felt her position, and became the more wretched the more her chances of escape seemed dark and hopeless.

But desperate persons resort to desperate remedies, as drowning men catch at straws. Jane thought upon the flowing dress that she wore. She thought that she would take it off, and cut it into long strips. She was too happy with her new idea,—so full of hopefulness for her escape—to think about the value of the dress, or the inconvenience of disrobing.

But she had nothing to cut it into strips with —but then she could tear it with her hands and fingers. And this she was about to do, when the handsome table cover attracted her attention. That would be better than her dress, for it was longer and stouter in material!

Jane began to smile again! In fancy she was once more abroad, and free from a villain's pursuit!

She took the green gold-striped cloth from the table, and folded it to the longest possible length. Then she methodically calculated how much of that length would be absorbed in fastening the cloth to the bell-rope—she would not deceive herself any more in the matter of the length, for that was the primary thing.

"If it won't do, I will have my dress too," she muttered to herself, while she held what length of cloth she had left after fastening it to the rope out of the window, to see how near it reached the ground.

Alas! the bell-ropes and the cloth, after they were fastened together, would not reach half way to the ground.

At this she was daunted at first, but the girl's courageous heart made amends for the inadequate length.

She would not supplement it by tearing up her dress—she would let herself fall the remaining distance. She would not hurt—and a broken leg or head was better than remaining an instant in this corrupt and corrupting atmosphere.

However, she had decided on taking all risks, and not cutting up her dress—for in her escape it would be very inconvenient to be without a dress.

But it would be far more inconvenient not to to be able to rise from the ground through the mishap of a broken leg! But Jane's courage led her from a due consideration of this contingency. She thought of it, indeed, but only thought of it in a manner that could hardly be considered serious.

The woman who hesitates is lost. This was the motto that was the basis of Jane's actions in the emergencies which arise, more or less, in everybody's life. With good heart, and much thankfulness that she had found a way out of the difficulties that her villain master had surrounded her with, she set to work to knot the cloth to the bell-rope.

But she had scarcely proceeded a step in her task before she was alarmed by some one at the lock of the door.

She dropped the cloth and rushed to the window, quite determined, high as it was, to let herself fall from it.

"But five minutes more, and I should have been ready with the rope! How unfortunate! Heaven guide me, and save me in my fall!"

This prayer for succour was no sooner uttered, than her ear was charmed by the voice of Ann!

"It's only me and a constable, Jane," announced the girl from the outside, while the policeman was applying the key to the lock.

But she had no sooner spoken than she was in the room, and in Jane's arms.

When the door opened, the policeman was the first to enter, and Jane for the moment thought that the voice of Ann had been counterfeited, and that her real perils were now to begin.

But no, it was her deliverance from perils that had come. No friends were ever so welcome to each other. They embraced again and again before they could give utterance to their feelings, which were of the deepest kind.

"We shall be all safe now, Jane!" cried Ann, with glee.

"Thank Heaven! thank Heaven!" responded Jane.

"Yes, you need have no further occasion to fear," said the detective.

"I was just going to leap from the window," said Jane, with a smile that reached the detective's heart, for he too was susceptible to the charms of a pretty girl, and when he went nearer to examine the blow on her brow, he felt mad to kiss her.

"Now the sooner we are up stairs, and take your evidence, the sooner you will be able to get out of this house, which I should think has been far from a pleasant retreat for you," said the detective with a smile.

They were soon again face to face with their cowardly tormentors—and after the scene already described, the detectives led their prisoners from the room to the stables, where the reluctant Butters was made to prepare the carriage, and saddle Mr. Duchesney's horse. This done, the prisoners were ordered inside the carriage; and while one of the detectives mounted the box and drove off, the other bestrode the horse and escorted them to the Gravesend lock-up for the night!

PRETTY JANE

OR, THE

VIPER OF KIDBROOK LANE

DUCHESNEY, WITH A BLOW KNOCKED BRUMMELL OVER THE CLIFF.

Riding along the beautiful Kentish roads and lanes to a prison at Gravesend, not in the least appeared to disturb Mr. Duchesney's serenity of mind. On the whole, (whether or not he affected the bravado, he only knew), he was jollier than ever.

He entered into a wild rambling conversation with the detective, who trotted his fine horse by the open window of the brougham, and who had become the most amiable of officers since Mr. Duchesney had slipped a couple of sovereigns into his "itching palm."

"I say, old fellow," he said to the pliable detective, "what an inconceivable pleasure there is in change!" Here he blazed away at his cigar, and puffed a volume of blue smoke into the face of the detective, who deferentially bent his ear to catch every word his rich prisoner said, and to make encouraging and flattering responses thereto.

"A fellow gets immensely used up in going the same daily rounds of pleasure," he continued. "There is something fresh and exciting in this!"

"Very glad I'm sure, sir, that you like it," said the agreeable constable. "And I can promise you that there's lots more changes to come yet."

"There's the crank, and the—"

"Cat for you," added the master, throwing himself back in the brougham, convulsed with laughter at the long and alarmed face the coachman pulled at the mention of a little wholesome flogging.

"He doesn't at all seem fond of cats," said the detective, supplementing Mr. Duchesney's remark. "But as this will be a second conviction, I think it is very likely that he will have to overcome his antipathy to those useful animals."

"I'm not convicted yet," said the coachman, whose steam had been completely taken out of him by this ugly conversation about prison "cats."

He knew, too, that second convictions were damaging things in the eyes of magistrates, and that the cat sometimes formed part of the punishment for "incorrigibles," as they are termed by the bench.

Brummell sat sad and silent. He looked upon his master's behaviour—which he did not look upon from a moral point of view, for had he done so he must have included his own also—to have been as silly as it was mean towards himself and his fellow-servant.

They had risked to serve him, and he had no right to have dragged them so regardlessly into so serious a scrape as this.

As he sat by his side, compelled to listen to his small talk and laughter, he hated him for the little show of feeling he exhibited towards those whose only crime was in serving him.

"You are quite a wet blanket upon the whole of my happiness, Brummell!" he exclaimed, rapping his servant smartly on the shoulder, which awakened him to say—

"If your happiness consists in inflicting wretchedness upon those who have incurred this disgrace—"

"Disgrace! call it a disgrace to suffer for a pretty girl? You are a gallant indeed! We are martyrs to love, nothing more!"

"The only difference between you and us being, that we are to have the martyrdom, while you have had the love—such as it was."

"I've had lots of love, with a vengeance!" exclaimed the master.

"That's your fault, sir."

"How so?"

"You alarmed the girls with your wild behaviour," said Brummell, without any attempt to disguise his dissatisfaction.

"My wild behaviour! I can only describe that as the height of impudence! Why the whole plot was yours!"

"But the acting was so bad, that the plot was seen through from the beginning," said the valet.

"Don't he speak well!" cried the coachman. "If he wasn't one of the prisoners he should be my adwocate."

"And you'll need one, too—"

"One, two—then that'll be three, if I can reckon," said the coachman, interrupting the horse-detective, for he it was who began to speak.

"And three won't get you off, playful as you are," observed the detective.

"What have I been doing on, I should like to know? This is my master's little affair—"

"That's right, shove it on to me," said Duchesney.

"He will find, sir, that every tub will have to stand on its own bottom," said the smooth-speaking detective. "But I cannot make that blockhead understand anything. Wherever did you pick him up, sir? and who gave him a character?"

"He brought me a written character from Colonel—Colonel—"

"Finchberry!" cried Butters, helping his master's memory.

"That's the gentleman he was living with when he stole the boots," said the detective, who was unnecessarily hard on the stableman, and seemed to have some old animosity against the man.

"Who said I stole them?" inquired the stableman.

"A British jury—is that good enough?"

"Not for me it ain't. Besides, there wasn't a Britisher among 'em—they were every one on 'em Londoners!" added the ignorant man, to the amusement of all; his geographical knowledge even causing a smile to mantle the aggrieved face of Mr. Brummell.

"I seem as good as a clown to yer all, 'pon my soul I do," he continued. "You've got no call to laugh as I can see, Mr. Brummell, for you're in the same swim with us."

"And by no means a pleasant swim," observed the valet, gravely. "But after I have set my transaction in the affair straight before a jury—"

"Don't depend on 'em—they're not to be trusted," said the coachman. "Didn't they find me guilty, when I told them I was hinnocent?"

"I care nothing about you," said the valet, the ill temper that his master had provoked extending to everybody. "Every one in this case I find is to be for himself. But I have no fear of getting through it."

"Then I'm sure the others will," observed the detective.

"I don't know so much about that," retorted the valet. "My previous good character will help me."

"It will not help you to get off; character influences the judge when he passes sentence—you may get six months instead of twelve."

"Six months, indeed! For what I should like to know? I worked for my master—"

"That's right, Brummell!" exclaimed the coachman. "So did I!"

"Mr. Duchesney was the exciting cause," continued the valet, forensically.

"No, no, the girls were the exciting cause," merrily interrupted the master. "Pull up at the next 'pub' you come to, officer, and let us have a nip all round."

"Sorry to say that it can't be done, sir," replied the detective, looking significantly in the face of the master.

"Why not? Here's the money, and we don't want to get out."

The detective then bent low from his horse, and whispered in Mr. Duchesney's ear.

"I see," said the master, when he immediately threw up his arms, dropped his head on his valet's shoulder, and with a very unpleasant kick at his coachman's stomach, which made Butters cry out, he lodged his legs in his lap.

"I'm ill! I'm faint! I die! Brandies all round—no, no—I'm delirious—give me brandy, every one of you! Brandy, or I perish! Don't stand staring at me,"—here he gave Butters another violent kick in the stomach, which made the man wince, and exclaim—

"It's no good a-kicking me—I ain't got no brandy!"

"Release his neckcloth, and unbutton his shirt," directed the detective; and Brummell, who was not up to the dodge, was completely taken in, and in the deepest anxiety threw open his shirt collar, and ran his hand through his hair to cool his head, while the coachman was about to pull off his boots, when the master, who objected to his proceedings with the boots, gave him such a dig in his ribs with the toe of his boot that set the man howling with pain, and he said, as soon as he could recover his wind—

" I shouldn't like to be your nuss, for long, I'm blowed if I should. What's to be done with him, hofficer? He's in your charge, remember."

" Oh! I'm in such agony!" he groaned, writhing and twisting, and throwing his arms about, which arms or hands he eventually managed to bring into contact with Mr. Brummell's nose, which was not anything so agreeable as a pinch of snuff, although it made him repeatedly sneeze and his eyes water.

" Have I no friend to get me brandy?" continued Duchesney, affecting the intensest suffering.

" If you'll lend me the hoss, guv'ner," said Butters to the detective, " I'll gallop back for some brandy."

" Will you really?" said the detective.

" Yes I will."

" No you won't," said the officer. " You don't get the blind side of me, so don't try it on."

" Brandy!" gasped the sick man.

" This ere detective won't let me fetch you any, nor he won't go himself, guv'ner," said the coachman, who, like Brummell, had not the slightest idea that their master was simulating illness, under the directions of the detective, as an excuse for the officer's getting him something to drink.

" Heaven's above, give me brandy!" roared the sick man.

" He wants it in a shower all over him," said Butters.

" I don't know whether you are aware of it, sir," said Brummell to the detective, " but the gentleman is very ill."

" That is obvious," he replied. " But I really don't see what I can do in it."

" Murder! brandy! thieves! fire! brandy! water—no, no, brandy!"

" He's quite delirious," said Brummell, with alarm.

" I'm going mad with pain!" he screamed, throwing up his arms, and as if by accident giving his valet a second slap on the nose, and his coachman another violent kick in his quantity of stomach.

" Oh! Oh! He's alive and kicking, I'm blest if he aint," said the coachman, rocking himself to and fro with real pain.

" Brandy! brandy!" roared the master, inwardly amused at the kicks and cuffs he was administering to his servants. " Brandy, don't I tell you!"

" I should be werry glad of some myself," said Butters.

" Hold his head up a little higher," directed the detective, addressing himself to the valet, who had his hand to his nose.

" I shall hold my nose a little higher, you may depend," he said, " or I shall soon have none to hold."

" Oh-h-h-h! I am so ill, and not a soul to succour me! Brandy! brandy! I've got ty-

phus and scarlet fever! I'm all over cholera, diarrhœa, and toothache! Brandy, or I die! I've got inflammation of the lungs, asthma, consumption, decline, and pretty Jane! Let me kiss her for her mother! Brandy! I'm in agony with congestion of the liver, the last rose of summer, whooping-cough and measles! Brandy! or I'll tear you all to pieces!"

" He's begun to rave," said the coachman, shrinking as far away from his master as the confined space of the brougham would admit. " Mind he don't bite you, Brummell."

" I shall take care of that as far as possible," returned the valet. " But he is certainly mad, either from excitement, fear, drink or pain. In either case it is unpleasant and dangerous, and I protest, sir, against being kept here with a madman."

" And I purtest, too!" cried Butters.

" Do you indeed!" sneered the detective. " What a dodge to get out of custody! But you don't."

" Then you must take the consequences," returned the valet.

" I've got hydrophobia—"

" Good Lord! look at the foam!" cried the coachman, but the foam was only in his imagination; however, his cry for the moment inspired Brummell, and the valet put his hand out to open the carriage door, when the detective drew forth a revolver, and said—

" At your peril!"

" He don't mean it, Brummell." said the coachman.

" You try him, and then I'll follow," said the valet, quite alive to the coachman's game, which was that Brummell should risk the danger of being shot at, but if there was no danger, and a good chance of escape, why then Butters would get up his bravery and follow him.

Both men, however, at sight of the pistol, sat quietly down, and kept their eyes fervently fixed on their mad master, who continued to breathe hard, and rave for brandy, and intermingle with his ravings a catalogue of diseases and a heap of miscellaneous nonsense, after the manner of a delirious person.

" I see that you are very ill, sir," said the detective.

" Oh, my friend, I'm dying—dying—"

" I hope not, sir," said the detective, while his fellow-prisoners secretly hoped that he was dying.

" Dying for brandy, you fools!" exclaimed Duchesney.

" You have quite relieved me," said the detective. " I thought it was a case of a coffin."

" And it will be, too, if I don't quickly get some brandy!"

" It is much against the law, but we shall pass a house in a few minutes, and then if you are not better you shall have some brandy."

" I begin to feel werry queer on the hinside myself," said Butters, pulling a wry face. " How is it with you, brother Brummell?"

" The prison doctor shall prescribe for you," said the detective. " Put the steam on, Ned," he added, to the detective coachman, " they're all getting ill inside."

" Gammon!"

" The governor is ill, and no mistake," replied the horse-detective.

"Oh, so ill!" groaned Duchesney, in quick response.

"Pull up at the Hop Pole for some brandy for him."

"And be so good as tell him to drive hard, for I'm sinking fast," said the master, and here he dextrously contrived to give the coachman a sly kick on his shin, which made the man howl again, but he could not resent it, for he believed that his master did not know what he was about, and therefore an irresponsible being.

"You're a purty inwalid, you are, a-kicking people's shins in that ere manner," he growled, while he rubbed his leg, but he wes only answered with a groan from the sick man, who was feigning illness unto death.

"Where is the Hop Pole?" inquired the detective from the box.

"I knows the Hop Pole werry well," said Butters,

"My mate is none the better for your knowing it, stupid!" said the detective.

"Who said he wur?"

"Brandy! I'm sinking under lock-jaw—the girl I left behind me—hydrophobia—"

"And hydrophobia it is too," said Brummell, who this time was fairly taken in. "You see in all his delirium he never calls for water."

"Torments of hell! who speaks of water? Bow-wow-wow! Bow-wow!"

Here he made snaps at his fellow-prisoners, until both of them seized him and held him down on the seat of the brougham.

"This is all through your a-mentioning of water—"

"Bow-wow-wow! Bow-wow-wow! Wow-wow-wow!" barked Duchesney, while he struggled to bite and rend the men who held him down.

"We mustn't mention water—"

"Bow-wow-wow! I'm in such pain across the kidneys. Brandy! My friend and a bottle to give him! Prussic acid or strychnine! Like a soldier die! Fatty degeneration of the heart—brandy!—hydrocephalus—hydrophobia—hydrometer—gasometer! Brandy, an' you love me, Hal!"

"It's a werry serous case, perliceman," said Butters.

"Anybody can see that," he snappishly replied. "Push a-head, mate, or it'll be a case of corpse."

"All right. But where is the Hop Pole?" again inquired the coachman detective from the other.

"You'll run your nose agen it presently," said the coachman, glancing out of the carriage-window. "I wish I had the ribbons, I'd bowl the lot on yer there in a brace of shakes. Right afore the door there's a pieee of water—"

The accidental mention of water again set off Duchesney on his barking, biting, and raving expedition. He kicked right and left, and both his servants came in for more kicks than ha'-pence, and were considerably bruised about the legs, and the brougham was full of yells and groans, and the noise much excited the mare, who, had it not been for the skill of the detective coachman, she would have bolted helter-skelter headlong down the steep hill before her.

She reared on high, taking up the shafts with her, while she foamed with passion, and her di-lated nostrils became blood red, and perspiration streamed down her sides, at the check the driver had given to her mad career down the hill.

The other horse, too, became a little restive, and curvetted from side to side, and showed his skill in rearing and snorting.

"He can't a-bear the snaffle," said Butters.

"He can't a-bear your yelling noise, so you'd best shut up," said the detective.

"I knows the hoss better than you do, and I was only telling yer."

"And I was only telling you to shut up. The Hop Pole, Ned, is a few yards to the left at the bottom of the hill."

"All right, mate," responded the detective coachman, who had not yet quite subdued the mare's proclivities towards a sensation.

"They does draw yer sich a fine glass o' hold hale at the Hop Pole, Mr. Brummell," said Butters, his memory travelling back a few years.

"It'll be some time before you put your beak into the pewter of the Hop Pole, I can tell you," said the detective.

"I don't know so much about that," growled Butters. "You seem to think I'm going to be hung."

"If you had your desserts you would," rejoined the officer.

Butters began to feel, as much as an uncouth nature like his could feel, that his body-guard was very hard upon him, and he gave such an appealing look to his fellow-servant, that Brummell was irresistibly impelled to remonstrate with the detective for his cowardice in taking advantage of their relative positions.

"Because, sir, that you are a detective, you need not be less a man," he said, looking straight into the rubicund face of the detective.

"Do you speak to me?" the latter asked, with a scathing scowl.

"That I did, sir," replied the bold Brummell. "And when I get the opportunity I shall speak to your superiors about your conduct to this man, who ever since he has been your prisoner you have been provoking to a breach of the peace."

Butters was overwhelmed with gratitude towards his fellow-servant, for his thus taking up the cudgels for him in this able manner.

"You have guv it him to rights!" he exclaimed, patting Brummell on the shoulder.

"D'ye hear, Ned," said the one detective to the other, "one of these fellows we have got in charge for abducting the girls, is going to report me for not treating them in a rose-lavender style! That's something rich, ain't it?"

"Was it that one who stole the top-boots?"

"No, the other, who has been carrying his head higher than his master ever since we lagged him."

"The chap who calls himself Samuel Brummell?"

"Yes. I daresay we shall yet find out something about this stuck-up Samivel Brummell. Many a prig tries to cover himself with bounce. Ha! ha!"

"If you were not an officer on duty, and I your prisoner, I would give you a demned good thrashing! I respect the law, not you."

"That's good, Mr. Brummell!" cried Butters. "You ought to be in Parliament, you ought.

You're a werry clever cove, and I'm obleeged to yer."

The detective tried the power of the handcuffs to silence their insubordination, as he deemed it. The sight of the jingling things weighed heavily on the speech and pluck of Butters, but Brummell defied them.

" Use them on me, at your peril !" he cried, holding forth his wrists from the carriage-window.

" When we get to the Hop Pole, you shall be adorned with the bracelets. Like convicts, I'll chain you both together."

" I didn't say nothink, did I?" he meekly asked, for Butters was no hero with policemen.

" Shame on you, Butters, that you should cringe and crawl to a fellow who has done nothing but insult you ! You would have been more of a man had you knocked him down."

" And got hung, perhaps !"

" Applauded, more likely," replied the Roman Brummell.

" Your strut and comb will yet be cut—and your hair too. Then you'll look such a guy ! And when the bread and water—"

Mr. Duchesney, true to the part that he was playing, began to scream for brandy, to recapitulate the numerous diseases he was suffering from—which ranged from the toothache to a gallopping consumption—and, in proof of his delirium, under which he did execution upon the legs of those in the brougham with him, he raved and talked about the most incongruous things.

" There's the Hop Pole, Ned," said the horse detective to the other, when they had reached the bottom of a narrow steep hill, embanked with high glistening white chalk sides or ridges, on the summit of which grew thousands of hardy wild bushes, which fringed the lovely meadows which sloped with its myriad lowing herd farther than the eye could reach.

The Hop Pole lay in a valley, at the foot of two hills. It was a well known house with travellers on the road, and was also popular with London workmen for their annual bean feasts, for the landlord was a jolly fellow, and a liberal caterer, and the rooms were spacious, and the grounds properly belonging to the house were of the most commodious character ; while the scenery at back and front, made up of hills, and hop-gardens, and woods, and farms, was unrivalled for its picturesqueness.

And besides the good hospitality always to be found at the Hop Pole, there were plenty of games and amusements to be had there ;—American bowls, skittles, foot ball, quoits, four corner, cricket, billiards, bagatelle, and two splendid bits of water for fishing and boating.

The landlord, too, was just what a landlord ought to be, a man of good general information —at all events as far as local information went. He was a Kentish man, and a very enthusiastic and devoted one. He knew and loved every inch of his county, and many a traveller has lingered late before the best parlour's winter night's cheerful fire to listen from his glowing lips recitals of county legends, battles, and the manners, customs, and peculiarities of Kentish people, which he always set forth to the best advantage, generally winding up with the assertion that the maids of Kent were the fairest, the men the bravest, and the county the most beauti-

ful and interesting, all England over, and all the world to boot.

Directly they had reached this memorable hostelry, the horse detective, without leaving his prisoners, ordered from a waiter who came out, a stiff glass of brandy and water for a gentleman that is ill.

" Make it two," roared Duchesney.

" Make it three !" supplemented Butters.

" Any more of this nonsense, and not any shall be had," said the detective, angrily.

" I'm in such dreadful torture ! Give me brandy or I die !"

The brandy as ordered was brought, and the sick man made an effort to raise himself from the seat of the brougham to take it, then with trembling hands he raised it to his lips—the rest may be conjectured.

" Better—better directly," he said, after he had drank it. " One of my paralysed sides has quite come round to its normal condition ; another glass, good friend, for the other side."

" No more, sir ; and I must trouble you for a shilling for the glass you have already had," said the detective.

" My money is in the pocket of my paralysed side, and I cannot move my hand or arm to get to my pocket. Another glass for Heaven's sake, and I will give you a sovereign !"

" I want none of your money," said the detective, who had already taken two sovereigns from his rich prisoner, " and I've a very good mind to cut you off from any more, however ill you may be, if you attempt to bribe me again."

Here a significant wink passed between the sick man and the detective, when the latter to blind the eyes of the other two prisoners, rode to his mate on the coach box, and said to him, with a knowing wink—

" What d'ye think, Ned, shall I get him another glass ?"

" He is downright ill, you think ?"

Duchesney gave a groan that rent the air, and the men stared, and the horses started.

" There, that'll tell you whether he is ill or not."

" Whatever is the matter with him ?" asked the coachman detective, who affected great particularity to know the merits of the case before he would sanction any further supply of spirituous liquours, for money too from Duchesney had likewise made him oblivious to his duties.

" It is quite impossible to say what's the matter with him. He seems to be suffering from everything."

" Yes, everything—that's my complaint ! And an awful complaint it is ! It's a judgment on me —I feel it is—for trying to lure those girls to sin. Give me brandy, and pray for me ! I am aching all over with everything. I've got diptheria now, and can't speak no more. Oh, sweet spirit hear my prayer, rhubarb pills, and tic-doloreux !"

" Look out for your nose and legs, Brummell, for master's delirious again," said Butters.

He kicked right and left, but his companions of the brougham were now too much on their guard to permit him to do much mischief.

" Better let him have another glass," said the coachman detective to the other. " And, hi ! d'ye hear? are you going to have anything yourself?"

"Yes, I shall have a little drop of Irish," was the answer.

"Order me a drop of the same."

"Nothink for us," observed Butters to his fellow-servant.

"Our refreshments are to come presently in the shape of a pair of handcuffs," returned the cynical valet.

"I say, sir," said Butters to the horseman, after he had tossed off his drop of Irish whisky, "don't be hard—we've come a long way—am in a deal of trouble about Mrs. Butters—"

"What about her?"

"Oh, sir, she will fret so, when she hears of this ere charge agen me of running arter two gals—"

"But she won't believe it, will she?" asked the detective.

"Won't she though! Mrs. Butters is a werry wicked jealous woman, and one of these creeturs who would b'lieve anything agen her husband, 'specially anythink about the gals."

"She must be an old fool to think any girl would have anything to do with an old frump like you."

"Not likely, I'm thinking," said Butters, swallowing the insult to his personal appearance with the hope of conciliating the detective to let him have a glass "o' hold hale," although both he and his wife could have contradicted the officer, for they could have told him, especially Mrs. Butters, that there was a certain young woman, who lived near the stables at Evesham House, who was too fond of Butters, and too forward in showing it, to please her.

"Come, sir, don't be hard on us—"

"Speak for yourself, not for me," said Brummell, with as much dignity as he could assume, "for I want nothing of him."

"Then you want about as much as you are likely to get," said the detective.

"What's the good of having the fat in the fire agen?" cried Butters. "And jist as he was agoing to melt, too! No good comes o' being windictive, Mr. Brummell."

"As I please about that; you are at liberty to do as you like."

"Lord help me, I wish I was! I'd get out of this ere carriage, and stand hold hales all round, and over again. But I'm in for it, and can't do as I like. But I'm werry famished for a glass o' hold hale—"

"Well, you've been middling civil," said the detective.

"I always am civil," interrupted Butters.

"That's a lie! You are only civil when it pays. I'm not blind nor stupid, and I think they would tell you the same at Scotland Yard."

"I'm sure on it," said the gentle Butters, so pleased with the friendly feeling that had sprung up between himself and his gaoler; and he flattered himself that after all a peck of his tact was worth a bushel of Mr. Brummell's cleverness.

"There's a deal of low cunning in you, Butters."

"Lord, sir! but I don't feel no sich thing," he replied. "But then perlicemen always know more than other people."

"Not one drop of ale do you have for that," said the detective.

"Whatever have I done now?"

"I would always rather any one called me a fool, than poked his fun at me, and imagined that I was fool enough not to see it. Drive on, Ned."

"All right, mate."

When the brougham moved away from the Hop Pole, Butters looked unutterable things at the churlish detective, who said to him—

"When you want anything from a detective officer, be civil to him, give him as little trouble as you can, but never fawn or flatter."

"I didn't."

"You did."

"But what about the hale?" asked Butters.

"That you don't have any, and let that be enough for the rest of the journey."

Butters now saw that his game was up—that they were trotting away from the Hop Pole—and that he could gain nothing by blarneying the detective, so he showed him his displeasure by grumbling in an under tone, but quite loud enough to be heard—

"Cold rabbit pie."

Nothing he thought could be more spiteful or insulting to a policeman's feelings, and being rather doubtful about his having heard him, he repeated the obnoxious calumny, and somewhat louder than before.

"I hear you," said the detective.

"You don't call that fawning flattery, does yer?"

"Shut up, you rascal you!" exclaimed Duchesney, who, after drinking his second shilling tumbler of brandy, he had fallen into a doze, and became very savage at being disturbed by his stableman. "Couldn't you see that your master was sleeping, blast you?"

"I didn't notice, guv'ner. I'm sure I didn't want to wake yer, for you've been kicking me about enough, so that I was glad to see you at rest."

"What did you wake me for then?" he asked, with bent fist levelled at his head.

"You waked yerself, I didn't wake yer, did I Mr. Brummell?"

"Oh, what one says the other would swear to," intervened the master.

"I object to that!" exclaimed the brave valet, his face full of passion. "And you have no right to make such an observation."

"You be ——! Do you think that I am afraid of you?" he exclaimed.

"Nor I of you, sir!" he retorted. "We stand upon an equality now."

"No, sir, you are still my servant," said the master.

"I decline the honour," said Brummell. "I serve no master who, for the gratification of his own selfishness, would heedlessly drag his servants to prison. Though I may get off this charge—"

"No you won't," said the detective.

"I am not speaking to you. And to you, sir, I have only to say—"

"Peace, you impudent fellow!" exclaimed his master, waiving his hand, then thrusting his head out of the window, he engaged in a whispered conversation with the horse detective.

"Whether you hear me or not, I shall say what I was going to say, and that is that you have played the poltroon with your servants! you have brought them into misfortune and disgrace, and left them to get out of it in the best manner that they could. What a master! except it be a master of meanness!"

"I'm werry much of your opinion," said Butters. "Only I should like to add that there is wages due—"

"Let him keep them; his money is of too dirty a character for me to handle."

"But I'm rayther short, and can't afford to be so generous."

"That's your business; the salary due to me he is welcome to—it will pay his counsel's fees, for he has not wit enough to defend himself."

"Nor I neither, Mr. Brummell, so that I want all that he owes me to pay a lawyer."

"You need not grieve about that; I'll help you."

"You *are* a trump!" exclaimed the stableman, with as much delight pictured in his face as if he had been tried and acquitted.

"But for your past character—"

"D—n them ere top-boots!" exclaimed the stableman, scratching his head.

"But for them, you would have got off, with a little special pleading. But I was fool enough to go deep into the matter with the girls, so I am safe to have them dead against me. As to you, they can swear nothing against you—"

"Except the driving on 'em down," said the stableman, encouraged by Brummell's hopeful talk.

"And that you did by my orders, which you had a right to obey, for I was the superior servant."

"In coorse I had," rolled out the stableman.

While the servants were consoling each other, and swearing to help each other in all possible ways, the master was endeavouring to make a further friend of the detective, whom he found very susceptible to money, of which there was plenty about. With his back turned upon his servants, and his head quite out of the carriage window, he whisperingly conferred with the detective upon the subject of bail, after slipping a third sovereign into his hand.

"There is a miserly solicitor whom I know in Gravesend; now if you could contrive for me to see him before you took me to the lock-up—"

The detective shook his head.

"Ah—you don't see your way to it?"

"Quite impossible," said the detective. "Had you been alone, there might have been no difficulty about it."

"It would have saved so much time if you could see your way clear to it."

"'Pon my word, sir, I don't see it," said the detective.

"Well, then, if it won't save time—which it will—it will very much relieve my mind in having secured bail."

The detective put on his considering cap, and then said—

"You want me to do a very risky thing."

"Find the way to do it, and I'll make it all right."

"That's beyond your power, if it goes wrong," said the detective. "But we are nearing the prison now, and if there's anything to be done it must be done at once."

"Yes, yes, there's no time to lose," said the master, eagerly. "How do you propose to manage it?"

The detective again fell into a brown study.

"Look here, I'll chance it," he said, after he had considered, and conferred with his mate on the box.

"That's a good fellow!" cried the master.

"Now then, where does this solicitor live?" asked the detective, and which question was answered by Duchesney giving him a card, containing the address of the solicitor.

"Why it's only four doors from the lock-up," said the detective, after he had scanned the solicitor's card, which the prisoner happened to have about him. "I wish it had been a little further off. Look here, I'll manage all you require without running me into any danger."

"Right you are. But how?"

"Directly that I have handed you over to the superintendent of the station, and got the charge entered, I will make it all right with him for you to see the solicitor at once in his private office."

"Good as far as it goes. But how to the deuce will the solicitor know that I am there, and that I urgently wish to see him?"

"I shall call on him myself immediately," returned the constable.

"But if he is from home?"

"There would be the same contingency in that direction if you yourself called upon him."

"Of course there would."

"But if he should happen to be out—which is not likely, for misers like to be home looking after their hoards at this time of the evening, except they can increase them by going abroad —why then I will do my best to find out where he has gone, and ride after him."

"You can do no more, I'm d—d if you can!" exclaimed the prisoner.

"Make your mind easy, you shall see him to-night if he's living."

They had now reached the cheerless entrance of the police-station, and when Butters looked at it he shrugged his shoulders, and audibly cried—

"Good Lord deliver us!"

"Halt!" cried the horse constable to his mate on the box.

"I wish the mare would bolt from that horrid place! and I b'lieve she would too, for she's a werry affectionate creetur, if she knew how nervous that place made me."

"Now then, out you go," said the detective to the servants, after their master had jumped out nimbly enough, and was escorted up the narrow stone passage by a policeman attached to the station, and then returned to show the like attentions to the other two prisoners.

"They don't seem in too much hurry, mate," said the policeman to the detective.

"I'm not going to break my neck for yer," said Butters. "Who are you?"

The policeman grinned, while he said, in provincial accents—

"Where did you catch them burds?"

"I wish I was a burd," returned the stableman, "I'd soon be on the fly."

"A Michaelmas bird, that's what he is," said the detective, holding back the door of the brougham for his reluctant prisoners to alight.

"Good with a bit of onion stuffing, eh?"

"Oh, no, he's good for nothing," rejoined the detective to the amusement of the policeman.

"So you've brought him to our school to be

reformed?" suggested the Gravesend police-man.

"Cold rabbit pie," sneered Butters, which was the severest retort he could make to a po-liceman.

"You'll get no such delicacy in here, so if that's your fancy you should have kept outside. What's he been up to, mate?"

"Running away with a couple of girls. Would you believe it?"

The policeman laughed immoderately.

"One thing he need never fear," said the po-liceman.

"What's that?" asked the detective.

"Why a girl's running away with him," he replied.

"I should like to punch your head," said the stableman.

"You shall when you come out. You're too fresh for me now."

"He'll be stale enough after awhile at the crank," observed the detective.

"Come on," said the stableman to the valet, "for I don't want to hear any more of their hignorance. Come on."

"If you don't, I shall quickly pull you out," said the detective.

"You want to make a row, that's what you want, afore the station door, and then say that we hobstructed a hofficer in the discharge of his dooty, and bring forrard that other perliceman as a witness," said the stableman, which was anything but alighting from the brougham.

"Are you coming out, you sweep?" inquired the detective, quite enraged, though it would be impossible to say for why except for the caprice of the moment, for whatever delay there might have been in the alighting was entirely traceable to himself and the Gravesend policeman.

"Here's a storm in a teapot!" cried Butters. "Who's afraid?"

"Go on, Butters, go on," said the valet, very languidly, for he was thoroughly wearied out with the whole day's proceedings.

"After you, my friend," said the stableman to the valet, "as the sooperior servant, after you."

"There, we've had quite enough of your non-sense," cried the detective, rushing forward, and seizing him with both hands by the collar of his coat, unceremoniously dragged him from the carriage to the pavement, and quickly hustled him along before he placed him beside his mas-ter, and before the stern-looking superintendent, who stood with pen in hand and the charge-book before him, quite prepared to make a record of the new case,

The local policeman escorted the scornful valet into the room, and before the superintend-ent, who now became full-blown with magiste-rial display.

"Is this gentleman the prosecutor?" asked the superintendent, when Brummell made such a stately head-erect entrance.

"Oh, dear no, sir, he is one of the prisoners, and the worst of them," replied the detective.

"Yes, I'm not the worst, am I, sir?" cried the stableman, delighted that the detective had declared a difference between them, and which difference had made him the lesser culprit.

"You are not my judge, are you?" asked the stiff-necked valet, whose quiet, dignified airs, and his rich broad-cloth dress, certainly invested him more with the appearance of a prosecutor than a prisoner.

"If I were your judge," replied the detective to the valet's question, "I should herring-pond you, and no mistake."

The valet, like a noble Rum'un as he was, gave him one of his looks (which did not appal), folded his arms upon his breast, and turned his back upon the detective.

"Now then I am quite prepared to take the charge," said the superintendent. "But where is the prosecutor?"

"There is no prosecutor," said the detective, much to the astonishment of the superintendent, who raised high his black bushy brows, as he exclaimed—

"What! no prosecutor?"

"No; they are all prosecutrixes," said the detective.

"Ah yes, I see," said the superintendent, who was a respectable military-looking man, and who was not at all offended at the detective's play-fulness which almost amounted to a "sell," "they are prosecutors of the feminine gender. But where are they? I should like to see the prosecutrixes."

"One of them is a noble lady—"

"By birth only, not by nature," intervened Duchesney.

"Do not interrupt, if you please," said the superintendent, calling up his authority.

"The lady I have referred to," said the de-tective, apologetically for Mr. Duchesney, who he was anxious to serve as much as possible be-hind his wife's back—for he had in his pocket some of Lady Mary's gold mingling and jingling with that of her hated husband's, and which was given to him as a bribe that he should do his worst to blacken the charge against Duchesney— "the lady I have referred to is this gentleman's wife."

"Oh, indeed," said the superintendent, ad-ding, with a little more deference in his tones, "Then I presume, sir, you are a nobleman?"

"By nature only, and not by birth," said Duchesney, with a bow and a smile.

"Noble by nature!" exclaimed the indignant valet. "Why, sir, he is the meanest scoundrel out, and the sequel of this case will show it!"

This assertion, delivered so boldly and ear-nestly as it was, startled the superintendent, who cast his eyes to the detective for an expla-nation, that is, if he had any to offer.

The latter slurred the thing over by lying.

"This man has been going on in this insolent manner ever since I took him in charge."

"Not me, sir," said the stableman, always looking out to give himself a lift over the hedge, even if it were at the expense of his friends, "not me, sir," he repeated, "but this other man," pointing to the valet.

"Hold your noise," said the detective. "I didn't say you, did I, you fool?"

"No you didn't, like a good fellow as you are," said the stableman, in carneying tones.

"We want uone of that blarney," said the detective. "You'll get no good by it from me, and that you know."

"I only said—"

"Say nothing until you are asked to speak. The girls are about to bring a very serious charge

PRETTY JANE

OR, THE

VIPER OF KIDBROOK LANE

LADY MARY AND THE DOCTOR DISTURBED BY THE SOUND OF FOOTSTEPS.

and one that all the judges punish with great severity."

"What are they charged with?" asked the superintendent.

"For a conspiracy to abduct away from their service two of Lady Mary Duchesney's maid servants—one of them, Jane, a most attractive girl—"

"That doesn't matter a pin, her attractiveness," interposed the superintendent.

"I know, sir; I just mentioned that by the way. And that they abducted these girls for felonious purposes."

"No doubt, if proved against them—"

"Which they can't do agen me!" exclaimed Butters.

"Will you shut up?" stormed the detective.

"I must defend myself" persisted Butters. "What did a hold married man like me want with two gals? All my felonious purposes are carried on at home with Mrs. Butters, and there would be a dreadful row in the house if they wasn't."

"Shall I take him to a cell below?" asked the detective of the superintendent.

"For gracious sake don't do that!" pleaded the stableman. "I only wanted to defend myself against a hinfamous charge."

"This is not the time or place," observed the superintendent.

"Oh, sir, he knows that very well," said the detective.

"Has he gone through this process before?" inquired the superintendent.

"Does he look like it?" said the detective, quizzingly. "Three months with hard labour that man has had for stealing a pair of top-boots. Would you believe it, sir?" he added, laughing.

"And who is the third prisoner?" the superintendent inquired.

"He is my valet," replied Duchesney, stepping forward.

"*Was* your valet," said the stiff-necked servant, emphasising the word in the past tense, "but your valet no longer."

"Not good enough now, you sweep, eh?" said the master, stung with the haughty demeanour of his servant. "How much misfortunes develope and level men! This man, sir," he continued, addressing the superintendent, "but a few hours ago would have licked the very boots I wear! But now that my rashness has led him and myself into a bit of a trouble like this, he becomes insolent! I paid him good wages—treated him as a companion more than a servant. See what a serpent I have been nursing!"

"He don't mean me, mind," cried the stableman, as he caught the superintendent's eye.

"Oh, you're a pair of time servers," replied Duchesney, with a scowl.

"You shouldn't say a word agen me," said the stableman. "I did everything right by you and the hosses."

"And the corn, too, I daresay," said his old enemy, the detective.

"I don't know what you mean, I'm sure I don't," ejaculated the stableman, talking very innocently, but looking very guilty.

"Is there any charge against him for stealing corn?" inquired the superintendent of the detective.

"None that I know of, sir," he replied. "No doubt there would have been had his master been as sharp as he has been goodnatured. He has had lots of opportunities to be dishonest with the corn—"

"But has he availed himself of them, and is he charged?"

The detective replied in the negative.

"Then I see no object in dwelling on it," said the superintendent. "My charge book would soon be full were I to enter records against persons who had opportunities to be dishonest."

"I merely made the remark out of sympathy to his master," said the detective, who was himself as dishonest as the man he was so fond of accusing.

"And I owe you one for that ere remark," said the stableman, ruffling up.

"And I would pay him now had he insinuated such a thing against me," said the valet, looking daggers at the detective.

"I really must call you to order, Mr. Samuel Brummell," said the superintendent. "Are you aware where you are?"

"In the pit of a theatre," was the astonishing reply.

"There's insolence for you!" exclaimed the detective.

"A what?" interrogated the superintendent, lifting his bushy brows, and darting austere

looks at the daring Brummell, who, to his great surprise, neither quailed nor trembled.

"I said the pit of a theatre," he coolly replied.

"I know you did, sir—I know you did," observed the superintendent. "But what did you mean?"

"That is nnother question," said the valet, as cool as a cucumber.

"Nothing but insolence you see, sir," said the detective to the superintendent, anxious to arouse the ire of the latter against the valet, that he might be instructed to remove him to the cells below.

"Yes, yes, I see his temper plain enough," said the superintendent. "It blows hot now, but I think we shall be able to cool it."

He then wrote opposite the name of Samuel Brummell in the charge-book, in blood-red ink, "Prisoner insolent."

"There, sir, do you see that?" asked the superintendent, losing his calmness and his dignity at the same time.

"Plain, as if it were written in blood," replied the valet, who kept tantalisingly quiet and cynical.

"The pit of a theatre indeed!" cried the spirit wounded superintendent. "The visiting magistrates will make you account for that observation—not made in a corner, remember—"

"Oh, I remember; my memory must be poor if I did not, seeing that the words have only just been spoken."

"You might yet regret having spoken them," remonstrated the superintendent.

"I might indeed, but I can hardly conceive such an event."

The superintendent looked at the detective, and the expression of his looks conveyed to the latter that he was asking him, as plainly as if he had spoken—

"This man is incorrigible. What is to be done with him?"

The detective quite understood that his looks carried that significance with them, and replied accordingly, by saying—

"Let me take him to the cells, sir. He's too much patter about him to be borne with."

"Truth offends you," remarked the valet.

"Complete the charge, and then take him to the darkest cell you can find," said the superintendent, whose decision appeared to give him as much satisfaction as the detective, who said—

"And I know one that's very damp as well as very dark; one that will remind him more of the bottomless pit than the pit of a theatre."

"You are a witness to all this, Butters, and I shall call upon you when the proper time comes round," said the implacable valet.

"Oh, pray don't bring me into it, Mr. Brummell," said the stableman, whose nerves were shocked by the mention of cells as dark as the regions of the bottomless pit where Satan and his host reign and suffer.

"Why what a coward you are!" exclaimed the valet.

"I know I am, so don't have nothink to do with me, for I'm sure to put you in the hole."

"You shall swear to what you have seen and heard, or perjure yourself," said the determined valet.

"He's use to that," said the detective.

"I'm sure I don't know what you mean by perjury," snivelled the stableman.

Another case was here brought into the station, and this additional business had the effect of making the superintendent concentrate his attention a little more upon the case in hand.

The detective placed him in full possession of the facts of the case, when it transpired that Lady Mary, a little while after the girls had been abducted, was determined to follow them, and for that purpose drove to the Eltham police-station and obtained the assistance of the two detectives, to accompany her in a post-chaise to Morley.

Bringing the officers with her from Eltham to Evesham House, she gave them a sumptuous entertainment, and then she disguised herself as the little old woman, and then drove rapidly after the girls. On the way she gave the detectives to understand a great deal about her relations with her husband, and further to understand that the more they could deepen the case against him, the more they would place her under obligations to him.

Now there is as much of the weakness of human nature in detectives as in any other portion of mankind. Oh! if Mr. Brummell had but known the bribery that had been about, and how much those men had disgraced themselves by yielding to it, no doubt but that he would have turned the tables on them, by getting them severely reprimanded, if not dismissed from the "force."

But "he saw it not, thought it not." These clever detectives had outwitted him, although some of the bribery money had passed from his master to one of the detectives under his very nose.

But the valet had not the opportunity to see the rich bribe and smiles full of meaning that passed from Lady Mary to the plastic detectives. There was one of those crisp water-marked bits of paper handed to one, which required no holding up to the light to be assured of its genuineness; while to the other she handed five sovereigns, which were an equivalent to the bit of "flimsy" which had been carefully folded and placed out of sight, but not out of mind, by the other officer.

No one better than Lady Mary knew the power of money. She had had a very large experience of its potency and its corrupting influences. She found all mankind accessible to it —clergymen, physicians, lawyers, rich and poor, men, women and children—her theory, founded on wicked experience, was that she could buy help from any one for the execution of any crime that her hellish imagination might conceive.

Lamentable to say, and as our readers know, this wicked woman had too much justification for her extraordinary opinions. But then Mrs. Oliphant and Joshua Ward, and half a dozen others of their mental and moral calibre, thank Heaven, were not types of the world we live in, if they were of the little circle which Lady Mary grovelled about.

Money no doubt is a very great power both for good and evil, and because Lady Mary chose to use it for wicked purposes with persons as hellish as herself, it would be a very wrong inference, and a very foolish one, to conclude that all money was used for debasing objects, and that all people could be contaminated with it.

But the views of so corrupt a woman are not worth the slight digression from our narrative. Let her sing as she likes, "Tan-ta-ra-ra, rogues all!" our experience teaches us that the world is peopled with myriads of people—and poor ones, too—who would scorn all her wealth rather than be a party to any of the wickedness she has been the author of.

Did she not know that though she bore a high name amongst the aristocracy, that by that very aristocracy she had been denounced as an outcast, and that not one of the nobility of England but what would have lost caste in speaking to her?

Her father, too, the noble Earl Ashford, had not he disowned her, and cast her from his house and his heart as a loathsome thing?

Her revered mother—where had the wickedness of her daughter brought her? To an untimely grave.

The Earl, too, began to show symptoms of passing away. The discredit his daughter had brought upon his house, and name oppressed him the more as he grew older. He wanted some one to lean upon, but there were none.

He sent for his solicitor one day, feeling himself worse than usual, and that his time grew short, and directed his attention to a clause that he wished to be inserted in his Will. The solicitor, a middle aged man, but somewhat eccentric in dress, read the following brief clause with as much surprise as feeling for his noble client, whose grey hairs were being fast brought with sorrow to the grave.

The memorandum was in the Earl's own handwriting, and was written so tremblingly that the man of law could scarcely read it, when he was bade by his client to read it audibly, while the Earl could not listen with more wrapped attention if had been his own death warrant that he had been listening to :—

"To my daughter Mary, now Mary Duchesney, I bequeath nothing but my tears and my hatred. I hereby disinherit her from all and every participation in my property personal or otherwise. The letter of the law compels me to mention her name in this my last Will and Testament, and I do so, but do so only to disown and disinherit her. She has disgraced her name as my daughter, and her sex as a woman. Her life has been one round of crime and dissipation; she broke the heart of the most devoted of mothers; she defies all the laws of man and God; she is sensual and devilish, and only glories in her shame. And I further bequest that the estate known as 'Marathon,' situate in Sussex, and which I had always intended to bequeath to my aforesaid daughter Mary, and on which estate God gave her life and the Evil One a spirit, be sold and the money invested for the benefit of such charities as I shall hereinafter name. And this I will and devise that my estate may be purged of her birthplace, and her very name forgotten in connection with my house and name, which she has lived only to disgrace and dishonour. May the Lord have mercy on her soul!"

After the solicitor had finished the melancholy document, he said—

"While I deeply sympathise with your sorrow, I really would not advise you to pour out your heart feelings in a legal document. You can disinherit her without that."

"Do not advise me, for I will have *my* way," said the Earl, sternly adding, "she merits all my displeasure, and the record of it! When my Will is published, let unhappy fathers, cursed with unruly children, pity me, and let wicked children take warning."

"I will not further trouble your lordship with my views."

"Thanks—thanks," said the Earl, his aged eyes suffused with tears.

"Your lordship's feelings are too strong and acute now for the reception of advice. But ere the Will can take effect a check may be made to the abandoned life of Lady Mary."

"Do you mean by death?"

"Death, illness, or the ascendancy of conscience," the solicitor suggested.

"Ah, my friend," said the Earl, "I can believe in her death, in her illness, but never in her awakened conscience! What is impossible cannot be. She has no conscience."

Nothing further passed between them on the subject. The solicitor did not consider it to be his duty, as he said, further to intrude his advice, but to carry out his instructions. The Earl's wishes were embodied in the Will, and the most stringent legal care taken to make the testator's desire to disinherit Lady Mary indisputable.

Before the Earl died, the solicitor's wife, who was a most excellent lady, called on Lady Mary, whom she saw in Mrs. Sterne's room. This lady, from the purest motives, told her about her disinheritance by her father for her misconduct, which she eloquently endeavoured to open her eyes to, and wound up by saying—

"But my belief is, and my husband's too, that if you would be more of a woman and a daughter—throw aside your evil associates—"

"Sink my individuality, in short; is not that what you mean, Mrs. Lindsay?" haughtily and pertly interrupted Lady Mary.

"If the individuality be bad and disagreeable, it is what I mean."

Lady Mary turned round, looked at Mrs. Sterne, who sat aside well pleased to listen to the sensible lecturing that was being administered to her abandoned mistress, and laughed immoderately.

Then she exclaimed—

"The idea! Whatever can possess the woman to think that I could alter my individuality? And if I could I should not, for I rather like it."

"Candidly. it is an abomination to every one else," said Mrs. Lindsay, rather hurt that her mission to Evesham House was likely to be fruitless as far as making any impression on the heart or mind of Lady Mary went.

"That matters not to me, madam," cried the latter. "The difference only between you and I is this, that while you strive to please everybody, I only strive to please myself."

"Let me tell you—"

"What! something more to tell me?" she gaily interrupted.

"Your smartness is but a poor attempt to cover impropriety."

"I thank you for your visit, Mrs. Lindsay," said Lady Mary, with a mock curtsey, "but as for your plain speaking—not that I care about it—not that it makes the smallest impression on me—I shall feel obliged if you will give me as little more of it as possible. I like you very well for a partner at whist, but as a lecturer on female propriety, I confess that you have failed to charm me, Give it up, my dear Mrs. Lindsay, for I do assure you that your pursuit of the avocation is a lamentable failure. By the by, how is your husband?"

"I know of nothing that he is suffering from but the knowledge of the unhappy differences between you and your father."

"Then he is not very bad, poor dear man," said the Earl's daughter.

"Why are you so censorious on everything that is named to you? I can assure you that Mr. Lindsay is very much affected to see your father going to his grave with such disturbed feelings about you, his only child."

"I can't help being his only child, can I?" she asked, continuing her vein of irony.

"But you can help being a wicked one," very happily retorted Mrs. Lindsay.

"Wicked, I suppose, because I am not like you, eh?"

"You have made that taunting remark before. Your wickedness is of an unspeakable kind," said Mrs. Lindsay, warmly,

"I am very glad to hear it, for it will save my ears being bored with it. Let us leave this nonsensical twaddle—"

"Oh, to speak thus of a father's grief!" exclaimed the solicitor's wife.

"My father's grief as you call it—"

"It bears no other name, and it is terrible to witness," observed Mrs. Lindsay, and she spoke with so much earnestness that it suggested to Lady Mary to inquire if anything had transpired afresh.

"You seem to be keeping back some news—is it so? Let me know all. I have plenty of nerve, and plenty of pluck, therefore you need not have any delicacy about communicating to me any event—however terrible it may be, and however interested I may personally be in it."

"News enough, I should have thought. to be told that your father had disinherited you," said Mrs. Lindsay.

"Pooh! that is not half a sensation for me," retorted the half haughty, half playful Lady Mary. "I don't want money or possessions, thanks."

"But your father—"

"Yes—well?"

Mrs. Lindsay was speechless. She had no idea of the hardened condition of heart to which she had fallen. It was quite plain to her that she was now the very incarnation of callousness and wickedness, which she attempted to carry off as much with smartness of conversation, as with bravado. Mrs. Lindsay and her husband had both done much to make a good woman of her, but they might as well have attempted to make a silk purse out of a sow's ear. The notorious fallen condition of her character, prevented Mrs. Lindsay, or any other woman who regarded herself, from making frequent visits to her. It had been some two years since she had seen her before, but now she thought she would give her another chance to amend her ways of life, and come to her father in the spirit of the Prodigal of Scripture, and cry "Father, I have sinned against Heaven and against thee, and am no longer worthy to be called thy son."

Mrs. Lindsay believed that Lady Mary was unusually fond of money, and therefore she was deeply surprised to find what little effect her father's disinheritance had upon her.

She knew that she had married a man whom she affected to despise merely that she might add to her possessions, and she now ventured to remind of it.

" Ah, I am daily reminded of that folly, and therefore I have no wish to add to it," she said.

" But surely you do not call it folly to bring peace to your father?" exclaimed Mrs. Lindsay,

" How can a wicked creature like me bring peace to any one? Besides, those sentiments that you have so often spoken to me about, my dear Mrs. Lindsay, have been so little in my way, that it really would be too much trouble now to change my course of life, which has always given me pleasure, although it has been wild and wicked, as contrasted with a humdrum everyday life."

Mrs. Lindsay lifted her hands, and shook her head, and then suddenly burst into a fit of tears.

" Pray do not weep, madam, for I am not susceptible to tears," said the hardened woman. " I can't remember that ever I wept in my life. I might have done so when a child, but I'll be bound to say that it was about something that having my own way was concerned in—was it not, Sterne? You know all about my childhood."

" Well, if your ladyship refers to me," said the housekeeper, as pleasantly and submissively as possible, " I must say that you were a very wilful child."

" Ah, yes, I thought so," said her mistress. " And the fruit is very much like the blossom, is it not, Mrs. Lindsay? But come, take off your bonnet, and take lunch with me, and then I'll row you about the lake."

" Other engagements will prevent my doing so."

" Then what in the name of fortune did you come for?"

" To tell you that your father was ill, and that—"

" He had disinherited me," interrupted Lady Mary, with much impatience. " Amen, so be it. But what can I do to alter these things? I am not fool enough to throw away a fortune if I could help it."

" You *can* help it, and you ought to help it," replied the solicitor's wife, firmly, while she added, " and one day you will regret that you did not help it."

" Sufficient is the day for the evil thereof," remarked Lady Mary. " Really you want impossible things from me."

" In what respect?"

" You ask me to alter my nature."

" What high-flown fallacies you cheat yourself with. If your cook spoils your dinner—"

" She shouldn't stop with me to spoil another, that's all," she quickly intervened.

" Then you would be unjust."

" Oh, yes, I'm sure to be wrong."

" But the cook, whether you dismissed her or not," Mrs. Lindsay continued, " would find out her error in spoiling the dinner, so as to avoid it for the future. It would be absurd to say that it was her nature to spoil her dinner, and that therefore she could not mend her ways. You would be the very first to reprove such folly."

" I should; but if cook came to me with an affair of the heart, and it might be a very unorthodox affair, why then I shouldn't. My evil, to use the world's phrase, has all sprung from an affair of the heart."

" An affair of the devil you mean," replied Mrs. Lindsay, greatly to the satisfaction of Mrs. Sterne, who gave her every now and then an approving nod.

But it was far otherwise with Lady Mary. The last observation of her plain-spoken visitor very much displeased her, and she chose thus to resent it :—

" I think, madam, you must have forgotten that you are only a visitor, and are taking advantage of that circumstance to say impertinent things to me. I decline to hear anything more from you. Good morning," she added, with a curtsey that betrayed more haughtiness than politeness, then in queenly style she left the apartment.

" She's mad," said Mrs. Sterne to Mrs. Lindsay, when they were left alone.

" Oh! what an infamous woman!" exclaimed the latter. " Bad—every way bad. She won't do good, even for that which is palpably for her own benefit. However can you live with such a monster?"

" Only for her mother's sake."

" Yes, to be sure, I remember now—you made a promise to the dear Countess. And very good it was of you. But had I made all the promises in the world, I could not have kept them. Live with such a woman as that I could not."

" I have had a hard fight with myself to continue here. I do assure you, ma'am, that her and her husband have made their establishment little better than a hell and a brothel."

" I can well believe it, and the sooner that I am out of the place the better for my character," said Mrs. Lindsay.

" Why should I stop here any longer, ma'am? The dear Countess fondly hoped that I could do her some good. But time has taught me that I cannot, and I have at last resolved to leave her to her own wicked impulses, which nothing now I am convinced but an interposition from Heaven can arrest her from."

" I quite think so too, I do indeed, Mrs. Sterne. She shall never see me again, for I feel that the attempt to bring her to a sense of her degradation is beyond human power. My heart bleeds for the Earl. But as far as the property is concerned, she is cut off without a penny, and such a fearful denunciation of her !"

" Indeed, ma'am. But I know that the poor old Earl deeply feels it."

" Feels it, Mrs. Sterne ! Why it will be the death of him, as it was of the Countess. My word for it that in a few weeks Earl Ashford will be no more. And it was this serious condition of his health which brought me here to-day."

" And what ingratitude you have met with !" said Mrs. Sterne.

" I might just as well have stopped away," rejoined Mrs. Lindsay.

" But there is always a pleasure springs from doing one's duty, however poor the results of the task that we have undertaken."

" I do assure you that it was only duty that led me here, and I regret to say that the sense of its performance is its only reward."

" Oblige me by giving my respectful duty to his lordship. If I can get to London next week I shall call and see him."

" And do not forget to call on me also," said the solicitor's wife. " We shall always be very glad to see you.'

" You are very kind."

" They say that women cannot keep a secret," said Mrs. Lindsay. " But that is a libel, and therefore I will trust you with one, and one that you are deeply interested in."

Mrs. Sterne looked all kinds of inexpressible things. A " secret!" Well, the word calls up in the mind of every one a " pleasing dreadful thought,"—indeed no word that we know of affects or calls into prominence a greater variety and contrariety of thoughts feelings and passions. The sound of the word stimulates hope and fear, curiosity and dread, wonder and vanity, terror and pleasure.

" You may rely on me, ma'am, that your confidence shall not be misplaced," said the housekeeper, " although I do not covet the trust."

" You need not be alarmed, Mrs. Sterne, the secret that I am about to impart will afford you nothing but pleasure, therefore you need not shrink from being the depositary of it."

Mrs. Sterne smiled all over, and amidst the smiles might be traced the question in the expression of her countenance, " Whatever can it be ?"

But her curiosity was quickly put at rest. Mrs. Lindsay did not long tantalise her breathless suspense, but at once told her that the Earl had left her a very nice little fortune.

When this became known to Mrs. Sterne she did not show that delight and pleasure which the solicitor's wife expected to see, which was soon explained when the old housekeeper said that—

" I always understood that the Earl had generously remembered me in his Will, and so did the Countess."

" Oh dear, no; something better than those, they were only small legacies," said Mrs. Lindsay.

" I always felt grateful for their handsome remembrance, and certainly never expected an addition to it."

" Well, then, the Earl has made an addition to it—enough to make a lady of you!"

The housekeeper stared with downright wonder. She looked incredulously at the solicitor's wife, who said—

" Oh, it is true enough. And I am very glad of it, for you have been a faithful servant to the Ashford family for a great number of years. But this is not telling you the degree of his munificence. Now don't be proud when I tell you."

" It will prove a bad gift, ma'am, if it makes me proud."

" There is no danger of that feeling with you. He has left you three hundred a-year, by codicil to his Will, and which was expressly added to denounce and disinherit Lady Mary, and to settle an annuity of three hundred a-year on you, my friend."

" I never heard of such a thing !" was her first exclamation.

" And not likely to again as long as you live," rejoined Mrs. Lindsay. " It is not every one that gets such a dip in the lucky bag of life as three hundred a-year, and nothing to do for it. But now I must leave you and the good news I have brought you to enjoy yourselves together. You will enjoy yourselves very well without me. But mind, if you do see the Earl or my husband next week, or any other time, you must not give the faintest allusion to it. You must know nothing of your good fortune, until after the Earl's death."

Thus for the present they parted, and we now return to that interesting group of prisoners at the Gravesend lock-up.

Since we left them, the savage detective, true to his word, had locked up Brummell in a very dark cell, where he could distinctly hear the waters of the Thames splashing about his silent gloomy cell, which he every now and then imagined must be submerged in the river. The stableman was placed in a separate cell, a trifle more comfortable than the one occupied by the valet.

Mr. Duchesney was very splendidly provided for in the superintendent's room, which was furnished like a private counting-house. Here was introduced to him Mr. Small, miser, solicitor, money-lender, and everything, indeed, at which he could make large profits with small risks.

He was an elderly, clean-faced, sharp-featured man, and, for one of his penurious habits, always respectably dressed.

Why of course he was a bachelor ! Did any one suppose that Mr. Small was going to work for a wife? If they did they did not know him. No Mrs. Small for him—for might there not follow a number of *small* children? And how was it possible that a poor man like him could keep a wife and children ? It was an extravagance not to be thought of, although he did own half of Gravesend, and quite rich enough to buy the other.

With all his wealth, the wretched old soul was haunted with the thought that he should die in the workhouse, and he was most desirous of impressing every one with this delusion of his, albeit every one knew that he was enormously rich. No one could please him better than by speaking to him sympathisingly of his poverty, and many needy people who wanted help from him, generally approached him with that dodge. And there was yet another dodge that he was susceptible to, and that was the state of his health.

No one could please Mr. Small better than any one meeting him, shaking him by the hand, and exclaiming—

" God bless my soul, Mr. Small, how well you do look !"

He had a terror of death—and what man with vast possessions has not ?

Garrick, when at the height of his fame and fortune, invited Dr. Johnson to inspect his valuable paintings and rich furniture. After the Doctor had inspected all that Garrick had to show him, he said to the great actor, tapping him on the shoulder—" Ah, David, David, these are the very things that make a death-bed terrible."

Mr. Small abhorred death, and he would almost shiver like an aspen if any one told him that he looked ill. He never forgave the unlucky wight who told him the truth in respect to his health or looks, and if he discounted for him at all it would always be at a higher rate of interest than he would charge a client who flattered his healthy appearance, and made the rich muckworm believe that he was to live forever and a day.

Weak men are easily cajoled into the things they crave for, at least those that their fears or vanities are concerned with.

Nothing is more grateful to the man who fears death—and no one did so more than Mr. Small—to be told that he looks as young as ever—that in years he would outrival Old Parr. At these sounds, so delicious to his fears, the miser would chuckle, rub his hands, pull himself together before the man who was laughing at him, and in other ways mock health and youth, until he would bring himself to believe that he was immortal.

How different death is looked at with the great and good !

How did Howard the prison philanthropist die ?

When the great man was dying he said—

" Death has no terrors for me ; it is an event that I always look to with cheerfulness, if not with pleasure ; and be assured, the subject is more grateful to me than any other. There is a spot near the village of Dauphiney where I should like to be buried. Suffer no pomp to be used at my funeral, no monument to mark the spot where I am laid ; but put me quietly in the earth, place a sundial over my grave, and let me be forgotten."

But the grovelling miser, whose little soul is stored up with his basely gotten wealth trembles at the name of death, that

Cure of the miser's wish, and coward's fear,
Death only shows us what we knew was near.
With courage, therefore, view the appointed
  hour,
Dread not death's anger, but expect his pow'r,
Nor Nature's law with fruitless sorrow mourn,
But die, O mortal man, for thou wert born.

But these beautiful and philosophic lines never reconciled a miser to death.

Some poet has wittily written the following upon this contemptible class of men :

Men say you are wealthy, but falsely I'm sure,
  And thus I can prove it, my friend ;
You have not a penny to give to the poor,
  Nor have you a penny to spend.
You keep, it is true, an abundance of pelf,
  But that's for your heirs, it is not for yourself.

Mr. Small could not see it. He had no heirs, and his friends—those who needed accommodation from him—flattered him that death was a very long way off from him.

Pollok, a sublime poet of the present day, thus truly writes of the miser :—

With eye awry, incurable and wild,
The laughing stock of devils and of men,
And by his guardian angel quite given up—

The miser, who, with dust inanimate
Held wedded intercourse. Ill guided wretch !
Thou might'st have seen him at the midnight
  hour,
When good men slept, and in light-wing'd
  dreams
Ascended up to God,
With vigilance and fasting worn to skin
And bone, and wrapp'd in most debasing rags,
Thou might'st have seen him bending o'er his
  heaps,
And holding strange communion with his
  gold ;
And as his thievish fancy seem'd to hear
The night-man's foot approach, starting
  alarm'd
And in his old, decrepit, wither'd hand,
That palsy shook, grasping the yellow earth
To make it sure. . Of all God made upright,
And in their nostrils breath'd a living soul,
Most fallen, most prone, most earthy, most
  bebased ;
Of all that sold eternity for time,
None bargain'd on so easy terms with death ;
Illustrious fool ! nay, most inhuman wretch !
He sat among his bags, and with a look
That hell might be asham'd of, drove the poor
Away unalms'd ; and 'midst abundance died,
Sorest of evils ! died of utter want.

When the detective called on Mr. Small, he found him in a very ill-furnished office, reclining on a long iron bed chair, which was arranged in close proximity to a ponderous iron safe—so close indeed, that the miser as he lay on his chair could rest his hand on the heavy handle of the safe ; and it was in this fashion that he usually went to sleep.

This evening, from what might be seen on the table, Mr. Small had been indulging in the cheap luxury of a red-herring, which were in season, and being sold very cheap. To save a fraction he had invested in a dozen, and there they were to be counted on the table by those who had the curiosity to do so, and making the apartment smell like a little Billingsgate.

This was Mr. Small's boarding and lodging apartment ; it was here that he ate his porridge breakfasts—his nondescript dinners—twopence-halfpenny was their maximum price—and his three a penny herring suppers ; and it was here also that he kept his iron safe, so, as Paddy says, that he might watch it while he slept.

His regular office, the room in which he saw his clients, adjoined this one, and was altogether a better affair than this ; it was light, spacious, had a large office-table in the centre, and otherwise contained good business furniture. In this room he made his money, in the other he saved and spent it, especially saved.

Without ceremony the detective opened the door and walked in, and at first was inclined to walk out faster than he came, for in the maddest manner the miser sprang from his couch to the detective's throat, exclaiming—

" What's your business, sir, here at this hour of the night ? To think that I had not locked my door against thieves ! I'm going out of my mind, that's what I am."

" This rough reception entitles me to say that you are utterly gone, and as a police officer I should only be doing my duty to arrest you for an assault or a lunatic. I feel indignant at such conduct."

"A police officer! I don't belive you," said Mr. Small.

"Ah, well," said the detective, calmly, "you are an old man, and for the sake of your friend Mr. Duchesney—"

"Why what of him?" he cried.

"He is in prison."

In the most unmitigated alarm he rather screamed than exclaimed—

"In prison! Why he owes me hundreds!"

"And he waits at the prison to arrange with you," said the detective, merely using this tact to get the miser on to the prison.

The relief that he was to be arranged with changed altogether the spirit of the miser, and he became quite docile and apologetic to the detective for his bull-dog treatment.

"I have become so irritable, sir, through so many severe and heavy losses, that at times I know not what I'm about. By one and another —not at all by Mr. Duchesney, who is a most honourable man—I have been reduced from affluence to absolute poverty. See how I live— a bit of red herring for supper,"—holding up the long bone of the fish that he had been eating— for one who was once the chief lawyer and financier of Gravesend. But don't say a word how you caught me, it would injure my prospeets with my clients."

"Oh, certainly not."

"Yet I don't care. No, I won't restrict you, sir. Poverty is not a thing to be ashamed of. Besides, I must come to the workhouse, and then it will all be known. Poverty, sir, is not easily hidden."

"It certainly don't require iron safes to hide it," said the detective, significantly.

This, to the miser, was an unpleasing allusion, but he got out of it, or fancied that he did, by saying—

"Ah, sir, that safe some years ago, would have repaid any burglar to have made a visit on the inside. It has held thousands in coin and notes, and tens of thousands in bills, deeds, and other securities. Therefore, sir, as a feeling man, you will pardon a tear or two, when I tell you that it contains nothing now but bankrupts' balance sheets, heaps of dishonoured acceptances, worthless deeds, and shares in swindling companies! Its chief value now is for its weight in iron, with perhaps a per centage over for workmanship. That safe reminds me of what I was— this remnant of herring of what I am."

"I want such a fine old safe as that, Mr. Small," poking a little fun at the miser, "what will you take for the safe, and all it contains?"

"It stands to me as a relic, as a sentiment, if I may say so, of the past, and my heart will not permit me to part with it."

"They won't permit paupers to have iron safes in the workhouse," said the detective, following the miser's retreats and subterfuges very close.

"No, no, I suppose not," said the miser, with just a little smile athwart his lips, for he saw that in his endeavours to get out of one little difficulty he had precipitated himself into another. "I did not literally mean the workhouse when I used the term, but merely as something to excite your sympathy. I hope to save a little

out of the wreck to keep me from the contingency of a workhouse, which must be a dreadful place for the poor."

"I could hardly believe that a millionaire lawyer could have played his cards so badly as to leave his grey hairs to the tender mercies of a workhouse."

"Only a little, just a very little beyond it, my friend," said the old miser, speaking in the most truthful and confidential tones to the detective, who knew all about the old rascal from Duchesney.

"I am very sorry for you, Mr. Small," he said, sympathetically, playing the gull.

"Ah! sir," cried the miser, "it breaks my heart to speak of it. Bu' what annoys me more than anything else is the incredulity of those who knew me in better days."

"Such a fall as yours is not an everyday occurrence, and people might well be pardoned for incredulity."

"Another thing—d'ye comprehend?" said the miser, nudging the detective's elbow with his.

"Can't say that I do."

"They want to save their breeches pocket— d'ye see?"

"Yes, yes, I see it plain now. You expected your friends to help you?"

"Of course I did, but they one and all got out of it by denying my poverty. Oh! sir, there's a nice lot of humanity about, I do assure you. The poor are the people to find that out."

"Yours seems to me to be a case for public subscription," suggested the detective.

"A famous idea!" exclaimed the miser, taking a pen from the table, and offering it to the detective. "Will you head the list with a trifle?"

The detective was now placed in a fix, but he smoothed his beard, and got out of it by adroitly saying—

"It requires more influential names than mine to start it. You should get the Mayor of Gravesend to head such a list as I mean, followed by the clergymen and bankers of the place, and indeed the gentry throughout the county."

"And I am personally known to most of them —that is, I was, but they don't know me now. You can sir, if you please, put your name down on the second page of the paper, and thus leave room for the influential names you have kindly suggested to precede yours."

"No, I don't see the object of that," said the detective. "My name, so early, would be of no value."

"Ah, but your subscription would," said the miser, cleverly placing the detective in fix number two.

"Oh, they are to be paid-up subscriptions, are they?"

"They would be no good to a poor man like me without," said the bland miser, who from the detective's hesitating yet friendly manner thought that he had caught a real victim.

"I begin to think that I have put my foot in it," said the detective.

"Not until the money is paid," replied the miser, closely pursuing his visitor.

"But I am not prepared," answered the latter.

"Kindly put down your name now, and pay me a little, ever so little, on account."

PRETTY JANE

OR, THE

VIPER OF KIDBROOK LANE

SHE CONFESSED HER PREFERENCE FOR ANOTHER.

"I think, Mr. Small, that you should consider the idea I have given you as an equivalent for my subscription," said the detective, who found himself very closely pinned by the miser, who was as much in sport as earnest, and who was thoroughly well posted up in human nature, which in his experience he found to be composed of equal parts of rogues and fools.

Nor did he spare himself in his classification, and to himself he acknowledged that he was a rogue, which he preferred to being a fool. If he turned fool, he should soon lose all that roguery had earned for him. God preserve me from being a fool, was the old man's constant prayer.

The detective, too, he classed with himself. He was no fool. He reckoned him up as one that you could get plenty of advice, plenty of ideas from, but not a penny of coin. The miser was determined to show him this, either directly or inferentially.

"I cannot live upon ideas. I should be fat if I could, for they are plentiful enough. Advice and ideas the poor never lack; they may be gathered from every tongue without stint or asking."

"Why but now, Mr. Small, you thanked me for the idea as heartily as if I had made your fortune. You have rather hurt my feelings."

No. 17.

"Why what a miserable man you must be to have feelings!" cynically exclaimed the miser. "Do you keep a conscience too?"

"I hope so. What makes you ask?"

"To hear what you would say. Idle curiosity, nothing more."

"To leave conscience—"

"I've done that long ago—and so have you, and all men that are wise."

"That won't do for me. I like a bit of a helm to steer by the rocks and shoals of life to the other shore."

"Whew! do you want to persuade me now that you are a religious man? Whew!"

"Oh, I don't want to persuade you to anything, except to sell me that lumbering safe, and the useless things it contains."

The detective plainly saw that he had touched upon a most disagreeable subject. The miser keenly looked at him to fathom his meaning; he saw a provoking smile playing about the lips and eyes of his detective visitor, which he construed to mean that he did not believe one word that he had told him about the safe and what it contained. Angrily he said—

"I have told you already about that safe. Besides, if I chose to sell, you have no money to buy."

"Oh, but I have though."

"People who keep consciences should not tell lies. But now, sir, you said that you had no money."

"Not to give away, I meant," said the detective.

"Ah, my friend, you are so much like other men," said the miser, with a chuckle. "Why should you expect other people to give me, or to do that, which you would not do yourself?"

"Because there are fools to be found who would believe in your poverty."

"Eh! And don't you?" asked the miser, excitedly.

"No, I do not. A plain question should have a plain answer."

"Well, I don't know that I should grieve about your opinions. Oh, so very rich I am!" he derisively chuckled, again dangling the herring-bone between finger and thumb.

"That's very fishy," said the detective, making a joke, "but it won't do for men of the world. This safe be my witness, but you are a rich man."

"It is a dangerous thing to excite an old man. I entreat you to say no more, or you will make me ill."

"Then you will not take my bid for the safe?" asked the detective, amusing himself at the miser's expense.

"You are not in earnest—you are laughing," said the miser.

"In downright earnest, I do assure you," retorted the visitor.

"You are not."

"I am," persisted the constable.

"I am very poor," rejoined the miser.

"More t'other," replied the detective, wondering what turn his friend was going to give to the conversation.

"The longer we talk the less confidence we have in each other," said Mr. Small. "We appear to know each other's business better than our own, and we are polite enough to contradict every word each other utters. What good can there be in continuing to converse? We had better part, or we might continue these provocations until they culminated in blows."

"Never fear," said the detective. "But look here, sir, how can you be poor—"

"What's that to you?" he angrily interrupted.

"Why Mr. Duchesney owes you a fortune!" exclaimed the detective.

"And should not that be your answer? Can I be owed a fortune as you term it, and yet hold it? Pooh! pooh! Can I have the cake and eat it too?"

This ambiguity on the part of the miser had not the smallest effect on the constable, who still entertained the opinion from what he saw, and what Mr. Duchesney had told him, that Mr. Small was a miser, and that he was very rich. But in order to terminate the conversation in that direction, which he had only continued for his diversion, he made no reply to Mr. Small, leaving the miser under the happy impression that he had completely satisfied him that he, the miser, was an unfortunate broken-down man.

"If I get Mr. Duchesney's money, I owe it all, and more."

"Ah yes, I see, so that you are bankrupt as well as beggar," said the detective.

"Exactly so!" exclaimed the miser, oh! so delighted that he had made, as he thought, another convert to a lie. "But it is very wrong of me, indeed it is, to keep Mr. Duchesney waiting so long. But I would rather that he had come to see me."

"And so would he too, I know. But being a prisoner—"

"Dear me! I had forgotten that. Whatever is he a prisoner for?"

"Why for—but let him tell you himself, sir, for I might tell you too much."

"Oh no you won't; don't be shy; I won't tell him that you have told me a syllable. Come I say let us be friends, and tell me what little game my client has been up to. Is there a woman in it?"

"A couple, besides his wife."

"Whew! his wife!—she's a Tartar. Well, but what was it all about? Tell me."

"A mere spree. But they are determined to punish him if they can. His wife you know is very bitter against him."

"So I have heard," said the miser. "But I never could understand for why. It was always a fog to me."

"Likes somebody else better," suggested the detective, with a laugh.

"Whew! that's what I've always thought, but never said so," said the miser.

"Oh, yes, you may rely upon it such is the fact," said the constable.

The miser lifted up his hands, while he exclaimed with much self-congratulation—

"Who'd be a husband!"

"I'm obliged to answer to the title," replied the officer, without a semblance of misery in his tones, but instead he wore a smile.

"Are you really a husband?" the old man asked, with as much surprise as incredulity.

"There is no getting out of it, Mr. Small."

"What! so wise a man as you a husband?"

"And never showed my wisdom more," said the constable to the miser's surprise.

"I can understand a youth marrying for the gratification of his passions, but I cannot understand that when he came to the years of maturity but what he regretted it."

"And so he would if he married only for the gratification of his passions," said the officer.

"What else would he marry for?"

"For love," answered the detective.

"Oh, you pretty little dear! A detective officer to talk of love! Come, I say, that won't do for me. I'm old, but I've got my understanding about me. It will not do."

"It's quite good enough for me," said the detective, in tones of the greatest happiness, which the old man noticed, and which much surprised him to see. "But I have yet to get back to Eltham, to-night, or my wife will scold me for being late."

"I thank the Lord! I have no one to scold me," the miser ejaculated.

"Ah, but you have though," said the detective, much to the surprise of the miser.

"How patly we contradict each other. Who, pray, is there in this world that has any right to scold me?" he inquired, half mystified as to the detective's meaning.

"Your bosom friend—she who made acquaintance with you at your birth, and who has lived and taken care of you ever since, though in every way you have reviled and insulted her."

"I never insulted a woman in my life, though I don't like the sex. Woman cursed man from the beginning, and she's been a curse to him to the end! Who could love them, except for passion's sake? From her creation she has been an intimate of the devil, and she seeks to draw men after her. I kept aloof from her, and when she tried her seductive arts on me I gave her back frowns for smiles. Now, sir, please let me know what bosom friend I have insulted?"

"Nature," replied the detective.

"That's your woman is it?" said the miser, a little relieved. "But when and how do I offend Nature? I look well—at least my friends say so—feel well, which is better still—and am up to a ripe old age. Nature, sir, resents pranks and liberties with her laws—do you see any of her resentment with me?"

"Where are your heirs to that iron safe?" asked the detective, rather too significantly for the miser's irritable feelings, when the slightest allusion was made to his possessions.

"You are mad, sir, quite mad! I thought so ever since I made your acquaintance with you."

"Thank you, Mr. Small, for your favourable opinion," the detective good-temperedly said.

"You are welcome, sir. At the same time I regret that you provoke me to a breach of good manners. Heirs to an old iron safe! Could I think otherwise than that you were mad. I should be thanked, you mean, that I have not added to the poor's rate by leaving my country a few heirs to the Union."

"Anything you like, Mr. Small, except stopping here any longer," said the detective.

"I have no desire to detain you, sir," said the miser. "The prison is but three doors from here, so I can go there unattended."

"Only that I promised Mr. Duchesney that I would bring you with me."

"In truth it is rather late for me to go out at all," said the miser, "only that I dare not but attend to any request from Mr. Duchesney, whom no one regards more than myself. Will you kindly step on to him, and tell him that I will be with him in a few minutes."

The constable took his leave, and the miser began to consider how he could leave his property with safety so late in the evening.

"That impudent fellow had a terrible eye for my safe," he muttered. "Why what a fool I was to leave my door open! No one should come here. Maybe this is a dodge to rob me. Ha! I will not go! Not likely, I think, that Duchesney is in prison down here. There is a robbery planned here, take my word for it, and I must be prepared."

He stepped to his iron bed-chair, and took from underneath the large square pillow a formidable-looking pistol, and well examined it, and then returned it to its hiding.

"May I never have occasion to use it," he said; "but Heaven help the man who provokes it. I must go, too, for said he not that Duchesney wanted to pay me? This shows that the stranger must know something of the relations between I and he. And how else could he have known it but from Duchesney himself? Therefore he must be known to my client."

He decided to go, and thereupon commenced examining window fastenings, and bolts and bars of safe and door, to the latter of which, when he got outside, he affixed a ponderous padlock, then locked it, and walked to the prison with the key grasped in his attenuated hand, while every step he took he looked back upon his two-storied house, to see that no one entered it, or loitered about it.

Before, however, that he closed the front-door upon himself, he called out to Margery Welden, who happened to be in the little underground kitchen—

"D'ye hear, Margery?—"

"Yes, Mr. Small—what is it?" she replied, from the foot of the stairs below, not at all in an unpleasant voice.

"Shan't be long, Margery—d'ye hear?"

"But wherever are you going so late, Mr. Small?"

"To make some money I hope, Margery."

"Mind you don't lose some, Mr. Small."

"Eh? what? what d'ye mean by that, Margery?" he asked, with a good deal of alarm in his tones. "Had you any reason for that remark, Margery?"

"Only that my mother used to say that she never knew of any good come of any business done after the sun went down."

"Your mother must have been a fool—d'ye hear, Margery?"

"Sure to hear disagreeable things, Mr. Small," she cheerfully answered. "But you wouldn't have said so had you known her."

"Stop a bit, Margery, stop a bit. Did she say what you told me?"

"That she did, often and often," was the chiruppy reply of Margery, in the firm belief that her mother was an oracle.

"Then your mother was often and often a fool—d'ye hear, Margery?"

"She wasn't that, Mr. Small," said the woman, who was little and old, but good in temper, spirit, and disposition, all three of which had daily trials from her capricious, cantankerous master.

"What has the sun, rising or setting, to do with money getting or losing?"

"She said that the sun was God—"

"Don't be a fool, Margery, as well as your mother! Why so are the moon, and the stars, and the flowers—and I and you, if that's all—every created thing is God, as much as the sun."

"But mother meant—"

"Bother your mother! D'ye hear, Margery?—when any one tells you that you shouldn't make money after the sun goes down is a fool! and he who tells you to make money whenever you can, is wise! and he who shows you how to take care of it when you have made it, is wisest of all. Look well after the house in my absence—"

"You may be very well sure of that, Mr. Small," said Margery, who here brought her dwarfish little figure, neatly arrayed in some light fabric of a silvery grey, her white hair smoothed each side her head, while her little-featured face was all smiles and cheerfulness.

"I am sure of it," said the miser. "You have served me for a quarter of a century with great fidelity, and shared a poor man's table without murmuring. You have suffered privations here—"

"Oh, no, Mr. Small, I haven't."

"You have, I say, and you must have suffered them out of compassion for me, and compassion melts the stoniest heart."

"Why no one could be kinder than you have been to me. No one would have kept me so long as you have, a little Tom Thumb like me, and I am only glad that I have kept so well in health—"

"It is the spare diet, Margery, that has done that."

"No doubt of it, Mr. Small," said the credulous little woman.

"Half the people in the world, Margery, dig their graves with their teeth."

"That I do believe," said the dwarf. "Then see how considerate of you, Mr. Small, to take care of my wages for me."

"Yes, Margery, I will never part with them, for your sake. Though sometimes I have run so short, that I have been tempted to borrow them, and of course if I had done so, I should have added some interest to your little capital, and kept them both together until you were dead, and then see what a fine grave and head-stone they would have bought! Why it would outshine all the others in Gravesend church-yard, and the Tribute that at my own expense I would have inscribed thereon would make it quite historic. And a faithful old servant like you ought to live in history—d'ye hear, Margery?"

The old servant was one of those very amiable souls that is strongly associated with idiotcy; and there are a good many people in this world of whom it would be more true to describe as idiots than as amiable. Such persons are an intolerable nuisance in society, and do incalculable mischief, for their amiability leads them to agree with everything that is spoken by the person that they are speaking to.

As a rule, too, these amiable people are chatterers and dawdlers—time wasters, without sense enough to be time-servers; they can find excuses for every villany, and the greatest rascal that ever breathed can find a friend with them if he will only touch their vanity, and flatter them by saying "what a dear good amiable soul you are."

Amiable people thirst insatiably for worship and society, finding none in themselves. But no amiable person must be reproved, or their angelic nature becomes demonised. Tell an amiable woman that she dresses ill—that she is an indifferent cook—that she talks too much in company, and pays too little attention to what others are saying,—then farewell to all her boasted amiability.

But her very soul is to be won away by sympathy; if she complains to you about her husband—be sure and call him a wretch, and express wonder how such a delicate amiable creature could possibly live with such a monster; if she complains of illness, which the amiable woman is sure to do—say she needs more care, rest, and quiet, and that she ought to travel, and live more generously; and if she says her husband says he can't afford it, just say that he can and he ought;—why for these things the amiable woman would run all over the parish saying what a nice man you were—never mind your having knocked down your own wife that morning, she don't know that, and if she did she would be sure to take your part against the wife, especially if the latter had too much sense and religion not to lend an ear to her fanciful ailments, and to have had the courage to have said to her when she had been speaking ill of the husband who was supporting her to the very best of his ability—

"My dear Mrs. L——, you act unwisely as a wife, to murmur a word against your husband, however bad he may be, and I always suspect the wife who does it; but no woman scandalises her husband twice to me. I will say this for husbands, that, whereas I have heard many women speak ill of them, and make confidants of other women as sickly-minded as themselves, I never heard a husband backbie his wife. The truth is, my dear Mrs. L., that if you knew other husbands as well as you know your own, you would be inclined to adopt my theory, which is, take husbands for all in all, they are pretty much alike, of course making due allowances for the circumstances by which each man is surrounded. But, Mrs. L., this is where your mistake through life lies; you go on a visit to Mr. A. or B., and you find him with his holiday clothes and holiday manners on to receive you. You find him full of politeness, gentleness and serenity; you are quite charmed with him, and wish the fates had apportioned him to you as your husband, instead of that brute you had left at home slaving for you.

"No doubt you found Mr. A. or Mr. B. all you say, and which is no more than other women have said of *your* husband, that he was an agreeable, kind, gentlemanly man. You set to work at once, and in the most ungenerous spirit, contrast your host with your husband, without for a moment reviewing the worldly circumstances of each.

"I will do that for you. Your husband is a

poor, proud, industrious man, who is doing daily battle with the world to support you and his children, and yet cannot, but through no fault of his own, keep from the harass of debt. Your friend is a gentleman of comfortable means, with an appointment as quiet and unvarying as the pendulum of a clock. And you find one all turbulence and irritability, and the other all serenity, smiles, and kindness, and with both ears at your service for your slandering tongue to inveigh against your husband. Had he not been so polite, perhaps unmanly would be the better term, he would have said—

"'Madam, I am disposed to believe all you say of your husband, but you have not yet told me the *cause* of the bad treatment. None, you say, but that I do not choose to accept. Quarrelling is not so remunerative or attractive that men indulge in it without a cause. It appears to me that your husband is in trouble, and that you ought not to be away from him. I may be wrong, you know, but as that is my opinion I shall act upon it, by advising you to return to your husband as fast as you can, and help and succour him, and pay visits in happier times.'"

"Have you fastened everything safe up stairs?" asked Margery of Mr. Small.

"Did you ever know me do otherwise?" the miser returned for answer. "Have you any reason for asking, Margery?"

"Oh dear, no," the amiable dwarf replied.

"You are not afraid are you?"

"Oh dear, no, Mr. Small."

"Bolt the door after me, then, keep your ears open, and let no one enter in my absence under any pretence whatever—d'ye hear, Margery?"

"Did I ever, Mr. Small?"

"Never."

With this last word the miser strode off to the prison, and quickly found himself with the lively Mr. Duchesney.

On the entrance of the miser, the latter threw up his hands and arms, and exclaimed—

"Why, Small, you look younger than ever!"

The miser blushed, and laughed, and wagged his head in youthful manner to and fro, while he said, coquettishly, "Come, I say, old fellow, no flattery."

"Oh, I don't flatter, Small. You are the only man that I found flattery fail with."

"That's about the truth I believe," said the cajoled man, taking the chief seat by the office-table, as directed by Duchesney, who invitingly pointed to it; "I believe it, because I feel myself to detest it."

In saying this the old man flattered himself immensely, and if he didn't know it, his friend Duchesney did, and he well worked his coin out of him through that agency.

The latter took a chair opposite the miser, and threw one leg across the other, holding his hat in his hand, while the miser came in without one, either the short distance did not necessitate it, or he became too much absorbed about the security of the possessions he was turning his back upon to think of such a trifle as a hat, or, more probable than either, he fancied himself too poor to indulge in such luxury.

The miser, however, looked very much more at home in the prison office than his client, as he sat in the high-backed chair, and with uplifted pen and finger, chatted pleasantly with his curly-locked client, who looked a rake of rakes.

"There's no mistake about your health—flesh as hard as marble, and as ruddy as a cherry," he observed, touching the miser's cheek with the point of his finger, "no pastiness about it. Best sign of all, see how well they are filled out. Do tell me how you contrive to make such a show of fine health?"

The rich old rogue swallowed it all like a lamb, and cheerily replied—

"I know of nothing that I do for my health, than live temperately in all things—neither drink nor smoke—and early to bed and early to rise—"

"And hands off the lassies O—eh?" said Duchesney.

"Most religiously. They won't have anything to do with me. But I say, these are nice quarters for a prison," he said, looking round.

"I'm indebted to a friend at court—"

"And a little palm oil, I suppose," interpolated the miser.

"You know me well enough, Small, I was never one to take something for nothing."

"Truly, you were always very liberal," said the miser, who was well secured, or he thought he was, for all the money that he had borrowed from the miser, which was a great deal at a most usurious rate.

"Well, just look here, my friend, I am locked up here in this demned place, with two of my servants, for a bit of a spree with a couple of wenches—"

"Petticoats were ever your bane," remarked the miser, with a sly twinkle of the eye.

"Oftener my antidote, Small. The world indeed would be a jest, were it not for the women. I don't mean vixen wives—"

"No, no, no, you've had enough of that cattle," said the soapy miser. "But what is the row all about?"

Duchesney, in his own characteristic language, related to him the whole of the facts, concluding with—

"Now the charge will be laid before the magistrate to-morrow, and if it is not settled there and then by a trumpery fine, the possibility is that I shall require bail, and I want you to be on the spot and prepared to give it. Of course I shall pay you for the trouble—risk there is none."

"Not so fast, my friend," said the miser, who was all alive O, and not to be caught, when bargains were about, "there is risk in every transaction in life."

"Do you suppose, old fellow, that I'm likely to bolt from a paltry case like this, and put my bail in for it?"

"We have no power over the moods of our mind, don't you see?"

"No, I don't! I only see that you think me capable of a mean action—"

"No, no, no!"

"But I say yes, and I am very much disappointed, after we have known each other so long, and had such stiff transactions together, that it should have resulted in such weak confidence. Am I honest?"

"To the backbone."

"Then why hesitate?"

"Don't be impatient, my dear sir. I have

to be prudent, that's all. I'm grown poor, and could not bear a loss."

"No, I know you couldn't," said Duchesney, which he knew would be very grateful to the miser's feelings to be considered almost a pauper. "But here there is no fear of a loss, my fine fellow."

"Well, I'll do my best to oblige Mr. Duchesney, as he is going to arrange to redeem the securities that I hold."

"Who says so?" asked the client, with much surprise,

"The messenger you sent for me—that you wanted to see me to settle."

"Yes, to settle the bail! He could have meant nothing else, for he knew of nothing about the securities."

"You should not have brought me here on such an errand at this time of night," said the miser, keenly disappointed.

But Duchesney after awhile got round him, and in the morning he was in the crowded court prepared to give bail should it be required.

Pretty Jane felt a little tremulous at the sight of the big wigs and the crowded court, but she gave her evidence sensibly, clearly, and not all the fire of counsel's cross-examination could shake, or in one particular contradict it. Whenever the prisoner caught her eye, it made her so indignant that she became positively eloquent.

When he was asked by the court whether he wished to ask the witness any question, his only answer was, that he would reserve his defence.

After Jane had made her statement, and which was confirmed in every word by Ann Orwell, who was not permitted to be in the court while Jane was giving her evidence, which was very damaging to Brummell and Butters, the latter of whom exclaimed, as Ann was leaving the witness box—

"You're a werry onproper young woman, that's what you are, to say sich things agen a married man."

Lady Mary was not present; she had got so drunk on the previous night, that she could scarcely stand on the morning of the examination, which resulted in commitment for trial at the county sessions.

Six months imprisonment with hard labour was ultimately Duchesney's doom, while Butters and Brummell were knocked down for three months.

Brummell was his master's chief enemy on the trial, and in defence of himself he disclosed some ugly truths against Duchesney, which resulted on the part of the latter to arouse the most revengeful feelings towards his high-minded valet servant.

Duchesney's counsel pleaded that it should be settled by fine; but the counsel that Lady Mary had instructed to defend her stoutly opposed such a settlement, and they were at once conveyed from the dock to their prison labour, refreshed by prison diet, amongst which they discovered more gruel, and pea-soup-looking-baths, than "hold hale" or champagne.

Butters was "werry" down about the affair, and did not at all take kindly to his duties, but his master and fellow-servant went to their work more cheerily, and by that means denuded it of half its terrors.

Everything, happily, comes to an end, which is a very good thing for those that are in trouble, as were the profligate master and his two servants. Their prison punishment exhausted itself—the penalty had been paid.

Duchesney when his sentence was over returned to Evesham House, to the great disgust of his wife.

Butters found it very uphill work to get along without a character, but through some timely assistance from his wife's brother-in-law, he contrived to possess himself of a London street cab.

Brummell was independent of service. His eye was on a rich elderly maiden lady, and her eye—the old fool!—was on him.

They were engaged to be married, and the day was fixed.

But every man has a destiny, and every destiny must be fulfilled!

But two days from his marriage-day he was unluckily rambling over some high Kentish cliff when he met his old master, who was flushed with wine.

Brummell was gay and happy, thinking of nothing but the good fortune that he was about to be the master of, but very little of the lady who was to bring it to him.

They were in that position on the cliff, that they could not escape each other, which Brummell would gladly have done, for he was in no quarrelling mood.

But Duchesney was possessed of the devil, a possession which he seldom left behind him. He was right glad to have some one to bully—some one to fight.

Who so good as Brummell, for whom he had conceived a terrible hatred? And here he was, most opportunely on the spot.

Had he followed his feelings, which he generally did, he would at once have pounced upon his throat; but he sprang up to him, and while ferociously menacing him with his eye and fist, he exclaimed—

"And have we met again, you liar?"

"You might be civil, or have passed on."

"Make no mistake about me—"

"I did though when first I knew you," said the cool Brummell, valet no longer.

"In what?" with passion he asked, confronting him closer.

"Why that I took you for a gentleman, and found you a blackguard!"

This was a hard hit, and was unmercifully felt by the master, and it more and more kindled his wrath.

He struck out at Brummell, but the cooler man warded it off, which caused Duchesney, who was soaked with wine, to reel to the ground, from which he was quickly on his legs again.

"If you want a round or two, you see it is to be had," said Brummell, and stupidly enough to get a little more out of the reach of his passionate assailant, went nearer the edge of the cliff.

Without a word of warning in reply, knitting his strength up to a pitch that he could not sustain, but which for the moment did deadly mischief, he closed in upon Brummell, and so quickly—that over the cliff he went, and in the great waters he found his death and his grave!

When Duchesney saw what he had done, he had no remorse, but he had plenty of selfishness, and that led him to the question how he might best cover his crime.

In case he should be seen his first object was to destroy all identification.

For this purpose he tucked his beard out of sight, buttoning his coat over it, and pulling up the collar of the said coat over his cheeks, bending his head and shoulders low, so as much as possible to give himself the appearance of age, and in this manner, neither looking to the right nor the left, he sloped away unperceived, and was never suspected.

Brummell had few friends, and no relatives that he was in communication with, therefore, with the exception of the lady to whom he was engaged, there were no inquiries after him, and she became satisfied after awhile that as he had gone let him go.

With her it had been more an affair of flattery than of the heart. The clever Brummell had flattered her that she looked young, and was really beautiful.

These sentiments, which she swallowed as facts, quite prepared her for giving her hand to Mr. Brummell when he asked for it, which was directly that he had ascertained the amount and conditions of her fortune.

Although Duchesney had escaped the consequences arising out of the death of Brummell, it was to meet with a violent death at the hands of his dare-devil wife.

Ever since that she had contracted marriage, she had hated the name of husband, and her secret thoughts, and a conference or two with her paramour, ran in the direction of his murder!

She had passed the time right merrily during his incarceration, but she failed to arouse in Joshua Woodward any inclination towards further murder.

He had already dipped his hands in the blood of his child, besides the torments that he knew his first-born, the Hunchback Boy, was suffering at the hands of that other criminal, Mrs. Oliphant!

"Look here, Josh," she said one evening during her husband's imprisonment, "you have become a perfect misery to me more than a source of pleasure."

"It must be so, for I am a misery to myself," replied the wretched man.

"Then hang thyself," rejoined the hard-hearted and insensible woman. "Pah! every one who is wretched should destroy himself out of mercy to himself as well as others."

"Oh! that I were dead!" he exclaimed, heeding but little her insensibility.

"Upon my word I wish you were," she cried. "Get a bottle of champagne, you fool, and drown your stupid sorrows in its sparkling bubbles."

"Do you forget that these hands, and your hands, strangled the sweetest child that ever lived!" he exclaimed, as he sat by the table in his room.

"I should be sorry, though, to remember it as you do. We thought it best to do what we have done—"

"I never did!" cried Josh, shaking his head, and burying his face in his hands.

"Snivel away! After all, like a good many other cowards, you care nothing for the deed, but are alarmed lest it bring you into trouble."

"It is not so with me, I do assure you. To show you so, I am anxious to give myself up, for my life is quite a burden to me. If it were not for you—"

"Stop there, please," she proudly interrupted him. "You have said that before, therefore I very well know what you were going to say—that you couldn't give up yourself without giving up me. Now let me consider that," she continued, promenading the room, with compressed lips, in deep thought. "Now I do not wish to be under any obligations to you, or any one else, therefore I do not choose to accept your consideration. Give up your wretched life—this hour if you like—and never mind me."

"Oh, yes, I must," said Josh, evidently with much feeling. "You have been very kind to me."

"Do not offend me by such commonplaces," she haughtily said. "Would I had never known you! But there—none but fools regret. Oh, I can tear you from my heart as easily as place you there! And I daresay I can find another lover. I am neither old nor wizened—"

"Oh, we should have been happy but for the murder!"

"And might be now, if you would be a man," she replied.

"To be happy now, I must be a fiend!" cried Josh.

"Then be a fiend—be anything but unhappy, for unhappiness is the worst of fiends."

"Let us do something to atone our crime!" cried Josh, with deep earnestness and contrition.

"What shall we do?"

"Take the Hunchback Boy, and—"

"And what?"

"Acknowledge him as our child," answered Josh.

"Oh! the little monster," she exclaimed, with horror in her tones, and shrugging high her shoulders.

"Let us forget that he is our child my dear Lady Mary."

"Too late, Woodward. It was a shame that that cursed Oliphant should have permitted it to live. A pretty baby-farmer she!" she added, with contempt and cruelty.

"She found out too much about you and your rank—"

"And nurtured the child to extort a permanent income out of me to keep the secret."

"She has confessed so much," said Josh.

"Oh yes, I know. The fool! I would rather have given her a permanent income had she destroyed the child—"

"Poor little creature!" sighed Josh. "But it ought not to be made to suffer for our sakes. His natural infirmities are surely enough—"

"Oh, I see how it is with you—the boy is getting round your heart. Ha!"

"Where he should be—for is he not our child?" he appealed again.

"Take the boy and travel, if that will make you happier," she said, with decision.

"I should like to do so. Would that I could take the two!" groaned Josh.

"Always wanting something that you cannot have," she said, with a sneer.

"Will you come with us, Lady Mary?" asked Josh.

"Certainly not. A hunchback boy and a wretched man, is not a cheerful party enough for me to travel with."

"But who is that man, and who is that boy?" asked Josh, in the most significant manner, while he well scanned her countenance.

"Were they ten times nearer it would not influence me, if they were not agreeable to me."

"Then I and the boy will go without you, for I cannot longer rest so near that barn !"

"Go—and leave the barn to me," she said.

"Oh! that I could. Wherever I go, there goes the barn. Nor can all the waters of the ocean divide me from it."

Josh wept again.

"I cannot stand much more of this nonsense," she said.

"You would have wept too, Lady Mary, had you seen that poor boy begging of me for mercy —and I—I—had none to give him, but chained him up in the barn !"

"Pray don't attempt to entangle me in your milksop feelings. Away with the boy, and may you find more happiness abroad than here. You can have plenty of money."

"But about Mrs. Oliphant ?"

"Send her to me, I'll arrange with her. We have now both decided, and a thing that has been decided upon should be acted upon at once. Go where you like—with whom you like —but go at once."

A few days' hasty preparation, and Josh and his emaciated son were steaming across the broad Atlantic. Lady Mary and a friend saw them from their starting point, and waved her hand-kerchief, which was her farewell adieu to her unhappy paramour.

The poor boy, who was a mere shadow of skin and bone, was delighted with the wonders of the ocean, and overpowered with his father's kind-ness. Josh told him his history, and they often and often on the voyage mingled their tears.

It was all too much for the poor boy's strength. His constitution had been completely shattered by his cruel nurse, and the new and happy life that so suddenly burst upon his wretchedness, oh! was too much for the tenement of his soul, which burst its feeble bounds, and went to God who gave it.

The death of the boy, who he was beginning to love, was too much for the father's already o'er-troubled brain. During the burial service that was read over the body of the Hunchback Boy before it was committed to the deep, and while they were lowering it to the waters, Josh climbed the vessel's side, plunged into the sea, and went down with the body of the boy to whom he had given life, and to whose death he had so largely contributed.

After the departure of her paramour, Lady Mary concentrated her wicked designs upon her husband to accomplish his death. Of course, in the room of Brummell, Duchesney had to pro-vide himself with another valet. The man was handsome, and gentlemanly in his bearing, and quickly caught the eye of the lady, and she in-stalled him in the place of Josh, and then con-verted him to help her in the murder of her hus-band.

Poison was resorted to, and it was adminis-tered in a basin of soup by the hand of his trea-cherous servant, and mixed by her bloody-minded wife, who had the cool daring to watch her vic-tim die !

She was akin in adultery and murder to an ancestor of hers, who married Lord Stroud, in the reign of the dissolute Charles II. This lady was much beloved by her husband, who dis-covered her in an intrigue with one of his attend-ants. On her knees she confessed her love for the servant, and Lord Stroud blew out his brains before her.

"And a good job, too !" cried Lady Mary, when she read this recital in her ancestral his-tory. "What did she want of a husband when she loved another, and lived with him ?"

Pretty Jane after the trial of her master did not remain long at Evesham House. She never liked the place nor its wicked mistress, although she was kindness itself to her. But no kindness would persuade her to serve in the house of wic-kedness. She left, and her footsteps unhappily led her to Greenwich, from whence a sad and shrouded fate attended her.

From this point of her history but little is known, but that on the morning of the 26th of April a policeman on his solitary rounds disco-vered her murdered body in Kidbrook Lane, and the last words she uttered in this life were "Let me die."

And die she did, poor young soul ! And she is now at peace in the village cemetery, mourned by thousands, loved by all who knew her, and her grave regarded with respect and honour— while he, poor wretch! who murdered her, whoever and wherever he may be, must carry about with him the pangs of hell ! Let him know for certain, that though he may escape the punish-ment of man, he cannot of God !

The mistress of Evesham House—what of her ? She in her turn became the victim to riot and drink. After the burial of her husband she and her new paramour went deep into cham-pagne, and inebriated as they were, they chal-lenged each other to a race, and for the purpose had their horses saddled. Off they tore, but Lady Mary could not keep her seat in the saddle —she fell backward over the horse, and was killed against a tree close by the old barn.

Her death, of course, was the ruin of that other wretch, Mrs. Oliphant. She had neither in-come nor character, and now bewails her inglo-rious fate in Eltham workhouse.

THE END.

www.ingramcontent.com/pod-product-compliance
Lightning Source LLC
Chambersburg PA
CBHW081153170626
46813CB00009B/3184